Real Like Daydreams

A Savage U Novel

J. Wolf

Copyright © 2022 by J. Wolf

Little Bird Publishing LLC

Real Like Daydreams

A Savage U Novel

All rights reserved.

No portion of this book may be reproduced in any form without written permission from the publisher or author, except as permitted by U.S. copyright law.

Photo by: Michelle Lancaster

Cover Design: Y'All That Graphic

Editing by: Word Nerd Editing, Monica Black

Proofreading by: My Brother's Editor

This one goes out to the ones who haven't stopped daydreaming.

Author's Note

Dear lovely reader,

Real Like Daydreams is not a dark romance, but it does delve into serious mental and physical health issues that I would be remiss not to tell you about before you read this story.

Those include:

-Depression

-Past instances of self-harm

-Scars from self-harm

-Recovering from a near-fatal car accident

-Ableist remarks from assholes

Please be kind to yourself when choosing whether or not to read this story.

xoxo,

Julia

Prologue

Seraphina

Sophomore Year

I'M ABOUT TO DO something stupid.

No, no. None of that.

This year, I'd been doing my best to ignore negative self-talk. Going to Seth's party wasn't stupid. How could going to my own boyfriend's party be stupid?

He told me to wait. He'll be so mad I didn't listen.

Yes, I was told to stay home until he texted, but Seth had a bad habit of not texting when he said he would, and it was already eleven. Sitting at home on a Saturday night while everyone else was out, including my forgetful boyfriend, seemed silly. Obviously, Seth had lost track of time.

He'd be happy I came, especially when he realized he had forgotten to text like he'd promised.

Although, it still wasn't clear why I hadn't been allowed to show up earlier. He hadn't really explained that one. But Seth was particular about a lot of things I didn't understand. He had "rituals" he attributed to being an elite athlete. I had my quirks too—who was I to judge?

I smoothed a hand over my straightened hair. Seth really liked when I wore it straight. And that was fine. Even though it took me a solid hour to tame my curls, I couldn't get enough of him dragging his fingers through them. He wouldn't touch my curls with a ten-foot pole. That *might* have been because he was grossed out by the amount of product I had to use so I didn't resemble my seventh-grade school picture—that was before the internet kindly informed me brushes and curls should never meet.

It was pitch dark as I set out toward Seth's off-campus house where he lived with five other football players. Fortunately, there were a lot of other people around, so I didn't feel like I was walking down a dark alley in the middle of the night. Just, you know, a conspicuously alone girl with no friends or boyfriend. At least, that was what I thought I looked like. I *did* have a lot of friends, they were just…somewhere else. Which sounded as believable as saying "my boyfriend lives in Canada, you'll never meet him, but he's totally real!" Yes, I was rambling inside my own head so I didn't have to think too hard about all the things lurking in the shadows between streetlights.

By the time I made it, my stomach was a mess of knots. I'd texted that I was on my way, but he hadn't read it. Something told me he'd probably set his phone down and couldn't remember where. Judging by the people spilling out the front door, it would be an easy thing to do.

I had to push through a wall of guys to get inside. Vaguely, I recognized them from the football team. They barely noticed me. Seth and I didn't have the same friends, and in the three months we'd been together, he'd only had me over once. His floors were sticky, and his roommates were smelly, so I didn't mind—especially after stepping on a used condom the one and only time I'd been here. In the living room. With bare feet.

I shuddered at the memory as I wove through the crowd. Not seeing Seth anywhere, I rose on my tiptoes to gain a better vantage. A giggling girl spun away from a growling guy, colliding into me. The contents of her Solo cup sloshed over the side, spilling down the front of my white dress.

"Oh my god, I'm sorry!" Using her hands, she tried to wipe away the pink liquid, but the only thing she really did was grope my boobs.

"It's fine. Don't worry about it." I knocked her hands away politely and leaned in so I didn't have to yell. "Have you seen Seth?"

She looked back at her growling boyfriend, who now had his arms wrapped around her middle and was attempting to devour her neck. By the breadth of his shoulders, I was certain he was another football player.

"Shawn, do you know where Seth is?" she asked.

He peeked up at her for a moment. "Uh...last I saw, he was still in the dining room."

"Great. Thank you." I whirled away from them before Shawn got back to feasting on his girl. They were cute and all, but I was a little jealous. Seth wasn't big on PDA and...well, maybe I was.

I made it to the dining room, a lot worse for wear. Sweat beaded my forehead, and the hair around my face had betrayed me, tightening into frizzy curls. My dress was soaked and molded to my chest, but I feared it wasn't in a sexy way at all. I'd also stepped in something sticky, so each step I took made a squelching sound. I was afraid to look down. If it was another condom, I might've cried.

A crowd stood around the circular dining room table where a game of poker was going strong. Seth wasn't one of the players, but he was watching from the other side while he talked to his best friend, Katie.

Katie and I were both in the drumline of Savage U's marching band. She was how I met Seth. They'd grown up together but had never been anything more than friends.

I knew that. I had accepted their closeness. Without Katie, I never would have met Seth.

So, why did it piss me off that she was here when I was told to wait at home?

Seth finally spotted me on the other side of the table. Instead of the smile I expected, his brows knitted in consternation. He leaned down to speak in Katie's ear then started making his way toward me.

She caught my gaze for a split second then rolled her eyes and looked away while shaking her head.

Before I could decipher her body language, a rough tug on my elbow had me whipping around to face a seething Seth.

My boyfriend was hot. There was no other way to describe him. Well over six feet tall, he had the tightly honed muscles of a star quarterback. His skin was smooth, smoky bronze, and his eyes were deep hazel with rich gold flecks. What got me first were his curls. Yeah, my boyfriend might not have liked my curls, but I adored his. He kept them short in an ebony crown on top of his perfectly crafted face. Square jaw, soft lips, cheekbones sharp enough to cut glass...Seth was a Greek sculpture come to life.

And he was all mine.

Except right now, he looked awfully pissed at me.

"What the fuck are you doing here?" he barked next to my ear.

I jerked back, surprised by the venom in his question. "It's after eleven. I assumed you lost your phone or forgot to text."

He took my shoulder in his hand and jerked me closer. "I told you to wait. I'm in the middle of something. I don't have time to babysit you."

Hurt jabbed at my chest. He hadn't forgotten, he just didn't want me here. "But you have time to babysit Katie?"

As soon as it slipped out, I knew it was the wrong thing to say. His hold on my shoulder tightened to the point of pain.

"Don't say her name," he hissed. "She knows how to conduct herself at parties. You, on the other hand, get so lost in your little girl daydreams, I have to keep watch over you."

"That isn't true." I blinked up at him, willing back tears. "You're hurting me." *In more ways than one.*

His grip loosened, but he gave me a little shake. "I don't have time for this, Sera. You need to go find a place to park your ass. I'll come for you when I'm done here."

"But—I seriously can't hang out with you and Katie?"

His eyes narrowed. "Are you jealous? You know I don't like that petty shit. If I tell you you're my girl, you don't question me."

I shook my head. "No, I know. I just want to be with you."

He shoved my hair back, looking me over. Disappointment etched his golden-god features. "Goddamn, you're a mess. Go sit down. I'll find you in a bit."

"Okay," I whispered, but he had already turned away, winding his way back to Katie.

I whirled around in the opposite direction, unwilling to watch their reunion. The trouble was, I didn't know where to go. Besides Katie, there was no one else here I knew. Seth and I hung out alone most of the time, or with my friends, including Katie. Although...it would've been a stretch to call us friends.

Wandering through the crowded living room, I grabbed a drink so I could take the edge off this miserable, infuriating humiliation. In my head, I gave Seth a time limit to find me. Thirty minutes. If he wasn't properly apologetic, he could find someone else to suck his dick.

Okay, that thought made me queasy.

I made it out to the enclosed back porch, which seemed to be the smoking spot—and I wasn't talking about cigarettes. Two seconds out here, inhaling the thick air, and I was practically floating.

Just as I was about to turn around and fight through the crowd in the main house, a guy sitting by himself on a rattan couch waved me over. I strode to his spot on the far side of the porch, tilting my head, trying to figure out if I knew him. It was pretty dark out here, and he was lost in the shadows.

"Hi?" My greeting came out as a question.

"Hey." He leaned forward, and the moon provided just enough light to gleam off his luminous, heavy-lidded blue eyes. "You looked lonely. You're welcome to sit, stay a while."

I bit my bottom lip, glancing behind me. Seth could come looking for me anytime—and I was just pissed and hurt enough not to mind if he found me sitting beside this stranger.

"I think I will." Smoothing the back of my skirt, I plopped down beside him and sank farther than expected, pulling a surprised yelp out of me. The couch had seen better days.

He chuckled. "Mind the first step, it's a doozy."

"A little warning would have been nice," I muttered, tucking my hair behind my ear as I adjusted myself on the cushions. "And really? A *Groundhog Day* reference? What are you, forty?"

That made him laugh a little harder. It was a slow, lazy thing, like dripping molasses. "Pot, kettle, and all that. Did you come here all alone?" he asked.

"Yes, but—" I started to tell him I was waiting for Seth but held my tongue. I didn't really want to talk about him right now. "I was supposed to meet someone, but I can't find them. How about you?"

"I know a few people. They're around. You seem more interesting than they are."

"That puts a lot of pressure on me."

"Are you saying you're bad company?"

"I enjoy myself," I answered.

"You seem trustworthy." His blue eyes swept over me, not even pausing on my stained dress. "If you tell me you're enjoyable, I believe you."

"Thank you." This stranger had taken my bad mood and tossed it in the garbage. Sure, Seth was in the back of my mind, but the sting eased as we exchanged easy banter. "So, you're just...what—sitting by yourself at a party? That's a little embarrassing," I teased.

He lifted a shoulder, his white teeth shining in the dark as he grinned. "I'm not by myself anymore. You're here."

"I don't know if I should stay."

"I'll convince you." He held his hand out in front of me. "Smoke?"

"What is that?" He definitely wasn't holding a joint.

He chuckled. "It's a vape pen."

Using my index finger, I nudged it a little. "It looks like a tiny flute."

He held it up in front of him. "I never noticed, but I guess I see it. Are you a musician?"

"Guilty. I suppose it's obvious. Who else would see a weed pen as a flute?" I peered down at the vape in his outstretched hand. "There *is* weed in there, right?"

"Mmhmm." He curled his fingers in to grip it and held it up to my lips. "Do you smoke?"

"I have, just not a lot."

The tip touched my bottom lip. He rubbed it back and forth, teasing me to open. It might've been crazy to take drugs from a stranger, but nothing was screaming danger. In fact, my stomach had untwisted while sitting here.

"I don't know what I'm doing," I murmured against the pen.

He tapped it gently on my bottom lip. "Inhale. Hold. Exhale."

"Let me see you do it first."

In the dim light, I could make out individual features, but not his whole face in combination. His smile was bright, wide, quick to appear. Those blue eyes, even under his heavy lids, danced with amusement. His hair was a little shaggy, but I couldn't tell if it was blond or brown. Maybe it was somewhere in between. I wanted to ask him to lean closer, to let me see all of him, but I bit down on my tongue. It didn't matter what he looked like. I had Seth.

The stranger placed the pen between his lips, showing me how it was done, then brought it to mine. When I put the end between my lips, my stomach dipped at the intimacy of sharing this with him. Our lips were in the same place. Tiny, microscopic drops of his saliva were now in my mouth. When he took another hit, mine would be in his.

I shivered.

"Are you cold?"

"No, I'm really good right now," I said.

"What's your name?"

"Seraphina."

He leaned back, a smoky exhale falling from him. "That's a big name."

"I'm a big girl."

He chuckled. "You're tiny."

I wasn't really tiny, but maybe, sitting down, I looked smaller than I was. If we'd been somewhere else, in another life, I would have flashed him my biceps of steel from my decade of playing drums.

"Big personality," I said. "Plus, I didn't really choose my name, you know. My mom liked it before I was even conceived. It means 'fiery one,' and since she's a redhead, she was hoping I would be too." I pointed to my hair. "Voilà! Wish granted. I don't know if I live up to my name, but I have the fiery hair."

He took another drag from the pen, sweeping me with his gaze. There was a solid minute of silence where we simply looked at each other. "You talk a lot."

"I know." I tried to tuck my hair, but the curls weren't having it. "Are you sorry you asked me to sit down with you?"

His answer was immediate. "Not even a little."

He passed me the pen again. I should have said no, but I didn't want to. While I inhaled, he stretched his legs out and tipped his head back, his face to the ceiling. I looked at him, his Adam's apple bobbing when he swallowed, wishing I could find a light switch to see him clearly. I didn't know why it was so important, but my hands twitched to reach out and trace the lines of his jaw.

"Did you get stood up, Dragon Girl?" he asked out of nowhere.

Startled, I took my phone out of my purse to check the time. I'd been here...a while.

And no Seth.

"Maybe."

He slipped the phone from my hand and tapped on the screen. I guessed I was high because I didn't bother to try to take it back. And it was fine, because he placed it in my hand when he was done.

"What was that?" I asked.

"Now you have my number—if you're ever alone at a party again and need company."

I opened my mouth to say...what? I didn't really know. And I'd never find out. Seth appeared out of nowhere and tugged me off the couch in one swoop.

"Who the fuck is that?" he gritted out, his head swinging back and forth between us.

The stranger raised his hand. "Just keeping your girl company."

Seth's hold on me was just past too tight. I knew I'd have bruises in the morning. He always forgot I didn't have thick, football player skin.

"Glad to hear you realize she's my girl." He lowered his chin, pausing, as if waiting for the stranger to challenge him. Of course that didn't happen.

"Have a good night, man." Seth jerked his head and dragged me deeper into his hold, then he swept me into the house before I could even say goodbye to my stranger.

• • • • ● • ● • • •

The next day, my thumb hovered over the new contact in my phone. He'd named himself The Phantom. I bit back a grin and tapped out a message.

Hi! Now you have my number too, so you don't embarrass yourself by pretending you have friends at another party again. You have a real one in me. Anyway, it was nice meeting you last night. Thanks for saving me. I had fun! Xoxo, Dragon Girl

I waited and waited, but I never got a reply. When days turned into weeks then months, I gave up on ever seeing my phantom again.

Chapter One

Seraphina

If I had my way, I'd be wearing sweatpants and a hoodie. My hair would be greasy, and I'd let my stress pimples fly. I just didn't care what I looked like.

My housemates, Laura and her girlfriend, Alley, were having none of it. They were one of those disgusting, maddeningly in-love couples who could have been on that Instagram account *Siblings or Dating?*. Blonde, tan, with perfect tits and even better fashion sense, I was like their scruffy little stepsister.

"This is your chance to show everyone you're unaffected," Laura said.

Alley nodded, swiping peachy blush onto my cheeks. "Time for a power move, girly. You're going to strut around campus looking hot as hell, living your best life. We do not give cheating boys the upper hand."

Laura rolled her eyes and tugged down the *V* of my T-shirt so more of my ample cleavage was on display. "Boys should *never* have the upper hand. It's not like they know what to do with it."

"I *am* affected," I protested.

We were in the bathroom of our shared rental house. My two best friends were preparing me to show my face on campus for the first time since winter break. My idea of preparation was sunglasses and a hoodie so I could pretend to be invisible. They went the opposite direction, putting me in a tight, vibrant purple tee and a sunshine-yellow swing skirt that barely covered my butt.

Laura wrapped one of my face-framing ringlets around her finger. "I'm affected too. I've been homicidal since Seth screwed the pooch—the pooch being Katie."

"Fucking Katie," Alley hissed from my other side.

"But you think I'm going to let either of them see that? I'm not. They are dirt beneath my feet." Laura pressed her cheek to mine, capturing my gaze in our reflection. "You are a goddess. All those idiots are going to see is a girl who just lost two-hundred-pounds of dead weight."

Alley nodded sharply. "Listen to my girl. In this house, you can fall apart, and we won't judge. Out there? You're the coolest girl on campus. Seth and Katie can go eat a dick. And they will when they see you. They'll choke on all the dicks they're going to eat."

I sucked in a breath and stared at myself in the mirror. My friends had magically de-puffed my eyes and disguised all the spots on my skin. This wasn't really me, but I'd look at it like armor. Beneath the makeup, perfect curls, and bright clothes was a broken, humiliated girl.

I glanced from Alley to Laura and forced myself to smile. "You're right. They don't deserve to see me hurting. I'm not going to show them what they've done to me. I'll lick my wounds in private."

Alley squealed and wrapped her arms around my shoulders. "That's my girly. Never let them know your next move."

I huffed a dry laugh. "What *is* my next move?"

Alley shrugged, flipping her golden hair behind her back. "Only you can say, but I know it's going to be fierce."

Yeah, that was a bridge too far for me to believe. Fierce wasn't really a word anyone would use to describe me. Ditzy, airheaded, flighty—those were more like it. At least, according to Seth. Since he'd lost the privilege of being inside me in any way anymore, I trampled on his voice echoing in my brain.

"Okay." I tugged up my shirt so I was only flashing a bit of tit, not my entire areola. "I think I'm ready."

Laura gave my butt a hard smack. "Damn right you are."

It had been three-hundred-sixty-seven days since Seth Michaelson asked me to be his girl, and thirty-three since everything fell apart. Today was the first day of the second semester of my junior year. I was twenty-one years old. Five feet, four inches tall. I had three classes today, one I would be sharing with Katie.

If my math was correct, Seth Michaelson and Katie Shin could eat an entire bag of dicks and then go fuck themselves.

And each other.

Because that was what they did.

· · · ● · ● · · ·

A few months ago, when signing up for this semester's classes, it seemed like a good idea to enroll in a modern music lecture with a bunch of my band friends. Music was my minor, so I needed the class anyway, and everyone said it was a cakewalk.

When I walked into the expansive lecture hall that could hold over three hundred students, I regretted my decision to the tips of my toes. Katie was there, sitting with a couple girls who also played cymbals, while a group of my actual band friends was clustered on the other side of the room. It was like the sharks and the jets—and they were all looking at me.

Raising my chin, I sauntered across the front of the room. On the inside, I was shriveling like an old, crinkled candy wrapper, but my outside was as smooth as I could get it. Once I started up the steps, Katie was no longer in my line of vision, so I didn't feel like I was going to barf or fly across the aisles to stab her with a dull pencil.

As soon as I sat down beside Dina and Stefan, my two favorite drummers, the hisses started.

"I can't believe that slut didn't drop this class."

"Whatta bitch."

"She's so ugly. Seth has no taste."

"Trashy. So trashy."

I hated all of it. Not that there was any love lost between Katie and me, but I didn't want this. *Everyone* knew, which led me to wonder how long they'd known.

I didn't want to know. Not now. Maybe in a hundred years when the sting wasn't so fresh, but not anytime soon.

"Guys, it's fine, really. I don't care anymore." I shot everyone my biggest, bravest smile. Laura and Alley would've been proud. I mean, they would have been even prouder if I'd flashed some nip along with it, but that wasn't happening. Stefan patted my arm, and Dina winced with sympathy. I supposed I hadn't been as convincing as I'd hoped.

Carson, the drum captain and biggest shit stirrer I'd ever met, got up from his seat and resituated himself right next to me. Wrapping his arms around my shoulders, he leaned in close.

"Baby girl, how are you? You didn't return my texts over break. I was worried," he cooed.

He wanted gossip. Carson had been voted captain because he was a damn good drummer, but also because he could blackmail almost every single member of the drumline. Not me, thankfully. Until the Katie and Seth scandal, I'd been living the least dramatic life ever.

"I'm good. Promise. I just needed to recenter myself during break, so I didn't really talk to anyone."

He clucked his tongue. "I get that. Dealing and healing. Classic."

We were both speaking in platitudes, but that was because the only thing we had in common was our love of marching band. It was the off-season, so there wasn't much left to say. The thing about Carson was he expected people to kowtow to him—and they did. In a certain set, being the drum captain was equal to being captain of the football team. Carson didn't discriminate on who he took to bed, and he was never short of people throwing themselves at him. I would never do that, but since I wanted to take over his position next year, I always played nice.

Apparently bored with me, his focus turned to the students still entering the lecture hall. He made a few snarky comments about outfits and hair while I ignored him. When he started snickering, he caught my attention.

"Oh my god, that's tragic," he murmured, elbowing my side.

I followed his gaze to a guy with a hood over his head slowly making his way into class. It was hot outside, so the heavy sweatshirt was enough to make this guy stand out. The fact that he was limping and using a cane put neon lights over his head.

"Tragic?" I asked.

He snickered again, and it wasn't a nice sound. "Don't you feel sorry for him? What do you think he's hiding under that hood?"

"I'd guess his face."

Carson guffawed loud enough to draw several sets of eyes his way. "I'd guess you're right. So, so tragic."

Fortunately, class started, and Carson shut his mean, gossiping mouth. Knowing him, he wasn't finished, though. He had to know everything about everyone, and I had a feeling he'd find a way to discover what was under that guy's hood.

• • • • • • • • • • •

By the end of the lecture, some of my tension had seeped away. Based on the syllabus, I didn't think this class would be very challenging. Plus, the professor was energetic and excited, so it should have been interesting and pretty painless.

Even though I had to share it with Katie.

And Carson.

And all the other people waiting for a show.

They wouldn't get one. No matter what.

My resolve lasted exactly thirty seconds. As I exited the classroom, my arm was grabbed, and I was nearly yanked off my feet.

"What the fuck, Sera?" Seth was in my face, his brown skin glowing with anger. "Did you block me?"

Shock at his sudden appearance froze me in place, my mouth parted in an *O*. Hundreds of other students were streaming out of the room around us, jostling me into Seth's chest.

"Let go of me," I whispered. "Let go of me right now."

There was no force behind my words, but I meant them all the same. I just couldn't wrap my head around him being here. We were done, done, done. Had been for over a month. And he was here, yelling at me for blocking his number? I felt like I'd stepped into an alternate reality where I was the bad guy, not my lying, cheating ex-boyfriend.

"What? You're not getting away from me until we talk." His hand clamped down on my bicep, squeezing too hard like always.

My nostrils flared, and I dug deep to plaster on my "cool, unaffected girl" facade. "Go talk to Katie."

He scoffed like he was unimpressed and gave me a shake. "Enough of that shit. You're coming back to my place, and we're putting this to rest."

"Absolutely not. It's already been put to rest. Was the moment you stuck your dick in someone else." Sucking in a breath, I raised my voice. "Get off me, Seth. I don't want anything to do with you."

We had an audience now. People weren't even pretending they weren't watching. We were probably a sight, a massive football player manhandling his much, much smaller ex-girlfriend in broad daylight. But no one said anything. No one stepped in.

"It was *one time*," he said lowly. "Meant nothing. You weren't there—"

We'd already had this exact conversation in private. I refused to rehash what we already both knew—especially where people could lap up shards of my broken heart like the sweetest candy.

"Seth, stop. Leave her alone."

This time, both of us froze. Katie had this sultry, raspy voice I'd always been jealous of. Now, it was nails on a chalkboard. How dare she come to my defense.

She wound around me to stand at his side, draping herself over his arm, and I realized she wasn't defending me at all. She saw her *bestie* making a spectacle that wasn't about her so she made it about her.

"Katie, not now." Seth's jaw was tight as he glanced at the girl attached to him.

"No, now is good. You chat with Katie. I'm done here." With my free hand, I gave him a hard shove. "Back off and get your hands off me. You're hurting me, Seth."

"You can't hurt her," Katie whispered, rubbing his shoulder. "Come on, let it go for now."

With a frustrated growl, Seth glared at me. It wasn't the expression of a lovelorn man. He was angry. Furious. This was the last thing I had been expecting today. I didn't quite know what to do with any of it.

"Fine." His fingers slowly loosened. "But you need to unblock me. We're not done, Sera. Not even close."

He let go completely, and I didn't waste a second. Ignoring all the gawkers and gossips, I hurried away as fast as my shaking legs would take me.

At the end of the hall, something pulled my gaze from the floor to the side. The guy in the hoodie was standing there, partially in shadow, his back against the wall. I couldn't see his eyes, but I was certain they were on me.

For reasons I would never know, I didn't want him to think that scene was me. I wasn't the girl who got into messy situations. I didn't let boys push me around. At least, I hadn't before Seth.

I paused in front of him. "I hope you enjoyed our pop-up theater. Watch for our performances around campus."

He slow clapped three or four times. "Bravo. I was almost convinced it was real. Would've been really embarrassing if it had been."

I forced out a laugh. "I know, right? Good thing it was totally scripted." I curtsied. Because why not? "Thank you for coming to the show."

And then I threw a smoke bomb and disappeared.

At least, that was the cool exit I'd made in my mind. Instead, I gave Hoodie Guy an awkward-as-hell wave and took the walk of shame the rest of the way down the hall and out the building.

• • • • ● • ● • • •

By the time I got home, I had a text. Even though I'd frowned and cursed the entire walk home, I smiled as soon as I saw his name on my screen, just like I always did.

ThePhantom: *First day blues?*

Me: *The high point was when I curtsied. Does that tell you anything?*

ThePhantom: *That's classy. Who was on the receiving end of this curtsy?*

Me: *Oh, just this guy in one of my classes.*

ThePhantom: *Oh yeah? Potential replacement for Seth? Or did the curtsy ruin it?*

Me: *Haha, no, I don't think so. I'm not looking for a replacement anyway.*

ThePhantom: *The guy earned a curtsy but he's not good enough for you? Sick burn.*

Me: *Oh my god, I didn't even see his face! He was just some guy with a cane.*

ThePhantom: *A pimp cane? Sounds like an even match to your curtsy.*

Me: *No, a cane cane. Like he has trouble walking on his own.*

ThePhantom: *Poor guy.*

Me: *Anyway, Seth showed up...*

One day out of the blue last semester, the phantom I'd met last spring had sent me a text. *Hey, Dragon Girl. Remember me?* As soon as I saw it, I'd found myself stupidly grinning. He didn't have any good explanation for not texting sooner or why he chose to message me when he did, but I hadn't minded.

His texts were sporadic. I could never predict when he was going to send me a message. Sometimes, it was daily. Other times, weeks would pass. But I pretty much always dropped what I was doing when his name appeared on my screen.

Well...his nickname. I still didn't know his name. I'd asked, and he'd told me since I had a boyfriend, we'd remain strangers who spilled their guts through text messages. I agreed because *I* was loyal to Seth, though I looked for my phantom at every party I went to and around campus.

I never, ever saw him, but I hadn't stopped looking.

I'd find him one day. For now, he was just the name on my screen and my favorite daydream.

Chapter Two

Julien

Sweat dripped down my forehead into my eyes. My shirt was stuck to my chest and back like a second skin. I balled my fists, flexing my fingers in and out, counting the beats of my heart.

"Repeat that to me." I injected calm into every syllable, though there was nothing calm about the war kicking up inside my head.

The receptionist behind the desk had the blandest expression. This was probably an everyday occurrence for her—breaking the already broken.

"I'm sorry, but you've reached your insurance cap for the year. If you wish to continue physical therapy, you'll have to pay out of pocket."

"And how much is a session if I pay out of pocket?"

I asked because I had to, even though any amount would be more than I could afford.

She tapped a few keys on her computer, then glanced up at me, still a wall of impassivity. "One hundred and fifty dollars per hour session. Would you like to keep your next appointment?"

I yanked my hoodie down lower on my head and squeezed my eyes shut. To some people, that wasn't much. They'd pay it in a heartbeat. To me, it was an obstacle I couldn't see my way around.

"Cancel it." I swiped my hand through the air. "Cancel all my appointments. I'm done."

There was no exiting in a blaze of glory. Not for me. These days, the most I could manage was a jaunty hobble with the support of my trusty cane—and after a PT session, there was nothing jaunty about my hobble.

I'd feel good tomorrow. Eyes on the prize and all that.

A black Escalade was idling out front, waiting for me. I threw open the door and hopped my ass inside, tucking my cane beside me.

"You good?"

I glanced over at my boy Amir and gave him a sharp nod. "Feel like shit, but I'm good. Thanks for picking me up."

I'd been going to PT for months and months, and this was one of the few times I'd asked Amir to pick me up. He'd been my best friend since we were kids, but things had changed since my accident. He could barely look at me, and when he did, I had to look away because all I saw in his eyes was heavy, heavy guilt, and I couldn't take it.

"You don't need to thank me, man. I've been offering."

I nodded. "I know. It's easier, living with Lock."

Even though that wasn't the whole truth, it wasn't a lie. I'd lived in a house with Amir and our friend Marco until I got hit by a fucking truck last spring. When I got out of the hospital over a month later, climbing stairs had been out of the question. My pauper ass got lucky, and I was offered a free room on the first floor of a house I now shared with two guys: Lock and Theo.

Amir nodded at the cane. "You could move back in—"

"Nah, I'm good where I am."

Stairs weren't so much a problem for me anymore. It was the fact that my best friend couldn't look at my scarred face without an expression of horrified guilt. Call me selfish, but that wasn't something I needed to see day in and day out. I had my own shit to deal with, and sometimes it got really fucking heavy. There was no room to try to lighten Amir's load.

"It's not the same without you. Just me and Marco. Too quiet. No one plays the piano," Amir said. "You know you can come play any time you want."

I shrugged. "Haven't been feeling very musical."

"Yeah." He sighed, tapping his hand on the steering wheel.

Silence stretched between us when there'd never been silence before. I'd known this guy since pre-K. In all that time, we'd never run out of things to talk about, even if it was just making jokes. I didn't know how to get back to that place, or if it was even possible. More than that, I didn't have the mental energy to try.

"You want to come over for dinner tonight?" he asked. "Zadie's cooking."

I almost accepted his invitation. A big part of me was tempted. Not just because his girlfriend, Zadie, cooked like a chef and had the temperament of an angel. It was more that I missed the hell out of the times we'd had in that house. The family dinners, shit-talking, fucking with each other. Then Zadie had come in and given us the soft we hadn't known we'd been missing. It'd been the best time of my life.

But I had to say no. Mostly because PT took a lot out of me, but also because nothing was the same and trying to relive those days would only be a stark reminder of that.

"I've got some studying to do."

He exhaled slowly through his nose, gripping the steering wheel a little tighter. "Hell must've frozen over for you to turn down my girl's cooking for schoolwork the second day of classes."

"I guess it did."

He gazed at me, giving me a look that would have intimidated most people. I'd been there when he'd learned to tie his shoes, so it was really fucking hard for me to be intimidated by anything he did.

"Is this how it's always gonna be? I'm gonna have to beg you for your time?"

"I don't think I heard you begging. If you want to try that, I'm game."

He didn't laugh, and neither did I. It sucked, but again, I didn't have the mental energy to make it right.

Amir finally pulled up in front of my house. I turned to him before I got out, pretending not to see his subtle wince when he looked at me straight on, and threw him a bone.

"I'm going to hit the gym with Marco after class tomorrow. I don't know your schedule yet—"

He held up his hand. "I'll be there. Text me the time. I'll make it work." His hand tightened to a fist. "Although, can't say I'm fucking pleased you already have plans with Marco and I knew nothing about it."

I chuckled. "Jealous, man? Really?"

He didn't laugh. "Yeah, I am. Don't leave me out, asshole." He gave my shoulder a shove, like he would have *before*. "Get out of my car."

That was the old Amir I knew and loved. The only person he'd ever handled with kid gloves was Zadie, but she was as soft as a feather and deserved that kind of treatment.

I saluted him with my middle finger. "Thanks for the ride, kid."

I felt better leaving his truck than I had when I'd gotten in and thought a lot of it had to do with the way our ride had ended. It was a taste of how things used to be, a flicker of hope we could at least get close to being back there.

Maybe the bone I'd thrown wasn't *only* for him.

• • • • • • • • •

In music class, I'd barely sat down before someone filled the seat beside me. It surprised me since no one wanted to sit in the front row in a lecture like this, but whatever floated their boat. I went about my business, paying no attention to the person next to me as I slid my cane out of the way and opened my laptop.

"Hey."

Spine stiffening, I stopped what I was doing and glanced over my shoulder. A guy with dark hair, wire-rim glasses, and slightly bucked teeth was sitting there, grinning at me.

"Hey," I replied.

"I'm Carson." He stuck out his hand, but I wasn't interested, so I ignored it. He barreled on anyway. "This class seems like it's gonna be a breeze. Do you know anyone who's taken it?"

"Nope."

I would've turned on my laptop, but this guy was all up in my business. In a purely subconscious move, I pulled my hoodie lower.

"Cool. A bunch of my friends from marching band are taking it together. You could come sit with us." He nodded at my cane. "I mean, if you can handle stairs."

"I'm good where I am."

I *had* been—until this kid showed up. He was after something, and I wasn't about to play whatever game this was.

"So, you *can* handle stairs?"

I grunted in response and crossed my arms over my chest.

"Were you, like, born this way, or did you get injured?" he pressed.

Who the hell was this dude? Sure, I'd heard whispers, and the rare little kid I ran across would ask what happened to me, but this was a first.

Before I could even formulate a response, he snickered. "I'm sorry. That's probably none of my business, is it? I saw you on the first day of class and got curious. My mouth ran away from me. I promise, I'm not this big of a dick on a normal basis."

I shot him a sidelong glance. "Look, I'm not really interested. I'm just here for class. I'd appreciate if you sat somewhere else."

Carson jumped like I'd startled him. "Wait—for real? You're telling me not to sit here?"

"Either you move or I do," I intoned.

"What the fuck?" he hissed. "You can't tell me where to sit."

Sighing, I leaned forward to grab my bag. "You're right. I'll move."

As I was stuffing my laptop back in my bag, Carson reached out, his hand coming straight for my face. Since I *really* didn't like anyone looking at my scars, much less touching them, my reaction was swift and violent.

I caught him midair, wrapped my fingers around his wrist, and slammed his hand down on his desk, pressing hard.

"Don't even think about touching me," I gritted out. "That's never going to happen."

He whimpered and squealed, attempting to tug out of my hold. He was stronger than I'd expected, but I kept him down.

"I got it. I got it. Let me go and I'll leave you alone," he said through clamped teeth.

"And you'll pretend I'm invisible for the rest of the semester. I don't want to hear your voice again," I warned.

"Fine, fine. You don't have to be an asshole about it. All I was trying to do—"

I squeezed my fingers into his taut tendons. "I know what you were trying to do—find out what's under the hood, huh? It's none of your fucking business. Now, get the hell out of here."

Tossing his hand into his lap, I peered at him from under my hoodie, the worst of my scars hidden in shadow. I didn't need to worry, though. The weaselly little idiot scrambled out of his seat as fast as his feet would carry him, leaving me alone, just how I wanted to be.

· · · ● · ● ● · · ·

After class, my anger had simmered, and I waited in the same spot in the hall I had the first day. I shouldn't have, but maybe my curiosity was as bad as Carson's. There was no big scene this time. No shouting football players. No bloodthirsty audience hanging on every salacious word.

There was just *her*. The curly-haired redhead who'd been at the center of it all. She was on her own, walking past me. Nothing could have surprised me more than when she stopped in her tracks in front of me.

If her smile had been the sun, it would have been bright enough to banish every single one of the shadows partially cloaking me. Thank Christ it wasn't. I needed those shadows to make me even mildly palatable to this girl.

"No show today. Sorry to disappoint my most loyal patron."

"Me?" I let out a dry laugh. "I've been to one show and I'm the most loyal?"

Her giggle was like a little kid's escaped bubble, floating impossibly high in the clear sky.

"Well, we're a new acting troupe, so we're short on fans. It's good you got in on the ground floor."

I tugged my hood lower. "Finally, something goes my way."

"Oh, hand over some of that good fortune. I could use it." She hitched her bag higher on her shoulder, hesitating for a moment. "Well, I guess I'll see you in class."

"Yep. Until then."

She pinched the hem of her skirt and did a cute little curtsy. "Until then, sir."

I watched her walk away, the ruffles at the bottom of her skirt flipping up on the back of her thick, smooth, muscular thighs. If I'd been my old self, I would have followed her—nah, strike that. I wouldn't have let her go in the first place, not without snagging her digits.

But that wasn't me. I waited until the hall was almost empty, then I wrapped my fingers around my cane and slowly made my way outside.

Chapter Three

Seraphina

Alley dove at me on the couch, sending me to my back, her boobs in my face as she tried to snag my phone. I stuffed it under my butt so she couldn't get to it then shoved at her shoulders.

"Get off me, you lunatic."

"Not until you hand over your phone." She wiggled lower, trying to wedge her hand between the couch and my butt. "Give it to me."

I tipped my head back and yelled. "Laura! Your girlfriend is feeling me up. Come get her!"

Alley wasn't fazed at the possibility of her girlfriend finding her mounted on top of another girl. She was single minded in her determination to get to my phone.

Laura sauntered into the living room, her arms crossed over her chest. "Alley girl, come on. Leave Sera alone. Remember the talk we had about personal space?"

Alley looked at Laura over her shoulder. "I'll give her personal space when she gives me her phone."

Laura cocked her head. "Personal space includes her phone. If she wants to goofy smile at her screen while she texts her mystery man, she's allowed to."

"Yeah." I stuck out my chin. "I'm allowed to. Also, I don't goofy smile."

"You so do." Alley climbed off me, but she was still eyeing me like she was seconds from jumping on me again. "I just want to know what he's saying to make you smile. To be honest, I haven't seen too many smiles out of you in a long while."

Laura wrapped her arms around Alley's waist and kissed the side of her head. "Don't question it, baby. Just be happy *someone* is making our girl smile."

Laura coaxed Alley out of the room, leaving me alone with my phone.

So, maybe I'd been texting with my phantom a lot more than usual. Alley and Laura had noticed, but I didn't want to explain who he was to them. Not when I wasn't sure myself. There was no way they'd approve or understand, but I needed this connection right now.

I scrolled through our messages, reading them over.

ThePhantom: *Better or worse?*

Me: *My day? Better. No Seth sightings.*

ThePhantom: *Are you ever going to tell me the deal with you and that dude?*

Me: *I have bad taste in guys, especially pretty ones, and Seth is exceptionally pretty.*

ThePhantom: *So, what you're saying is you're extremely shallow?*

Me: *Yeah, that's what I'm saying. But for real, I don't know. I feel like I'm coming out of a year-long fugue state. When I look back on the things I let slide with him, I don't even recognize myself.*

ThePhantom: *Guess you'll forgive a lot if he has a pretty face.*

Me: *I was just kidding. You know that, right?*

ThePhantom: *Not sure I do. What was it that kept you coming back for more then?*

Me: *I'm still trying to figure that out, to be honest. Don't be disappointed in me, okay? I couldn't stand it if you were.*

ThePhantom: *Send me a picture.*

At the time, I'd been distracted by posing my body in just the right way and snapping a picture of the upper curve of my hip. Sometimes, I sent him shots of my room or pretty clouds. Other times, it was pieces of myself—secret parts I only showed to him.

Now that I was reading our messages back, I wondered if my phantom was disappointed in me. Did he truly think I was shallow? That thought struck a pang in my chest that I had to rub away.

I read through the rest of our messages from today.

ThePhantom: *Damn. DAMN. Are you sure we really met? I swear, if I had seen those pretty hips, I wouldn't have let that douche drag you away from me.*

Me: *I think I'm insulted you don't remember me.*

ThePhantom: *I'm just playing, Dragon Girl. You know I'd never be able to forget you. But I gotta say, the shadows did you no justice that night.*

He sent me a picture of himself then. My breath caught as I stared down at my phantom's wide, tan hand resting on the flat of his taut, bare stomach. His thumb hovered over his belly button, and his fingers stretched low, almost pointed toward the *V* that disappeared beneath his low-riding pants.

Me: *Gulp.*

ThePhantom: *Bahahahaha...you're so fucking cute.*

Me: *I'm blushing so hard right now. Don't send me pics like that without warning me first!*

ThePhantom: *See? So fucking cute. Send me more pictures.*

Me: *No, sir. You got your one a day. Anyway, I need to go to class. You're on your own with your hot muscles.*

ThePhantom: *And my naughty pictures of you. Whatever will I do?*

Me: *Gulp, gulp, gulp.*

As I got to the end of our messages, Alley stormed back into the room, her hands on her hips.

"That's it. I'm done being ignored. We're going to the gym," she declared.

I hopped up from the couch and stuffed my phone in the tiny pocket on the side of my leggings. "I'm ready. Let's go."

She wrinkled her nose. "That was easier than it should have been."

"I can argue with you if you want."

She huffed. "Fine, but let's argue on the way."

Savage U had two student gyms. I would be frequenting the one with the pool since I had an adaptive exercise class there twice a week. Two birds, one stone, and all that.

Alley and I were lifting free weights while Laura jogged her ass off on a treadmill on the other side of the gym.

"Okay, babe. Time for squats," Alley announced.

I stuck my bottom lip out. "But you're going to be mean."

"That's right—and that's why you like to work out with me." She handed me a dumbbell and picked up one for herself, clutching it to her chest. "Time to drop it like it's hot."

Holding the dumbbell in the goblet position, I kept my core tight and lowered into a deep squat. Alley was right, I *did* like working out with her because she forced me to challenge myself. If I'd been on my own, I probably would have half-assed my way through.

"Oh, wow." Alley licked her lips, staring at something across the gym. "Look at that deliciousness."

My gaze followed hers to three guys using the circuit machines. One was doing pull-ups, another arm curls, and the third seemed to be cheering them on. The guy on the leg press had a hood over his head. My breath caught.

"I think one of them is in my music class." We slowly rose to standing, and I looked over at her. "And, hello, you're a lesbian—why are you checking out guys?"

She gave me a look like I was crazy. "I can recognize beauty when I see it. Doesn't mean I want the *D*. Which one's in your class?"

"The one with the hoodie. He always wears one."

The guy doing pull-ups was lanky and tall, with smooth, rich-brown skin, and close-cropped hair. He smiled at something his friend said, flashing a perfect set of white teeth. The other guy looked like he could have been Middle Eastern, with midnight-black hair, an amber complexion, and a scowl that would scare the devil away. Even when he smiled, he was somehow still scowling.

She hmphed. "Too bad it's not one of the other ones. Hoodie guy seems like the weak link."

I shook my head at her. "That's really rude, Al. I think he has scars or something he's hiding. That doesn't make him the weak link."

She straightened out of another squat. "You're right. I was so mesmerized by his hot friends, I got stupid for a second."

"I'm telling Laura you're getting stupid for boys."

She flipped me off. "Go on, tell her. Then ask her what her favorite kind of porn is."

I dropped my dumbbell with a clang, drawing eyes in our direction. "I don't want to know that," I hissed. Hoodie Guy had turned my way, along with his friends. Not knowing what else to do, I gave him a wave. The tip of his chin was barely perceptible. His friends glancing from him to me and back, however, was more than obvious.

"It's male-male, by the way," Alley whispered. "My girlfriend loves the *D*."

She made me giggle so hard, I couldn't even bend over to pick up my weight. Alley rubbed my back, quietly laughing too.

"I like this version of you so much better than the sad girl you've been lately."

Sobering, I rested my sweaty head on her shoulder. "I can't guarantee I won't slip back into being a sad girl again."

"I know, and you're allowed to feel however you want to feel, I just hate that you're sad over douche canoe Seth. He doesn't deserve the sunshine he stole from you."

Remembering my phantom's words, I asked, "What does it say about me that I was with him for so long?"

"It says you were charmed—because he's more than capable of being charming. And maybe you got lost for a while, but you're back now, so cut out the pity party. You're not getting out of doing squats."

Whip cracked, I bent over to pick up my dumbbell, then dropped it like it was hot. When I glanced up, Hoodie Guy was turned my way again. I flashed him a grin. He only gave me another nod before looking away.

I was a kinesiology major with plans to go to PT school for my graduate degree. What that meant was a lot of my classes were practical now that I was a junior, including my adaptive exercise course.

This class was twice a week, one day in the pool, the other on dry land, learning exercises and various ways to adapt therapy for different injuries. Floating around the pool and hanging out in the gym wasn't the worst way to earn college credit, that was for sure.

Except Katie was in my class, and that *was* the worst since it was such a small group. I'd hopped in the pool before realizing she was already in there and ended up emerging beside her. When I tried to swim away, she caught me by the arm.

I shrugged her off. "Don't."

She held her hands up. "I was just going to say you don't have to go."

"I do. I don't want to be anywhere near you."

She had the audacity to roll her eyes. "You knew Seth and I were close when you went after him."

My eyes bugged at her. "Um. I—what? So, it's my fault you fell on my boyfriend's dick?"

She sighed. "That's not what I'm saying."

I shook my head. "I don't care what you're trying to say. I'm going to the other side of the pool, and I'd really like it if you could pretend not to know me. I'll do the same. I have nothing to say to you, Katie."

Her brow arched. "You shouldn't be such a bitch to Seth. At least let him apologize. He made a mistake."

I almost threw up from how disgusted I was by the things coming out of her mouth. More than that, I was furious she thought she had the right to say *anything* to me.

"Says the mistake." I shook my head, so angry, I wouldn't have been surprised if the water around me started to boil. "Honestly,

Katie, you and Seth can have each other. You're both garbage people—it's a match made in heaven."

I turned and swam away before I lost my mind and pushed her under the water. From the icy look she shot me, she felt the exact same way.

Throwing my head back, I blew out a heavy breath. This was only the first week of the semester—it would get easier. Everything was still fresh. It wouldn't always be this difficult. Seth and I would go back to being strangers, and Katie would be another percussionist in the marching band. I didn't even have to play with her until summer. By then, all this drama would be ancient history.

With my head tipped back, I opened my eyes, my gaze landing on the glass wall overlooking the pool. There he was. The guy in the hood, standing on an unmoving treadmill. I couldn't see his eyes, not from this distance, but I knew he was watching me.

Lifting my hand, I waved. His head canted to the side. Curiosity had me wishing I could see his expression, but he turned away and stepped off the treadmill. Taking one last glance at me, he barely raised his hand then walked away, disappearing into the depths of the gym.

What was that about?

Chapter Four

Seraphina

It was finally the last day of the longest week ever. I just had to get through one more class. One. More. Class. Then I could go home, bury myself under my covers, and not emerge until Monday morning. I deserved a slovenly weekend. Alley and Laura might not agree, but I was prepared to fist fight them to achieve my dreams of laziness.

That was what was in my head as I waited for class to start. Daydreams of pillows, cozy beds, and my smut-filled Kindle. Yes, sir, thank you, sir.

"Dude, are you okay? Are you freaking out?"

Carson slid into the desk beside me. We were in a small classroom where the discussion section of our music class was being held. This one would be taught by the TA instead of the professor.

"Totally fine," I said absently, still stuck on my weekend plans.

He clucked his tongue. "Katie is such a bitch. I mean, first she goes after your man, then she starts telling people she wants to be drum captain next year when everyone knows that's your spot."

That ripped me out of my soft pillow and smut fantasies. I whipped around to face Carson. "What?"

He tilted his head and blinked puppy-dog eyes at me. "Oh yeah, girl. She's actively campaigning. I mean, personally, I'm a little leery of a cymbal player being drum captain, but she does have leadership qualities..."

I stared at him, dumbfounded by the words spilling out of his mouth. Katie wanted to be drum captain? Since when? She barely managed to show up to practice on time, and she played with as much enthusiasm as a bored toddler.

It was Carson's wavering that really sent a wave of panic through me. Since we met my freshman year, and I'd boldly informed him of my plan to become drum captain my senior year, he'd been behind me, one hundred percent. And now...?

"I thought you were backing me. Are you—have you changed your mind?"

"Well—" Carson tapped his chin, "—I'm not saying I won't back you, but now that Katie is throwing her hat in the ring too, it's only fair for me to consider you both. I have to set an example to everyone else, right?"

I'd shove her stupid hat down her traitorous throat. She wasn't taking my position. I'd earned it, I deserved it, and Katie couldn't have one more thing that was mine. I'd give her a thousand Seths—she couldn't have this.

"Carson," I breathed. "I'm—really?" I was at a loss. There were a lot of things I was insecure about, but my place in the band wasn't one of them.

His placid expression did nothing to soothe my nerves, and it was readily apparent he wasn't trying to. A lot of people thought of marching band as the nerd brigade, and maybe we were, but let me tell you, nerds could be mean as hell, Carson being the prime example. He got off on waving his power around so much, he should have been part of the color guard.

"What's fair is fair," he replied nonchalantly, as if he wasn't jamming a dagger in my back.

Just then, his attention went to the door. Hoodie Guy walked through, his eyes sweeping over the class. He paused on me, only for a moment, before going to the other side of the room and taking a seat in the back.

Carson clutched the edge of his desk, his knuckles going white. "Do you know that asshole?"

He did nothing to modulate his voice. Everyone around us had to have heard him calling Hoodie Guy an asshole.

"Why?" I asked.

"Because he looked at you like he knows you."

"We've talked briefly...twice. Why are you calling him an asshole? Do *you* know him?"

He gave his head a sharp shake. "I know he's an asshole who needs to be taught a lesson."

Again with the loud talking. The guy with the hood seemed to be unaware...or at least ignoring Carson's ranting. I sank down in my seat, my cheeks burning hot. I wished I could get up and move or tell him to shut up, but I didn't have that kind of power.

At least he quieted down when our TA started class, but I could practically hear his wheels of vengeance turning. My own were turning too. I only half paid attention to the discussion, the rest of me ruminating over Katie's new campaign of terror. I guessed calling her a garbage person might have been a mistake, but damn, she deserved it. That was more apparent now that I knew she was gunning for drum captain.

In the middle of class, Carson slid me a note.

Sera,

There's a way you can have my full backing, and I will rally everyone else behind you. I want to make a bet. Tell me if you're interested.

-Car

I scrawled yes on the bottom and slid it back to him before I could change my mind. Carson had a thing for making bets. Last year, he bet a trombone player he couldn't convince his parents he was engaged in a torrid affair with his instrument. Another time, he made a bet with a trumpet player to dump his flutist girlfriend for a week then see if she would take him back. She did not, unfortunately for him. Carson always got something out of the bets, no matter who won or lost.

His next note detailed what he wanted me to do. I held my breath as I read it.

Get the asshole in the hoodie to fall for you. Date him through spring break then publicly dump him. You do that, you get drum captain. You don't, we'll just see how it plays out between Katie and you. Your deadline for deciding is the end of class today.

Stomach sick at the very idea of doing this, my eyes flicked up to the guy across the room. His head was bent over his laptop, tapping out notes while staying in his own, solitary bubble. He was surrounded by other students, but he held himself apart, as if he was somewhere else.

If he hadn't spoken to me this week or watched me in the gym, I'd have said no immediately. Even with that, getting this guy to fall for me seemed like an impossible task. And then dumping him? I really didn't know if I had that in me.

But then, he glanced up. From his personal shadows, his eyes connected with mine. I couldn't help the smile that tipped my lips, and I swore, he smiled back. It was barely there, but the low swoop in my stomach at the sight was undeniable. It was like he'd invited me into his bubble for that brief second.

It popped when Carson nudged me, jerking his head toward the note. Hoodie Guy's attention trained on his laptop, and I stared down at the bet.

Could I really do this?

I couldn't imagine hurting another person to get ahead. Nothing was worth that. And that was only a consideration *if* the guy across the room let me get close enough.

Then I thought of the way my chest had caved in at seeing the pictures of Katie riding Seth in the back of his car. How completely into each other they'd been. Then spending winter break with my perfect parents, who had never quite understood me, pitying my bouts of tears, and watching for more serious signs of slipping into a darker place. Hiding every sharp object when they thought I wasn't looking. And my older sister, Ophelia, giving me trite words of wisdom, while her Ken Doll fiancé, Michael, stood behind her, looking almost lifelike.

I'd never be as pretty as Katie, or as glamorous as Ophelia. I'd always be the quirky daughter my parents joked must have been the result of a hospital mix-up. I accepted that and made the best of who and what I was.

I wouldn't accept not being drum captain.

Katie couldn't have this. She wouldn't win. I wasn't going to let her.

I'd figure out a way to make it so the other person who got hurt was Katie...and okay, maybe Seth too. I really hoped he suffered.

I wrote my response to Carson and tossed it on his desk.

I'm in.

It was probably the worst decision I'd ever made—besides Seth—but it was done now. I was committed.

The wicked grin Carson gave me did nothing to settle my nerves. Oh, he was definitely going to get something out of this.

• • • ● • ● • • •

At the end of class, Carson shot me a wink, then booked it out of the room while I lingered. The guy in the hood made his way toward the door, and I tried to be casual about ending up right in front of him. I glanced at him behind me, giving him a grin.

"I'm sad to tell you, our theater troupe has broken up."

He jerked at the sound of my voice, like he hadn't noticed me there. I slowed my steps so I was beside him. He kept his head straight.

"Will I be getting my investment back?" he asked in a low, flat tone.

"No. It's our policy that we don't refund words of encouragement. And since that's all you ever gave us—" I tossed my hands up, "—you're shit out of luck. By the way, I'm Sera."

"Okay."

Well, damn, I had known this wasn't going to be easy, but I hadn't expected to hit a brick wall so soon.

"You know, it would be nice if I could call you something other than Hoodie Guy..."

"You're talking about me?"

I shrugged. "Only to the voices in my head. And of course, I was having your name engraved on a plaque as our most prized patron. It was going to go beneath a statue of you...but my dreams were dashed."

He didn't laugh. In fact, he barely reacted.

"I guess if you don't tell me your name, I'll make one up for you. What do you think about Dudley?"

He huffed, so I supposed he didn't like Dudley.

"All right, how about Draco?"

"Not Harry?"

I grinned. "I was getting there, it's just that I read this Draco and Hermione fanfic last night and—"

"It's Julien," he muttered, interrupting me. Thank *god*.

"Julien? That's your name?"

"Yes. Did you need something?"

Walking ahead of him, I pushed open the door to outside and held it for him. He hesitated before going through it, like he expected it to be booby-trapped or something.

"No, I don't need anything. Do you?" I asked.

He scoffed, his head down. "Nope."

I trailed beside him down the ramp to the sidewalk. "I saw you at the gym yesterday. Do you go there often? I prefer to run outside, but my roommate—the hot blonde girl I was with—likes to torture me with squats. I mean, I think my butt and thighs are big enough, but she says there's always room for growth."

This was truly how I flirted—it was a miracle I'd ever had a boyfriend, to be honest—but even I knew better than to talk about my butt with a man I barely knew. He could see for himself I had...you know, a lot going on back there. I didn't need to draw attention to it. Or open it up for discussion.

"I'm there a few times a week," was all he replied.

"Nice. Maybe we could work out together. I won't sic Alley on you. She'll make you do squats and no one—"

He swung his cane out in front. "Squats aren't really my thing."

"Yeah. Wow." I slapped my forehead, but I kind of wish I could punch myself instead. "Of course they're not." Craning my neck, I peered at his butt. "You already have quite the dump truck. You don't even need to do squats."

I had no idea what I was doing. It was like I was an alien pretending to be human and this was my very first interaction with one. Nothing I was saying made sense. Sure, they were words, and objectively, they were in the proper order, but they had nothing to do with reality. I felt terrible for subjecting Julien to this.

"A dump truck?" he asked.

Julien was tall and rangy, and based on what I could see through his loose clothing, he did not, in fact, have a dump truck ass. He seemed to be in perfect proportion actually. I almost said that, but I bit my tongue, attempting to gather my wits.

I touched his arm, and his muscles bunched beneath my hand. "I swear, I've talked to people before. I have no idea why I'm bungling this all up. I'm sorry, Julien."

He calmly removed his arm from my grasp. "Do you need something?" he asked again.

I was stumped on how to prolong this interaction. Somehow, I had to lure Julien into my web, but I was no femme fatale.

Clearly.

Maybe after a weekend in bed, I'd wake up a new woman. A new, sexy woman who didn't say anything awkward or embarrassing.

"Nope. If you don't want me to walk with you, I can follow behind you. It's just that we're going in the same direction so..."

"I don't want you to follow me."

"Good. It wasn't a real suggestion."

He laughed. It was short and quiet, but it was real. And for reasons unknown to me, his barely there laugh made my chest tight with pleasure. I wanted to hear it again, maybe louder next time.

He let me walk with him until we reached the street where I had to turn left and he had to go right.

"Have a great weekend," I said.

"You too."

It was only when I got home, flung myself down on my couch, and let my brain go quiet that I started to freak out about the bet I'd agreed to.

What had I done?

Slipping my phone out, I texted the only person I wanted to mull this over with.

Me: *I did a bad, bad thing.*

It took him a while to reply, but I was used to that. I scrolled through a few emails and watched some TikToks as I waited. When his message appeared on the screen, my heart stuttered.

ThePhantom: *If you tell me you got back together with Seth, I'm not going to be happy with you, D.G.*

Me: *No. That would be a stupid thing. What I did...or agreed to do, I should say, is bad. So bad.*

ThePhantom: *Please, kill the suspense and tell me.*

Me: *I took a bet to try to date this guy in my music class.*

ThePhantom: *Hmmm...a bet? Why would you take a bet? And who's the guy?*

Me: *Remember the guy with the cane I told you about? The one I curtsied at?*

There was another long pause before he answered. Sometimes that happened. I'd accepted it as a fact of life when texting with my phantom. He breezed in and out of our messages like his ephemeral namesake.

ThePhantom: *So, you took a bet to date a poor guy with a cane. Doesn't seem like the Dragon Girl I know. What's in it for you?*

Me: *Couldn't the guy be what's in it for me? His name is Julien, by the way. I'd rather refer to him by his name.*

ThePhantom: *All right, all right. Tell me the truth now.*

Me: *You'll judge me, but I'll tell you anyway. Katie wants drum captain. She's campaigning for the position. Carson said he'll back me if I take the bet. I'm just vengeful enough to do it.*

ThePhantom: *And drag some schlub in with you? Not sure that's cool. There needs to be something in it for the guy or else you shouldn't do it.*

Me: *Isn't my company enough? And I thought we were calling him Julien from now on.*

ThePhantom: *Normally, I'd say yeah, but not this time. You're getting the drum captain position, so the guy should get something too.*

Me: *Do you hate me for agreeing to this?*

ThePhantom: *Hate is a strong, strong word. How are you feeling about yourself?*

Me: *Not great, but you know, it's been a while since I've felt great about myself.*

ThePhantom: *See, now that makes me sad. Send me a pic. I'll compliment you.*

I wasn't in the mood for snapping pictures of my body today. Not after all this. What kind of person agreed to date someone on a bet? Not for a noble, selfless reason, but for the sake of revenge? Even my phantom was ashamed of me. I could feel it through his messages.

I took a picture of the lollipop earring dangling from my ear and sent it.

ThePhantom: *Cute, always, Dragon Girl. Like those earrings.*

He sent me a picture of his ear. He had two lobe-hugging silver hoops. I didn't really know why, but I was sort of surprised by that.

Me: *Mega cute. Now, tell me what I should do.*

ThePhantom: *Do the bet. Make it worth the guy's time. Don't be an asshole. You okay? I don't like you getting down on yourself.*

Me: *Yeah, I'm okay. It's been a long week.*

Maybe my phantom read between the lines, sensed my slide into misery. He didn't let me go. We texted for another hour, until Alley and Laura got home and shamed me off my phone. Each time I said goodbye to him, it was getting harder and harder not to ask him to meet in person. But if he wanted that, he'd say, and I didn't want to ruin something so important to me.

So I plugged my phone in, swallowed the words I couldn't say, and put on my shiniest smile. If I did it enough, it would be real. At least, that was what I kept telling myself.

Chapter Five

Julien

Tossing my phone aside, I tipped my head back on the couch cushions and rubbed my gritty eyes. I had wasted a lot of my Saturday. I should've been getting changed to head to the gym, but my body wasn't cooperating. It was like my muscles were aware they weren't going to be getting PT anymore so they'd decided to lock up in protest.

Tight all over, I ached. Even my jaw was fraught with tension. But I couldn't really blame that on the accident. That was purely my stressed-out brain.

The front door opened, and the click-clack of heels followed by boots thumping against the hardwood floor told me who'd entered the house without me having to open my eyes. A few seconds later, I became aware of a presence perched on the coffee table in front of me.

I cracked an eyelid. An icy blonde stared back at me with pursed lips.

"Hey."

"Hey yourself," Elena replied. "I'm impressed you left your hovel under the stairs."

"First, let me point out that your dad owns this house. If it's a hovel, that's on him. Second, I only left my hovel because the house was empty." I opened the other eye, giving her a pointed look.

She leaned forward, elbows braced on her knees, her chin on her fists. "Aren't you adorable, pretending you don't want to spend all your spare time with me. I almost believe it."

Chuckling, I let my head fall back again. "I'm trying to find the motivation to head to the gym."

"Should I poke fun at your scrawny muscles? Will that help?"

"Elena." Her boyfriend and my roommate, Lock, came into the room, sinking down on the other end of the couch. "Leave Julien alone."

She gasped, like she was offended. I knew for a fucking fact she was incapable of offense. "I will do no such thing. I'm seriously hurt you suggested it."

He rumbled a laugh, and the look he gave his girl was pure adoration. I looked at her like that too—minus the sex vibes. At first glance, Elena Sanderson came across as just another shallow daddy's girl. She had the look and money to pull it off. Beneath that, though, was stark, raw kindness. Since her dad owned this house, she'd been able to arrange it so I could live here, rent-free. She'd hardly known me when she'd offered the room. Just saw I was in need and couldn't pay and handed it over, no strings *or* pity attached. This rich, pretty girl had never once made me feel beholden, nor had she told anyone.

I cracked a grin. "You don't get offended and you know it."

She sighed, checking out her nails. "Getting offended is boring. Who has time for that?"

With a growl, Lock reached out, grabbed her wrist, and yanked her onto his lap. He was the size of a mountain while she was more of a gazelle, but somehow, they fit.

Taking her new position in stride, Elena draped an arm around her boyfriend's neck and situated herself so she was sideways on his thick legs.

"Julien," she cooed.

"Elena," I deadpanned. "What mischief are you about to get up to?"

"No mischief. I'm inviting you to a *we survived the first week of school* cookout."

"On our deck," Lock added.

I huffed, amused. "You're inviting me to my own house?"

She rolled her eyes. "Yes. And don't annoy me or I'll rescind it." She stretched her long leg across the space between us, nudging me with her toes. "Accept the invitation."

"Who's coming?" I asked.

"The usual suspects." She leaned forward, her eyes narrowing. "Why? Do you have someone you want me to invite? A new love interest? Are you going to give your flower to a special girl? If you are, I really should meet her first. I'm not sure I trust your judgment."

Squeezing my eyes shut, I scrubbed at my face. Elena had this long-running joke about me being a born-again virgin since it had been so long since I'd had a girl—and fuck if it wasn't the truth. I didn't find it so funny anymore, but this girl had done too much for me to jump down her throat, so I laughed it off.

"Nah. I haven't found my perfect ray of sunshine yet."

Her humming reply set off a low-key alarm. Enough for me to sweep her with my gaze. Lock shook his head, murmuring for her to be a good girl.

She kissed his cheek and whispered something that was probably unspeakably dirty, based on Lock's flushed cheeks. I cleared my throat and glanced down at my phone to give them privacy, even though they gave me no such consideration. Ever. Not that I begrudged their happiness. I didn't. *Someone* deserved to be happy.

"So, it's a plan. You'll be on the deck this evening, and you will have bells on," she ordered.

"If bells are required, I'm out."

She kicked me again. "Shut up and just show up. You'll have fun."

• • • ● • ● • • •

I used to have a small circle. Me, Amir, and Marco. That was it. Girls came and went, there were guy friends that hung around, but the three of us were a unit. Then Zadie happened, and with her came her friends.

My backyard, with its mostly dead grass and pretty damn spacious deck, had turned into a badminton court, Theo and Helen on one side, Marco and Elena on the other. Lock was at the grill, and Amir and Zadie were inside. Zadie was cooking while Amir most likely watched her like a creeper and grabbed her ass whenever she came within his reach.

Expanding my circle wasn't so bad. If I'd been my old self, I'd have been enjoying the hell out of the festivities. Instead, I was on the deck, a beer in hand, watching it all happen from the periphery. This was better than the months I barely left my room, though. A lot better.

"This kind of stuff reminds me of my childhood," Lock said suddenly. "The summers, at least, when things slowed down."

"Must've been nice."

He bowed his head. "Yeah. You?"

My laugh was desert dry. "My childhood was nothing like this. It was just me and my mom in an apartment. No sitting outside on a nice deck, grilling. She made hot dogs on the stove. Cut them up in my mac and cheese if she was feeling fancy."

Lock cracked a grin. "Ah, I'd forgotten about hot dogs in mac and cheese. Childhood memory unlocked."

"Mmm." I took another long pull of my beer and let my gaze wander back to the yard. Elena was on Marco's back, encouraging him to charge Theo and Helen. Helen had her racket over her shoulder like a baseball bat. Theo's hands were in his pockets, rocking back on his heels, unbothered as his girl protected him.

"Do you need a ride this week? Or is Amir taking you?" Lock asked.

I shook my head. "I'm done with PT."

Turning away from the grill, Lock folded his thick arms across his chest. His nostrils flared as he looked me over.

"Why?"

I wasn't getting into the wonders of my health insurance with him. "I graduated."

He canted his head, his eyes landing on my trusty cane. "I find that hard to believe. Are you quitting?"

"Nope."

"Do you need—"

I slammed my bottle down on the glass table. "I don't need anything, Lock. I appreciate all you've done, but I'm square now. If I need a ride, or anything else, I'll ask. Can you give me that? Let me be in charge of myself?"

His stare was heavy and assessing, and I was an asshole, but I wasn't backing down. My independence was stolen from me the minute that truck made contact with my body. I didn't regret pushing Amir out of the way and taking the hit, but there had been times I'd wished I'd never woken up in the hospital. Those thoughts came less and less often, but they were still there, lingering in the back of my mind.

"I can give you that," Lock said lowly. "As long as you know you can ask me for anything you need."

I twisted my bottle around in a tight circle and nodded, watching the condensation slide down to the table instead of making eye contact. "I do know that."

After a long beat of silence, Lock turned back to the grill.

That silence carried on for a solid minute before it was interrupted by a squeal of delight from Elena. She charged across the grass with her arms out. Swiveling in my chair, I followed her path. Two blondes came at her, wrapping her in a group hug. That wasn't what had me sitting up straight, though. Right behind them was a little redhead, curls piled on top of her head. She was pulled into the hug too.

Fuck.

Why did Elena know absolutely everyone at this school?

More importantly, why was this girl—Sera—at my house?

The four of them started in my direction. I got up from my chair, but there was no way I'd get inside before they reached the deck. And here I'd been, feeling comfortable enough to be outside without my hoodie on. Everyone here had seen my face at its worst. The way it looked now was a vast improvement from the beginning. But I was—I guess vain was the word—enough not to have any desire for strangers to stare at my scar-mottled skin.

I made it to the door before Elena halted me by calling my name. "Julien," she sang. "Come meet my friends."

I kept the scarred side of my face toward the house, letting my overgrown hair fall forward so it covered as much of my cheek and jaw as possible.

"Hey," I gruffed. "I'm heading inside."

Elena wrapped her fingers around my wrist, peering up at me. "These girls are cool," she whispered. "I wouldn't put you in a bad situation. The blondes are a couple, and the redhead rivals Zadie for sweetness. Come on, Jules. Stay. Don't disappear."

A gasp from behind Elena has us both turning. Sera had both hands over her mouth, her light-brown eyes wide as she looked me over.

"Julien?" she squeaked. "You're here."

Elena hooked her arm with mine. "You know my bestie?"

"Not really," I answered.

At the same time, Sera nodded, her eyes still wide. "We have a class together."

The blonde from the gym sputtered a laugh. "Well, which is it?"

Her girlfriend elbowed her. "Chill, baby."

Sera dropped her hands to her sides, glancing at her friends over her shoulder. "We have a class together but we don't really know each other. I just...kind of tried to force my friendship on him yesterday, and he wasn't into it."

Elena barked a delighted laugh. "This is better than anticipated." She squeezed my arm. "Why weren't you into being friends with Sera? Was it the marching band thing? I promise, she doesn't *always* talk about it."

The gym blonde snickered. "Not *always*." Her eyes met mine. She did a bang-up job at not staring at my scars. "I'm Alley, by the way. And this hot girl is Laura, my wifey."

"They're not really married," Sera said. "I mean, they will be one day. They promised I could be the maid of honor *and* the best woman and there's no takesies backsies, so it's going to happen. Just not yet."

Alley and Laura giggled at Sera's stream of consciousness. I stayed silent while my stomach churned. I didn't *do* this kind of casual social interaction anymore. I couldn't really remember how to act. Discomfort crawled up my skin. If Elena hadn't been holding on to me as tightly as she was, I'd have mumbled an excuse and booked it back to my hovel.

Sera held up the dish in her hands. "Is there somewhere I can put this? It's dessert. For later."

Elena gave me a soft shove. "Julien will show you where to put it in the kitchen."

The kitchen was on the other side of the sliding glass door. It wasn't a mystery. It was on the tip of my tongue to say that, but I didn't need to be an asshole to this girl.

"Come on," I gruffed and headed inside.

Zadie was standing at the island, chopping up vegetables, while Amir, as expected, sat on a stool watching her. They both looked up, their attention on the girl behind me.

"Zadie, Amir, this is Sera. She has a dessert she needs to put somewhere."

Amir stayed seated, assessing the girl, the situation, all of it. That was him. Always on guard. Zadie, though, she came for Sera with her arms out—and that was her, always welcoming and kind.

"Hey. It's nice to see you again," Zadie said.

"You too." Sera leaned in, giving Zadie a one-armed hug. "Now, where can I put this? It's carrot cake."

"You know each other?" Both Zadie and Sera jumped, and I cringed. My question had come out harder than intended.

Sera spun around, smiling like I hadn't just pummeled her with my voice. "We met through Elena."

"We've had some girls' nights. Are Alley and Laura here too?" Zadie asked.

Sera nodded. "Yep. Do you think they'd let me go somewhere fun without them?"

They were giggling, happy to see each other, and I couldn't fucking relax. My skin kept crawling like there were a million ants all over me. The scars on my face felt like they were burning from a too-bright spotlight.

It pissed me off I couldn't be normal. This wasn't me. I was trapped in a stranger's body. An angry, depressed stranger who didn't want to be around anyone, or talk to anyone, or accept the hand he'd been dealt. I didn't know how to be this person.

Amir was studying me instead of his girl. His hands were clenched tight on the counter, knuckles white with tension. He wouldn't look away from me, scanning all my exposed skin. His guilt was a tangible thing, pouring out of him and onto me like vats of molasses. Cloying and thick, sometimes it was impossible to breathe when I was around him. And that made *me* feel guilty. And sad. Really fucking sad.

"I'm gonna go get my hoodie," I muttered.

I left the kitchen and kept my head down.

As always.

Chapter Six

Seraphina

My plans of staying in bed all weekend were thwarted before noon. Alley and Laura stole my covers so I had to wake up and drag myself to the gym. Then the three of us got a text from Elena inviting us over for a cookout. I might have declined, but my roommates were bullies and didn't let me.

As I stood in the doorway of Julien's bedroom, I regretted coming.

He was sitting on his bed, facing away from the door, his head in his hands, a hoodie strewn beside him. It was obvious he wasn't comfortable having us here, and I hated that we had unknowingly put him in this position.

I knocked softly on the door. "Hey."

His head lifted, but he didn't turn around. "Hey."

"I take it you didn't know we were coming."

"Nope."

"I'm sorry. If I had known us being here was going to make you feel uncomfortable in your own home, I definitely would have declined. I'd say we'll go, but I doubt I can drag Alley and Laura away. I can make excuses for you if you want to stay in here, though. I'll even sneak you some food if you're hungry. The cake I made is really good. It's the only thing I know how to make, but I have to say, I've perfected it."

He was quiet for a moment, his shoulders tense and high around his ears. Releasing a long, slow exhale, he relaxed the slightest amount.

"What excuse would you make?" he gruffed.

"Hmmm..." I leaned my head against the doorjamb, thinking. "I could tell everyone you have a sudden bout of food poisoning and can't leave the bathroom."

I am a disgusting human. Why would I say that?

"Plausible, if not embarrassing," he replied dryly.

"Oh yeah, totally gross. Let's see if I can think of a better excuse. What if I tell them you've been hiding a secret phobia of grills and can't take it anymore? Or I could say you ripped your pants. Seeing as it was your last clean pair, you can't leave your room or you'll be flashing everyone your ass."

He twisted around, his eyes narrowed. The lighting in the room was dim, filtering through the slats of his blinds, hiding most of his scars. I'd seen them outside, though, and they were pretty bad. Worse than I'd expected.

"All of your excuses seem to further embarrass me," he said.

I stepped into his room, which was stark and tidy. The walls were empty. The bedding was tucked tight in the corners. He had a sleek cherry dresser and a nightstand beside his bed. Aside from the hoodie on top of the covers and a book on the nightstand, nothing was out of place. It barely looked lived in.

"It was all I could come up with on the fly." I pointed to his bed. "Can I sit?"

He hesitated, then bowed his head. "Have at it."

I took a seat on the end of the bed and pulled one of my legs up, turning my body to face him.

"Julien, I have to tell you, your room is kind of sad."

"Is it?" He glanced around like he'd never seen it before. "It's okay."

"It's not the kind of place I'd expect a lover of the arts to reside. It's a little depressing, if you ask me."

The good side of his jaw ticced. "I didn't."

"What?"

"Ask. I didn't ask your opinion of my room."

He'd said it so softly, it had almost sounded kind. Too bad he'd chastised me. And he'd had every right. I'd been making another useless attempt to flirt by teasing him and had come off as a bitch.

"Yikes. I'm really bad at this."

"What?" he asked.

"Talking to you. I'm okay with other people, but everything I say to you comes out all wrong." I picked up his hoodie, rubbing the soft, worn fabric in my hands. I almost lifted it to my nose—because I was a weirdo—but stopped myself.

"Why do you keep trying?"

"I probably wouldn't, except you made me laugh on a really shitty day after a really shitty incident, and that's hard to forget. And I don't know if you've figured this out about me yet, but I'm a naturally talkative person. Give me a brick wall, and I can make friends. I suppose you're kind of like a brick wall—minus the witty comments on occasion. Maybe that's the real reason I keep trying. I'm jonesing for the wit."

He started to shove his hair back then reversed his actions, pulling more of it forward. I wondered what he'd been like before. He might've always been grumpy, but something told me he hadn't. I would never know the old Julien, though. The one in front of me was who he was now.

"That's a lot of pressure on me," he replied.

"I don't mean it to be."

I brought Julien's hoodie up to my nose and took a long sniff. I froze, suddenly aware I was doing the exact thing I'd been stopping myself from doing the last ten minutes. It was too late. His hoodie smelled like laundry detergent, with just a hint of something cool and spicy. I liked it so much, I tried to sneak another whiff, but Julien fully turned my way, watching me with wide eyes.

"Did you just sniff my hoodie?" He sounded incredulous—which made sense. Sniffing a perfect stranger's clothing was worth incredulity.

"No." In a panic, I tossed it at him. "Honestly, why would someone do that? What a weirdo."

"That *would* be really strange if a girl wandered into my bedroom uninvited and started sniffing my clothes."

I shook my head. "Good thing I'd never do that."

He shoved his arms into his sweatshirt and pulled the hood over his head. "Good thing."

A sudden memory hit me. I'd been to this house once before. Not inside, but on the front porch.

"We've met before," I declared.

His shoulders rose around his ears. "Have we?"

"Yes. Last semester, Elena and I went out and got way too drunk. I dropped her off here because she insisted. You answered the door. You were super grumpy. I actually cried because you were so mean."

He pulled his hood around his head even tighter. "I remember that. Not the tears. You dropping her off."

"I held the tears in until I left." I touched his arm. "But don't worry, I cry at the drop of a hat when I'm drunk. One time, Laura ate the last piece of cantaloupe, and I burst into sobs. I really, really wanted that cantaloupe."

"Did you stab her in her sleep?"

Gasping, my hand flew to my chest. "What do you take me for, Julien? If I were to stab someone, I'd make sure they were looking me in the eyes as life fled their body."

He stared at me. I stared back, giving him no indication I was totally fucking with him. I liked that I'd disarmed him enough, he was giving me a full view of his face without constantly tugging on the strings of his hoodie.

The unmarred half of Julien's face was all sharp planes and angles. High cheekbones and razor-edged jaw, there was a fierceness about him. The other side looked like it belonged to someone else. His cheek was puffy, distorting the shape. A purplish scar tugged at the side of his mouth, trailing to the corner of his jaw. Another line slashed from the side of his nose, diving into branches that reached all the way to his hairline. And there were smaller, puckered scars on his forehead, his eyebrow, above his upper lip. It was hard to see, knowing the pain that must have come attached to his injuries—pain he possibly still carried.

"Have you done that before?" he asked.

"Stab someone?"

He inclined his head.

"Will you be disappointed if I say no?"

"I'd be relieved since we're sitting in my bedroom. Alone."

I poked at my biceps. "I'm glad you're recognizing I could easily overpower you and take you down."

"Is that what you think?"

"It's what I know. I carry twenty-five pounds of drums while I march all over football fields. I can easily take a grown man down if I need to."

Thank god Alley wasn't witnessing this atrocious display of attempted flirtation. The problem was, I was enjoying talking to Julien, so I kept forgetting I was supposed to be seducing him into a relationship.

"*Really*? I think I'm going to take you at your word."

"Not surprised." I shrugged. "I'd be intimidated too."

He rubbed his mouth, but I didn't miss his faint chuckle. The sound spread heat across my chest. Earning a laugh from Julien, no matter how small, was a victory.

He muttered something about crazy girls challenging him to a fight and shook his head, his eyes flicking to mine.

"Marching band? Hmmm. And drums?"

"That's right."

We did the staring thing again. His pretty gray eyes swept over my face. His mouth was set in an almost straight line. The scars at one corner pulled his lips down. I wished he'd smile so I could see how crooked it was, but also because I wanted to make him smile.

"You're not..." He rubbed the top of his head.

I waited with bated breath to find out what he thought I wasn't. Before he could finish, the door swung wide, knocking against the wall. Elena and Alley filled the doorway, giggling.

"There they are," Elena said.

"Very interesting." Alley tapped her chin. "Hi, guys. What's happening in here?"

I hopped up from the bed, both annoyed at their interruption and relieved. Chances were, whatever Julien had been about to say hadn't been complimentary. I talked a big game, but my ego was pretty fragile right now. The last thing I needed was for my shortcomings to be pointed out.

"Just talking. Is the food ready? I'm starving."

"Nothing," Julien murmured at the same time.

Alley and Elena glanced at each other and then me. Elena stepped into the room and gave my hair a fluff, eyeing me with skepticism.

"The food's ready," she said. "We were just wondering where you had disappeared to."

"Well, here I am, but not for long. I could eat my weight in hot dogs." I glanced down at Julien. "Are you coming?"

"Yes, he is," Elena commanded. "Both of you are."

El led the way outside, Alley trailing behind her. I paused at the doorway, biting my lip.

"You know, you don't have to wear the hoodie. I—"

"I know I don't." Julien's rebuke was sharp and immediate, like a slap to the face. And, man, did I feel it. "I don't need to be told that."

"Right. Sorry. I'll go." Spinning on my toes, I fled his room, only slowing in the kitchen. There, I leaned against the counter, letting my heartbeat settle.

This was never going to work. I couldn't even get Julien to tolerate me, much less like me enough to date me. If anything, I was making backward progress, sliding from indifference to blatant dislike.

Tempted as I was to grab my carrot cake and go—it *was* an exceptional carrot cake—I decided to stay and leave Julien alone for the rest of the night.

• • • • • • • • •

Since Elena lived right next door with Helen and Zadie, I'd met them both a few times. Zadie was soft and sweet, fiercely intelligent, and funny in a quiet way. Helen was a red-lipped, badass, skateboarding, brunette beauty. She was tough but friendly. And Elena was...well, she was something else. Outwardly, she was the typical California golden girl. When she opened her mouth and her snark emerged, it was obvious she was anything *but* typical.

If I didn't have Laura and Alley, I would have been jealous of the three of them. But as I sat on the deck, drinking a hard seltzer and diving into my second hot dog, I contemplated merging our groups. Three blondes, two brunettes, and a redhead sounded like the start of a joke—*or* a ridiculously amazing and somewhat scary girl gang.

"We should form a girl gang." Oops, that had slipped out. All eyes swiveled to me.

"Who?" Helen pointed at all the double-X-chromosome-having people on the deck. "Us?"

I nodded.

Elena leaned forward on Lock's lap. "I'm intrigued. Helen, Zadie, and I already have matching bats. Obviously that would be a membership requirement."

"My bat is *not* pink," Helen corrected.

"You have a pink bat. You just refuse to carry it because you're a—"

Lock covered Elena's mouth with his hand. "Be nice," he murmured.

Elena bit his finger before removing his hand. "I was going to say she's a rebel. What did you think I was going to say?"

He gave her an affectionate look, and she sank back into him, cupping his scruffy cheek in her palm.

"Okay, I can do bats." Alley rubbed her hands together. "Do we get to smash things?"

"Not people," Zadie stated. "But things, I would be into smashing."

Amir circled his arms tighter around her, pulling her into his chest and whispering something that made her blush. That was cute. He was kind of scary and intense but still...cute.

Laura snapped her fingers. "I read about this place where you can break shit. You get all geared up and go to town, smashing plates and old cars."

Elena gave her nails a casual inspection. "I love breaking shit."

All eyes turned to me. Helen asked, "Is that what you had in mind?"

I shrugged. "I don't know what I had in mind, but that sounds perfect."

Theo, Helen's stupidly handsome, blue-eyed boyfriend, clucked his tongue. "Three of you with bats is bad enough. Now we're multiplying that by two?"

Marco, the guy from the gym who'd been doing pull-ups like it was his job, eyed me up and down, a slow, lazy smile pulling at his lush lips. The men on this deck were making me sweaty. Too much hotness in one place.

"You're trouble, aren't you?" he asked in a smooth, smoky voice. "Riling up these girls like they need to be more riled."

Because I'd already finished one hard seltzer and was starting in on another, I raised an eyebrow and dipped my voice low.

"I don't think there's such a thing as too riled—only men who can't handle it."

His chuckle was silk against my skin. "Oh, damn. I think you have that right, baby girl."

I almost missed what he said. The sliding glass door had slid open, and Julien stood there, watching me as I did a far better job at flirting with his friend than I had with him.

Tamping unnecessary guilt down, I toyed with one of my ringlets. "I tend to get a lot of things right."

Marco hummed, taking a sip of his beer, a playful smile still tipping his mouth.

My eyes flicked back to Julien, and I nodded to the empty chair beside me. I'd purposely chosen it since it was in the darkest part of the deck, where the lights didn't quite reach. He'd have shadows on his scarred side if it was what he wanted.

He hesitated, scanning for another empty chair and finding one near Marco. He didn't have to sit beside me. I wasn't going to make a spectacle out of it. I held my breath, though I was pretty certain he'd sit by his friend.

Julien grabbed a plate of food and a beer, then he scanned the deck again. I breathed a sigh of—well…not relief, but something else maybe—when he came my way, claiming the spot next to me. I was even more pleased that he'd ditched the hoodie inside.

After a minute, he turned his head, eyeing me. "What number hot dog is that?"

I picked it up, taking a little bite. "Only number two. Sadly, I think I overestimated how hungry I was. I won't actually be able to consume my weight in hot dogs."

"Two is pretty legit, though."

I scrunched my face. "Did you think I was finished? I'm only getting started." Because I refused to be cool or sexy or anything attractive around this guy, I stuffed almost half a hot dog in my mouth, stretching my cheeks out like a chipmunk.

Julien laughed a loud, boisterous laugh, his mouth curving into a crooked grin. Just like that, it didn't matter that I was constantly embarrassing myself in front of him. That one laugh made it worth it.

The chatter around us quieted, and everyone turned in our direction. I froze, my mouth full of hot dog, and Julien's laughter sadly died down as quickly as it had come.

He took a long pull from his beer bottle, and I chewed as fast as I could, crossing my fingers I didn't choke since that was the direction this evening was definitely going.

After an awkward pause, conversation started back up, though Julien stayed silent, even as Marco flirted with me and I bantered back.

After eating a third hot dog, I joined in a game of badminton. Alley almost took out my eyes with a birdie, but I dodged it at the last moment, knowing how vicious she could be. Unfortunately, that meant face-planting in the dead grass. Marco helped me up because he was a gentleman. *And* I was pretty sure he wanted to get in my pants.

Flattering, but detrimental to my Julien-seduction plan.

So, I ran away, into the kitchen to fetch my carrot cake. I brought two slices out on the deck, where it was only Julien and me. Zadie and Amir had disappeared to parts unknown, while the rest were playing a badminton death match in the dark.

"Do you want some cake?" I asked.

Julien took the plate wordlessly, his head bowed. I sat beside him, digging into mine. The cream cheese frosting hit my tongue, and I groaned.

"This is my grandma's recipe," I said.

"It's good."

"I know. She tried to teach me to cook and bake, but this was the only one that stuck. She started calling me carrot cake. That, or CC for short, until she died last year."

He made a noise that almost sounded like amusement. "That's cute. I like it."

"Yeah. She always made me feel special with little things like that."

"Sorry you lost her."

"Me too. She was the only one in my family who really got me."

He let that statement lay, which was okay. We were barely more than strangers. Laying my family trauma on him wasn't really appropriate.

After a minute, he cleared his throat and pushed back his chair. "I'm going to go inside."

Startled, I launched to my feet. "Oh. Are you sure?"

He rose a little slower, grabbing his cane and plate. "I'm sure." He started past me, then stopped right beside me, his eyes sweeping over me in the dark. I found myself holding my breath again, wondering what he might say, if he might finish the sentence he'd started in his bedroom.

"Have a good night, Sera."

I hid my disappointment with a bright smile. "You too, Julien. See you Monday."

With a sharp nod, he turned and walked away as I sank back into my seat. That hadn't been perfect, but it hadn't been as big of a disaster as I'd thought it would be.

On Monday, I'd have my game face on. No more stuffing hot dogs in my mouth or sniffing hoodies. I was going to make this guy fall for me if it was the last thing I did.

Chapter Seven

Julien

I wasn't surprised to see Sera already sitting in the front row of our music lecture when I arrived. What did surprise me was my lack of annoyance. When she waved, I didn't have to fight the urge to turn around and leave.

She didn't bother me the way someone like her should have. Someone happy, filled with sunshine and a bright future. That was evident just looking at her.

So, what the hell was she doing, trying to hang out with someone like me?

Something else was at play here.

I sat down in the empty chair next to her, nodding. "Hey."

"Hey. How was the rest of your weekend?"

"It was fine. You?"

"Well, I didn't harass anyone else, so I'd say the end was better than the beginning."

I glanced at her. Her lips were pressed in a tight line. "You didn't harass me, if that's what you're implying."

"That was definitely what I was implying. I'm sorry, anyway. I think I'm just in a weird space with the breakup of my acting troupe and all."

I scoffed, almost smiling. "Oh, right. The acting troupe."

She tsked, shaking her head. "How soon they forget. You went from our top patron to completely blanking on us. I'd cry if I weren't all out of tears."

"From the breakup?"

Her nod was solemn. "Of the troupe."

"Obviously."

A chorus of laughs and snickers from a few rows back sent a trickle of unease down my spine. I shifted in my seat, refusing to turn around. Sera did the opposite, twisting in her seat and scowling.

"Do you know them?" I asked.

She sighed, turning back around. "Yes. A few people from marching band are sitting back there, and I'm pretty sure they're laughing at me. I love my band, but damn, the gossip mill can be vicious."

"They're gossiping about you?"

"Most likely. That's what happens when your boyfriend sleeps with his best friend, who is also in band. Everyone knows, they take sides, and they squeeze all the drama out of the subject they can. It's pretty exhausting, which is why I'm sitting down here, beside you, instead of with them."

I winced. My friends had their faults, but that kind of shit didn't fly. "And you love those people?"

Her hands spread out on her closed laptop. "They're not all like that. And when I'm drum captain next year, I will not play around. There will be no toxicity in my drumline." One hand balled into a fist. "I guess I should say *if* I'm drum captain."

Our conversation was cut off by the start of class. The lecture was on ska bands from the nineties. Out of all my classes, this one was going to be the least painful. An hour of being immersed in music would always be my idea of a good time.

Beside me, Sera tapped her finger along to the beats, a smile curling the corners of her mouth. She was even more immersed, bopping her head and doing her thing, seemingly without a care for who was around her.

I wondered when she was going to tell me what she wanted from me. She wasn't being this friendly because she found me delightful. Even I could acknowledge I was a grumpy son of a bitch and not particularly fun to be around. I had my reasons, but that didn't make being in my company any easier.

There were ulterior motives here, I just had to wait for her to let me in on them.

She turned her head, catching me looking. I didn't try to hide my stare. Instead of being put off by my frown, she wiggled her shoulders and mouthed the lyrics about never having to knock on wood.

I remembered when it was easy to be free like that. To not care who looked at me. To *want* people to look at me. My stomach coiled with jealousy. Sera still had something I'd lost and would never get back. *Fuck*, it was hard to look at her.

With a heavy sigh, I turned away, keeping my eyes on the professor for the rest of the lecture. I hated this. I was trapped in this existence, this failure of a body, this hideous face, and there was no end in sight. This was me now, but I was fucking grieving over who I used to be. Sometimes, that grief hit me out of nowhere, like when a sweet, carefree girl mouthed the lyrics to a ska song in the middle of class. I couldn't fight the rising anger in my gut. It burned and raged, but there was no one to direct it toward.

When class ended, I muttered a quick goodbye and got out of that room as fast as my no-good legs would take me.

Too bad it wasn't fast enough to miss the darkness that curtained over Sera's sunny face as she watched me go.

• • • • ● • ● • • •

A week with no PT, and I was feeling it. My hip and leg were tight as I walked on the treadmill. Marco was beside me, powering through his miles like a machine. Being around him was easy. He had times when he was as intense as Amir, but he didn't carry any guilt. Marco powered through life the same way he did his miles.

He took his earbud out of his ear. "You hear from Amir, bro? Is he showing up?"

I shook my head. "Nah. I didn't mention the gym to him."

His stare was hard. "You didn't mention the gym? Why not?"

"He doesn't need to be here, watching over me. He's got other things going on."

"That's a load of bullshit and you know it. The kid needs to work out too. He wants to be around you. Two birds, one stone, man. What's the real reason?"

Marco was running a six-minute mile and wasn't even winded. I couldn't even be mad about it. I'd *never* been the machine he was.

"Did you see him working out last week? Or was he spotting me on every fucking machine?" I swiped sweat off my forehead with the back of my hand.

"That's what he was doing?"

I nodded. "That's what he was doing."

Marco went silent, his mouth tight as he ran. Then he heaved a sigh, shaking his head. "He's gotta cut that out."

"That's not happening. He looks at me, and I know what's going on in his head. He wishes I never pushed him out of the way. He wishes he was the one who got hit, even though he probably would have died. Luck is the only damn thing that saved me that night. There's no moving on, not when he has to look at me to do it."

Marco kept running, his head forward. I walked, even though my leg was screaming at me to stop. If I was going to have a limp forever, at least I'd be strong. At least I'd have stamina.

At fucking least.

"He might wish that," Marco murmured. "But it's only for a split second. I know he's glad you're both here. Maybe he'd wish it less if it seemed like *you* were moving on, you know? If it seemed like you were happy. Maybe if you had a girl like he does. I don't know, man. All I know is you can't keep pushing him away. He loves you like a brother."

"You're both my brothers. That's never gonna change. But this is who I am now."

Marco stopped, letting the treadmill keep going, his feet on the sides, and looked at me.

"Have you talked to Amir about any of this?"

"You know I haven't. I already know what I know. No sense in pressing on open wounds."

Puffing up his cheeks, he blew out a long breath. "Man, this is some shit. Something's gotta give."

That it did. Avoiding my best friend for the rest of my life wasn't really an option. I'd get hit by a dozen trucks to get back to where we used to be. But I was flying blind here, trying to figure out my own new, encumbered life. That didn't leave room for figuring out how to fix my shit with Amir.

Marco started running again, and my attention drifted to the windows in front of me overlooking the pool a level down. I knew what time it was. She'd be there, taking her class. I knew that, and still, when I spotted Sera walking along the side of the pool, pulling the back of her one-piece bathing suit out of where it had ridden up her round, perky ass, my breath caught in my throat.

Even from my high vantage, I could tell the squats she said Alley made her do were working. Her thighs were thickly muscled, and when she walked, her ass bounced with each step.

Marco being Marco, a connoisseur of women, noticed too. "Damn. I didn't know all that was happening back there on Saturday."

I grunted, my hands tightening around the handrails.

He looked at me, not missing anything. "Oh, shit. Are you into Little Miss Ass-Is-Hot?"

"I don't know her." That wasn't going to stop him, though. Marco could be a dog with a bone, never giving up even when he was wrong. "I was just noticing the same thing you're noticing. Pretty little ass on that girl."

He was looking at me while I watched Sera lower herself into the pool.

"You should hit that up," he said.

I shook my head. "Not for me."

He clicked his tongue against his teeth. "Too quirky, right? I feel that. I'd probably overlook a lot for a girl with that kind of ass on her."

Scoffing, I fought off a grin. "Says the dude who fucked Vanessa for a full semester. Vanessa, who had zero personality or sense of humor. I'll say you'll overlook a lot."

Turning his head, he revealed his pearly whites. "Fuck yeah. I'm as shallow as they come and don't deny it."

Marco kept running, and I walked through the pain, even as my physical therapist's voice scolded me in the back of my head.

Watching Sera splashing in the pool made it a hell of a lot easier to grit my teeth and keep going.

Chapter Eight

Seraphina

As much as I loved swimming, my hair didn't appreciate chlorine. After class, I headed straight for the showers, dodging Katie, who seemed to still be under the impression I wanted to hear anything she had to say.

I found I didn't care about her anymore. Over the year Seth and I were together, her very existence used to fill me with jealousy. But I supposed I'd been spending most of my time waiting for the other shoe to drop. Now that it had, I really couldn't get it up to spend much thought on her at all.

I mean, I was pissed she thought she could be drum captain when she had no leadership skills and was a mediocre percussionist at best. She'd soon be relieved of that notion, though...once I figured out how to lure Julien into my sultry and seductive web.

A giggle bubbled out of me under the water. Sultry and seductive. Hilarious.

Still laughing to myself, I turned off the shower and squeezed my hair out. Then I wrapped a towel around my head, another around my chest, slipped my feet into my shower flip-flops, and padded over to where I'd left my bag on a bench.

Using a wide-tooth comb, I got the snarls out of my hair, then scrunched in some curl cream and tossed it back. I reached into my bag for my clothes...and came up empty. Frowning, I peered inside.

Not only were my clothes missing, my wet bathing suit was too. There were zero pieces of fabric in my bag, though all my toiletries and hair stuff were right where I'd left them.

What the fuckity fuck?

Vaulting to my feet, I whirled around, checking my surroundings. Nothing on the floor. I yanked open all the unlocked lockers. They were barren. And of course, the locker room was completely empty, so there was no one to ask.

Slumping down on the bench, I racked my brain, trying to figure out my next move. At least I had two towels. I wasn't completely exposed, but the towel around my body barely covered my butt. There was no way I could walk home like this.

Alley and Laura were across campus in classes. If I waited here, I bet they'd bring me clothes. That was what I'd do, since obviously I wasn't going to be leaving the locker room like this.

As I got my phone out to send an SOS text, the locker room door creaked open.

"Sera? Is there a Sera in here?" a girl's voice asked.

I hopped up and waved. I didn't recognize the girl peeking her head through the cracked door, but I took her knowing my name as a good sign. "I'm Sera."

She jerked her thumb over her shoulder. "There's a guy out there who asked me to check on you. He seemed concerned, but I don't know..."

"Oh, okay. Thanks."

With a sharp nod, she disappeared as quickly as she'd come, letting the door bang shut behind her.

My brow furrowed, I crossed the tile floor and cracked open the door.

Seth was right outside, pacing. When he saw me, he stopped, his eyes wide.

Bad sign. The girl knowing my name had been a bad sign. I had to get better at reading them.

"Sera. I've been waiting out here to talk to you. I got worried when you didn't come out." His eyes swept over me. "Why are you in a towel? Go get dressed. You shouldn't be standing there where anyone could see you. Your fucking pussy is almost on display."

It was funny to me now, watching Seth's concern quickly switch to control. I hadn't noticed it when we were together, but my view of him had been too myopic. Now that I had taken a hundred steps back, the big picture became clear: Seth was an asshole.

And still, *still*, having him close like this, acting interested in me, panged low in my stomach. It was undeniable he'd hurt me many, many times while we were together, and I wasn't over it. I hated him, I truly did, but I also ached with sadness. I'd once loved him, and he'd taken that love, slurped it up, and found it lacking.

Found *me* lacking.

"Why are you here?" I asked, keeping the trembles out of my voice.

"I told you. I'm here to talk. Where are your clothes?"

My eyes narrowed. "Someone stole them. You wouldn't know anything about that, would you?"

His jaw dropped like he was appalled. "What the fuck? Absolutely not. Someone *stole* your clothes?"

"Mmmhmm. Strange, right? Who would have done something like that?" I retreated away from the door, ready to close it on his smug, handsome face. "Anyway, I need to go text my friend to bring me new clothes. See you around."

His hand shot out, keeping the door open. "Fuck that. I've got some spare clothes. You'll wear them, I'll drive you home, and we can finally talk."

"No. I have nothing to say to you, and I don't want to hear anything you have to say. Please, leave me alone. We're done."

He kept pushing, completely ignoring my request. "I don't accept that."

"Too bad. Go talk to Katie." Movement behind him caught my eye. Julien was across the hall, watching the show from the shadows. "Move out of the way. My friend is here. Julien!" I called.

Seth reared around to see who I was waving over. Julien approached, his movements slow, tentative, his head swiveling to check out the situation.

"Hey, Jules. Thanks so much for coming. Can you believe my clothes disappeared? You have some extras, right?" I rounded my eyes, attempting to convey he needed to say yes, no matter what the real answer was.

"Of course I do." He unzipped his gym bag and pulled out a hoodie and shorts. "Here you go. I'll wait out here for you."

Relieved, I grabbed the clothes from him, ignoring Seth's presence, even though I could feel the waves of anger seeping out of him. I hoped it was eating him up inside. He had to understand he didn't have control over me anymore.

"Sera," he hissed. "Who the fuck is this guy?"

Leveling him with the hardest gaze I could manage, I pressed my mouth into a firm line. "None of your business. Now, let me close the door so I can get dressed."

Surprisingly, he let go, but as the door swung shut, I saw him twist toward Julien. My stomach dropped. Oh god, if he hurt Julien, I'd never forgive myself.

But Seth was all bark. Being on the football team, he couldn't afford to get in fights, but more than that, deep down, I was pretty certain he was a coward. He'd talk shit all day and night, but when push came to shove, he always acted like he'd been joking. I'd seen his act more than once. I just hoped he didn't look at Julien as an easy victim.

I threw on Julien's basketball shorts and tugged on his hoodie before slipping my feet back into my flip-flops and tossing my bag over my shoulder. Then I yanked open the locker room door and—

Stopped in my tracks.

Seth had his hands up in a defensive position, backing away from Julien, who had somehow made himself look bigger, tougher, more intimidating. He was in Seth's face, gritting out something too low for me to hear. He used his cane to shove at Seth's middle, like a damn cattle prod. Seth fell back and back and back, even though he was arguably stronger and should have been able to stand his ground.

Julien raised his voice enough for me to finally hear. "If I find out you've been fucking with her again, I won't be as friendly as I am right now. Get the fuck outa here, man."

This was...well, it was breathtakingly sexy. If I'd been wearing panties, they would have been wet. Crap, was I making Julien's basketball shorts wet? That was not okay.

Seth made an ugly, scrunched-up expression, then nodded and walked away with his head down. Julien stood there like a sentinel, watching until Seth disappeared from sight.

I took a step forward, and the locker room door swung shut behind me. Julien spun around, his face flushed crimson, his brows dipped low over furious eyes. He took a moment to inhale a deep breath then strode toward me, stopping right in front of me.

"Are you okay?" His concern came out hard and rough.

I nodded. "I'm fine. Pissed off, but none the worse for wear. I'm sorry for dragging you into my drama. I wasn't thinking when I called you over. That was so dumb of me—"

He grabbed my shoulder, cutting me off. "Don't apologize to me. I wouldn't have gotten involved if I weren't willing."

The breath I sucked in was shuddering. Julien took notice, squeezing my shoulder and watching me warily.

"I'm sorry anyway. Even if you won't accept it. Normally, audience members don't get pulled onstage, but one of our performers went rogue." My joke fell flat. Julien didn't even pretend to find me amusing, and I guess it really wasn't all that funny. I tucked my damp hair behind my ear. "That won't happen again."

The good side of his jaw ticced. "Don't worry about it, Sera." He canted his head toward the exit. "You going home?"

"That was my plan."

"I'll walk with you. Let's go."

Our path through campus was filled with silence. Julien was most likely happy about that, but I was sinking into a pit of negativity, and I really didn't want to go there. Plus, I'd made zero headway on convincing him to fall for me.

"Thank you for the clothes." I draped my hood over my head. "I feel like you now."

He huffed an almost laugh. "I'm not wearing a hood."

"Don't think I didn't notice. Why not?"

"It's hot as hell and I'm trying to get used to not wearing it all the time."

"Good thinking." I pushed my hood off. "By the way, I don't know if you were wondering, but that was my ex. He cheated on me before winter break, and I blocked him everywhere so he couldn't contact me. He seems to think I need to talk to him, to listen to his explanation, but I disagree. I'm almost certain he set up that situation back there so he could swoop in and save the day."

He stared straight ahead, but tilted his head toward mine, showing me he was listening. "Are you disappointed I didn't let him?"

I snorted at his ridiculous question. "Absolutely not. I would have walked home naked before letting him play the hero."

He shot me a quick, grumpy look. "Not an option, Sera."

"Well, obviously." I tugged on my hoodie strings. "Because you were there to save the day—which I am not thanking you for."

He turned his head then, scanning me from head to toe. "You look better in my clothes anyway."

I peered at his ass, then looked over my shoulder at mine. "I don't know about that, but I definitely fill them out more."

"I thought I had a dump truck ass," he said dryly.

"You can't hold any of my nervous rambling against me, Julien. You have to let that go."

That got me another sharp look.

"Why were you nervous?"

"Because I want you to like me. And I don't know if you know this, but you're sort of a hard nut to crack."

There was a long pause as we stopped at an intersection, waiting for the light to turn so we could cross. A few students waited with us, pressing Julien and me closer.

He peered down at me. I was glad he'd lost the hoodie, at least for now. Maybe he was getting more comfortable with me. I hoped that was the case.

"Why do you want me to like you?" he asked. "We're strangers."

"We were, but not anymore." I smoothed my hands down the sides of my thighs. "I'm wearing your clothes, after all. I'm assuming you don't give them out to just everyone. And anyway, I want you to like me because I like you."

A loud laugh burst out of him. This one, I didn't like. It was bitter and humorless.

"You like me? Why the hell would you go and do that?"

A few people stared at us—at Julien—but the light turned and we were able to start walking again before he noticed. Or maybe he noticed and just refused to acknowledge them.

"I don't know. It just happened. It probably had to do with our first interaction."

"We barely exchanged words."

I elbowed his arm. "You're not talking me out of this. Despite your bouts of grumpiness, I've liked talking to you. And it gets easier each time we do it. So, I think we should probably continue. Maybe over coffee or dinner or something."

I did it. I probably should have built up to asking Julien on a date a little more, but since it was my first time, I wasn't exactly smooth about it.

"No, I don't think so," he said lowly.

That was a gut punch. I knew he wasn't falling in love with me or anything, but wow, I hadn't expected to be turned down so swiftly.

"Um...okay." Feeling twitchy, I hooked my thumbs in the straps of my backpack. "Would you tell me why not?"

He breathed slowly out of his nose. "Because I don't believe you want to go on a date with me. I've given you no reason to want that. So, either you're grateful for me helping you out back there and are trying to repay me—which is unnecessary and unwanted—or you have an ulterior motive."

My heart leaped into my throat. Swallowing a few times didn't lessen the tightness holding back my answer. I didn't know what to say. Both of those things were true, but I really did enjoy hanging out with Julien. When I'd accepted the bet from Carson, I'd expected this whole fake dating thing to be a trial, but now, I was mostly looking forward to it.

"Um—"

We came to another intersection. Julien faced me, his nostrils flaring. "Cat got your tongue, Sera? You honestly expected me to believe you have some sort of thing for me? Unless you want to tell me what that offer was really about, we're done here."

My mouth opened, closed. "Julien—"

When it came down to it, I didn't want to lie to him, but I couldn't possibly tell him the truth. I didn't know what to say. Even if I had, the knot in my throat was too big for words to pass. So, I stood there, mute, blinking up at him. He stared back at me, with his storm-cloud eyes and crooked frown, shaking his head like he was disappointed in me.

"That's what I thought. I'll see you around." Julien stalked off in the opposite direction, leaving me standing there, at a loss.

That was when I checked our surroundings and saw how close I was to home. This was where Julien and I had parted last week too.

I couldn't believe how badly I'd bungled that interaction after everything. To be fair, it was my first time ever attempting to ask a guy out, and though I'd rushed it, I thought I'd done okay.

Obviously, I'd been wrong.

And it made me sad Julien couldn't believe I genuinely wanted to spend more time with him. Because I did, despite the bet. I found him interesting, and he made me laugh. We could be friends, for sure.

Well, could have been. Not now. I'd screwed it all up.

I shook myself back to the present, where I was still standing alone on a street corner. I could hear my mother's voice in my head, scolding me for getting lost in yet another daydream.

Snapping out of it, I slinked home with my tail between my legs, defeated and utterly bottomed out.

• • • ● • ● • • •

Seeing a text from my phantom didn't bring me out of my crap mood. I'd been slamming cabinets in the kitchen for the last hour since I'd gotten home, hungry but not finding anything I wanted to eat. Fortunately, neither Alley nor Laura was here to judge me. Or ask questions. Asking questions would have been worse.

ThePhantom: *Hey, Dragon Girl. How's life? Raining hellfire down on campus?*

Me: *It's fine. How are you? Can we talk about you for a change?*

ThePhantom: *Hey...what's wrong? You sound upset.*

Me: *You don't know what I sound like because you met me once, almost a year ago. You probably don't even remember my face. Don't you want to see me in person? Or am I only palatable through a screen?*

Obviously, I deleted that self-effacing stream of consciousness that would definitely cause my phantom to block me and never speak to me again.

Me: *I made a mess of things with Julien. We were having a good conversation, and I pushed for a date. Naturally, he rejected me.*

ThePhantom: *Why naturally?*

Me: *Naturally because I seem to be in a downswing right now. Nothing's going how I want it.*

ThePhantom: *Are you getting down on yourself, D.G.? Are you having bad thoughts?*

Me: *Of course I am. How could I not?*

ThePhantom: *The kid who rejected you probably knows he's not good enough for you. And the piece of shit who cheated on you definitely knows he's not good enough for you. What those assholes did has no bearing on your awesomeness.*

Me: *Nice words, Phantom, but the common denominator in both those cases is me.*

ThePhantom: *Imagine I'm shaking some sense into you right now.*
Me: *I'll give you my address, you can do it for real.*
ThePhantom: *Nah, I think you probably need a hug more than shaking. I don't like when you get down on yourself. You've gotta be kinder to my girl.*

It was when he said things like this that I desperately wanted to ask why he never suggested we get together in person. He called me his girl, worried over me, had wanted to tear apart the world when Seth cheated, but he didn't want to see me, when we lived in the same town and went to the same university. I always came back to it being my fault. I'd revealed too much about myself in the beginning—my past struggles with depression, my darkest thoughts and urges. He would never see me as more than that.

Me: *I try, promise. I'm just having an off afternoon. The thing with Julien really threw me for a loop.*
ThePhantom: *I thought you were going to make a deal with the cane kid anyway. Did you try to make a deal?*
Me: *No, I didn't. I like him. I'm not sure if it's more than friendship, but I do like him. I really did want to spend more time with him. Leading with the bet seemed like a dead end.*

It took so long for my phantom to respond, I almost gave up and assumed he'd faded back into the ether. But my phone finally chimed with a text from him.

ThePhantom: *Lead with the bet. Offer him something or let him ask for something. I think he'll take it. Who wouldn't want you as a fake girlfriend?*
Me: *I think I might have to lick my wounds for a while. I don't know if he'll even talk to me again after today's debacle.*
ThePhantom: *I doubt it was as bad as you think. You could charm the pants off a man in a kilt, Dragon Girl.*
Me: *That is patently false and we both know it. But thanks for the attempted confidence boost.*
ThePhantom: *I'm your cheer section. Always. Now, I'm gonna need you to go for a walk, or eat something sweet, or call a friend. Can you do that for me? Can you pull yourself out of this?*

My heart contracted in my chest. I'd never been so honest with anyone about my struggles as I had with my phantom. Well, except the therapist my worried parents had thrust upon me my senior year of high school. The thing was, I trusted my phantom more than I'd ever trusted the therapist. Maybe it was the near anonymity of it all.

Me: *I can do that if you send me a pic first.*

I waited a minute, then two, before an image came through. My breath caught at the sight of his sinewy forearm, the veins popping as he flexed. What was it about veiny forearms? Liquid pooled in my mouth as I stared, zooming in and out.

Once I was finished drooling for the moment, I took a picture of my hand too. Only, mine was positioned in front of my mouth, my index finger caught between my teeth, pulling my bottom lip down.

ThePhantom: *Fucking shit, are you trying to kill me?!*

Me: *You started it.*

He faded away then, just like I'd known he would. That was okay, though. He'd succeeded in snapping me out of my downward spiral. I tucked my feet in my shoes and grabbed my wallet.

Walk, sweets, phone a friend, then I'd figure out how I was going to fix things with Julien. I was determined.

Chapter Nine

Seraphina

Carson snagged me outside the lecture hall, yanking me away from the door.

"What the hell?" I tugged my arm out of his iron grasp. "What are you doing?"

"I think I should be asking you the same question. What are *you* doing, Seraphina? I thought you accepted the bet, yet I don't see you and Mr. Broken Bones all loved up. Are you backing out? That would be incredibly disappointing. I'd honestly hate for Katie to become drum captain next year, but she has a strong contingent of supporters..."

He folded his arms across his chest, giving me his best imperious, bitchy look. This guy was so damn power drunk, he made me sick. I really hoped the real world slapped him in the face. But he was rich, with a powerful family, so probably not.

"I'm not backing out," I said firmly. "I'm sorry if it takes me a little time to get a guy to be into me, but I'm working on it."

Sort of. I hadn't actually come up with a plan yesterday. I wasn't even sure Julien would speak to me today. But I was going to keep trying.

His nostrils flared as he glared at me. "You managed to bag Seth and he's on the fucking football team. I think you can seduce a hobbling-ass—"

I held my hand up, beyond irritated. "You're my friend, Carson—" Gag, he wasn't. "—but I'm not comfortable with ableist insults. I don't know what you have against Julien, but please stop with that kind of talk around me."

His narrow jaw clenched so hard, I worried for his veneers.

"Fine, Sera. Have it your way. I'll be watching your little faux-woke ass closely. If I get even a hint things between you and your special boyfriend aren't real, like you decide to tell him about the bet, I'll throw all my support to Katie."

With that final threat, Carson spun on his toes and marched into class. My entrance was slower, with less flair. Eyes were on me as I took a seat in the front row, and I tried my best to ignore them.

Julien slid into the seat beside me at the last moment. I turned to him, offering a shaky smile. He eyed me for a long, drawn-out moment, then lifted his chin, his mouth in a firm, straight line.

Thick tension created a barrier between us. I wanted to whisper something funny to him, but I couldn't think of anything to say. Fortunately, class began, and we got to listen to big band music today, so I was swept away in that for a while. I noticed Julien's fingers moving on his desktop, like he was playing piano, and wondered if he was a musician.

His fingers were really nice. Long and thin, but strong. His nails were neatly trimmed, and the veins in the back of his hand popped.

Unable to help myself, I leaned closer to him. "Do you play piano?"

He stiffened for a moment, looking down at me from under his hood. "I did."

"You stopped?"

"Mmm."

That wasn't much of an answer, but if he *had* stopped, I felt sorry for him. There was nothing that could make me quit music. Even when I'd hated life so much, I wished for it to end, music had kept me going.

But Julien and I were not the same.

• • • ● • ● • • • •

As we flowed out of class, I stuck beside Julien. My brain was still whirring to come up with what to say, but there was nothing.

Outside, he came to an abrupt halt, turning to face me. "Do you have something to say?"

I nodded sharply. "Yes. Do you think we could grab a coffee and talk for a minute?"

He cocked his head. "Are you going to be honest with me?"

"Yes." As honest as I could be, which might have to be all the way honest. It didn't seem like Julien was going to accept anything less.

"Then, yeah, we can go sit down somewhere."

Somewhere ended up being the student union where there was a Starbucks. Julien ordered an iced coffee and a cookie. I got a matcha latte and drooled over his cookie.

There was pink icing on it. I was jealous, okay?

He broke off a piece—a really big chunk—put it on a napkin, and slid it to me across the two-seater table tucked as far away from other students as we could get. My cheeks heated, both from the unexpected sweet act and the fact that he must have seen me eyeing his cookie like a starved animal.

I pushed it back toward him. "Oh, I couldn't possibly accept this."

From his personal shadows, he raised a brow, then reached out as if he was going to take it back. "No problem. I'll eat it."

He slowly drew the napkin back to his side of the table, and I swore I was going to cry. Five minutes ago, I hadn't even wanted a cookie. Now, I was desperate for this one.

"You're really taking it back?" I stuck my bottom lip out. "That's sort of rude, Julien."

He guffawed, his hand freezing in place. "Are you saying you *do* want it?"

"Of course I do, you maniac." Holding my hand out, I made a come-to-mama motion with my fingers. "Give me the cookie."

He canted his head, as if he was waiting, but I didn't quite know what for, so I wiggled my fingers again, which made him chuckle.

"Is that really how you ask for something you want?"

Oh, he wanted to play. Well, I guess I'd already been playing, so he joined in my game.

Leaning forward on both elbows, I did my best sultry impression. "Please, sir, may I have some of your cookie?"

Julien watched me, his eyes grazing my face. Then he picked the cookie up, reached across the table, and held it to my lips. I rubbed my mouth back and forth along the jagged edge, then slowly opened. He pushed it inside, hitting the tip of my tongue.

My tongue darted out, pulling the cookie in farther, and my teeth sank into the soft frosting. I groaned at the first taste of sugary sweetness, playing up my pleasure a little more than strictly required, and bit off a big piece. Julien's lids went heavy for a moment, his eyes on my mouth as I licked away the crumbs from my upper lip.

"Good?" he asked.

"Delicious. Thank you." I took a sip of my matcha, my cheeks like twin fireballs, telling me, perhaps, once again, I'd taken things too far.

"Never would have pegged you for the type," he said.

"The type?" I pressed on my chest, bracing myself for his reply.

He nodded, taking his time answering. "Yeah. The cookie-loving type. I thought you were a carrot cake girl."

My hand flattened on my breastbone as my heart started up again. "Only most of the time. I do have a thing for stealing other people's desserts."

"By first pretending you don't want them?" he asked me dryly.

I giggled. "I didn't expect you to actually take it back."

I couldn't tell if he sighed or laughed under his breath. Either way, he wasn't really smiling, and his attention had diverted back to his cookie. He broke off another piece, pushing it my way, then took a big bite of the remainder.

His eyes flicked back to mine after he swallowed. "You wanted to talk?"

"Yes." Sitting up straight, I squared my shoulders and lowered my voice. "I need to date you until spring break."

He didn't move a single inch. I wasn't even sure he was breathing. That was okay. I was being silly and needed to start over once again.

"God, no, sorry." I rubbed the center of my forehead. "Let me explain."

He snorted softly. "Please do."

I had nothing to lose. Clearly, Julien thought I was a ridiculous person. I'd made a fool of myself in front of him more times than I could count. So what was the harm in laying everything on the line and letting him come to a decision? If he said no, I'd leave him alone. No harm, no foul.

"Okay, my cards are going on the table. I was bet to date you until spring break and then break up with you. This guy in marching band, Carson—he's the drum captain this year—he likes to make bets like this. I think he thinks of himself as a puppet master, when really he's just an asshole."

Shaking my head, I inhaled as deeply as I could, needing to get back on track.

"I said yes because he offered to help me get something I desperately want. And I thought, maybe you and I could hang out, and I could convince him we were dating. Since you obviously saw right through me, I decided to tell you everything. So, here I am, telling you everything. I would like to fake date you until spring break. Obviously, I wouldn't expect you to do it for free. I have some money saved or...I don't know, I could make you daily carrot cakes, or buy you dinner every night. I could do anything you need."

As he shifted forward in his seat, Julien's hoodie fell back enough to give me a full view of the feelings playing on his face. Well, if there had been anything other than blankness there, I would have seen it.

"Anything? You mean, if I agree to this, I could ask for nightly blow jobs and you'd agree? Or could I ask for you to crawl under the table now and start your repayment?"

His hands were steepled under his chin, as if he was seriously contemplating his own question, while I was one second away from dumping my matcha out on his head.

"No. You absolutely can't ask that." My hands shook as I pushed against the edge of the table, scooting my chair back. "Obviously, this was a mistake. I'm sorry I brought it up. From now on, I'll leave you be."

Julien's hand shot out, catching my wrist before I could stand. We stayed like that, in stasis, staring at each other. As each second passed, the clouds parted in his eyes, and he exhaled.

"I'm being unnecessarily shitty because you surprised me. Stay. We can talk."

"And you won't bring up blow jobs? Because that was definitely not—"

Releasing my wrist, his hands went up in front of him. "I know it wasn't what you meant. I'm sorry for being an asshole and acting like that was on the table when I knew it wasn't."

I blew out a long breath. "This is so weird, I know. You hardly know me, and here I am, trying to drag you into fake dating me. I don't know why I thought I could ask you to do this. More importantly, I'm not sure how I could have been deluded enough to think you might agree to it." I shoved my curls off my forehead. "Let's just forget about it, okay?"

His eyes were on me, cool and steely. "I don't think I can. Tell me what you want badly enough to do this."

"You make it sound like I'm taking on a burden, fake dating you. I was thinking it might be fun, especially now that you're in on it. Well...fun for me, since I kind of enjoy our interactions."

His expression stuttered before he reined in his features, regaining his usual, mildly disgruntled look.

"How?"

I shrugged. "You're all grumpy growly most of the time, but when I get you to crack, it feels like a big accomplishment. It's kind of addictive, to be honest."

His fingers drummed on the table. "So, I'm your experiment?"

"No. You're Julien, and we're getting to know each other. Maybe I'm the only one who's enjoying any of this, I don't know, but it definitely won't be a hardship for me to spend more time with you." My teeth dug into my bottom lip. "The thing I want is to be drum captain next year. It's decided by vote, and Carson has always promised to throw his support behind me. Now, someone else is interested in the position, and Carson is waffling, so…"

"So, you'll do this crazy shit to make sure you have him on your side?"

"Yeah. And I know this whole idea makes me seem like the biggest bitch alive—using someone to get what I want. Hell, maybe I am. But I promise to make it as painless for you as possible, and I'll pay you…or—"

"Sera." He said my name so suddenly, it sliced through the tense air between us. I clamped my mouth shut and listened. "You gotta stop offering me money. It's pretty fucking insulting."

My eyes widened. "I don't mean it as insulting. It's not like I know your financial situation. I just don't have much to offer besides my killer carrot cake or the cash I saved from my summer job as a camp counselor."

He huffed a humorless laugh. "Why can I easily picture you as a camp counselor? I bet you were the favorite."

My mouth twitched. "It was middle school band camp. I promise you, middle schoolers don't like anyone, including me. But I had fun being extra peppy just to annoy them, which was very easy to do."

He slumped back in his chair, quietly assessing me while stretching his legs out under the table, his feet sliding on either side of one of mine. I tried to pull back, but he kept my foot wedged between his. Nothing in his expression betrayed he was keeping my foot prisoner, but there was something playful about the whole thing that made my stomach flip.

We were getting off track again. It was time for business.

"Okay…" I tugged on one of my curls. "Well, is there any way I can get you to agree to this? Or should I give up and use my camp money to pay someone to bump Carson off?"

His eyebrows winged. "Oh, we're talking big, big camp money. Why didn't you say that?"

I snorted. "No, I just think I could convince someone to do it on the cheap."

The unscarred corner of his mouth tugged upward. "Tell me about the class you're taking in the pool."

I started, my head jerking back. "The pool?" It took me a moment to understand his question, given the abrupt change of subject. "Oh, on Tuesdays? It's an adaptive exercise course. We're learning exercises to do with patients who have physical disabilities."

He nodded. "You're planning on being a physical therapist?"

"Mmmhmm. I'll go to PT school when I graduate." I frowned at him, confused at this line of questioning. "Why?"

He turned his head, and I would have thought he was ignoring me if not for his feet moving to a staccato beat around mine.

"My insurance ran out. Can't see my regular physical therapist anymore. I'm thinking, as repayment for playing along with this bet, you give me PT in the pool once a week." He finally turned back to look at me again. "That's what I want from you. If you agree, I'll be the fucking best fake boyfriend there ever was."

"But I—" I clamped down on my lip, my forehead scrunching. "But, Julien, I'm not a physical therapist. Not even close. I can't—"

He opened his hands on the table. "This is my price, Sera. I've been in PT long enough to have an idea of what I need. It's not high level anymore, so I'm confident you can figure it out if you put your mind to it. If you really want this whole drum captain thing—if you want to beat Carson and the naysayers—take it or leave it."

"But—"

I was at a loss. What he was asking...it was unthinkable, wasn't it? I couldn't possibly help him...could I? I mean, I'd interned at a rehabilitation center for two years, and when my grandmother had broken her hip, I'd helped her with at-home exercises, but this? I could make things worse—no, chances were I *would* make things worse.

"Julien, I'll hurt you."

His jaw worked back and forth. "I'm already hurting. There's nothing you could do that could possibly make things worse."

I'm already hurting.

That simple, blunt statement took the wind right out of my self-righteous sails.

"You're in pain?" I asked.

He lifted a shoulder. "I'm used to it, but yeah, I really don't want to talk about it. You're in or you're out. If you're in, we can get into that. No sense in *me* laying my cards on the table if you're just going to gather yours and take them home."

The fact that I was even considering this was insanity.

I'm already hurting.

It was almost impossible to say no to that. Almost...because I had to. My experience as an intern and taking care of my grandma wasn't even a fraction of one percent of what Julien needed.

When I didn't reply right away, he jerked his chin and pushed back from the table, releasing my foot.

"All right. Then that's it. I hope you have a nice life, Sera." He grabbed his cane and started to rise.

I should let him go.

I reached across, and this time, it was me snagging his wrist to halt him. "Wait. Wait. Let's talk about this. I'm not saying no."

"Are you saying yes?"

I was definitely going to hate myself for agreeing to this. I wanted that drum captain position so bad, I could taste it. I would have given it up, though, if he hadn't said those words. *I'm already hurting.* Now, I couldn't seem to make myself walk away.

"Julien...I'm saying yes, but with the caveat that you understand I'm not a therapist."

To that, he cracked a crooked grin, though it was more sardonic than amused. "Yeah, Sera, I understand that."

Heat rushed to my cheeks, and I pressed my hands to my face to stifle the rosy bloom.

"Obviously. What I mean is...I can't take the place of your therapist. I'll try to help you find relief—"

He held his hand up. "That's all I need."

I had to stop myself from pulling my bottom lip between my teeth again. I was bound to gnaw a hole straight through it. Julien agreeing to this hackneyed plan was supposed to calm me, but my anxiety ratcheted up a hundred notches.

Sucking in a breath, I attempted to make myself seem self-assured by pushing back my shoulders and raising my chin.

"Good. Then we'll start next week after we go over the specifics of your injuries."

He took out his phone, tapping on the screen. "Sure. I'm sending you a message through Savage Talk. Sera...what's your last name?"

I laughed under my breath at the ridiculousness of the situation I'd gotten myself into. Here I was, with my new fake boyfriend slash illegal physical therapy patient slash coconspirator, and he didn't even know my last name. For that matter, I didn't know his either.

"It's Ellis. Seraphina Ellis. And yours?"

His thumbs moved over the phone screen, his brow furrowed. He looked up at the same time my phone chimed. I took it out, finding a message from Julien Umbra through the university's internal messaging system, Savage Talk.

Hi, Seraphina Ellis, this is your fake boyfriend. The best fucking fake boyfriend there ever was.

- *Jules*

"Jules," I whispered to myself.

He heard me, though. Of course he did.

"My friends call me that. I figured, since we're a couple lovebirds now, you might want to call me that too."

His words were cute, but his stiff shoulders and tight jaw belied his message.

"We'll probably take the lovebird thing slow," I said.

Suddenly, it was dawning on me that I'd have to do some very real acts of affection to be in a fake relationship with this man...at least, in public.

"Sure. It's your game." Grabbing his cane, he braced himself to stand. "But if I have a say in all this—"

"You do," I rushed out.

"Then we should start with some hand-holding after our discussion on Friday. Maybe a glance or two."

My stomach tightened and swirled. "Okay. Hand-holding and glances. I'm game."

That earned me another crooked grin, this one slightly warmer. "Then it's a date. I'll be seeing you, Seraphina Ellis."

I swallowed hard. "See you soon, Julien Umbra."

My eyes stayed trained on Julien's back as he walked away. Once he faded from view, I swallowed hard, falling back in my chair.

What the hell had I just done?

Chapter Ten

Julien

There was a stir when I sat down at my desk on Friday. Since the accident, I'd gotten used to causing stirs. This one was different, though, and it had everything to do with the little redhead beside me.

My *fake girlfriend*.

God, I hadn't had a girlfriend—real or otherwise—since high school. The inner workings of being in a relationship were a mystery to me. But that didn't matter. All I needed to get right were the outer workings. Appearances were everything.

Says the man cloaking most of his face in shadows.

Leaning over the side of my desk, I ran my fingertips down the length of Sera's arm, tracing over the bones on the top of her hand.

"Hey, you." I kept my voice low, but above a whisper. If people wanted to hear, they would be able to, and that was what this was all about.

Sera's eyes swept to mine. A few corkscrews fell into her face, framing her forehead and blushing cheeks. This girl could blush. She did it at the drop of a hat—or the brush of my fingers.

"Hey, Jules." She winked and made it kind of adorable.

"Yeah," I breathed out. "That's how you do it."

She twisted in her desk, resting the side of her head on her fist. "Are you having second thoughts?" she whispered.

I nodded. "Thirds and fourths too."

Her mouth opened into a perfect *O*. "Really?"

"Nah. Not really." I picked up her hand, rubbing my thumb along her knuckles. "We're doing this thing. How am I doing so far?"

Her chin quivered before she got it under control and beamed. "Very charming. Ten out of ten."

"I aim to please."

When I left Sera two days ago, although I'd agreed to go forward with her plan, I still had doubts. Heavy doubts. Elephantine doubts. Attention was the last thing I wanted to draw to myself, but that was what I'd undoubtedly be getting being with her, fake or not.

I'd never wanted a lot, never asked or prayed for much. My mom's good health was the only thing I ever got down on my knees and begged for—and that had gotten me nowhere. But when Amir stopped by to hang out last night, it'd been awkward as hell. Like we'd just met instead of being friends for life. He watched me like I was about to jump off a bridge any second, and that was mad, mad uncomfortable.

Hanging out with Amir was what kicked me over the edge. I thought back to my conversation with Marco at the gym. He'd told me if Amir saw me moving on, finding a girl and happiness, he'd be able to move on too. Maybe we'd be able to get back to the people we'd been...or at least close. That was what I wanted more than pretty much anything.

So, I was all in. I'd promised Sera I was going to be the best fucking fake boyfriend there ever was—and that was what I'd be for her. And for me. She was a good girl. This wasn't going to be a hardship by any means.

Except for the attention. That was going to take a lot out of me. Not Sera's, though. Surprisingly, I didn't mind her eyes on me. It didn't feel like bugs were crawling along my skin when she walked beside me. Never once had I felt pity from her. Curiosity, sure, but I really didn't believe she pitied me.

At the end of class, I gathered my things and held my hand out to Sera. Her eyes met mine. There was trepidation there, but only for a second. She slipped her fingers between mine, weaving them together.

Exhaling, she smiled up at me, but stayed quiet for once. A few people called her name, telling her to have a good weekend. There were some pointed stares at our joined hands, but only one person approached.

"Hey, Sera." The obnoxious kid who'd tried to talk to me during lecture last week blocked our path out of the room. Carter or Conrad or some other shitty name. His eyes darted from Sera, to me, to our hands, and he smirked.

"Hey. Ready for the weekend?" she asked, giving him a wide smile.

"Oh, I was born ready."

"Me too." She bounced on her toes. "Well, we'd better get going. See you, Carson."

After a long beat, he stepped aside. "You too, you little cutie. And call me. Seems like we have some things to talk about."

She tucked her hair behind her ear. "Sure thing. Bye."

He finger waved as we passed him, and I felt his eyes on our backs all the way down the hall.

When we got outside, she squeezed my hand. "Don't let go yet, okay?" she murmured. "I might be paranoid, but I'm imagining Carson having spies everywhere."

"I wasn't going to let go." I squeezed her hand even tighter. "So, that was Carson, huh?"

"Yeah. That was Carson." She puffed up her cheeks and blew out a breath.

"I met him once, before class. The kid tried to pull off my hood."

Her eyes rounded. "Are you kidding me?" She slammed her palm against her forehead. "And I bet you told him off. Well, that explains why he chose you as my victim."

"You're right, I did. He's an idiot."

She giggled, neither agreeing nor disagreeing—which I took as agreement, because I was right.

"Are you headed home?" I asked.

"Yes." She turned her head, lifting her chin. "You? Are you going home?"

"That was my plan. Maybe we should walk together."

She half smiled. "That seems like something two people who are dating would do." Her fingers wiggled between mine. "I'm sorry my hands are so rough."

"I didn't notice." I held our joined hands up, checking hers out. They were small, but not dainty and calloused. "They are rough, but you don't have to be sorry."

She snort-laughed and tried to tug her hand away from me. I held firm, bringing it to my chest.

"That's so rude, Jules," she giggled.

"I only agreed with you. Should I have said your hands are as soft as angels' bottoms?"

Her head jerked back, but she was still laughing. "Bottoms? Really? I think I'd rather you agree that my hands are rough than be told I have ass hands."

"Good, because that's what I did, so you should be happy."

She snorted again. "I feel like I just got reverse-psychologied. Well played, Julien. Well played."

"My mom taught me to always compliment ladies. Seems I've learned my lesson well."

Her eyebrow arched. "I think I'm going to need to have a chat with your mom about your definition of a compliment. I have a feeling the message got lost in translation."

I got two minutes of levity. Two minutes of feeling like my old self. Like I could laugh, make jokes, not think about the pain shooting up my leg, or that the only way I could get a girl these days was if she took a bet to go out with me. Heaviness crashed into me, a smack-in-the-face reminder I wasn't that person anymore.

"You find a way to talk to dead people, let me know."

The urge to drop her hand and walk away was strong, but I'd made a promise to her. A lot of shit was out of my control, but this, I could be in charge of. I'd keep my promise to Sera.

She hissed under her breath. "If I do, you'll be the first one I tell," she said gently. "Well...after I convene with my grandma, but I'll keep it brief. Just a 'how's the afterlife, I miss you, please don't be mad I added a squeeze of lemon juice to your frosting recipe.' *Then* I'll let you know."

I shook my head, the ache in my chest cracking. It was like Sera had reached in, taken my sadness, and shook it up with her own brand of—god, I didn't even know what to call the way she spoke and the things she said. Whatever it was, she managed to fragment the melancholy that always came when the topic of my mom came up.

"Think she'll be pissed about the lemon juice?" I asked.

Her thumb softly stroked the side of my hand. "Nah. Not my grandma. She'd pretend to be offended for maybe five minutes, then she'd make a remark about how innovative young people are these days. And she'd say, 'My CC always marches to the beat of her own drum—literally!'. She always said that."

"She sounds like she was the shit."

"She was. The raddest of the rad." Her elbow poked my ribs. "I'm just going to assume you don't want to share a mom memory, right?"

I swallowed hard. "Not right now."

"I understand."

We stopped at an intersection, facing each other. Sera was close to a foot shorter than me, but like her hands, she was no delicate flower. Beneath the thin straps of her tank top, the muscles in her shoulders and biceps were softly defined. Her top clung to her round, perky tits and the faint curve of her stomach, resting at her flared hips.

She had to tip her chin up to look at me. The sun hit her just right, making her light-brown eyes almost clear. Freckles dusted her button nose, which stood out as adorable in the center of her other sharper features. Her jaw was square, capped with a round, pouty chin. Her mouth was wide when at rest, and even wider when she talked, and her lips were a peachy velvet. Her cheekbones were high and angular. When added up, none of her features really made sense. It was when she smiled it all became clear. Everything went soft and rosy. That button nose fit in with apple cheeks and happy lips.

This wasn't the first time I'd noticed how pretty Sera was, but I hadn't allowed myself to take such a long inventory of her features.

Now that I was her fake boyfriend, it was within my rights to stare at my fake girlfriend. She was staring right back, so I knew she didn't mind—although, what she had to look at wasn't nearly as pretty.

"Should we talk about what this relationship is going to look like?" Her lips rolled inward. "We didn't really discuss any of that. I mean, I think the hand-holding is good. It's really good, so we should keep doing that. And walking home from class together is definitely an authentic touch. But what else?"

"You tell me. This is your show."

"I don't want anything to happen you're uncomfortable with." Her brow pinched in the center. "Well, it would be weird for us to suddenly be loved up, so I think we're fine where we are for a week or two."

"Is that what you did with Seth?"

"No." She tugged on my hand, urging me to start walking with her again. "He wasn't big on PDA. Well, not with me. With his best friend, Katie, he was always hugging her, draping his arm around her—ugh. I know you're wondering how I could have stayed with him for so long. Believe me, I'm wondering that too. I guess he was good at making me the center of his attention when she wasn't around, and I was dumb enough to think that meant something."

"That guy's a dick. You know that, right?"

Understatement of the century. Her ex was all big and strong, but outside the locker room a few days ago, he'd proved himself to be a coward, backing down the second I got in his face. And I'd gotten in his face because the things he had to say about Sera were foul. He was under the impression he owned her. That him sticking his dick in someone else was just a blip in their relationship. A guy had oats he had to sow, right? Sera would get it. He just had to let her be mad for a bit. He said everyone important on campus knew she belonged to him, and once she saw she didn't have any other choice, she'd come crawling back like the little bitch in heat she was.

That was what he said.

It had taken all my self-control not to pick up my cane and brain him with it. The only thing saving him was the fact that I never wanted Sera to hear any of the shit coming out of his mouth. She'd probably heard enough of it while they were together.

"Oh, I know. I won't be fake breaking up with you to run back to him." She sighed, her shoulders curling. "Let's go back to us. So, a week of hand-holding?"

I squeezed her fingers. "I think I can handle that."

"Maybe, during week two, you might put your arm around me?"

"That's fine."

She sucked in a breath. "What if—"

"What?"

"Well, Carson isn't going to make this easy. What if we have to go somewhere other than class? Like a band dinner or a party or something? Would you be into that? I know it's asking a lot."

A year ago, I was at every party. Not even to drink, I just liked the atmosphere. The people laughing, dancing, yelling, chilling. I'd go, find a spot to sit, and watch it all go down. Now, the suggestion had my heart pounding in my chest. None of that held any appeal anymore.

But I sucked it up.

"If this was real, I'd be wherever you went," I said thickly. "I'm banking on you not being a party girl. That's not really my scene these days."

Her giggle was half sad. "Somehow, I could've guessed that. But I was thinking, if we do go to a party, we might have to kiss. Not like, make out or anything, but light kissing. And we wouldn't *have* to, but—"

"It's all good, Sera. I'm down for whatever. Like I said, it's your show."

We stopped at the intersection where we always parted. She rubbed her lips together, like she was gearing up to kiss me right here where we stood. She smiled instead.

"Any plans this weekend?" she asked.

"Home. Gym. Sleep. The usual." I tipped my chin. "You?"

"Bed and reading a lot of filth. My plans got ruined last weekend. I need my fix of angsty smut."

"Angsty smut? I need more information."

She narrowed her eyes. "Are you making fun, or do you really want to know?"

"I'm asking you to tell me what you're going to be reading."

She leaned closer, one hand on my chest. "It's Dramione fan fiction. I'm addicted, Jules. I think I have an actual problem."

"Dramione?"

She pushed up on her toes, bringing her lips close to my ear. "Draco and Hermione from *Harry Potter*. The one I'm about to start is supposed to be really dark and super spicy."

"Send me the link."

She dropped back down on her heels. "Really? You're going to read it?"

"Why not? Isn't it normal to share interests with your fake girlfriend?"

Her mouth fell open for a moment before snapping closed to curve into a pleased smile. "I don't know if it's normal, but it's never been my experience. Well, obviously not the fake part. You're my first fake boyfriend. I meant the sharing interests part. *That* hadn't been my experience. You don't have to read it just because I am."

I shrugged. "Send it to me. I'll let you know what I think."

Her mouth did the open close, open close thing again, then she nodded decisively. "I'll send you the link. But don't tell me if you hate it. We never have to talk about it again if you do."

Chances were, we'd never be talking about this again. But I didn't have anything better to do, and I was interested in what got Sera's mind revving, so I'd give it a try.

"I'll see you around, Sera."

We'd been holding hands the entire time we were standing there. When I finally let her go, she pressed forward, wrapping her arms around me.

"A hug seems like the way to go for a new boyfriend," she mumbled against my chest.

It took me a second, then I circled my arms around her, giving her a loose hug back.

"I think you're right." With a pat in the center of her back, I ended the embrace and stepped away. "See you."

Her cheeks were pink, eyes wide, but she didn't seem upset, which meant I was good to walk away.

"Bye, Jules."

With a nod, I turned and headed toward my house. Before I got far, Sera called out to me.

"Don't forget to watch out for the link I'm sending you!"

I raised a hand, letting her know I heard, then I glanced back. She waved, her curls and tits bouncing, she'd done it so enthusiastically.

There was no question I was in over my head with all this, but for the first time in a long, long time, I wasn't in any rush to get back to my room and hide from the world.

That was new.

It might have meant nothing,

Then again, it could have meant everything.

Chapter Eleven

Seraphina

I CAME TO AN abrupt stop outside the arts building Monday afternoon. I should have been hurrying, since I was running late, but my feet didn't seem to want to move.

Julien was propped up against the wall beside the stairs. His head was turned, and the unscarred side of his face was bared to the sun. His hood was down, and his sandy hair swooped across his forehead. There was something about his stance, the lighting, the perfect sweep of his hair, that made my stomach flip.

He could've been James Dean, rebelling without a cause right in front of my eyes. He even had the snug white T-shirt thing going on—beneath his zippered hoodie, obviously.

I must've stood still for too long and caught his attention. Slowly, he turned my direction, cocking his head at the sight of me. Since I really didn't want to explain why I wasn't moving, I strode forward, meeting him at the bottom of the ramp.

"Hey, you," I said brightly. "Are you waiting for me?"

He held out his hand, pulling me close. "Of course. What kind of fake boyfriend would I be if I didn't?"

I bit my tongue instead of telling him Seth had never once waited for me. I also didn't add that Katie had taken the class too, and sometimes when I arrived, they hadn't even saved a seat for me.

Yep. I'd put up with that nonsense, but Julien did *not* need to be aware of what a doormat I'd become.

We almost made it into class without incident, but not quite. Katie arrived at the same time we did and eyed our joined hands like they confused her.

"Does Seth know about this?" she asked. "You know he isn't going to be happy, right?"

Instead of responding to her stupid questions, I scrunched my face and brushed by her, holding my hot, fake boyfriend's hand tight in mine.

When he sat down, Julien leaned over, brushing my hair aside to speak low into my ear. His warm breath on my skin sent little tremors down my spine.

"What the fuck was that?"

I turned slightly, my cheek almost pressed to his. "That's the girl. Seth's bestie."

"The one he cheated with?"

"Mmmhmm."

He breathed a laugh. "And she's telling you he won't be happy you're moving on? What kind of fucked-up relationship do those two have?"

When I smiled, my cheek pushed into his. Neither of us moved away, allowing the contact to continue.

"A really fucking fucked-up one."

"Glad you got out of that whole thing, Seraphina."

And maybe it was my imagination, but I was pretty certain he purposely brushed his cheek back and forth along mine before moving into his own space beside me.

• • • ● • ● • • •

When the lecture was finished, we walked out together, and I was thankful he was there with me. An angry Seth was waiting right outside the door, and if I had to guess, I would have said his bestie had sent him a text, alerting him of my new relationship status.

"Oh boy, looks like there's going to be an encore of our acting troupe," I mumbled, my stomach sinking to the ground.

"I'm not going anywhere," Julien assured me.

"Seraphina," Seth snapped. "We need to talk."

"Absolutely not. Like I keep telling you, talk to Katie."

Julien and I continued past him, but Seth wasn't letting us go. Sidling up beside me, his hand fell on my shoulder, and he dipped down to hiss at me.

"Stop walking and talk to me. You owe me an explanation."

By some miracle, I kept my face mostly impassive. "No. I don't want to, and I don't owe you anything. Please, just stop."

Julien released my hand, sending me into a panic, then his arm slid around my waist, tugging me tight against his side, away from Seth. We came to a standstill in the middle of the hall, which wasn't a good thing since three hundred people were trying to stream past us at the same time.

"I think you heard her," Julien gritted out above the steady din of voices. "And I think you and I already had a talk about Sera. Walk away."

Seth threw his arms out, nearly hitting a girl with glasses. She dodged him, shooting him a nasty glare and flipping him off, filling the little pocket of evil in my soul.

"You can't be serious, Sera. You're telling me you'd rather be with this guy, who can barely fucking walk, than *me*?" Seth pounded his chest like the meathead he was. "Is this some revenge thing? Fuck the ugly guy so I'll feel bad about myself? It's not going to work."

Every word that left Seth's pretty mouth turned him uglier and uglier, until he looked like an ooze-dripping pimple to me. He'd hidden this ugliness from me when we were together. He had to have. There was no way I would have stayed otherwise.

Right?

"Contrary to what you seem to believe, not everything has to do with you." My voice rose higher than intended, but I was spitting mad at the way Julien had gone stiff at my side. His hold on me was brittle. I knew he'd let me go as soon as he could.

Seth scoffed. "The hell it doesn't. It takes two people to break up a relationship. I never agreed we were done. I gave you space, but that space wasn't for you to go out and fuck around. That was for you to get over your issues and come back to me so I can show you how sorry I am I messed up. You walking around campus with another guy, even if he's all screwed up and shit, does not fly with me."

I held my hand up, done with this. "Let me make this perfectly clear to you and everyone pretending they're not listening. I'm done with you, Seth. I will never, ever get back together with you. We have been broken up for over a month, and that's not going to change. As for Julien, you could only dream of being as amazing as he is. If that isn't clear enough, how about this?" I curled all but my middle finger into my palm. "Go fuck yourself, Seth."

The way he gawked at Julien and me as we went by him sent even more delight into my evil pocket. The thing was going to be overflowing soon.

Julien was stiff and silent, his fingertips digging into my waist. I would have asked him to loosen his grip, but I was afraid I'd lose him entirely. I took the discomfort so I could keep him close.

"I'm sorry," I murmured to Julien. "I'm so, so sorry."

"I'm fine. Don't worry about it." His words were rote, as if he'd said them often.

Once we were outside again, around the corner from the arts building, away from prying eyes and angry exes, Julien's arm dropped from my waist like lead.

"He doesn't know what he's talking about," I started.

Julien nodded once. "Good on you for telling him off, but I gotta get out of here. I'm meeting up with Marco, so I'll see you around."

I let him go, even though disappointment shot through my chest like fiery arrows. Julien and I hadn't made specific plans to hang out after class, but I'd kind of been hoping we might.

If I could have gone back, I would have punched Seth in the nose the second he showed up. He ruined everything, like always. I didn't give a damn what he said to me. But the insults he casually tossed at Julien were unconscionable. And the fact that he'd done it in front of so many people and would likely not bear any social repercussions made it a thousand times worse.

I had no clue what Julien was feeling now, but it couldn't have been good.

I braced myself to be very real dumped by my fake boyfriend.

My mother called me on my way to the gym on Tuesday. I'd chosen laziness over working out with Alley, and for once, she'd taken pity on me and allowed it.

She and Laura had told me it was because I'd been doing so well over the past two weeks, they'd barely had to peel me out of bed at all. Of course, the two of them had spent most of this past weekend at Alley's parents' house, so they missed my unkempt, pajama-wearing, snack-eating self lazing about in my room while devouring another fanfic.

They would not be proud if they knew about that. Neither would my mother, for that matter.

"Hello, chickadee," she cooed.

"Hey, Mama. What's up?"

"Just checking in, honey. Are you keeping your chin up?"

"Most of the time."

She tsked. "Have you seen Seth?"

"A few times."

"And what did he say? Did you let him apologize?"

Here was the thing about my mother: she loved me, but she wasn't always on my side. I spent all six weeks of winter break alternating between sobbing in my bed and rage exercising. Mostly sobbing, though. Thank goodness we weren't a D1 school so I didn't have to worry about playing bowl games. I had needed that time to recover.

My mother was witness to all of it, and between stroking my hair and whispering comforting, but trite words, she asked questions. For example, she wanted to know if one cheating incident really was worth splitting up over. She asked if Seth was sorry, if he wanted me back. And when he called the house, she tried her damnedest to get me to speak to him.

Because he was handsome, rich, popular, and played football. He charmed my parents, looked good in pictures, and balanced out my quirkiness. My parents had breathed a sigh of relief when they met him. Seth was their ideal boyfriend for me, even if he did stick his dick in someone else.

"Mom." I sighed into the phone. "I'm not forgiving him. I need you to understand it's over. Stop pressing me on this. It's not fair to me."

"Well, I don't think it's fair to not hear Seth out, but of course, I understand your side of things. I just think you need to consider whether you'll truly find someone better than him. He's a little immature and made a mistake, but he was so sorry when I spoke to him—"

Knife. Gut. Intestinal spillage.

She'd always been this way, loving, always, but tended to be my fair-weather fan. When I did something she liked, or made a choice she would have, she was my biggest cheerleader. The opposite was true when I didn't—which happened more often than not.

"Please, please, I'm asking you not to bring him up anymore."

I could almost feel her displeasure shooting at me through the ether.

"Fine. I won't. You know my feelings on the matter."

"I do." And because I was a little bit dumb and a lot bit impulsive, I kept talking. "Anyway, I'm seeing someone else. His name is Julien, he's a pianist, supersmart, and so, so sweet. It's new, but—"

My mother squealed. "Why didn't you *say* that? Oh my god! Julien? Is he French? I love that name. Is he cute? Send me a picture, honey!"

"Mom..." I giggled softly at her overenthusiasm. "It's new. When it's less new, I'll send you a picture of us together. Okay?"

If I hadn't been fake dumped. Having not heard from Julien since he left me yesterday, that was looking more and more likely. Then again, I hadn't contacted him either, giving him the space he deserved.

"I'll be waiting with bated breath, Seraphina. I don't know how I didn't notice before, but you sound so much happier than the last time we spoke. I can only imagine that's Julien's doing. I already like him."

"Maybe," I said softly as the gym came into view. "Listen, I need to get ready for class. I'll talk to you later."

"Of course. Oh, wait. I wanted to remind you that you need to find a dress for Ophelia's bridal luncheon. She's requested you wear something knee length, in kelly green or violet. And not too fitted. You know how she is about your backside."

My teeth slammed down on my tongue so I didn't say all the things speeding through my mind.

"Fine. I'll go shopping. Give Dad my love."

By the time we hung up, I felt like I'd been dragged by my hair behind a wild horse, over broken glass, then hugged by angels.

It made sense in my head, and I was used to their raw, painful love.

There was nothing like family.

Chapter Twelve

Seraphina

Something told me to look up. A niggling in the back of my brain, the weight of eyes on me, a sudden awareness—*something*. When I let my eyes drift to the bank of windows overlooking the pool, they immediately found his.

Julien was on a treadmill in the gym, between his friends Marco and Amir. They were running hard, while he was walking. He nodded to me when our eyes met. I couldn't stop the wide smile from spreading across my face.

He'd been watching me during my class in the pool, probably for a while since it was almost finished. My stomach did this little happy dance at both the sight of him and knowing he'd been watching.

I beckoned him to come down to the pool. He cocked his head, telling me he saw me, but his countenance was neutral, so I had no idea what he was thinking. Then he broke contact altogether, turning his head to speak to Marco.

That was okay. I needed to pay attention to the rest of class. Otherwise, I'd likely inadvertently drown myself.

· · · · ● · ● · · ·

Bending down, I grabbed my towel from one of the chairs by the pool. I wrapped it around my chest and squeezed the water from my hair. Then I grabbed my bag to head to the locker room where I would *not* be showering.

I turned around and jumped when Julien was right behind me. "Oh my god, you just shaved ten years off my life." I pressed a hand over my thrashing heart.

His mouth twitched. "I said your name. I don't think you heard me over your humming."

"What humming? I don't hum."

One eyebrow winged. "You can deny it, but you were humming so loud, you couldn't hear your own name."

My hands went to my hips. "Oh? And what was I supposedly humming?"

"The poetic masterpiece of Cardi B and Megan Thee Stallion, 'WAP.'"

"That"—I hummed about my wet-ass pussy for a second—"okay, that sounds like me, but I didn't even know I was doing it. God, do I hum all the time? Is it always 'WAP,' or do I hum other inappropriate songs?"

Julien huffed a low laugh and grabbed my arm. "Never heard you hum before this. I'll let you know if it happens again."

"Thanks, pal." I sighed, looking him over. In gym shorts and a formfitting tee, he looked good, if not sweaty. But I couldn't really get a read on his mood. "So, are you dumping me now or later?"

He cocked his head. "Did I fall asleep and wake up after spring break?"

"No, but I'm assuming you wish you did. The whole scene with Seth was so—" My lips pressed together as gut-clenching anger clogged my throat.

"Embarrassing?" he supplied without a shred of intonation.

"Yeah, exactly. You must think I'm the absolute worst for ever being with someone like him. I'm deeply embarrassed by it all."

His head jerked. "*You're* embarrassed?"

His tone and emphasis on certain words gave me pause. "Well, yes, of course I am. Why wouldn't I be? You're doing me a favor and got dragged into the drama I wish wasn't my life."

He scoffed, looking away. "No big deal."

It struck me that he thought I'd been embarrassed by him. That the things Seth had said about him had made me feel ashamed of having Julien as my boyfriend.

I wasn't a perfect person. Julien's scars had taken me a minute or two to get used to. But if this were real, if he were my actual boyfriend, I'd be proud to be with him. Even fake, I was proud.

"It's always a big deal when someone's an asshole to you, Jules. I'm glad you're willing to speak to me. I was bracing myself to be dumped and blocked."

He shook his head. "Nah. I need my PT. Can't dump you yet."

I sucked in a breath, relieved, but now nervous all over again. "Okay...well, on that note, I wondered if you wanted to get in the pool with me now. That's why I waved you down here. I wasn't even thinking about swim trunks, but—"

He jerked his thumb over his shoulder. "I have trunks in my bag. Pool time sounds really good. I'll go change and meet you back here."

While Julien was in the locker room, I left my towel on a chair and got back in the mostly empty pool to float around. A couple people were swimming laps on the other end, but it had pretty much cleared out by the time class ended.

Julien strode out on the pool deck a few minutes later. His head was down, so he didn't notice me nearly going underwater while checking him out. With my feet under me, I watched as he tossed his towel down next to mine, propped his cane against the chair, and made his way to the steps.

Julien's torso was long and lean, with tightly defined abs and a light dusting of hair between his pecs, trailing down the middle of his stomach. His trunks rode low, low, *low* on his narrow hips. Each step he took caused the lines of his *V* to ripple and flex, drawing my eye even lower, to the hint of a bulge behind the loose fabric of his shorts.

I squeezed my eyes shut. *No lusting after your fake boyfriend, ma'am.*

"Is there a reason your eyes are closed?"

Julien's voice came from close by, and from the splashing sounds, he was coming toward me.

"You have abs for days," I squeaked out.

A breath of a chuckle burst out of him. "Uh...I never thought of them that way, but—hold up, is that an explanation as to why your eyes are closed?"

I cracked an eyelid. Julien was right in front of me, frowning. The water was almost up to his pecs, covering most of his sleek, scandalous skin.

"Can we actually not talk about that? That would be deeply wonderful." I chanced opening both eyes. Julien was still frowning and studying me like he was trying to figure me out.

"Would that make you happy?" he asked.

I nodded hard. "Yes. Very happy. You'd be the best boyfriend ever." I added *fake* in my head to remind myself that was what this was.

"I wouldn't want to miss the opportunity to be the best boyfriend ever." The slight curve of his mouth was the only hint at humor. Otherwise, he was dry as a bone. "So, now that you have me here, what are you going to do with me?"

He had to be doing this on purpose, right? He was fucking with me, drawling out that sexy line. Based on how hot my cheeks flamed, I was surprised the pool didn't start boiling. Unable to think of anything else to turn the attention off me and my red-hot cheeks, I shoved a massive wave of water straight at Julien, splashing him in the face.

He sputtered and backed away from me, wiping the water away with his forearm. His eyebrows were angry slants as rivulets made their way down his tight cheeks and jaw.

"I'm sorry," I began. "I didn't mean—"

Suddenly, I was struck by an avalanche of pool water. I started to fall backward, my arms shooting out at my sides, pinwheeling in the air. Just as I was about to go under, Julien wrapped his arms around my middle, pulling me upright.

We were chest to chest, both of us panting, dripping wet. Raising my chin, I stared up at his face, which was turned down to look at me. My hands were on his chest, his holding on to my waist.

"My hero," I breathed.

His head angled to the side. "Don't think I can be your hero when I'm the one who tried to drown you."

"I started it." My palms slid down his wet skin just a little, pressing into the taut muscles. Under my right hand, his pulse thumped a staccato rhythm. My fingers tapped the beat lightly on his chest. "You asked me what I'm going to do with you."

"I did. Do you know?"

"Hmph." I smiled, but I didn't dare admit the filthy idea that had just passed through my head. "I was thinking we'd just swim around, maybe stretch a little, and you can tell me about your accident. I mean, I feel like I should probably know the extent of your injuries if I'm going to attempt to help you."

He turned away, his body stiffening. His jaw ticced as his molars ground together, but he didn't answer me. Then again, I supposed I hadn't asked a question.

"It's up to you, Jules. If you don't want to talk, that's fine. We definitely don't have to do that right now," I assured him.

He slowly turned back to me. "I'm good. I don't like talking about it. I've said the same words over and over and over to doctors, I've avoided saying the words to nosy assholes."

He let the last part of his statement hang in the air, leaving me to guess he thought I was one of the nosy assholes. That stung, maybe because it was a little true, but also because I didn't want Julien to see me that way.

"I'm curious, I don't deny that. If we were closer and had known each other longer, I might ask. But under normal circumstances, I wouldn't be digging around in your business, I promise. And I get that you've had bad experiences with people. I don't want to make you feel that way."

His brow crinkled. "You're getting me wrong, Sera. Just because I don't like talking about it doesn't mean I don't get why you're asking."

Reaching out, I grabbed his hand under the water. "Come to the wall. We'll do some stretches and you can tell me whatever you want to tell me. Okay?"

He didn't pull his hand away until we got to the wall, then he placed it next to mine on the concrete edge of the pool, his pinkie brushing mine. I led us through some very, very basic stretches, using the water as resistance. I really didn't want to hurt him.

I'm already hurting.

If I made his pain worse, I'd never forgive myself. Not that he'd tell me. I had a feeling Julien had become adept at masking his pain. He certainly didn't show it any time I was with him. And I knew a *lot* about masking pain.

"It was an SUV, not a car," he said.

It took me a moment to understand what he was talking about. "That hit you?"

"Yeah." He cleared his throat. "He hit me going full speed. I don't know how I survived it. I don't think I should have."

"I'm glad you did."

His head bowed, but he otherwise didn't acknowledge I had spoken. "I'm half titanium now. They had to rebuild my face and the left side of my lower body. I had a shattered pelvis, broken femur—"

He went on, listing the injuries to his leg and pelvis. The placement of rods and screws the doctors had used to put him back together. My chest ached as he spoke robotically about his surgeries and the initial recovery process. Maybe that was the only way he could talk about it. It was so much. *Too* much.

Emotion clogged my throat. I listened, giving him my full attention, but my heart broke for him. The crazy thing was, I'd been at intake meetings during my internships. I'd heard and witnessed injuries far more catastrophic, and though I'd been sad, I hadn't been devastated in the way I was right now for Julien.

"I won't ever walk normally," he finished. "I've accepted that."

I had to swallow a few times before I could speak. "At least you have a fancy cane now."

I wanted to fling myself to the moon for saying that. *At least you have a fancy cane? Come on, Seraphina, what the hell kind of response was that?*

Julien laughed. It was short and quiet, but it was definitely a laugh. "That's a bright side I hadn't looked at before: accessories. Although, I don't think my cane qualifies as fancy."

"No." His stainless steel cane was pretty utilitarian. "We could bedazzle it, though. Or paint it?"

His eyes were warm when they met mine. "I'm going to pass on the bedazzling. When I have some spare cash one day, I'll look into buying one that's less grandpa looking. It's not really a priority right now. Not something I think about."

I scrunched my nose. "Of course you don't."

He tilted his face toward mine and dropped his voice to a rough whisper. "I've got other things on my mind, like being the best fake boyfriend ever."

That made me grin. I whispered back, "Oh, you are. Top marks in fake boyfriendry. Really stellar performance."

"It helps that there's no audience."

"Tell me about it. When I was with my old acting troupe, we had this one audience member who made me so, so nervous."

He shook his head, blowing out a breath. "Now I know you're still acting. There's no way I ever made you nervous. You're like a brave little ball of energy, bouncing around with confidence."

I took his opinion of me as a compliment, and even though it wasn't all the way true, I liked knowing he saw me that way.

"I'm for real. And I'm insanely nervous right now, which is why I'm saying incredibly insensitive things."

"Why are you nervous now?"

The whole time Julien had been talking, we'd been in motion. I stopped my leg movements and turned my body to face him. He mirrored my pose, propping his bent arm on the side of the pool.

I chewed on my bottom lip, flicking my eyes to his. That warmth was still there, like the summer sun breaking through storm clouds.

"Because I think I'm in over my head with you." I twisted my mouth. "No, I know I am."

"You couldn't take a look at me and see how bad off I am?"

"No. I can't look at you and see where you started. I feel like I'm going to make things worse."

Julien puffed out a breath. "Not possible, Sera. I promise you, I'm well fucking aware of my body these days. I know the signals when something isn't right. I'll let you know before anything goes too far." He tapped my hand. "I'm not asking you to work miracles. You know that, right?"

"I know. I just kinda wish I could."

The corner of his mouth hitched. "I more than kind of wish you could. But if I've learned nothing else, it's to keep my expectations low." He skimmed the surface of the water with his palm. "This feels good right now. I'm not worried about falling on my face or struggling through pain. That's pretty much as good as it gets for me."

"Julien," I breathed.

He took a step back, then another. "I'm gonna get dressed. You too?" He had me all topsy-turvy, but I nodded. "All right. I'll wait outside the locker room for you."

I watched him climb out of the pool, fighting back the urge to help him, knowing he'd hate it. Julien was stronger than I could ever imagine being—both physically and mentally. The muscles in his back rippled as he leaned on his cane and dried himself off with his other hand.

My stomach dipped dangerously low.

It wasn't pity or melancholy I was feeling while my gaze was glued to Julien's back. This was something entirely different. This was attraction, but more than that, I was pretty sure I had a crush on my fake boyfriend.

Fuckity fuck.

Chapter Thirteen

Julien

By the time I got home, I was wrecked. A full day of classes, gym time, the pool, and walking home, and my body was holding up the middle finger, telling me to fuck off.

After the time I spent with Marco and Amir, then Sera, I needed to shut my bedroom door and decompress. Not that listening to Sera chatter was hard. Honestly, she could go all night and I'd be right there with her. The girl could *talk*, but I found most of what she said compelling.

I'd set her off on the walk home. Holy fuck had I set her off. I caught myself grinning thinking about it.

"So...did you happen to read any of the story I sent you?"

I glanced at her as her shoulder brushed against mine. She didn't move away like I'd expected, keeping the light contact as we trailed down the sidewalk, in no hurry on our trip across campus.

"I did. That cat, Neville, is the love interest, right?"

She stopped walking, and when I turned back, she shoved my shoulder. "You're messing with me. Tell me you're messing with me."

"I'm not, I swear. Neville's got hero vibes written all over him. People overlook him because there're all these other loud, powerful guys around him. Meanwhile, he's quietly becoming a badass. So, I just gotta assume, since Hermione is smart, she chooses him."

Sera blinked at me and blinked at me, then she threw her arms up, groaned, and stalked down the sidewalk. Laughing, I caught up with her, grabbing her elbow.

"I'm guessing by your violent reaction I'm wrong?"

She practically hissed like an angry cat. "I told you it's Dramione fic! That means Draco and Hermione. It's not... God, I don't even know what Neville and Hermione's 'ship name would be! It doesn't exist!"

"Nevione sounds good to me. Or Hermville."

"Hermville!" She sounded like she was in legit pain. "You have to be fucking with me, Jules. No one 'ships Neville and Hermione. That is not a thing."

"I don't know what to tell you. They make sense to me. This Draco kid isn't shit. Who'd want that guy?"

Her little hands balled into tight fists. "I'm regretting ever letting you read it."

After all the heaviness in the pool, arguing over fan fiction with Sera made me want to throw my head back and cackle. I hadn't felt like this in a long-ass time.

"Come on now, Seraphina. Aren't I allowed to have my own opinions? Half the fun in reading a book together is debating our opinions."

She folded her arms across her chest. "This isn't fun for me. Does it look like I'm having fun?"

"I don't know, but I'm enjoying the hell out of it."

Her eyes slid to the side, glancing at me. When she saw me grinning at her, she immediately uncrossed them, hooking one around mine.

"Fine. You can 'ship them, but you're up for some big heartbreak if you think they're going to end up together."

And then she ranted for a solid five to ten minutes about exactly why Neville and Hermione were not a thing and would never be a thing.

At the end of it all, I'd applauded, Sera had given a grudging curtsy, and I'd left her with the promise to never bring up Hermville again.

But I might've been lying. Miffed Sera was all kinds of adorable. She got all pink cheeked and huffy, her curls bouncing when she stomped her feet. Yeah, Hermville was definitely going to come back out to play.

I locked the front door of my house behind me and started toward my bedroom when Elena sauntered out of the kitchen, drying her hands on a towel. I should've guessed she would be here, but there was always a fifty-fifty shot. She and Lock seemed to try to switch up where they stayed, her place or his. Looked like tonight it was his.

Her eyebrow arched. "What are you smiling about?"

Fuck. I hadn't even been aware I was. "Nothing," I muttered.

"Oh? I was hoping that smiley face had something to do with a sassy little redhead Lachlan and I spotted you with when we were driving home. She was all tucked up against you—"

"Nothing," I grunted.

"Nothing?" she echoed.

My knee-jerk instinct was to deny it, because that was the truth. Sera and I got along, but none of the other stuff was real. She wasn't into me, and I was in no place to consider starting something real with anyone. Who knew if I ever would be.

Then I remembered I was supposed to be convincing Amir I'd moved on so he could too. I couldn't exactly pretend to have a girlfriend around him and not everyone else.

I cleared my throat. "It isn't nothing. It's something new."

Elena clamped down on her bottom lip. She wasn't very good at hiding her excitement. I should've felt guilty lying to her, but damn, I was done with guilt. I had so much of everyone else's weighing on me, I couldn't muster up the energy to produce my own.

I shook my head. "Go ahead and react like you want to."

She bounced on her toes, full on beaming. "Julien! You have amazing taste in girls. I knew you'd adore Sera. She's such a peach, how could you not?" She craned her head over her shoulder. "Lachlan! Julien and Sera are together."

He stuck his head out of the kitchen, glanced at her, then briefly at me, giving me a chin tip. "Nice girl. You know Ellie is going to crow about this forever."

"She is?" My eyes went to El. "You are?"

Her big blue eyes rounded, and she grabbed my shoulders. "Do you not realize I invited her here for *you*? She finally lost her loser of an ex and is ready for a nice guy. That's you. You, Julien Beauregard Umbra, are not at all ready for that quirky, sweet angel, but she will be so good for you." She held up a finger. "Don't doubt me.

You walked into this house with a shining bright smile because of Seraphina."

I crossed my arms. "My middle name is William."

"Who cares? That isn't the point. You have to let me gloat."

I held a hand out. "I don't think I can stop you."

Lock came into the living room, wrapping his arm around his girl's shoulders. He looked at me, amused by Elena's lack of chill.

"We're making dinner. Join us," he said.

My room was calling my name. I'd been planning to dig up something to eat later, when I didn't have to socialize like a real human. Plus, Sera had emailed me an "intake form" she insisted I fill out like a real patient, and I was under a strict time limit to get it done. But if Lock was offering, he was sincere, and I'd spent too much time on my own since the accident. The form could wait.

"Sure." My gaze locked on Elena. "No quizzing me on Sera, though."

She pushed her bottom lip out. "Fine. That's fine. Absolutely fine."

"You don't mean that," I said.

She flashed me an Elena Sanderson snarl. "Of course I don't."

"Compromise with me. Press Sera for the details when you see her. She likes to talk."

And she was probably a hell of a lot better at faking things than I was.

Elena rolled her eyes. "Don't think I won't. I'm like your godmother now. I deserve to know everything."

I followed her and Lock into the kitchen. "Just feed me. Maybe I'll let something slip."

Sera thought it was fucking hilarious that Elena had put me under the microscope. I hadn't expected any other kind of reaction from her. Then, she'd pointed out that since our friends were under the impression we were dating, that meant spending time together on the weekend—y'know, actually "dating."

That was how I ended up in her car, on the way to a mall.

The fucking mall—a place of nightmares on the best day, and I hadn't had one of those in a long, long time.

"Tell me why I agreed to this again," I grumbled.

"Because you'd like to keep your best-fake-boyfriend-ever badge."

"And you need a dress? Don't you have dresses?"

She sighed, her hands squeezing the wheel. "Of course I do, but you don't understand my mom and sister. They aren't anything like me, really—especially Ophelia. She's a perfectionist and flips her shit when things don't go exactly as planned. My mom isn't so rigid, but she's very image oriented, so she's allowing my sister to rain terror down on us. Mind you, this is just a bridal luncheon—whatever the hell that is—but I have been ordered to wear kelly green or violet—oh! And nothing tight because my sister finds my big butt offensive."

I choked on my own goddamn spit. "You're shitting me."

Her fingers tapped on the wheel. "About what?"

"All of it? Your sister finding the size of your butt *offensive*?"

"As my mother so eloquently reminded me."

The heel of my hand pressed into my forehead. "*Fuck*. You're serious?"

"Mmmhmm. It isn't a huge deal. I mean, not anymore. When I was a tween and teenager, I pretty much hated everything about my body, but I'm over it now."

There was absolutely nothing wrong with the way Seraphina looked. *Nothing*. She was small and powerful. And yeah, her thighs were thick, and her ass was round and full, but there was nothing offensive about it.

"She's jealous," I stated.

Sera snorted. "She isn't, I promise. Phe is a delicate little flower. Everyone always says how beautiful she is, and they've always called me cute. My sister is the opposite of jealous of me."

"Mmm. That's why she wants you to wear a bag—she's *not* jealous of your hot ass."

That made her giggle. "She isn't, Jules. She would probably faint if she heard you saying that. Faint then make an emergency phone call to her therapist to work through the trauma of being called jealous of *me*."

I shrugged, watching her smile. "I don't have a sister, so I don't know how those relationships work, but her making you wear a dress that doesn't show off your curves tells me all I need to know about her."

"We'll just have to agree to disagree."

· · · • · • · · ·

Maybe I had some optimist left in me after all. I'd found the silver lining to the day: the mall Sera drove us to was outdoors, so at least I could catch some rays between stores.

Hooking her arm through mine, Sera studied the map of the mall. I wondered if she realized what she was doing, holding on to me when no one we knew was around. I didn't mind. She felt good tucked by my side. And if I had to endure a day of shopping, at least I had this.

"Do you have brothers?" she asked out of nowhere.

"What? Why?"

"I don't know. You said you don't have sisters, so I wondered if you're an only child or have brothers."

We were strolling by stores. I had my hood draped over my head and sunglasses on, my face turned down to Sera. No one stared, but there was a slight tingling of unease at the base of my spine that never went away when I was out in public.

"I have a half brother, but I don't know him well. We share a dad. That's about it."

"How old?" Sera asked.

"Twelve...no, I think Beckett's thirteen now. I'm not much of a brother to him."

"Did your mom and dad have a bad breakup?"

My jaw clenched like it always did when the topic of my parents' relationship came up. "No, they were never together. She cleaned his family's house. He knocked her up, paid her off, then married a woman his parents approved of a few years later."

"Oof." She rubbed her hand up and down my forearm. "I take it you and your dad aren't close either."

"I haven't spoken to him in nearly a year. What does that tell you?"

She pulled me to a stop and patted my good cheek. "It tells me he's dumb—*and* he's missing out on knowing you."

I let myself lean into her hand. "Think we're going to have to agree to disagree."

Her eyes narrowed. "Using my own words on me, are you? Rude." Her hand slid from my cheek to my chest, her fingers clenching my T-shirt. "Just for that, I'm going to try on all the kelly green and violet dresses I can find—and you're going to give me your opinion on every single one."

Chapter Fourteen

Seraphina

Shopping with Julien wasn't unpleasant at all. At least I wasn't with my mom or, god forbid, Ophelia. I still had nightmares about back-to-school shopping with them. Phe was only two years older than me. By the time we were in high school together, everything about me mortified her and she let me know it.

My ass was too big.

My legs were too stocky to wear shorts or skirts.

Only nerds were in marching band.

My curls were an absolute tragedy.

Her list of the things wrong with me was taller than I was. At that age, it had been really, really difficult not to internalize a lot of it.

But that was history. Mostly. Leaving home and not having to listen to Ophelia's constant stream of criticism day in and day out had been a big part of beginning to actually like myself.

Julien stood by while I grabbed all the dresses close to the approved colors. He had to hate this, but he was being a pretty good sport. Plus, he'd told me I had a hot ass, which made dragging him out with me worth it.

I slipped into the changing room while Julien sat in one of the available chairs to wait on me. First, I tried on a loose shirt dress, and dramatically threw open the dressing room curtain to show him.

He barely even looked at me. "No. Turn around and try again."

My face fell as I looked down at myself. "I look that bad?"

"The dress...it's too big. You're wearing a fucking sack. Turn around and try again."

Julien seemed to be legitimately offended, so I turned myself back around and pulled on a different one. This dress was midi length and A-line. Ophelia was always telling me that was my cut. I completely ignored her advice when I shopped for myself, but this *was* her event, so I could play nice.

I came out of the dressing room and did a spin. "How about this one?"

Julien groaned. "Are you forty? No. That's not for you."

"Really?" I held out the full skirt. "I kind of thought it was nice."

"It isn't."

It went on like that for two more dresses. Julien hated everything. I was surprised by how vocally opinionated he was. Finally, I ran out of options, so we left the shop empty-handed. My stomach was twisting a little, worry and annoyance gnawing away at my insides.

In the second shop, Julien asked me my size, then he searched through the racks, and I stood back, watching. He handed me his choices and sat down in a chair like a kid waiting to be entertained. I, naturally, was the jester.

The first dress was a strapless raw silk emerald-green sheath. It looked really hot on me, so I immediately knew Ophelia would hate it. I snapped a picture of myself in the mirror so I could remember how good I looked then went out to show Julien.

Holding my arms out, I did a slow three-sixty, giving my hips a sway as I spun.

By the time I turned all the way around, Julien had sat up straighter in his chair. "Yes. Get that one."

I smoothed my palms down the material covering my hips. "I can't."

"Because your sister will be seething with jealousy?"

I rolled my eyes. "My sister is beautiful. She can be mean, but she isn't jealous. Not of me." I twisted back and forth, catching my reflection in the mirror at the end of the dressing area. "I would wear this in a heartbeat on another occasion, but not her bridal luncheon. Did you choose any dresses that aren't formfitting?"

Julien stared at me for a long beat, his jaw clenched, his fingers curled around the arm of his chair. "Maybe. I don't know. I have a feeling you're going to end up in a purple garbage bag anyway."

I walked up to him and leaned down, bracing my hands on his shoulders. "Don't pout, Jules. You have excellent taste in dresses. I love this one to the bottom of my heart."

He didn't try to hide the way his eyes lingered on my cleavage before rising to my face.

"I hope you're telling the truth. If not to me, then yourself." He gripped my shoulders and turned me around, giving me a little shove toward the dressing room.

I muttered to myself as I tugged off the beautiful, perfect dress. Of course I was telling the truth. Why did he keep insisting Ophelia was jealous of me? That couldn't be further from the truth.

Before I put on another dress, I checked out the amount of material each one had. Anything that was a sheath, I nixed, leaving only one option. This one was strapless too, but the skirt was a lot fuller than the others. The zipper was a delicate thing, and my blunt, drummer's fingers weren't getting the job done.

I stuck my head out of the curtain. "Julien, I need help."

A moment later, his voice came from the other side of the curtain. "What can I do?"

I reached out, grabbed his wrist, and pulled him into the little cubicle. "I can't get the zipper up." Spinning around, I showed him my back. I'd gotten it halfway up, but it wouldn't go any farther. "Can you do it?"

He grunted his assent, and in the mirror, I watched him dip his head to glare at the zipper like it was his mortal enemy. His hands rose slowly, his warm breath feathering across my shoulder. He gave the zipper a gentle tug, pulling it up to the center of my back where it stopped. The tips of his fingers brushed along the top of the dress, skimming over my bare skin. My breath caught, and I stood stock-still, staring at his reflection. His brow pinched as his fingers inched across my shoulder blades.

Then his eyes met mine in the mirror.

I wanted to spin around so I could try to understand what was going on in his mind, but my feet were glued to the floor. Besides, Julien was so close, if I turned around, I'd end up pressed against him.

Which wouldn't have been the worst thing in the world.

At all.

"Pretty," he murmured, letting his hands fall. "Get this one."

It took me a moment to break from his gaze and check myself out in the dress. I'd have to wear a cardigan in front of Ophelia—she would bemoan my strong shoulders being on display—but otherwise, it was perfect. The top was fitted to my chest and nipped at my waist, and the skirt flowed away from my body, hiding the lower curves without hiding everything else.

"I don't know if it's on the approved color list. I think this is more of an emerald not kelly—"

Laughing, he took my shoulders in his hands and gave me a shake. "Shut up and buy the dress. You look beautiful in this. If your sister has a problem, tell her to go fuck herself."

I gasped playfully. "At her own bridal luncheon?"

His hands trailed up the side of my neck, then back down to my shoulders. "What the fuck is a bridal luncheon anyway?"

I smiled at him in the mirror. "Mystery of the universe." I brought my hand up to cover his. "I need your assistance getting out of this thing please."

He let out a heavy breath, warming my skin, then used the same gentle touch to lower the zipper. This time, he didn't stop midway, sliding his fingers along with the zipper all the way to the bottom.

My mind's focus had pinpointed the spots on my body Julien's fingers grazed—which meant I wasn't paying attention to anything else. So, when I was completely unzipped, I didn't think to hold the dress up. In fact, the thought didn't occur to me until it was pooled at my feet and I was standing in front of Julien in nothing but a nude thong.

My eyes flared. His breathing stopped. We both froze. Well, his eyes didn't. They moved to my near nudity reflecting in the mirror.

It couldn't have been more than three seconds. My mind kick-started, and I crossed one arm over my tits, the other attempting to cover my hips. Those seconds stretched out for an eternity as Julien dragged his gaze over me.

"Shit," he muttered. "Sorry. Fuck. I'll go. I'm going."

He basically threw himself out of the cubicle, the curtain swaying behind him. And when he was gone, for some reason, my chin started to tremble. I was only a little embarrassed, mostly because of the scars on my hips. But I didn't think he'd noticed, and that wasn't why I was shaking.

What was this? My belly was in tight coils. My heart thrummed wildly, like I was coming down from an orgasm. Or, more accurately, like I'd gotten super close to coming, only for it not to happen.

My little nude thong was doing its best to disguise how wet I'd gotten. And now I had to go back out there and act natural.

Fortunately for me, Julien probably thought I was half-nuts anyway. He wouldn't be surprised if I blushed madly and acted like a lunatic.

• • • • • • • • • •

The ride back to Savage River had been mostly silent, and I refused to allow a little nudity to set us back to square one. So, instead of taking Julien home, I made him have lunch with me at the *T*, an old-fashioned diner with the best apple pie ever.

When I ordered pie, Julien's silence finally broke, which I'd been expecting.

"That isn't lunch. Order something else first." He looked up at the waitress, her pen poised over her pad. "She'll have a cheeseburger too."

I almost kicked him under the table but stopped myself. The man had enough leg pain without me adding to it. I wouldn't hesitate to stab him in the hand with my fork, though.

I beamed at our confused waitress. "Pie and ice cream please. I don't want a cheeseburger."

She scribbled that down and zipped away from our table before Julien could say anything else. I gave him an even brighter smile. He scoffed.

"You can't eat pie for lunch," he groused.

"Watch me. I'm going to do it in just a few minutes."

His eyes narrowed. "You'll be hungry in an hour. You need real food."

"You're cute, Jules, but the pie here is gigantic. I'll be lucky if I'm hungry before tomorrow." I straightened my silverware, my pulse quickening as I forced myself to speak again. "Are we going to talk about what happened in the dressing room?"

He groaned and cupped his forehead. "Nah, I think I'm square."

"I'm sorry if my boobs made you uncomfortable. I wasn't paying attention and my dress just...fell off. Though, to be perfectly honest, I hadn't been expecting you to unzip me all the way like that, so it's at least sixty percent your fault."

"Please, Sera, stop talking."

"Don't be embarrassed, Julien. I'm not. They're just boobs. Well, I guess you also saw my butt since my underwear barely exists. But we all have bodies, right? It doesn't have to be a big deal. I'm fine with it. See? Isn't it obvious how fine I am? Totally and completely fine."

He raised his head slightly, peering at me over his hands. "Are you torturing me because I saw you naked? Is that what this is? I'm being punished for those three seconds of bliss? I don't see how that's fair."

Bliss. He called seeing me almost naked bliss. It was probably a figure of speech or whatever, but as a girl in dire need of flattery, I was taking that word and tucking it away for later.

"I'm not trying to torture you. I want things to go back to how they were before, prenudity—when we could actually speak to each other. Can we do that?" I batted my eyes at him, hoping that would help. "*Please*?"

Before he could answer, a big group entered the diner. They filled up the waiting area, and since there were so many, their chatter was loud enough to draw attention.

My stomach sank when I recognized Katie at the center. A few drummers, people I thought were loyal to me, surrounded her, laughing at whatever she was saying. Katie wasn't even funny. I had no idea why the hell they were laughing. The group wasn't comprised of all drummers, but there were enough to make my stomach twist.

A waitress motioned for them to follow her. They would be walking right past Julien and me.

I lunged across the table, grabbing his hand and lacing our fingers together. "Look at me adoringly. Act like you're incredibly happy to be with me. Think about my boobs if you have to."

His eyes widened for a split second, and I nodded, encouraging him to go along with me and not ask questions. To my relief, he did, rubbing his thumb over the top of my knuckles and softening his gaze.

The corners of his mouth turned up, and I knew what was on his mind. My cheeks were on fire. My thighs were pressed tight together. I should have been panicked, not turned on, yet here I was, even wetter than before.

"Hey, Sera."

Dina and Stefan waved as they passed, which set off everyone else. Well, not Katie. She sneered and rolled her eyes but kept her mouth shut. Being a bitch to me wasn't going to ingratiate her with the rest of the drumline, nor would it win her votes.

When they were seated a few tables away, I let out a sigh, and Julien squeezed my hand.

"Are you upset you weren't invited out with them?" he asked.

I shook my head. "No. I mean, I was invited. I didn't know they were coming here, but Dina—she plays bass drum—asked me this morning if I wanted to have lunch with some people from band.

We spend so much time together in the fall, when the season's over, we make an effort to get together every so often." I waved my hand. "You and I already had plans, so I told her no."

"Shouldn't you be campaigning?"

I huffed a laugh. "They know me, Jules. There's nothing I can really do now. If they've spent three years playing with Katie and me and still choose to vote for her, they were never my people, you know?"

"Then why do you need Carson's support?"

"It's not really that I need his support. I need him not to turn on me and twist reality so Katie looks like the best choice. I've seen him ruin people on a whim."

He tensed, his shoulders rising around his ears. "He's not going to fuck with you."

"He won't. Not when I have the best boyfriend ever, right?" *Fake.* I had to keep repeating that in my head.

Our waitress appeared at the end of our table with our orders. I wiggled my fingers between Julien's, and he slowly let me go so the waitress could set down our plates.

As soon as she left, I picked up my fork, and Julien chuckled. My eyes flicked to his amused face. "What?"

"That *is* a giant piece of pie."

"Oh, I know."

"You're going to eat all of it?"

I waggled my brows at him. "Every. Single. Bite."

And then I showed him exactly how much I loved this pie.

Stuffed full and happy from a really great day with my fake boyfriend, I collapsed on the couch and took out my phone to spend some time mindlessly scrolling. Laura wandered into the room, pushing an earring into her ear.

"You're back?" she asked.

"Yes. I ate a piece of pie—"

She held up her hand. "You ate that gigantic pie in front of your boyfriend?"

I rubbed my stomach. "I did. He was proud of me."

I never, ever, *ever* would have considered eating like that in front of Seth. He would have been appalled and refused to touch me after. When I ate anything other than a salad around him, he basically grimaced. Julien had been the complete opposite, applauding me when I cleaned my plate.

"Please tell me you didn't ask him to rub your food baby," Laura begged.

I held up my fingers a half inch apart. "I was this close but refrained. I have a feeling he would have been up for it, though."

Both hands went to her hips. "I'll sic Alley on you if you even entertain ever doing that. Speaking of Alls, I'm running super late. We have that jazz festival thing her parents got us tickets to."

I held up my phone. "I've got TikToks to watch. Have fun."

She ran out the door, and I picked up my phone, smiling to myself. A text came through moments later, and I was surprised to see it was from my phantom. I hadn't heard from him in a while, and I hadn't really thought too much about texting him. But I was glad to see his name on my screen.

ThePhantom: *Hello, Dragon Girl. How are your adventures going?*

Me: *Hello, ghost boy. Adventures are swell. I bought a dress and ate pie.*

ThePhantom: *Wow, that does sound swell. Did you save me any?*

Me: *Absolutely not. Tell me, how are you?*

ThePhantom: *I've been busy.*

Me: *That's all you have to say? Busy doing what? Do you have a girl?*

ThePhantom: *I've been seeing someone. Probably not going anywhere, though. How's your cane-boy?*

I'd expected to be at least a little heartbroken, if and when my phantom ever told me he had a girlfriend. Searching inside myself now, there was a twinge of disappointment I couldn't deny, but I wasn't devastated. Not the way I would have been a few weeks ago, before Julien. That was most likely a problem in itself, but I'd deal with that when the time came.

Me: *You're just going to tell me you have a girlfriend and not elaborate? This relationship is super one sided.*

ThePhantom: *She's a good girl with a smart mouth. Too smart to like someone like me.*

Me: *You always get after me for my negative self-talk. Don't do that. If she's as smart as you say, she'll see the good in you. I could talk to her and explain how you were with me during one of my darkest times. Or I can write a testimonial for you to show to all future, potential girlfriends. "I don't know his name, but he is unfailingly supportive when push comes to shove."*

ThePhantom: *That's sweet. Don't know how convincing it would be, but sweet. You want to know my name, Seraphina? I thought we weren't doing that.*

Me: *No, I guess we're not. It's funny, I always wonder if you're in my classes, watching me. I feel like I'd recognize you if I saw you again, but probably not. It was so dark that night, and you plied me with weed.*

ThePhantom: *LOL...pretty sure it was you asking for it.*

Me: *Maybe. Anyway, to answer your question, Julien is doing well. He helped me pick out a dress today.*

ThePhantom: *Send me a pic.*

Me: *Is that allowed? Would your girl appreciate that?*

ThePhantom: *Not of your tits, silly. Of the dress. Do you have a pic?*

Me: *Only of the one I didn't choose. Here you go.*

I cropped the mirror picture so it was only from the mouth down and sent it to him. It wasn't like I was naked. If his girl saw it, hopefully she wouldn't mind.

ThePhantom: *Hot little Dragon Girl. You should've bought this one.*

Me: *That's what Julien said. But my sister would have murdered me.*

ThePhantom: *Cane-boy sounds like a smart guy. Still faking it with him?*

Was I? The moment in the dressing room hadn't felt fake. And when he'd held my hand across the table in the diner, we'd both been reluctant to let go. Of course, he could have been pretending for my sake. I honestly had no idea what was going on inside his head.

But the fact of the matter was, even though I was developing feelings for him, we were still faking it. He wasn't my boyfriend. I wasn't his girlfriend. We were spending time together because of a bet. A stupid, idiotic bet I regretted accepting every single day. But that was reality.

Me: *Still faking it.*

Chapter Fifteen

Julien

I was an idiot.

A stupid, motherfucking idiot.

I had dug myself so deep in my idiocy, there was no way up or down. I was stuck here, without any idea how to get out.

My thumb hovered over the delete button on my phone, but there wasn't a chance I was actually going to hit it. With a sigh, I brought the screen closer, looking at the picture again.

She should've bought that dress. If I had any extra money, I would've bought it for her. But that was the point, wasn't it? I didn't have shit. No money, a broken body, a fucked face, and, to top it all off, I was a liar.

Shit had gotten out of hand, and I'd let it. But I never thought I'd be in this position. I never considered Sera having cause to speak to me in person, let alone us spending all this time together.

It was supposed to be one message after she stumbled to my door last semester, blind drunk, and dropped Elena off. I'd made her cry—unintentionally, sure—but guilt had nagged at me until I messaged her the next day.

It didn't stop at one.

She'd be pissed if she ever found out—and I wasn't about to tell her. Her phantom was going to slowly fade out of her life. Now that she had gotten rid of Seth and dealt with the grief of losing her grandmother, she was good. Steady. She didn't need him—me—anymore anyway.

I was snapped out of my self-loathing when someone slammed into my shoulder. Twisting around in my desk, I came face-to-face with that jackass, Carson.

He held his hands out. "Sorry, man. I wasn't paying attention to where I was going. I didn't fuck you up any worse, did I?"

I felt nothing but irritation that this guy existed and I had to see his ugly mug three days a week. The shit he was saying to me meant less than nothing.

"It's all good," I replied, shifting forward in my desk to wait for class to start.

"Oh, cool. That's cool. Where's your girlfriend, by the way? Isn't she usually here by now?"

"Sera will be here soon," I said levelly. I hadn't seen or spoken to her since Saturday, and I was oddly anxious for her to show.

"How are things with the two of you? She's my girl, so you better treat her right."

Nodding, I worked on opening my laptop, hoping Carson would read social cues and take a hint.

"She's a good girl," I answered when he didn't leave.

"Have you gotten to see her drum?"

"Not yet." Flashes of her on TV during football games didn't count.

Carson tsked. "That's a shame. But hey, there's a drumline party Friday night. You guys should come. Everyone's been *dying* to see how cute you guys are together." He nodded toward the stairs. "I'm going to dash. I'll text Sera all the details."

I was alone in a class of three hundred for less than a minute before the little dragon girl slipped into the desk beside me, rays of sunshine beaming out of her. She greeted me, leaning into my shoulder. Curls spilled forward onto her chest and across her forehead. Her arm wrapped around mine, and her hand was flattened on my forearm.

"So, it's officially week three. Is it okay if I kiss you today?" she whispered.

I had to stop myself from flinching. That wasn't going to convince everyone what we had was real. And they were watching us, like always.

Since I'd made a promise to Sera, I ignored the weight of one hundred stares and put on my devoted-boyfriend mantle. Reaching around her, I palmed the back of her head and drew her face to mine. When our lips were a hairsbreadth away, I stopped, rubbing my nose against hers. Her breath shuddered.

"A little one, because if you were really my girl, kissing would be between us, in private."

I brushed my lips across hers, barely touching. She grinned into my mouth.

"Are you shy, Jules?"

"Not shy." My fingers threaded into her curls. "But if you were my girl, and I started kissing you, we'd need privacy for what would inevitably happen next. There's no way it would stop at kissing, and I would never share what happened between us with anyone else. That would be for you and me only."

The noise she made sounded an awful lot like a whimper. She pressed herself into my arm, her forehead knocking into mine.

"That was incredibly sexy," she whispered. "Good job destroying my underwear. It's going to be fun to sit through class while I'm absolutely wrecked."

"What?" I barked lowly. "What did you just say?"

She snorted and let her head drop to my shoulder. "Oh, you heard me, you tease. That was like listening to my erotic fiction app."

"*What*?" I repeated.

"Oh my god, Jules. There's this app Alley told me about with women's audio erotica. It's like porn for your ears. And what you just said to me could have been lifted straight from one of those stories."

If I could have banged my head against my desk without drawing attention, I would have. This girl had no idea what she did to me. The things that came out of her mouth scrambled my senses.

"You'll have to send me the link," I said.

She raised her head, her cheeks blushing furiously. "Oh, we're going to listen together. I want to see just how not shy you are."

"That sounds like a dangerous situation, Sera."

She smacked her forehead. "Oh my god, you're right. What am I thinking? You've got me so hot and bothered with your sexy-time voice, I'm being thoughtless. Obviously, you don't want to listen to ear porn with me when you know I'm all throbby."

Grimacing, I squeezed my eyes shut. "Please stop talking unless you want me to be sitting here with a hard-on."

Her gasp was soft next to my ear. "Are you serious? Jules, are you getting hard right now? From me?"

"Shut up. Right now. *Please.*"

She snickered, brushing her mouth along my earlobe. "Are you kidding me? I feel so powerful right now. If I keep talking, are you going to—"

I turned my head and pressed my lips to hers. Hard. She let out a little moan, then opened her mouth slightly, inviting my bottom lip to slot between hers. My teeth dug into her lush flesh, nipping at her until she forgot about the torture she'd been inflicting on me.

"Stop being a bad girl," I murmured, pulling back.

"I'll try really hard," she said, followed directly by another snicker. There was absolutely no chance she was going to try.

With her taste on my lips, I found I didn't fucking care. I'd sit through the next hour with my dick trying to punch a hole in my jeans. Because bad-girl Seraphina was something to behold.

"Not too hard, I hope."

• • • • ● • ● • • •

On the way home, Sera's fingers woven between mine, I remembered Carson's invite.

"You hear about a party on Friday?"

"Mmmhmm. I'm considering going." Her head turned sharply toward me. "Wait. How do you know about it?"

"Your bestie, Carson, invited me along. Said people are dying to see us together." My fingers stretched between hers. "Sounds like a test."

"Did you tell him no?" There was worry behind her question, which made me angry. This kid, Carson, had far too much power over her. I really didn't like the way he made her squirm like a worm on a hook.

"I didn't say much to him, but I'll go with you if you want me to."

Her eyebrows lowered. A look of concern softened her features. "You will? Are you sure? I know I asked you before, but you really don't have to do anything you're not comfortable with."

"Do you want me there?"

She nodded without hesitation. "I do. It should be fun. Lots of playing music, which I miss so badly during the off-season. Wait, does that sound fun to you? I always forget not everyone loves the sound of twenty drummers going at it at the same time."

"It sounds entertaining, if nothing else."

We were at a crossroads. Literally. The place where we always parted. Today, I didn't feel like going home and sitting in my room. I wasn't really ready to say goodbye to Sera either.

"What are you doing now?" I asked.

"Not sure yet. You?"

"I was considering making a visit to my piano. Are you interested?"

"Yes," she said immediately. "Where is your piano?"

"What if I said San Francisco?"

"I'd say we better get going if we want to be back in time for class tomorrow."

I tugged her forward, toward my old house. "My piano lives with Amir and Marco. I haven't played it since the accident but listening to you talk about missing playing drums reminded me."

"Reminded you that you missed it?" She looked at me like I had seven hundred eyeballs on my forehead—like she was disgusted I could give up music.

"Mmm. I've put it out of my head. Music has pretty much eluded me while I've been recovering. That piano bench had been my happy place since I was a kid. I didn't want to taint it with the black clouds I've been carrying around with me, you know?"

"Not really." Her laugh was short and dry. "Oh, that's probably not the supportive answer you were looking for. Honestly, music is my refuge. I've been to *dark* places mentally, and never stopped playing. Then again, I haven't been through what you have."

"Thank Christ for that. I'd never wish this on my worst enemy."

She tightened her grip on my hand, holding it against her stomach for the rest of the walk to Amir and Marco's place. I was counting on them being out for the next couple hours. Amir and Marco had internships that kept them busy, even though I didn't know their exact schedules.

The house was quiet when I unlocked the door. Stepping inside was a punch to the gut. The memories in this place were strong and almost all good.

The piano was in the living room, off to the side of the entryway, tucked in a bay of windows overlooking the street. I walked into the room, seeing it the same and different all at once. I hadn't been here since before. The last time I sat at this bench, I'd been whole. I was better now, but I wasn't the same man I'd been. The cane in my hand was an easy reminder of that.

When I sat down and ran my fingers over the keys, however, *they* were the same. Cool and smooth, I could close my eyes and be any age. Two, pounding away with my fists. Four, stretching my short fingers as wide as I could. Six, reading music. Ten, practicing for a recital. Thirteen, learning a song by Bruno Mars to impress a girl. Fourteen, playing for my mom when she couldn't get out of bed. Fifteen, crying while I played in my new room at Amir's house. And now, twenty-fucking-two, wanting to erase twenty years and pound my fists over the keys because I was so damn angry and there was *nothing* I could do about it.

Sera's warm hand pressed against the center of my back before she sat down beside me, her fingers skimming the keys. The sides of our bodies were glued together, sharing the small bench. Her thigh was hot and comforting against mine. She reached across me to put her hands in the center of the piano.

"Can I play?" she asked softly.

She'd been watching me. I didn't know what she saw, but it got me her gentle voice, so I must've looked seconds away from losing it.

"Yeah. Go ahead." I shifted to the side, giving her more room.

She started with "Chopsticks." Even though it was a children's warm-up song, the first note sent something tumbling in my chest. She kept playing, switching to a real song.

"Coldplay?" I grunted, recognizing "The Scientist."

"Mmmhmm. My parents took me to their concert once."

"And you just know how to play?"

She giggled. "Obviously not. I taught it to myself after the concert. Well, not how to play piano. I started lessons when I was in kindergarten. Believe it or not, I've always liked making noise. My parents were trying to channel it into something more constructive. I like playing piano, but unfortunately for them, I fell in love with drums." She elbowed me as she played. "When did you start?"

"I don't think there's a time I can remember not playing piano. My mom taught lessons on the side." I ran my palm over the antique oak. "This was her piano. The only thing she ever really owned."

"And you left it here when you moved?"

"Told you...didn't feel the music."

She stopped playing and covered my hand with hers. "Look at you, Jules. I don't think you know it, but you've been smiling since you sat down. I think you need to play."

I brought my other hand up to my face, and the hell of it was, there was a smile there. Jesus Christ, I hadn't even been aware of it. But now that she'd said it, I felt the looseness in my shoulders and the absence of the ache in my chest.

"What should I play?"

She propped her chin on my shoulder and hummed. "Impress me."

I chuckled. "I was just thinking about the Bruno Mars song I learned to impress a girl when I was thirteen."

"Did it work?"

"I got a kiss."

Her laugh bubbles, popping next to my ear. "You player, kissing at thirteen? I didn't even snag one until I graduated high school. No one wanted to kiss me because I was a giant geek. Not that I'm not now, but it was far worse then. At least I know how to use gel in my hair now."

I huffed. She'd probably had guys with their tongues lolling out following her around the halls of her high school and had never even noticed. In fact, I was positive about that.

"You should've learned to play Bruno Mars. It always works," I said dryly.

"It wouldn't work on me now that I know it's your seduction method."

"A kiss is hardly a seduction."

She tapped my bottom lip with her fingertip. "My kisses are worth a lot more than a song you learned for another girl." She straightened on the bench, the corners of her eyes pinched. "Not that you're trying to earn my kisses, obviously. Anyway, play me some Elton John. Do you know any Elton John? I feel like that's a classic piano—"

I cut her off with the opening chords of "Tiny Dancer." Nostalgia and rightness pressed in on my bones, replacing the ache with the feeling of home. It wasn't the song—I didn't give a shit about Elton John—but the sounds my fingers were making.

Sera melted into my side. As the song went on, her head fell to my shoulder and one of her hands curled around my leg. I didn't get lost there. If anything, with her warmth and my mother's keys, I was found. Even then, I reminded myself all of this was fleeting. This feeling wouldn't last. Sera would get up and move away. The song would end. I'd lock up the house and go back to my new, quieter one. And after this, it would be even harder to accept my new reality. I knew that, but I didn't stop playing or ask Sera to stop touching me.

One song blended into the next. I played Bruno Mars to make Sera laugh—which I succeeded in doing—then moved onto Chopin. Sera was as quiet as she'd ever been. I'd catch her fingers drumming against her thigh in my peripheral, but otherwise, she was still as marble.

If I could have stopped, I would have asked her to play with me. This sharp desire to mingle my sound with Sera's—who was practically music personified—jabbed at me.

Maybe I'd ask in a while. I just needed to get through this song. And the next. Needed to feel and not think.

I was out of practice, but I could have played all night. If there hadn't been a clatter in the entryway, I wasn't sure what would have stopped me. But the sound of something falling onto the wood floor by the front door had me ripping my hands away from the keys and twisting around.

Sera was rushing to help before I even registered that it was Zadie standing there, surrounded by the groceries she'd dropped.

"You're playing," she rasped, pressing her hand to her chest. "Julien, you're playing."

Sera bent down, picking up the reusable bags. "I'll take these to the kitchen," she blurted out. "I'll just...I'll be back." Then she disappeared, leaving me with Zadie, who was slowly approaching me.

"Hey." I glanced back at the piano. "Sorry for coming over without calling. I didn't think anyone would be here. We'll go."

She stopped in front of me, dropped to a crouch, and took my hands in hers. "You know you don't have to ask. Thank god Amir isn't here to hear you even suggest that." Her smile was wobbly. "He's going to be so happy you were playing. Have you been here other times, or...?"

I shook my head. "Nah, this was the first. I wanted to show Sera the piano. I wasn't even sure I was going to put my hands on it."

"How'd it feel?"

"Like I stepped back in time." My breath came out heavy and shuddering. "We should go."

"Please don't." She squeezed my hands tighter. "I'm making dinner tonight for the guys. You and Sera should stay. Please, Julien? I'm making lemon bars. I know how you feel about them."

I almost laughed. How I felt about them was probably criminal in forty-eight states. It had to be legal to marry desserts in at least two, right?

"Best thing I've ever tasted, but I don't think I'm in good enough shape to battle Marco for my fair share."

We'd almost come to blows over Zadie's lemon bars. All her cooking had gotten us out of control when it came down to it. Those were good times, but they were too closely tied to my fucked-up present to be anything but bitter memories. All the sweet had been sucked away.

"You could trip him with your cane," Zadie suggested.

I shook my head. "Look at you, Ms. Bloodthirsty. Amir's wearing off on you, huh?"

She lifted a shoulder, her lips curving. "Only a little." She stood straight, my hands still in hers. "Will you stay? Please, Julien?"

I should stay and put things to right with Amir. This was my life now, and I had to accept it. I knew that. I didn't deny it in my head. But I was crashing. Going from feeling so fucking good, like I was who I used to be, back to this broken body and distorted life was such a mindfuck. Anger mounted in my belly, If I stayed, tried to slot back into a place I didn't fit anymore, there would be no holding it back. None of these people deserved my rage.

"I gotta get Sera home. Thanks, Z." I pushed to my feet, wrapping an arm around her shoulders. "Next time, I promise."

We both knew that promise was as real as fool's gold.

Zadie blinked up at me, her pretty blue eyes shining. "He misses you."

"I see him every week at the gym."

She kept staring at me like I was an idiot. "That's not what I mean and you know it."

Amir missed the kid he grew up with. He missed my jokes, my easy laugh, my carefree nature. He missed someone who no longer existed.

"I know it." I dropped my arm, and Sera peeked out of the kitchen. I jerked my head toward the front door. "Time to go."

Past time. My lungs were flat, a wave of panic filling the empty crevices. I needed out of this house before the black at the edges of my vision took over.

She came out of the kitchen, smiling at Zadie. "I put most things away for you. I hope I did it right."

Zadie told her not to worry, even as I tugged her toward the door. She followed, yelling her goodbyes until I pulled the door shut, cutting them off from each other. With her hand in mine, I hurried us away from my old house, hazy eyed and short of breath.

"Jules, are you okay?"

"I'm fine."

Sera wrapped her fingers around my bicep. "Are you sure? You don't—"

"I'm fine, Sera. Leave it."

The bones in my knee rubbed together the faster I walked down the sidewalk, sucking away what little air I had left in my lungs. I needed to be in my room, silent and dark. If I could just get there, clear this panic out of my system, I'd be good.

"Julien, I'm worried. You can talk to me. Tell me what's going on and I—"

When I snapped, I wasn't in the driver's seat anymore. Fuck, I loved Sera's voice, but in this moment, when I wasn't sure I wanted to take another step, let alone wake up in the morning, I couldn't take it. Her concern for me was like an ice pick in my ear.

"Holy shit, can you not hear me? I said I'm fine. That means you need to stop asking. Preferably—stop speaking altogether. I'm not your fucking boyfriend or your sad little project. You keep pecking and pecking at me, and I'm going out of my mind. Leave me the hell alone. Just... *God*, can't you see I don't want you around me? Can't you see that?"

She shoved away from me. And when our connection was shattered, she shoved me again. I fell back a step, then another, barely catching myself from falling on my ass.

"What is wrong with you?" she cried. "Why would you—?"

She clamped her lips together and spun on her toes, her legs carrying her fast in the opposite direction. Seeing her go, getting smaller and smaller, pulled me out of my panic enough for me to grasp what I'd just said to her.

I called her name. Bellowed it. But she didn't miss a step. Within seconds, she was gone, faded in the distance before I could even put one foot forward.

It was all I could do to get myself home, locked in my dark bedroom.

But the relief I'd been looking for wasn't to be had. Not when Sera's stricken expression was seared into the back of my eyelids, on every curve of my brain, in the chambers of my heart.

I hated myself most of the time, but never, ever Sera.

And I'd treated her like I did. If she never forgave me, I wouldn't blame her. I didn't even begin to know how to make things right with her.

Staying away from Sera would be the best thing for her, but I owed her my presence...if she still wanted it.

Chapter Sixteen

Seraphina

My nervous, angry belly was the only thing keeping me afloat. Who knew anger was buoyant? It had to be, because all I wanted to do was sink to the bottom of this pool.

Julien climbed down the steps, his head bowed. The only communication we'd had since he'd torn me to shreds was a message telling me he'd be here for his PT session today and would apologize in person. I almost told him to fuck off, but I couldn't bring myself to do it. I cared about him too much, understood too well the sadness and helplessness writhing inside him, to write him off completely.

"Sera—"

I held up my hand to stop him. "When we're done. Let's just get through this session first." I studied a spot over his shoulder. "I read your intake form. I want to work on loosening your pelvis and hips this time. Nothing should hurt, so you have to tell me if it does. Do *not* power through. I need to know."

A long beat of silence passed before he nodded. "Okay. Let's go."

The lapping of the water against our bodies and splashes as one or both of our hands collided with the surface became the conversation between us. Julien swayed toward me, and I cut backward, giving myself space. He reached for me once, and when I pretended not to notice, he let his arm fall underwater.

Julien followed my directions, rotating and lifting, his injured bones and ligaments working hard against him. I watched his face, the tightness around his mouth and at the corners of his eyes. It was hard to tell if it was from pain or frustration.

This was what I wanted to do, but working with someone I knew and cared about was more difficult than I had anticipated. The need to do right by him, to help him, was almost overwhelming.

"I need to put my hands on your hips for this part," I said, circling around to his back. "Is that okay?"

His shoulders were stiff, but he twisted his neck to glance at me. "Of course it is."

My touch was too tentative at first, holding on to the sides of his hips. I should have been in front of him, but that was too intimate and I was too pissed off at him, so we'd try it like this for now.

"I'm going to put pressure here. I want you to push against it." I tipped my head down to watch his lower half under the water, my forehead grazing his slick, warm back. Both of us made a low sound, somewhere between a grunt and a moan. I wanted to laugh, but I wasn't quite there yet.

"How's that?" he asked.

"That's good. How does it feel?"

"Doesn't hurt."

"There's a lot between pain and feeling good, Jules."

He didn't have anything to say to that, putting all of his might into pushing against my hand. And when I asked, he pushed the other way. His shoulders were still tense, and the muscles along his spine were flexed tight. He wasn't using his words to tell me how he was doing, and from behind him I couldn't use facial cues.

Sucking it up, I circled around to his front. He raised his eyebrows but didn't question me.

I positioned myself in front of him, placing my hand on his lower belly. *Way* too intimate. I wasn't thinking like a PT. I was thinking like a woman incredibly attracted to this man and the flat plane of his taut abdomen felt like the perfect slide I wanted to go down.

Swallowing hard, I placed my other hand on his hip. "Now, rock to the right."

I moved Julien through the stretches, observing his face through all of it. He was so good at wearing a mask, it was impossible to tell anything from his expression. And when he lowered his chin to stare back at me, I forgot what I was looking for anyway.

The gray in his eyes was desolate, empty, like a ghost town covered in the ashes of the past. So unlike the man who had played "Tiny Dancer" for me yesterday. This wasn't his normal grumpiness. It was far beyond that, and I hated seeing him this way. Even though he'd been an ass to me, had wrecked me, hurt my tender feelings, sent me reeling. If not for the messages from my phantom, I might have spiraled down to the dark place I retreated to when the world became unbearable.

ThePhantom: *Tell me a story, Dragon Girl.*

Me: *I'm not in the mood.*

ThePhantom: *What's wrong, you? Did someone hurt you? I'll kill them.*

Me: *You wouldn't. And I don't really want to talk about what's wrong.*

ThePhantom: *I would. And that's fine. I'll tell you a story about your grandma.*

Me: *You're going to tell me a story about my own grandmother? I can't wait.*

ThePhantom: *Belinda was engaged to this guy, Phillip. Nice guy, but a dud. That's what she called him. He wanted her to stay home, have his babies, and make his house nice. But Belinda realized she didn't want any of that. When a rock band played at her town's carnival, she fell hard for the drummer. Belinda said goodbye to Phillip, packed a bag, and went on tour with the band.*

Me: *Did she marry the drummer?*

ThePhantom: *Do you think Belinda would do something so boring? No, our girl became the drummer. And one day, she had a granddaughter with flaming-red hair. A dragon girl. Belinda knew from the start this girl was her soul mate. When Dragon Girl picked up drumsticks for the first time, it was confirmed. Belinda told her dragon girl if someone didn't understand her or like who she was or* *said something cruel to her, she should pick up her drumsticks and drown it all out. She said to always be louder than the bullshit.*

Me: *I can't believe you remember all that.*

ThePhantom: *I remember everything you've told me. Now, go find some fucking drumsticks and drown it out. Can you do that for me?*

Me: *I'm going. Thank you for reminding me who I am.*

My grandma had been the best, coolest, most accepting person ever, and when she died around Thanksgiving, my phantom had talked me through my grief. He'd let me tell him an endless stream of stories about her. He'd been there any time I texted, ready to listen. It was more than my own boyfriend had done for me.

Of course, he had an excuse. While I was away for my grandmother's funeral, Seth had been incredibly busy having sex with Katie.

Ugh.

Last night, my phantom had pulled me out of my pity party. Instead of crying in my bed over what Julien had said to me, I let Laura and Alley take me out to dinner, then we watched too many episodes of some cheesy dating show on Netflix. *That's* who I was—not a sad girl who couldn't get out of bed.

"Are you sorry?" I asked suddenly.

Julien jolted, his lips parting without making a sound. I continued talking, unable to stand the silence stretching between us.

"If you're sorry, and you didn't mean what you said, I'll probably be able to forgive you. Just know I won't be your punching bag—ever—but if you tell me you need space, I won't keep asking like I did last night."

He cleared his throat. "Of course I'm sorry. You didn't do anything wrong. That was all me." He brought his hands to my shoulders, slowly curling his fingers around them as he dipped his head to peer straight into my eyes. "I'm sorry, Sera. No matter what's going on in my head, I will never, ever speak to you like that again. You didn't deserve it, and I don't *want* you to take that kind of treatment from anyone, let alone me."

I nodded, my breath hitching. "I'm going to probably be a little mad at you for a while, but I'll forgive you. You're on serious probation, though. I've been far too forgiving in the past because I have this thing where I want to be liked and will bend over backward to be accepted. I'm not doing that anymore. In fact, I've decided to enact a two-strike policy on people I let in my life. One, I might be able to get past, but if we get to two, it's done."

"Sera..."—his palm slid from my shoulder to my nape—"if anyone doesn't like you, they're stupid. Me losing my temper with you had nothing to do with not liking you and everything to do with being overwhelmed and pissed off and lashing out like an idiot."

I clutched his wrist, giving it a squeeze. "I figured that's what happened. It doesn't excuse it, but I understand."

He grimaced, his mouth tight and flat. "I don't want you to excuse me. I was a dick to you after dragging you there with me in the first place."

"You didn't drag me, and I loved being there with you until the end." I blinked up at him, my stomach swooping at the intensity staring back at me. "Do you want to talk about it now?"

"I don't know. Not really, but maybe."

That made me laugh despite myself. "I think we're done in the pool. I'm going to get dressed. If you decide you want to talk, we can. It's up to you."

But I was really hoping he'd take what I was offering. More than anything, I wanted to know him.

• • • • • • • • • •

We were walking in the dark, holding hands. The things Julien was saying weren't romantic, and the hand-holding wasn't real, but my heart hadn't gotten the memo. I had to force myself to stay grounded in reality, when all I wanted was to get lost in a daydream. This was fake. Holding hands was for effect. Twenty-four hours ago, Julien said awful, hurtful things to me I was still working on forgiving. There was no way I could pretend the blue glow of the security lights we passed every twenty feet was mood lighting. My feet were going to stay firmly planted.

"You know how some people say they're not friends, they're brothers?" He glanced at me, and I nodded. "For me and Amir, it's close to the truth. My mom died when I was fifteen. I had the option of living with my dad and his family, but I never considered it. Amir told me to get my ass to his house, so I did. His parents weren't around, and they didn't really give a shit I was there anyway. We were family, always had been, since the first day of preschool. He'd shoved this kid who had stolen my Play-Doh, and the rest is history."

I snorted a laugh. "Oh god, that's so freaking cute."

His chuckle was low, soft. "Yeah. We were both rude little shits."

I tightened my hold on his hand. "Sorry about your mom."

"Me too. She didn't have an easy life. Came here by herself from the Czech Republic, worked her hands raw as a maid, raised a hellion on her own, then died a slow, painful death. She went easy at the end, though, knowing I had Amir."

I pressed my arm against his, letting him know I wasn't going anywhere.

"So, what happened? Why did your accident drive the two of you apart? I don't get it."

Jules stopped walking and pulled me to sit down on a bench beneath a bright streetlight. We both twisted our bodies to face one another, his arm slung over the back of the bench, my knee bent on the seat.

"It wasn't an accident."

My mouth fell open, and I grabbed Julien's arm. "What? What wasn't?"

"Amir has an older brother, Reno. He's kinda big in the shady parts of Savage River. He runs a fighting ring, drugs, girls... Anyway—Amir worked for him up until last spring, and he made some enemies. Shady business is gonna attract shady people."

"Um, okay...I don't know what to say."

Shaking his head, he exhaled. "You don't have to say anything. I had to tell you that part for the rest to make sense. Amir's out of that life now. I don't want you thinking—"

"I don't think anything. I barely know Amir, but Zadie is the sweetest human alive. If she loves him—if *you* love him—I'll trust you guys are good judges of character. I'm just glad he's done with all that."

"He's done, yeah, but I'm the lasting repercussion." He slid his arm out from under my hold and took my hand in his, sliding his fingers between mine. "This cat who had a beef with Amir came barreling out of nowhere in his souped-up truck. Had to be going fifty or more. I shoved Amir out of the way, and even though it happened in a split second, I knew I was going to take the hit. And even knowing what I know now, I'd do it again a thousand times over."

A flash flood of dread and fear filled my chest. "Holy shit, Jules. How did you survive that?"

"No idea. I probably shouldn't have." He dropped his head, his sigh ghosting across our joined hands. "I can't be around him anymore. When he looks at my scars and the way I walk, all I see is regret—him wishing I hadn't pushed him out of the way. I can't even talk to my fucking brother anymore without feeling his guilt over my situation. Like the sight of me absolutely destroys him."

"Jules," I breathed. His frustration and pain were palpable, and so completely understandable.

"How am I supposed to accept who I am now when I've lost my best friend because of it? It eats me up, you know? And being back in that house...god, it felt good at first, but when Zadie showed up, it was like the way everything had changed slapped me in the face."

"I'm assuming you haven't said any of this to him?"

His laugh was dry and breathy. "Nah. I'm only wrapping my head around my reasons for needing to be away from him. At first, I thought it was because I didn't want to be pitied, and maybe that was true then. But now...I don't know. I really don't know if we can ever get back to where we were."

My nose tickled. The backs of my eyes burned. I had to bite down on the inside of my cheek to keep the tears at bay.

"You're being quiet, Sera." He rubbed his thumb along my knuckles, soft and sweet. "You're sad for me?"

That was what did it. His quiet concern pulled the plug, and I burst out with a sob. His eyes rounded in alarm, which made me laugh even as a few errant tears slipped down my cheeks.

"I'm sorry." I held up my hand. "I keep thinking about tiny Julien and baby Amir scrapping in preschool and it's killing me that you guys have this rift." I swiped at my cheeks, sniffling. "I don't know what's wrong with me."

He turned his head, but I swore I saw a grin playing on his lips. Then his shoulders started to shake, and I knew it. This motherfucker was laughing at me.

I slapped his shoulder. "Stop it."

His head dropped. He was full on laughing now, not even trying to hide it. I groaned and tried to yank my hand out of his, but he pulled it to his chest. So, I pinched him—which wasn't easy because he was all lean muscle, but I managed. Julien didn't even flinch. Instead, he laughed harder.

"I hate you, asshole."

He looked at me from under his hair, and his bright, delirious grin made my heart flip. I'd definitely never seen him smile like that. Never, ever.

"You're so fucking cute. So angry and adorable." He reached out and tugged on one of my curls.

Even though I wanted to be mad, Julien was laughing. I'd made him laugh, and he'd shown me his beautiful, crooked smile. Who gave a damn if he was laughing at my expense? I really and truly didn't.

"You should laugh all the time, asshole. It's a nice sound."

That made him chuckle again, which sent me into a fit of giggles. I guess I'd forgiven him. How could I not? He'd been through hell, his life had been upended, and he was still trying to figure out who and where he was.

He was still on probation with me. His reasons for what he did were not an excuse.

But I liked him. I wanted to make him smile all the time. As much as I disliked Carson and the bet I'd been strong-armed into taking, I didn't dislike in any way that it meant I got to spend this time with Jules. Even if our friendship—or whatever this was—was brief, I was more than happy it was happening.

He cupped my jaw with the lightest touch. "Thanks for letting me explain. I know I fucked up and don't deserve your understanding, but I'm really grateful to have it. I mean that, Sera. You're cool as hell. I'm lucky to know you."

My nod was quick and sharp. "Yeah, you are."

He shook his head, hiding his grin from me behind his shaggy hair. "Come on, trouble. Let me walk you home."

We strolled the rest of the way across campus, holding hands under the moonlight, even though no one was around to see us. I had to kick my inner daydreamer in the teeth when I started getting ideas that maybe this was a little real for Julien too.

Daydreams were bad.

They got me in trouble.

Rational, reality-based thoughts only from now on.

No daydreams.

Chapter Seventeen

Julien

I'd been promised a small, laid-back party. Given Carson had been the one to make that promise, I hadn't actually expected it. Then Sera led me into the backyard of an off-campus house where maybe twenty or twenty-five people were drinking and chilling.

Small.

Laid back.

I was uncomfortable as hell.

Small and laid back meant I couldn't blend. There'd be eyes on me—at least until people got too drunk to care.

Sera's hold on my hand was firm, and she positioned herself in front of me like my protector. It pissed me off while my belly warmed from how adorable it was. Ten months ago, it would have been the opposite. I'd have been the one protecting her, leading her into a party, showing her off with confidence.

For Sera, it was easy to be the leader of our pair. For me, having her out front was a direct hit to my shaky ego.

Carson came toward us, his arms outstretched. "If it isn't the cutest couple at Savage U." He clapped me on the shoulder. "Welcome, welcome to my humble abode, man. Find a drink, have a smoke, get to know everyone. If you're still around in the fall, these are the people Sera will be spending ninety percent of her time with."

He shot Sera a wink—because they both knew I wouldn't be around in the fall. He was a bullshitter, doing it right in front of me. This kid was the most disrespectful piece of shit around.

"I'm looking forward to the drumming," I answered.

Sera pushed out a stale giggle. Pretty sure she liked this cat even less than I did. "And the drinks, right? That's what I came for."

"Absolutely, little lady. Let Uncle Carson stir you up a concoction of something delicious and lethal." He raised an eyebrow at me. "Are you able to drink?"

I had no idea why he thought I wouldn't be able to, so I didn't bother with a response. Given the fact he didn't pause for one, I sensed it was a dig on me rather than an actual question.

For the sake of Sera, I let it slide. She needed that drum captain position, and I was here, by her side, because of it. I wasn't gonna screw it up for her, even if I wanted to rip that little shit fuck apart.

• • • • • • • • • •

Sera's cheeks were flaming bright red, and her giggles were coming easier and easier as she sipped her drink and bounced to the music. Some of the other drummers were playing around on a couple sets of quads and quints. We were tucked together on a love seat, enjoying the show.

Sera's arms went up, directing the pace. "Come on, Dina, give it to me," she called to the girl behind a set of quads.

Dina twirled her drumstick in the air, whooping back at Sera.

I leaned into her. "You want to be up there, don't you?"

She knocked her head against mine. "I'm not leaving you alone."

"I'm good, Dra—Sera." Shit. A couple hits of a blunt, and I almost called her Dragon Girl. I needed to get myself together. "I wanna see you up there. Show me those skills, baby."

Snorting, she threw her arms around my neck and pressed her mouth to my ear, whispering softly, "You're the best fake boyfriend ever."

I turned my head, my nose grazing her hot, velvet cheek. "You make it easy."

We were putting on a show for her friends and that asshole Carson. They'd been watching us all night. Sera had kept herself glued to my side, and I hadn't minded. In fact, I'd have liked it a lot more without the audience.

It made me wonder if this was what she'd been like with Seth or if she was putting on a character. I'd never know the answer to that, so my ass would have to daydream about it.

When Sera hopped up, I swatted her butt. She squeaked, then wiggled it at me. I went for her again, but she jumped out of my reach, spinning around to laugh.

"Be nice, Jules," she admonished.

"I'm always nice to you, Seraphina."

Her teeth dug into her bottom lip. She took a long time just standing there, looking like she was thinking about letting me give her plump little ass another smack. Tipsy Sera was flirty and even cuter than when she was fully sober—and that was saying a lot since she was *incredibly* adorable always.

After a dragging moment, she finally shook her head and ventured over to the drums, swaying her hips the whole time. In the red sundress that barely grazed the bottom of her ass when she was standing still, swaying Sera was a dangerous, tempting thing.

For a while, she stood behind her friends, clapping and cheering them on. Two drummers were playing a game of Simon, one pounding out a beat, the other copying it.

One of Sera's friends, Stefan, whom she'd privately told me was cool, stopped by with a fat blunt he was willing to share. Stefan didn't talk much, which I appreciated. Sera picked up a set of drumsticks, and the two of us watched the girls go to town on the drums.

The way they were banging on their tenors would probably be frowned upon in another setting, but no one blinked tonight.

"You guys are cute," Stefan said.

I tipped my chin at him. "Thanks, man."

He rested his ankle on his opposite knee. "She brought her ex to a couple of these. He barely ever touched her or talked to her. We all talked about how shitty he was to her. Like, did he even like her? No one really understood their relationship. I mean, he's a dick, and she's awesome. But it's pretty obvious how much you like her. Everyone sees it and appreciates it, because we all love Sera, you know?"

I nodded at my girl rocking out to her own beats. "I know. I don't get why she was with that guy either."

Sera hadn't revealed much to her phantom, but enough for me to build a picture of exactly how she'd been treated by her douchey ex. To be fair, though, I hadn't needed her messages. The first time I met her, I'd seen the kind of boyfriend he was to her.

There was a small commotion behind us. I twisted around, to see three girls coming down the path along the side of the house that led to where we were in the back. The one in front I recognized immediately as the little bitch that got caught riding Sera's ex. She obviously had a hard-on for Sera, because she was all pinchy eyed and stony mouthed as she watched Sera living her best life on the drums.

As she started to pass me, clearly headed for my girl, I stuck out my arm to stop her.

"Don't even think about it," I hissed.

Affronted, she looked down at me, her mouth wide open. "What the hell?"

"If you're contemplating getting in my girl's face, the answer is no. If you're here to have a couple drinks and chill, have at it—but you're not going to mess with my girl."

She crossed her arms over her chest. "Oh, please. No one thinks you're actually together. Whatever this is, it's obviously Sera's misguided attempt to make Seth jealous, which is so laughable."

Stefan made a shooing motion. "Be gone, hellbeast. You weren't even invited."

Katie rolled her eyes. "You don't know what you're talking about. Carson personally invited me. And why wouldn't he? He knows I'll be taking his position next year. I have to bond with my people."

Stefan held up his middle finger. "Bond with this, Katherine. Absolutely no one wants you to be captain. I don't even think *you* want it."

She huffed. "As I said, you don't know what you're talking about." Her attention shifted back to me. "Seth isn't finished with Sera. God only knows why. If I were you, I wouldn't get too comfortable. He'll get her back."

She stalked off, leaving me frowning after her. What the hell was that? That chick fucked her bestie but was still trying to pawn him off on Sera?

Stefan patted my shoulder. "Don't even try to wrap your head around it. Katie and Seth have the strangest, most incestuous relationship ever. All of us stopped trying to figure them out freshman year."

"Is there a chance she'll win drum captain?"

"Pfft." He shook his head incredulously. "Not happening. Like I said, we all love Sera, and after living under Carson's reign of terror, we want her in charge next year. Katie might have a couple strays on her side, but there's no chance she'll win."

Lowering my chin, I studied him through the subtle haze of the beginning of my high. "Why's Sera worried then?"

"Because she wants it. Because Katie has a big mouth and everything that went down with Seth put a big dent in her confidence." He pressed one hand to his heart and held the other up. "Scout's honor, Sera has nothing to worry about."

After a minute or two, Stefan hopped up to join the drummers, leaving me with the end of the blunt, which I was happy to take off his hands. By the time Sera came dancing toward me, flicking her hips to the rhythmic beat of the drums, matching the beat of a song playing on the speakers someone had dragged outside, I was feeling absolutely no pain.

She stopped in front of me, holding her hands out. The warm air had heated her skin, giving her a rosy glow all over. Her cheeks were shining, and her hair wove in fiery circles around her face.

"Come on, boyfriend. Dance with your girlfriend."

"I'm not much of a dancer these days."

"All you have to do is stand there and hold me. I'll do all the work." She bent forward, bracing a hand on my shoulder. "If you don't get up, I'll be forced to dance on your lap."

A laugh shot out of me. "Is that supposed to be a threat?"

She tilted her head, sending her spirals over one shoulder. "It's however you want to take it. A threat or a promise. I don't have any experience giving lap dances, but I think I'd be good at it."

Swiveling in a slow circle until her ass was in my face, Sera's hips rolled in sensuous waves. If she sat down on me now, there was no hiding my reaction to her moves.

She peered back at me over her shoulder. "What's it going to be, baby?"

Having no real choice, I pushed myself up to stand, my front dragging along her backside. She went still as my chest collided with her back and one of my hands gripped her hip.

"Take it easy on me," I murmured beside her ear. "I'm out of practice."

I'd never been much of a dancer before, and even less now, but I trusted Sera to be gentle. Besides, with her moving like she was seconds away from fucking, no one was going to be paying attention to me anyway.

She spun around, her hands hitting my chest. One slid to my nape, tangling in the overlong hair there.

"Thanks for dancing with me, Jules. No one ever dances with me."

"I'm not much of a partner, but you ask, I'll always dance with you."

That pulled a beaming grin out of her. She lunged forward, her lips pressing against mine in a hard, fast kiss.

"God, you're really good at this," she cooed. "How'd you get so good at this?"

"At what?"

"Being my boyfriend." Her head fell back and her spine arched as she pressed her pelvis against mine. There was no question she felt my hard-on, but instead of putting space between us, her lower body undulated in time to the Latin song.

"You make it easy."

She was singing along to the music, missing the answer to a question she'd probably already forgotten she'd asked. Sera soaked up the rhythm around her, becoming part of it. It was all I could do to hold on to her. But she never let go of me either, her fingers playing with my hair, scratching the skin on the back of my neck. Her other hand ran around my chest, down my side, and back up again. I wasn't much more than a prop, with my cane in one hand so I didn't fall on my ass, but she made me feel like her partner.

A slower song came on, and she pulled back, giving me an assessing look.

"Do you want to sit down?"

My brow crinkled. "Do you?"

She shook her head. "Can you put your arms around me and sway? I love swaying to slow songs. I want to sway with you, Jules."

"I can do that."

I propped my cane on the seat behind me and wrapped my arms around Sera's waist. She curled her arms around my neck and pressed herself tightly to my chest. A soft, shuddering sigh fell from her lips as she laid her head on my shoulder. We didn't do much more than rocking in a leisurely circle, but from the way Sera kept nuzzling into me, she liked it.

It took me half the song to let my muscles relax. Another quarter to really breathe. Then I dropped my head, resting my cheek on her hair. She smelled like cinnamon and the sun. Mixed with the weed in the air, I was right back to the first time we met. Another party, another life.

"This is so nice," she whispered.

"What's nice?"

"This. You. I'm going to pretend it's real until the song ends, okay?"

Swallowing hard, I nodded. "That's all right. Pretend all you want to."

When the music picked up again, Sera broke away from me, grinning. "Thank you for doing that. You were probably miserable, but I enjoyed myself thoroughly."

"I wasn't miserable." I swiped a hand over my face and cleared my throat. "Are my services no longer needed?"

"I'm gonna go grab a drink. I'll grab a refill for you." She danced away, stopping a few times to shimmy her shoulders and shake her ass with her friends.

While she was gone, Stefan stopped by again. He seemed to be the hookup among this crowd. Judging by his endless supplies of blunts, I was surprised I didn't recognize him from hanging with Amir. Stefan must've had another supplier, one with good, high-quality shit.

He nodded at the cane in my hand. "Are you good standing? Dancing?"

"Oh yeah." I exhaled the smoke from my lungs. "I'm not even sure I have legs anymore."

He let out a thick, smoky laugh. "Oh shit, me neither."

Sera reappeared from nowhere, thrusting a Solo cup in my hand. "I made this for you. Tell me if it's delicious."

She leaned back on Stefan, her head on his shoulder, spine arched so the rest of her barely touched him. He circled her shoulders loosely, stumbling back a step.

I took a sip, watching them over the rim of the cup. I didn't like him holding her, even if it was friendly. My claim on her was too flimsy for me to be secure enough to see another man with his hands on her.

Stefan plopped his *J* between her lips, holding it while she puffed, and it was all I could do not to grab her away from him and carry her to the top of a skyscraper to King Kong. Possession rode me hard, and I had no right to it. But I was tripping hard enough not to care what kind of rights I had. Right now, Sera was mine, and everyone around us needed a reminder. She blew smoke into Stefan's face, giggling, her gaze alighting on me. "You didn't tell me how your special drink is, Jules."

My brow winged up. "You want a taste?"

"Yes. Give me some."

Reaching out, I pushed on the underside of her chin, tilting her head back. "Open your mouth."

She complied, her pretty lips parting for me. Stefan watched us with interest, flicking his gaze back and forth between the girl he was holding and me as I took a long pull from my cup.

Closing the small space between us, I held Sera's nape and tipped my chin down, aligning my mouth with hers, then let the liquid in my mouth trickle into hers. Instead of sputtering and closing her mouth like I thought she would, her lips widened and her tongue darted out to collect the raining sweet alcohol.

Our noses touched as I spilled into her mouth. Droplets dotted her lips and chin. Her eyes were wide, locked on mine. Behind her, Stefan groaned, reminding me he was there.

Unfortunately.

Sera let out the softest whimper when she'd taken all I had to give. "You want more?" I asked.

She licked her wet lips. "Yes please."

I drained more of the drink, then tugged Sera out of Stefan's arms and into mine. Her fingers dug into my shoulders, grasping my T-shirt as I fed her again. She took it so eagerly, practically lapping at the stream. This time, when I ran out, she pushed up on her toes to lick the little drops off my lips.

I fisted her curls, yanked her as close as she could get, and sucked her bottom lip into my mouth. She moaned and let go of my shirt to cup my face. Her tongue found mine, both cold and coated with sweetness. She licked into my mouth, and I responded, sucking on the tip, swallowing down every last drop, uncovering her natural flavor. Infinitely sweeter and more addictive, I lapped it the fuck up, letting it fill the empty, aching crevices inside me.

Sera pressed forward, giving me all her weight. And fuck me if I didn't stumble backward, hitting the edge of the wicker love seat behind me. If I'd been stronger, more steady, I would have stayed on my feet. But that wasn't me. I went down hard, bringing Sera with me, our lips wrenched apart as we fell.

Thankfully, the chair was pretty cushioned, and I'd caught Sera, her body sprawled across me diagonally, shaking with giggles.

"Oh shit," she squeaked. "Are you okay?"

Too toasted to properly assess whether I'd damaged my already damaged body, I worked on pulling her upright. She was all loose limbed and wiggly, so it wasn't an easy feat, but I got her sitting sideways in my lap and held her there.

Taking her chin in my hand, I tilted her head left and right. "Are *you* okay? I took you down."

"I'm so okay." She slapped her palm on my chest. "You know, you're a really good kisser. So good. I'm pretty sure we traumatized Stefan for life, but I have no regrets."

"No?"

"No." She fitted her face into the side of my neck, her breath hot on my skin. "I'm pretty sure I just let you spit in my mouth. I must like you."

"I was only sharing my drink."

"And spit."

"A little spit."

Her lips touched my throat. "Chef's kiss to the drink thing. Very sexy, Jules. If anyone questioned whether we were real before tonight, they won't anymore."

"Right." I patted her thigh. "I'm going numb here. Up you go."

Numb was the opposite of what I was. But Sera's reminder that the heat we just shared was one-hundred-percent fake had my throbbing dick rapidly deflating.

Giggling, she rolled off my lap, tucking herself beside me.

She laid her head on my shoulder and sighed. "Thank you for being my friend. You're the best, you know?"

I grunted, which made her giggle even more.

"I think I'm a little drunk," she said.

"A little?"

She took my hand in hers, toying with my fingertips. "Only a little. I'll definitely remember every moment of that kiss." Her thumb ran along my middle finger. "Hopefully we'll have a reason to reenact it. I don't think I can go the rest of my life without at least one more of those dirty, delicious kisses."

I was going to let this lie, but then her head popped up. "Wait—you didn't say. Do you think I'm a good kisser too? Here I am talking about repeats, and you might be thinking I have a tongue like a slug and lips like...I don't know, marshmallows."

"Marshmallows don't sound bad for lips."

Her nose scrunched. "I couldn't think of anything. I guess my lips could be like slugs too. Do I have slug lips?"

I pressed my thumb into her bottom lip. "Nothing like slugs."

"But am I a good kisser?"

"You don't have anything to worry about."

An understatement, but I was in no position to tell her she kissed like she talked—free, uninhibited, too much and not enough all at once. Sweet and spice swirled with sexy and cute. Ever since our lips had parted, I'd been considering diving back in for more.

But I didn't say that, and Sera stopped asking.

There was no more kissing or touching or dancing—which was for the better—but the night still ended up being the best I'd had since *before*. By the time I made it home, I almost felt like me.

The last thought I had before I fell asleep wasn't filled with dread like it had been since last spring.

As I drifted, pink, sassy lips carried me the rest of the way to a deep, very close to contented sleep.

Chapter Eighteen

Seraphina

Julien's head was bent over his laptop, his hair curtaining his face. He was studying, and so was I. It just so happened, I was studying him.

My excuse was I was hungover and the dull ache in my head made reading for too long difficult. The truth was, I couldn't get over the fact that Julien was in my room, sitting at my desk.

I'd been needy this morning when I woke up feeling a little like death. Shoving my pride aside, I'd messaged Julien that I wanted to hang out with him. To my surprise and sheer delight, he messaged back saying he was coming to me and bringing food.

There'd been a moment when he showed up I felt like a total dick because my room was on the second floor of the house, but Julien handled the stairs just fine. It took him a little longer, but he did it without complaint.

And he brought me a greasy, delicious breakfast.

My greedy eyes zeroed in on the bags in Julien's hand. "What did you bring me?"

He held them up. "Oh, these? You wanted a salad, right? I hope so."

"I'll murder you. Don't test me."

That made him laugh. "Right. Don't mess with the hungover girl."

"I'm not hungover. Just grumpy."

"Mmmhmm. You know I was with you last night, right? I saw what you drank."

"Don't shame me." I lunged at the bags, but I was moving slowly because I might have been hungover, so I missed. *"Why are you torturing me?"*

He held his arm out, beckoning me with the flick of his hand. I went to him, tucking myself under his arm. He finally handed me the bags, which were warm from the contents—hash browns, egg and cheddar breakfast sandwich, and bacon. Lots and lots of bacon.

"Thank you, Jules. You're my new best friend."

"I'm honored, although it seems like you're easily bought."

I snuggled into him as I dug into the first bag. "No, I already liked you a lot before this. A lot, a lot."

He'd fed me and then stayed. Alley and Laura had been in and out of the room, swooning over how cute we were, even though he was on one side of the room and I was on the other. Granted, it was a small room, so there weren't more than six feet of distance between us, but still. I was on the bed. He was sitting at my desk. Not very coupley. Though, neither Alley nor Laura commented, so what did I know?

Julien tucked his hair behind his ear, only for it to flop forward again. He exhaled and shoved it away again with more force. I liked that he was comfortable with me and didn't try to cover up with his hoodie or purposefully hide behind his hair.

He glanced up, catching me watching him. I averted my gaze, pretending to focus on the book in front of me. It was super smooth. There was no way possible he realized I'd been creeping on him.

A minute later, I gave in to temptation and peered up from my book. Julien had shifted in his chair to face me. Our eyes locked, and there was no hope of pretending this time.

"You keep peeking at me." He rolled his shoulder, wincing slightly.

"I'm having trouble concentrating and you're more interesting than my reading." I tipped my head toward him. "Is your shoulder hurting?"

"Stiff, but I can handle it."

I pushed my book aside and patted the bed in front of me. "Come here. Let me help you with some stretches."

He hesitated for a beat, then sighed and shut his laptop, crossing the small space between us. He sat on the edge of the bed, facing away from me. I got behind him on my knees, lightly touching his shoulder.

"Is this from the collision?" I refused to call it an accident anymore, since I knew the truth. There was nothing accidental about what had happened to Julien.

"Yeah. It's not bad, but I spent months on crutches, and now, using the cane, I'm still off." He turned his head, giving me his profile. "You don't have to do this."

"I know that, but I want to. I'm not promising miracles, but I think I can help a little. At band camp, people used to line up for my shoulder massages."

He huffed. "Guys, right?"

I tapped the top of his head. "I know what you're implying, but believe it or not, I had a mix. My fingers are *that* magical."

His muscles were tight under my fingertips. I rolled them gently and pressed his neck to the side to give him a nice stretch. He grunted, but didn't tense, so I wasn't hurting him. As I worked, kneading in a circular pattern, more soft, low grunts fell from Julien. By the way he clamped his mouth shut immediately each time, the noises were involuntary.

"Does this feel good?" I murmured.

"Mmmhmm."

His joined hands slid down his legs, inch by inch, and his head fell forward, his hair slipping over his face again. He left it, arms relaxed and limp at his sides. Seeing him like that filled me with a deep satisfaction.

Shuffling forward on my knees to get a different angle, my front brushed against his back. I felt his traps jump then slowly unclench as I massaged and stretched him.

"Still good?"

"Fuck yes. I see why you had a line."

I wanted to press my lips to his nape, but I restrained myself, biting hard on my bottom lip. "If you're nice, I can make this a regular occurrence."

"I can be nice to you, Sera, but that doesn't seem like enough of a payment." His words were slurred, almost drunken. In my head, I was running a victory lap. I only wished I could see his face, but his hair was hiding it from me.

"I have an idea, but you might not like it."

"Anything," he vowed. "Anything you want. I'm your fucking minion."

Giggling, I ruffled the top of his hair. "Let me braid your hair so it's out of your way."

He tensed again, but I pressed on his shoulder, easing it down. "I don't know if—"

I fitted my face beside his, his short whiskers scruffing against my cheek. "Just while you're here with me, Jules. I want to see you while I'm peeking at you."

"Why?"

"Because I like your face, and your stupid hair keeps hiding it from me."

He shoveled his fingers through his hair and twisted around to look at me. "You don't like my hair?"

I patted the top of his head. "Your hair is lovely, but it's annoying me. And I think it's annoying you, based on the number of times you've tucked it behind your ears."

His nostrils flared as he exhaled. "You really wanna braid my hair?"

I nodded eagerly. "I really do."

I pointed to the headboard, telling him to sit with his back against it. Since his shoes were already off, he climbed all the way onto my bed and situated himself, stretching his long legs in front of him. I grabbed a couple ponytail holders and a comb and sat on the bed beside him, frowning at my low position.

This wasn't going to work.

Shifting again, I got on my knees, leaning over him. Not the most comfortable, but it would do. Julien sat statue-still as I combed out the section I wanted to braid. His hair was silky and thick between my fingers. I indulged myself, stroking it for longer than necessary, but he didn't complain. He wasn't in the same languid state he'd been while I'd rubbed his shoulders, but his eyes were shut and he was tilted toward me, as if asking for more.

"Was your hair always long?" I asked.

"It's longer than it was before. But I haven't had it short for years."

"Has anyone ever done this to you?"

He breathed out a laugh. "Never."

"Good. I get to claim my position as the first."

"Most likely only."

I let my knuckles drag down the unblemished side of his face. "I doubt that. A lot of girls would be happy to get their hands on your hair. It's beautiful, if not stupid from time to time."

I had no doubt before his injuries, Julien easily pulled. Once he realized he wasn't the beast he saw himself as, once his confidence came back, he'd have girls falling all over him once again. And as much as I wanted him to regain his confidence, the thought of him moving on and finding someone—or lots of someones—made my stomach churn with jealousy.

His hand flexed on my comforter, wadding in his fist. "My hair, sure. The rest of me, that's doubtful."

"I don't believe that."

But there was something I'd been meaning to ask him. When I went over the intake form I'd forced him to fill out, I'd included questions about sexual function, since patients with pelvic injuries sometimes had issues. He'd left it blank, probably decided it was none of my damn business—and it wasn't since I wasn't an actual physical therapist. Last night, though, when our bodies had been as close as two people could get without actually fucking, it had been clear to me getting aroused wasn't a problem for Julien. Not in the least. Still, I wondered...

"Doesn't matter what you believe."

"Julien..."—I cupped his jaw—"have you been with anyone since...?"

"No," he gritted out, his brow dipping low over his closed eyes.

"Are you concerned about function? About your range of motion or—?"

His eyes flew open. "Stop it, Sera," he barked. "Cut that shit out."

An idea sparked, and my mouth ran away with me.

"Because if you're concerned, we can work on it. I mean, if you want to, while we're doing this whole fake boyfriend-girlfriend thing, we can...experiment. Find positions that work for you."

The grimace that took over him made me want to crawl under the bed and hide. He was actually *pained* by the idea of having sex with me. I should have never said anything. I'd been so caught up in the high of dancing and kissing last night, and having him in my bed today, that I wasn't thinking. Of *course* he didn't want to do that with me. Everything we'd done last night had been for show.

"Why would you want to do that?" He turned away from me, staring at the wall across the room. "You feel sorry for me? You're offering to pity fuck me now?"

"Just forget it." I covered my face with my hands. "God, I'm sorry. I thought it would be fun, but I clearly wasn't thinking."

The room went dead silent, apart from my ragged breathing. I braced myself to feel the bed moving and to hear Julien's retreating footsteps, but that never came.

"Fun?" His fingers closed around my wrists, pulling my hands down. "You want to...experiment, to fuck, for fun?"

"Yes. Well...I did. Not now, obviously."

Cuffing both of my wrists in one hand, he used the other to lift my chin so I had no choice but to look at him. My cheeks were burning. I wished I had the capacity to melt myself into a puddle and float away, but I remained corporeal under Julien's scrutiny.

"How would it work?" he asked. "What would we do?"

I considered him for a moment, a boulder of self-hatred and nerves sitting in my throat.

He shook my bound wrists. "Sera. How would it work?"

"I guess...maybe, I would ride you the first time, and if that went well, we could try it other ways. I haven't really thought it through.

It doesn't matter anyway. I don't know why you're making me embarrass myself further right now."

The breath he took was shaky and deep, but he was no longer recoiling. Julien studied the flames in my cheeks and my teeth worrying my bottom lip to smithereens. He clucked his tongue and used his thumb to pry my lip free, then rubbed back and forth over the wet, abused surface.

"It's not because you pity me?" he rasped, his jaw flexing.

"No. I don't pity you, asshole. You can just tell me no and we can move on. That would be ideal, wouldn't it?"

He blinked slowly, his pupils blooming. "You're sitting here calling me an asshole, yet I'm still hard as stone."

My gaze dropped to his lap. He wasn't lying. "Jules," I breathed. "What—?"

His hand slid to my nape, pulling me forward. With me beside him on the edge of the bed, there was nowhere to go but on top of him. I went slowly, so he could stop me if this wasn't what he really wanted. He kept coaxing me closer, so I straddled his thighs, pulling the bottom of my sundress down to cover myself as much as I could. It was strange, given what we were talking about, but I was in a vulnerable position and a scrap of a dress was all I had to armor myself.

"This is for science, right?" he asked.

I nodded. "And for fun. It should definitely be fun."

"I can do fun." He touched my arms, ghosted along my sides, and settled his hold on the flare of my hips.

"Then stop looking like you're going to your own funeral." I scrunched my nose, disgruntled by this whole thing. I was clearly no seductress, and Julien wasn't helping in any way. I couldn't read him, other than the bulge pressing against me.

"I feel like I've fucking died and somehow made it to heaven, Sera. My beautiful friend is offering to have sex with me, out of the blue, for fun, and I'm still catching up. Forgive me if I'm not reacting as I should. I feel like my brain and dick are going to simultaneously explode."

That was what I needed. Julien made me laugh and called me beautiful. *My beautiful friend.* Falling forward on his chest giggling, we ended up nose to nose. Julien slid his back and forth against mine and then he tipped his chin, until our lips touched. There was a moment's pause, like we were both acknowledging this was the point of no return.

The rumbling growl that preceded Julien's lips crushing mine in a searing hot kiss, traveled straight to my belly, and then crawled down to my core. His tongue slicked over my lips and tongue, like a promise of all that he could do to me if I allowed it to happen. And god, I hoped this experiment went well so we could try everything.

He shoved up the back of my dress, palming my butt. I was in comfortable cotton panties today—the full coverage kind that *some* people might refer to as granny panties—but he didn't hesitate to slide right under them and grab handfuls of my flesh. Squeezing and kneading, he groaned into my mouth as he explored my body, running the tips of his fingers along the valley of my ass, and forward into my wet heat.

I worked my way under his T-shirt, finally getting my hands on all the smooth, tan skin I got to see every week in the pool. The divots of his muscles provided routes for me to trail over, but I couldn't stay on course. I wanted to touch him everywhere.

I had to remind myself this wasn't about me. This was about Julien. He was the one who needed to know what worked for him and what didn't.

Pulling back from his mouth, I sat up and shrugged off my cardigan. He reached for the spaghetti straps of my dress, raising a questioning eyebrow. I nodded, giving him permission to lower the straps. The fabric caught on my peaked nipples. He gave it a gentle tug, exposing my little breasts.

From the hungry, reverential expression Julien wore, he didn't find me lacking.

And when his mouth covered one of my nipples, I forgot that I had ever found myself lacking either.

He sucked and licked, swirling his tongue around my nipple until I threw my head back and moaned at the ceiling. He made it easy to forget this wasn't about me. I badly wanted him to keep going, to put his mouth on me absolutely everywhere.

"Julien...Jules..." I cupped his cheek to make him let go of my nipple. He dragged his head away, peering at me from under heavy-lidded eyes. "I'm going to grab a condom, okay?"

His brow lowered. "What?"

"Condom."

I scrambled off of him, opened the drawer of my bedside table and ripped a foil packet out of the box. Tossing it on the table, I wiggled out of my underwear and kicked them aside.

Julien had his thumbs hooked in his waistband, tugging his pants down his hips. I sucked in a breath when his cock popped out and thumped heavily on his belly.

"You're huge." My eyes flew to his. I swallowed hard. "You're huge, Julien."

He stroked his length from root to deep-purple tip, eyeing me lazily. "It'll fit. Come back here. I wasn't done."

"I will, I just—" I placed my hand on top of his, curling around his fingers. We locked eyes as he pumped and heat flooded my lower belly in a desperate, needy way.

"Fuck, Sera." He clamped his jaw hard and stroked his cock even harder.

"Julien...I want to feel it. Let me—" I snatched up the condom, tore it open, and nudged his hand aside. When I grabbed his thick base, he shuddered, and the slit at the top wept precum. "Oh god."

It was all I could do to get the condom on with my trembling hands. Julien was no help as he gripped my comforter with all his might. A few fumbles, and he was sheathed. I positioned myself on top of him, rubbing his rigid length between my folds. I was soaked, and he hadn't even really touched me there.

"I need to be inside you, Sera." He held on to my hips, digging his fingertips into my flesh. He didn't try to take my dress all the way off, and for that, I was grateful. "No more teasing or else this is going to be over before it starts."

"I need it too." Rising up on my knees, I angled the tip of him toward my entrance, then slowly took him inside. He stretched me like I'd never been stretched, the burn only adding to the otherworldly experience.

I had to rock back and forth, working myself down, until I took all of him.

Attempting to remember why we were doing this, I focused on Julien's expression, which was tight and pained.

"Am I hurting you?" I rushed out. "Oh god, am I sitting on something tend—"

"No," he said sharply, exhaling. "No, you're not hurting me. It's—" He brought his hands up to my face, and then down to my breasts, over my stomach, and back to my hips. "It's been a long, long time. You feel so fucking incredible, Sera. There is no possible way I'm going to last long enough to make this good for you."

I shook my head, denying he wouldn't make it good. It was already good. "I love how you feel inside me. I'm not worried about how long you can go. Just—let me fuck you, okay?"

He let his head fall back against my pillows and released a breathy laugh. "There's no way I can say no to that."

Julien held on to me as I started to bounce. I went slow, so I wouldn't hurt him, but the groans he was making weren't from pain, spurring me on.

"Do you want to try to thrust from below, Jules? Or is what I'm doing good?" I was panting, even though I wasn't overly exerting myself yet. It was just that...with Julien inside me, there was no room for unimportant things, like oxygen or rational thoughts.

"Jesus, fuck." His teeth ground together. His eyes were all over me. "I can't—Sera..."

I took his hand and placed it on my breast. "Please," I whispered. "Touch me however you want. Take what you need."

He rolled my nipple between his fingers at the same time he raised his hips, hitting a spot so deep inside me, it sent my eyes rolling back.

A guttural moan left Julien, and he fucked into me again, meeting me every time I lowered.

My belly tightened, taking me by surprise. We couldn't have been going at it for more than a few minutes, but my climax was already creeping up on me. This never happened. But I'd never, ever felt anything like this either.

"Sera," Julien hissed, capturing my attention. "Oh fuck, Sera. I can't—"

His hips slapped into me frantically, then he held on to my waist, shoving me down hard. He was shaking, the tendons in his neck standing in stark relief. I could only watch him, try to keep up with him, let him take over.

His bellow echoed off the walls and my brain and my heart. His neck arched as he came, throwing his head back. Time suspended as I watched pure bliss take him over and rode the waves of it with him. Seeing him coming, witnessing Julien racked with pleasure because of *me*, was almost as good as experiencing it myself. I thought I could see this a thousand times in a row and never get tired of it.

When his body unclenched, I was still on fire, but I rolled off him to lie on the mattress by his side. His eyes were closed, chest rising and falling as he panted. The heaviness between my thighs and the ache in my belly had me rubbing my legs together.

His eyes opened suddenly and quickly shuttered. "I'm sorry."

"I'm not."

His brow pinched. "That wasn't any good for you. I just couldn't—"

"Are you kidding me? It was unbelievable for me. I am so turned on now, I'd be surprised if my eyes aren't crossed. I'm seriously considering kicking you out so I can finish myself."

He went motionless, except for his eyes, which were still guarded, but sweeping over me in a constant vigil. "How would you do that?"

I licked my bottom lip and inched my hand between my thighs to cup my swollen pussy. "I have a little vibrator that sucks my clit."

"Where is it?"

I pointed to the table on his side. "In there."

Without hesitation, he twisted his upper body to open the drawer. There were a couple toys in there, but he chose the right one. My favorite.

He got rid of the condom and rolled onto his side. "Spread your legs."

My breath caught. "What are you doing?"

He leveled me with a heated stare. "You just gave me something so big, I don't think I can put it into words. There is absolutely no way I'm not going to give you as many orgasms as your beautiful fucking body can take. Spread your legs, Sera."

My legs fell open without any conscious decision of my own. Julien lifted my dress, but only to uncover my pussy. It was like he somehow knew without me saying I wasn't comfortable being fully naked. Not yet.

Those thoughts were swept away when he stroked his finger through my folds and plunged into me. My hips rose, trying to keep him inside, take him deeper. The heat in me grew with his attention.

"Julien," I whispered, reaching for his face. He let me touch the scarred side, let me stroke my fingers along his mottled skin, leaning into my touch.

"Your cunt is perfect." His fingertip rolled my hard clit around in slow circles. "Perfect."

"My cunt is needy right now. If I don't come, I might get mad."

I'd never said the word "cunt" out loud. Then again, I'd never propositioned a man, nor had one ever used one of my toys on me. This was a day of firsts with Julien. He was breaking me out of my shell by making me feel beautiful and desirable.

He tore his eyes from between my legs to meet mine. The corner of his mouth drew upward. "We can't have that. I don't like making you mad."

I'd been distracted by his cocky smirk, so when my vibrating rose made contact with my clit, I nearly flew out of my skin. The feeling didn't abate as he held it there, in the exact spot I needed. My nails dug into his sinewy forearm, bracing for what I knew was coming.

"You like that? Does that feel good?" he asked.

"Keep going."

"Don't worry, pretty girl. I won't stop until you get yours. I want to see you come. Show me what it looks like when you come so many times, you can't help but cry."

"Okay," I quivered. "Okay, Julien."

My first orgasm came swiftly, with a sharp, precise missile of pleasure, splitting me apart. Julien whispered to me, encouraging me, telling me how beautiful I looked as I came. With his low, sonorous voice in my ear and the never-ending suction of my toy, one orgasm rolled into another. My legs shook, completely out of my control.

After that, Julien sucked and kissed my nipples, then dragged his lips over my skin to my shoulders. His upper body pressed down on mine, and the weight of him while his tongue laved my throat sent me over the edge once more.

My cries were ragged, desperate. My body wouldn't stop trembling, but still, I wanted more. Julien gave me everything. Between the toy, his touch, his mouth, and his words of praise, I lost count of how many times I came. One piled on top of the other, until I was nothing more than a sweaty, writhing mess on my sheets.

And when I finally said no more—and meant it—Julien dropped the toy, gathered me into his arms, and kissed my lips like a sipping hummingbird. So light and delicate, exactly what I needed to help me come down.

We lay in silence, my thundering heart filling my ears. My fingers were tangled in Julien's hair. His were tracing lines along my spine.

"Are you okay?" he asked.

I tilted my head back to frown at him. "I just came a thousand times. I'm definitely okay. Why wouldn't I be?"

He tapped my nose, my lips, my chin. "I'm making sure I didn't cross any lines."

"You didn't come close to crossing my lines." My eyebrows pinched. "Did you have fun?"

A brief pause, then a laugh boomed out of him. He rolled onto his back and swiped the back of his hand over his forehead.

"Seraphina." He shook his head, then turned to me, stroking my cheek with his knuckles. "Yes, I had fun. Too much fun. I'm afraid you think I'm a two-pump chump."

I propped myself up on my hand, biting back a grin. "I don't know. There's something extremely hot about a man being so turned on, he can't hold back."

He glared at me, but I sensed the playfulness behind it. "I'm not always like that. It's just been a long, long time, and you're *you*. Jesus, if I'd known you were going to spring a sex experiment on me, I would have jerked off at home a hundred times so I didn't make a fool of myself."

"You didn't make a fool of yourself." I scratched the back of his neck. "I want to keep going with the experiment. Do you?"

"Now?" He actually sounded raring to go.

I sputtered a laugh. "Not now. I think my vagina needs a little rest. But soon."

"Soon." His eyes danced over me. "What I need to know is what scientific journal you're going to submit your findings to."

Snickering, I flopped on his chest. His arms locked around me, keeping me there. I thought maybe I liked this version of Julien the best. Sated and relaxed and very, very tactile. I smiled into his hot skin.

"Shut up, Julien."

"All right, Sera. But next time, I'm on top."

Chapter Nineteen

Julien

Sera was floating on her back when I descended the steps into the pool. I had to fight back a grin seeing her like that. It was so on brand for her. All by herself, not a care in the world who saw her, letting the water take her where it may.

When I was almost standing on top of her, her eyes popped open, and a wide grin stretched across her face. We hadn't been able to spend a lot of time together since Saturday. Her parents came down to hang out with her the next day, and although we saw each other in class on Monday, we both had actual studying to do, so we didn't hang out after.

I'd been apprehensive all day, worried things had changed or she regretted having sex with me.

That she wouldn't want to do it again.

The smile she gave me took the edge off my troubled mind.

"Hi, Jules," she chirped louder than necessary. Then again, her ears were below the surface so she couldn't hear herself. "You're here."

She held her hands out to me, so I took them, pulling her upright with more force than needed so she collided with my chest. I caught her shoulders, but instead of setting her away from me, I pulled her even closer. When her arms circled my waist, something in me settled.

"Did you think I wasn't coming?" I peered down at her. A curl was plastered across her forehead. I brushed it back and cupped the crown of her head. "I live for our pool sessions."

"We didn't really talk about it, so I wasn't one hundred percent, but I'm glad you're here. How are you feeling?"

Ah, so we were getting down to the business at hand. It made me proud how seriously she was taking her role of physical therapist. I couldn't say if the exercises we did each week made a huge difference, but I looked forward to it more than anything else. That was big for me. It had been too long since I'd had something to consistently look forward to.

"I'm feeling good. My neck and shoulders are still loose from your magic fingers."

"And your hips and pelvis?" She slid her flattened hand from my back around to my front, pressing below my navel. My dick twitched in a way that would have been entirely inappropriate with a real therapist. Luckily, that had never been a problem with Demetri.

"Could be looser," I bit out.

She frowned up at me, clearly taken aback by my sudden surly tone. "Did I ask the wrong question?"

I grabbed her hand and moved it down a couple inches until she covered my rising hard-on.

"Sorry. My dick's confused around you now. I feel your hand slide down and can't help getting hard. Not your fault—and I'm not mad at you."

She sucked in a breath and expelled a giggle. "Oh, okay. You're grumpy because you're horny." She squeezed me, pressing her tits into my chest. "We didn't really get to talk about the experiment. Did that position work for you?"

She wasn't even using a seductive tone, but her hand on my dick and the words coming out of her pretty pink mouth were quickly making me lose my grip on my control—and it had been tenuous to start.

"I think you know I had no problems with that position. In fact, it worked a little too well."

"Stop." She swatted my chest with her free hand. "I'm asking about pain and comfort."

"While holding my dick," I deadpanned.

Her brow winged. "I can be both a caring professional and a dirty, naughty, fake girlfriend."

"You're right. You're excellent at both." I caught her wrist. "But if you don't stop, there's going to be a code white in this pool and it'll be all your fault."

Her eyes rounded. "Oh god, is that a thing? Are we all swimming around in jizz?" She slapped my chest harder this time. "Please tell me that's not a thing."

I caught her slapping hand too, holding both up to my mouth so I could bite down on her fingertips. She wiggled but made no real effort to escape as I methodically went finger by finger to sample them all.

Her breathing became audible as her mouth hung open. "This might be working to help you calm down, but it's having the opposite effect on me."

I stopped at her right ring finger and glanced at her flushed face. "Yeah? Are you making a mess of your bathing suit?"

"Probably. Luckily, it's easier for me to hide and I won't make a mess of the pool." She pushed away from me, swimming backward toward the wall. "Come here and do your exercises with me. If you do a good job, we can discuss my messy bathing suit in more depth."

The smug grin she shot me told me she was proud of her wording and the way she was essentially leading me around by my dick. The thing she didn't understand and would never be able to grasp was she'd owned me for months. Getting to feel her from the inside and kiss her everywhere meant something entirely different to me than it did for her.

She had fun, and so did I.

I was grateful her experiment proved I wasn't entirely broken.

But for her, fun and experimentation were where it ended. She reminded me of that every time she called herself my fake girlfriend.

The truth was, I was wrapped up in Seraphina Ellis. I wasn't proud of the things I'd done or how I was continuing to deceive her, but I wouldn't take back the months we'd had as two virtual strangers behind our screens.

If I thought for a second Sera would want to take this fake dating and flip it to real, I would have to tell her. I would have to own up to a few things and explain my reasoning behind my actions. I would have to take the chance of losing her.

I'd lost so fucking much, I didn't know how to lose one more thing. One more person.

So, I stayed quiet, kept the truth buried inside, and let myself enjoy being close to her for as long as it lasted. There was no question what I was doing was wrong and selfish, but I wasn't going to stop. I couldn't.

· · · • · • · · ·

An hour later, we climbed out of the pool.

An hour spent with Sera's hands all over me. The mix of professional and *accidental* slips into my trunks had been torture. I left the water in a hell of a lot more pain than when I'd entered—and it was all centered below my waist.

I wrapped my towel around me, but it did little to hide my erection. When Sera bent over to grab her towel, I pressed against her ass, wedging myself between her cheeks. She arched her spine and ground her lush ass into me.

"Go to the bathroom." I wrapped my arm around her, pulling her up straight. "Go to the unisex bathroom and wait for me. I'll be right back."

She turned her head, peering at me over her shoulder. "Here? Really?"

I nipped at her earlobe and whispered, "We still have to discuss your messy bathing suit, don't we?"

"Yes," she breathed. "We definitely do."

She darted out of my arms and spun, walking briskly toward the bathroom between the two locker rooms. Once she was inside with the door closed behind her, I slung my bag over my shoulder, grabbed my cane, and made my way at a slower pace, looking around to ensure no one was watching. As badly as I wanted to lose my mind and get inside Sera as soon as possible, I'd go home with blue balls before allowing anyone else to have an inkling of what we were about to do. That was for her and me. No one else.

Fortunately for me and my dick, the pool was pretty empty, save for a couple lap swimmers. I cracked the bathroom door open, finding the lights off. Sera stood there in her flip-flops, bathing suit, and towel, chewing on her fingernails, illuminated only by the flashlight on her phone.

"I read that having sex standing up is really good for people with pelvic injuries," she rushed out. "Do you think we could do that?" From the quiver in her voice, she was interested in the idea for more than scientific purposes.

"Doing your homework, huh?" I pulled a condom out, then dropped my bag by the door and propped my cane against the tiled wall. "Lose your towel."

With a breathy inhale, she let the towel fall. Her phone lit up the outline of her. My mouth watered for the details. To see the nipples I knew were pebbled. To know if her bathing suit clung to her slit where she was soaked. More than any of that, I longed for the feel of her.

Leaving the condom on the edge of the sink, I slid my hands under the straps of her bathing suit and lowered them slowly, allowing her to stop me if she wanted to.

"Take it off me, Jules. I need it off." It was more of a whine, but I took it as a command and tugged her damp suit down her body. She helped me when it got caught on her flared hips, wiggling to get it the rest of the way off.

She was hiding herself from me. I didn't like it, but I understood it…probably more than anyone else could. She had insecurities, parts of her she didn't think were pretty. She was wrong. Every part of her was pretty. But she wasn't ready to believe that, and now wasn't the time to try to convince her. As much as I wanted to study every dip and curve of her in the light, I would wait. The time would come, but it wasn't now.

Stepping forward, eliminating every inch of space separating us, I took her mouth and palmed her ass. She plunged her fingers into my hair, pulling me down so she could lick at my tongue. It was messy and fuck hot. The hour of foreplay in the pool hadn't only affected me.

Holding on to the sink behind her for balance, I fitted my thigh between hers. Her pussy was hot and slick. She sank down, rubbing back and forth while she moaned into my mouth.

"You're wet for me." I bit her bottom lip, gathering her taste.

"Told you I was." She snaked her hand down to my cock, giving it firm, slow strokes. "I forgot how big you are." Her mouth trailed to my throat, sucking the spot above my collarbone.

"You forgot?"

She giggled into my neck. "I had to block it out or I wouldn't have been able to think about anything else." Tipping her head back, she blinked her cloudy eyes at me. "Are you going to give me a reminder? I think I really, *really* need one."

"I'll give you a reminder. Turn around, hands on the sink."

She complied, bracing her hands on the square porcelain and arching her back. Watching me in the mirror, she spread her legs and reached between them to cup her pussy. One finger easily slid inside her, moving in and out at a slow, dragging pace. I could barely look away to deal with the condom, but fuck, I needed to get inside her more than I needed to breathe.

"You're gonna cause me to make a fool of myself again, Sera." I tossed the foil aside and closed the space between our bodies. She removed her hand, placing it back on the sink, making room for where we both wanted me to be.

"I would never think you're a fool. Well…if you don't start fucking me, I might—"

I slammed into her, cutting off whatever she was going to say. Her mouth fell open, and our eyes locked in the dim reflection, though it was a difficult task to keep mine open.

"Gonna fuck you hard now."

She nodded, pushing into me. "Okay. Do it."

My talk was bigger than my game. I wanted to fuck her hard, but my body was untested. I started slow, taking deep, forceful strokes, working my length all the way in before pulling out to the tip. When I was almost out of her, I slammed forward again, taking both of our breaths away.

"Again." She widened her stance. "Again, Julien."

Since it felt good—better than good, fucking ridiculous—I continued that slow, torturous withdraw followed by a quick, powerful advance. Her slick inner walls clung to me, drawing me forward, trying to keep me deep inside her. That was where I wanted to be, to stay.

"Like that?"

She moaned. "God, yes. *Please.*"

I found my pace, leaning over her back to brace one hand on the sink beside hers. It was as much for balance as it was a need to get closer.

That was a lie.

The need to be closer to Sera superseded all else at this moment. If I couldn't see her skin, I'd absorb the feel of it with mine. My chest pressed into her back as my hips collided with her plush ass. Our faces were parallel, rubbing and parting with the waves of our bodies. She turned to the side to suck on my bottom lip.

I palmed her sweet little tit, the tight skin around her nipple like braille. This was going to be my favorite story. I couldn't get enough of her breasts. My mouth was watering for them now, but I settled for sucking on her shoulder, which wasn't settling in any way. The fact that I was allowed to put my mouth on this girl, that she *liked* it, still hadn't fully sunk in.

"Julien." She drew my name into a song, dulcet and breathy. "Keep going."

"I will."

My teeth latched onto the side of her neck, followed quickly by my tongue to soothe the hurt away. I sucked and licked jagged lines all the way up to her jaw then back down again. My marks were all over her, and she smelled like me now. Possessive satisfaction had me slamming into her harder. When my body agreed with my mind's decision, cooperating for fucking once, I kept driving into her.

"Touch your clit, pretty girl. Need you to come on my dick this time. I have to know what it feels like to have you squeezing the hell out of me." I curved my tongue around her ear and bit the shell. She shuddered against me, pushing the side of her head against my mouth.

Her arm slipped from the sink to play between her legs. As soon as she made contact, a long, high moan climbed up her throat and echoed off the tiles.

"Are you going to come for me, Sera?"

"Mmmhmm."

Her insides were slick and lush, wrapping around me, holding me. Her walls swelled, inviting me deeper and deeper. Her ass cushioned my manic thrusts, our skin slapping each time. It was all I could do to hang out, but I had no choice. I needed her coming around me. Had been thinking about it to the point of distraction.

"I'm so close," she rasped. "Please don't stop."

"Never," I promised. "But I need you to get there. I can't breathe until you get there. Want to hear those moans. Want to feel this sweet ass shaking and your belly tighten. Need it, Sera. Need it so bad, pretty girl."

"Oh god, Julien." Her head fell forward as the rest of her started to tremble.

My control was at a razor's edge. I clenched the sink, digging my fingertips in hard. The slight pain distracted me from the pure, exquisite torture happening to my cock. Sera's pussy fluttered and clenched around me, so close to drawing out my climax, but I caught myself.

This was her time. Mine would happen, but not until she got exactly what she needed.

"Julien," she cried again, angling her head to the side. "Kiss me now."

Falling over her, our mouths connected. My tongue swept between her lips to taste her moans. Her insides contracted. Her mouth fell still, breathing her pleasure into me. It was all I could do not to let go, but I had to experience this with her. Christ only knew if I'd have another chance to feel Seraphina falling apart around me.

Cupping her throat, I sucked on her lips and licked along the line of her jaw. The high-pitched keening cries that fell from her only made me harder, needier. And when she breathed out my name as her orgasm started to subside, I gave in, leaving the tender kisses behind to hold on to her hip and rut into her wet heat.

It didn't take long before the impossible pressure in my lower abdomen exploded. I plunged inside her as far as I could go, my front sealed to her backside. Panting on her shoulder, I wrapped my arm around her middle, keeping her close as tremors racked through me.

"Fuck. Shit, Sera," I growled.

She let out a breathy giggle. "I know."

"God." My head fell against her nape. "We weren't quiet."

"We didn't even try."

"I'm sorry."

"Don't be." She turned her head to press her cheek to my forehead. "Unless I get arrested or kicked out of school, then maybe we can talk apologies."

Sweeping her damp curls aside, I touched my lips to her cheek. "Not gonna let anything happen to you."

There was enough light coming from her phone for me to see her expression had grown serious. "I know that. I trust you."

I didn't deserve her trust, not after deceiving her, but I'd take it, because like I said, when it came to Sera, I was selfish like that.

Chapter Twenty

Seraphina

Alley and Laura were doing their best to force me to watch a Turkish romantic drama they were currently obsessed with, but I couldn't seem to concentrate. Every time I shifted on our monstrously cushy and large sectional sofa, I felt a twinge between my legs and got caught up in remembering the way Julien had taken me in the bathroom. I'd *never* done anything like that before. We were lucky not to get caught, but the chance had been well worth taking.

I was deliciously sore, boneless, and wondering when we could work on our experiment again.

Soon, I hoped. It was crazy how quickly I'd become hooked on sex with Julien. It had never been anything I'd craved. I'd kind of assumed I wasn't much of a sexual creature, considering how lackluster my sex life had been with Seth. He'd wanted it all the time, but a gust of wind could have gotten him hard—and he obviously wasn't very discerning about who his partner was.

My phone vibrated in the pocket of my sweatpants. Alley and Laura were too engrossed in their show to notice me slipping it out to check my message.

I'd never once been disappointed to hear from my phantom, but I had to admit, I was just a little bit. Not because I didn't want to talk to him, but because I'd been hoping, in the back of my mind, it was Julien messaging me.

ThePhantom: *It's been too long since I've heard your thoughts, Dragon Girl.*

Me: *I thought you were giving me up for your girl. How are you?*

ThePhantom: *I could never give you up. Just thought it would be right to ease up on the pic sharing. Do I need to ask for a hip pic?*

Me: *You don't need to ask, and you're right, no more nakey pics. I'm glad you aren't giving me up.*

ThePhantom: *You're gonna have to be the one to walk away, D.G. Now, tell me your thoughts.*

Me: *I guess I shouldn't tell you I was sitting here pondering my very bad sex life.*

A few minutes went by without a response from him. I probably shouldn't have brought up sex. We'd been flirty and some of the pictures we'd shared had bordered on the naughty side, but we'd never gone any further. Not that I was trying to now.

Finally, he replied, and I breathed a sigh of relief.

ThePhantom: *You're having sex? And it's bad? That's unfortunate. Is cane-boy not giving it to you good? You're worth a thousand suns. Don't settle for anything less than what lights you on fire.*

Me: *While that was very sweet and supportive—thank you for that—I was thinking about Seth, actually. I guess I should have said my past sex life.*

ThePhantom: *Ah, yeah, you should've led with that. Why are you thinking about that dick? Is he sniffing around? Finally figured out what he lost?*

Me: *No, he's gone quiet, which is a little worrisome. But maybe he's moved on. Anyway, I wasn't really thinking about him, per se. More like the mediocre sex we had. Since I had no experience and he had a ton, I always blamed myself for how blah our sex was.*

ThePhantom: *Why am I not surprised he's bad in bed? Why am I also not surprised you blamed yourself?*

Me: *Because you know me, duh. But recently, I've done some things that have led me to the conclusion I was very wrong.*

ThePhantom: *Is my little D.G. getting some?*

Me: *Yes. Some very good some. And that's all I'm going to say because I feel weird sharing what I already have.*

ThePhantom: *I get that. Seraphina, I'm happy as hell at how good you sound right now. You're treating yourself the way you deserve. That's all I've wanted for you.*

Me: *That's what I want for you too. Tell me about your girl. Is she head over heels for you or do I need to write that testimonial?*

ThePhantom: *Don't know about head over heels. She's still too smart and beautiful for me. We could be moving forward, though. Time will tell.*

Me: *She'd better treat you how you deserve. I don't think I would have survived those dark months without you. Hope you're showing her how special you are.*

ThePhantom: *You're making me blush, D.G. Cut that shit out.*

Alley caught me in the act, screeching my name and threatening to take my phone if I didn't pay attention to the show. So, I said goodbye to my phantom and sank down into the couch, twinging with reminders of Julien.

· · · ● · ● · · ·

The rest of the week passed by too quickly. Without more experimentation, sadly. When I wasn't in class or being whipped into shape in the gym by Alley, I was working on a paper for my women's history class. The time I spent with Jules had been confined to our walks home, which were spent almost entirely debating the Dramione fic we were both still reading—and by debating, I meant Julien made ludicrous statements and I was forced to explain, in great detail, *why* they were ludicrous.

But honestly, it was my second favorite way to spend time with him, because I never failed to coax laughter out of him, and when he let go and lost himself in laughter, he was absolutely stunning.

"Seraphina!" My mom whacked my arm. "Stop daydreaming and come chat with Michael's mom and sister."

My mom had a strange tendency to refer to people by their roles. I'd met Beth and Catrina—my sister's fiancé's mother and sister—a handful of times now. My mom was well aware of this, since she'd been there each time. But I didn't bother questioning her and plastered on a smile. This was Ophelia's bridal luncheon. It was not the time to make waves.

Ophelia was standing with her future mother- and sister-in-law, blending in with them seamlessly. Her stark white dress with its starched collar and A-line skirt was perfect for the country club set—her goal in life and where her luncheon was taking place. Beth was in pink, Catrina in green, and their dresses were eerily similar to Phe's, save for the color. My sister had even blown her curls out straight and flipped the ends, just like Beth's.

Poor Michael was marrying a girl who was going to morph into his mother within a year or two.

Or maybe not-so-poor Michael. He might've been into it.

Phe hooked her arm through mine, squeezing me tight in what I took as a warning to be *normal*. "And here's Sera. Doesn't she look so pretty in purple?"

When I'd arrived, Phe had asked me why I hadn't chosen something in green since it was more my color. I wished I'd bought the dress Julien had loved. My sister would have swallowed her tongue.

Beth gave me a crisp smile. "Absolutely darling." Her eyes ventured up to my hair. "It's nice you chose a simple dress, given how...wild your hair is. Tell me, have you ever thought of straightening it?"

Phe had turned into a boa constrictor, coiling around my captured arm. "Sera isn't really into doing much with her looks. She doesn't like to devote time to herself that way. Too busy with her marching band."

That last part was said like a dirty word.

My mother flared her eyes at me, sending me the very clear signal I was not to argue or defend myself.

Catrina, the sister, tittered behind her dainty hands. "Oh, how I wish I could be that way."

Her mother jolted. "Why would you wish that?"

She waved in my direction. "Think of how much time you'd save if you were comfortable leaving the house like that."

I couldn't stop my flinch. I wanted to, loathing that anyone could see how violently her remark had landed. It couldn't even be called a jab, since it hadn't been said with malicious intent. Catrina, the girl my sister was soon to be related to, had taken a look at me in my pretty dress, my grandma's locket around my neck, curly hair that had taken me an hour to tame, subtle makeup, painted nails, and had found me wanting.

I barely knew this girl, but her comment sliced into the mushy, bruised part of me that never seemed to fully heal. That was probably because every time I swung too far into self-love and acceptance territory, I was always yanked back into self-hatred and discomfort by a "*well-meaning*" comment from my loving family.

Phe patted my arm. "Sera looks lovely. She just has her own style."

My mother's movements were subtle, but when she ended up partially in front of me, I knew it was no accident. She wouldn't speak up for me, so her way of protecting me was to steer the conversation in another direction.

It was something, but it wasn't enough. And she wondered why I hadn't come to her when I was so hopeless, I hadn't cared if I woke up each morning.

• • • ● • ● • • •

The luncheon passed quickly.

Okay, that was a bald-faced lie. It was interminable, with a thousand courses and small talk with Michael's cousins, who I'd been seated with for some unknown reason.

All I wanted to do was tear out of this stuffy country club and go home, get in my regular clothes, and bang on my drums to remind myself of who I was.

Ophelia clinked on her glass with her spoon, drawing all eyes on her. She'd been seated at another table with several of her sorority sisters, along with my mother, Beth, and Catrina. The seating arrangements confused me, but I wasn't about to complain about not being close to any of them.

"Thank you all for coming, and more importantly, thank you, Beth, for hosting this luncheon at your club." Ophelia bent down to squeeze Beth's narrow shoulders. "There's so much planning that has to happen between now and our wedding next spring, but one of the most important things to me is who will be standing by my side on my big day—besides Michael of course."

She paused for laughter, which was politely given, then produced six gift bags from beneath the table and beamed at the women sitting around her.

"With that being said, I'd love to ask some of the most important women in my life to be my bridesmaids."

I braced myself to stand and act happy. Not that I *wasn't* happy for my sister. She was getting the life she wanted, the perfect family and doting husband. I'd stand by her and support her in this, because as much as I complained about her, I loved her, and I didn't doubt she loved me too. She just had a shit way of showing it sometimes.

The gift bags went to her sorority sisters first. They all squealed, like they were so surprised to be asked. There was no way I could match that level of enthusiasm, but I supposed I had to at least try.

When she got to her last bag, it was a darker purple and a size larger than the others.

"I've saved the most important job for last." She clutched the gift bag in front of her. "My maid of honor will be by my side the whole way, like she has been from the start."

I pushed back to get up, and despite everything, tears pricked the backs of my eyes. Okay, so maybe I was happier for Phe than I expected to be.

But the strange thing was, she didn't turn in my direction. In fact, she swiveled around to face Catrina, and all I could do was watch as my sister rejected me in front of an entire room of finely dressed women.

"Catty-cat, we hit it off the day we met, like two peas in a pod. I couldn't ask for a better sister." Ophelia held the bag out to her. "Would you be my maid of honor?"

I didn't move or breathe or blink. It was hard to do those things with a caved-in chest. The world went on around me, more squealing, hugs, celebration, while I sat, immobile and uncomprehending.

I couldn't ask for a better sister.

Everyone was up, out of their seats to mingle again, and still, I sat. My fingers twitched on the skirt of my wretched dress. If I'd had the strength, I would've ripped it to tatters. I hated this dress, this place...myself.

Someone pulled the chair out beside me and sat down. Lilac perfume hit my nose before my mother spoke.

"How are you doing, chickadee?"

"Fine." Except my bones were frozen. How did I get them to move?

She sighed. "Ophelia has a certain vision for her wedding that Catrina understands. The girls from her sorority do too. You can't be mad at her for wanting her dream wedding."

"Of course not." I wasn't mad. I wasn't anything. This was a dream. It didn't feel real.

"She didn't mean what she said, about not being able to ask for a better sister. *You're* her sister, and she loves you very much. We all do."

"I know." Did I? Maybe I didn't know that. Why wouldn't my body move?

My mom leaned into me, taking my chin in her hand. "Honey, I'm sorry. I can see you're hurt. To be honest, Ophelia has hurt my heart with her decision too. I think she'll regret it in the future, but there's nothing I can say to make her change her mind. We just have to be there for her and support her from the stands, okay?"

"Like a fan."

"No, Seraphina." She dropped her hand to my shoulder, giving it a gentle rub. "Like family. We don't always see eye to eye, but we love each other."

"I think I'm going to go now."

"You can't leave before the luncheon is over. People will talk."

Finally, I made my head turn to lock eyes with my mom and clutched my grandma's locket for strength. My bones were thawing, along with the feelings. The hottest one was indignation, and it was righteous.

"Do you not think people will talk about how Ophelia's actual sister was seated at a different table then shut out of the bridal party? Because I do. I think everyone will be talking about it." I stood up from my seat, grabbing my wristlet and the favor bag in front of my place setting. "Tell Ophelia I'm so very happy for her and wish her the best."

My mother sputtered. I would definitely be hearing about this later, but she would never make a scene in a place like this, so I flounced out of that room, my head held high and my crushed little heart spinning like a top in my chest.

Chapter Twenty-one

Seraphina

As soon as Julien opened his door, tears welled in my eyes. "Hi," I squeezed out.

His brow dipped low over his stormy eyes. "Sera?"

I crossed my arms over my middle, listing toward him. "I'm sorry to bother you. I was hoping I could come inside. And maybe you could hug me, because I really kind of need that right now."

He pulled me into the house, closing the door behind him, and led me directly to his room. Without saying a single word, he wrapped his arms around me and held me snug against his chest. I pressed my face into him, rubbing back and forth, settling my cheek over his thumping heart.

"You could never bother me," he said softly into my hair.

That was all. He didn't ask for me to explain or try to soothe me with words. Julien held me tight, breathing with me as we swayed. There was never even a fraction of a second in all the minutes we embraced that it seemed like he wanted to let go. I wasn't a burden to him. He held me because I needed it. And maybe, just maybe, because he wanted to.

Tears flowed in slow streams down my cheeks, wetting Julien's shirt. We were stuck together, bathing in the salty puddles I made.

"I've made your shirt so wet," I rasped.

"I don't care."

"I think there's snot mixed in with my tears." I sniffled, trying not to be embarrassed.

"I really don't care, Sera." His fingers tangled in the back of my hair, tipping my face up. With his other hand, he wiped my cheeks, then leaned in and pressed a kiss to my forehead.

"I don't like you sad. You're breaking my heart here." He surveyed me, cocking his head to check me from different angles. All I wanted to do was dive back into him and hide away, but then I noticed him leaning on his good side, and it struck me he didn't have his cane in his hand. He'd dropped it beside him to hold me.

"Can we sit on your bed?" Without waiting for an answer, I took his hand in mine, pulling him with me, then threw myself down in a heap. Julien was less dramatic, positioning himself on his side right next to me, draping his arm around my middle. I snuggled into him and sighed. My tears had ebbed, but I was still so damn raw, I needed to be close to him or the wound my sister had inflicted wouldn't be bearable.

"I had a bad day." My voice was small and tinny. Julien heaved a breath and tucked me flush against him.

"Tell me what I can do to make it better," he gruffed, like he was angry.

"Just stay with me. Please?"

"That goes without saying." His lips touched the top of my head once, twice, three times. "Sera...fuck. You're tearing me up."

Digging my face out of his armpit, I blinked at him. "I'm not meaning to. I know I shouldn't have come, but you were the only person I wanted to see. I can g—"

"Don't you dare say that. You can't go. I won't let you." His declaration was firm, as if his word was law. "Sera...tell me who to kill. I'll do it."

That had tears pricking my eyes again. I had to bite down on the inside of my cheek to stop myself from crying. He wasn't angry at me—this man was angry *for* me.

I shook my head. "No one has ever defended me except my grandma." I knocked my forehead into his chin. "She was the best, just like you."

"The one who called you CC?"

"Yeah. That was my grandma."

"You can tell me about her if you want." Soft, so soft and careful he was with me.

"Really?"

"Of course. I want you to tell me about her."

My grandmother had been my favorite person in the world. She was in my thoughts, always, and though I missed her bitterly, talking about her didn't make me sad. If anything, it brought back some of the brightness she'd cast on me when she'd been around. I spilled everything there was to know about Belinda Ellis. I told him the story of her running away from Phillip and becoming a drummer. And then I told him about the time my mother flew with Phe to San Francisco for a weekend to shop for her prom dress so my grandmother took me glamping and we joined a drum circle.

He listened so intently, I wondered sometimes if he was breathing.

"I'm really glad you had her."

"Oh, me too. I wouldn't have survived without her."

Since my tears had subsided, I sucked in a breath and told Julien what had happened at the luncheon today. "My sister announced her bridesmaids. In front of this room of lovely women, she chose seven to stand up with her at her wedding—and I wasn't one of the seven. I wasn't even invited to sit at the table with her and my mother."

Julien went rigid, his hold on me tightening. "*What?*"

"I was surprised—that was the worst part. I hadn't braced for that kind of rejection. Ophelia and I have never seen eye to eye, but I thought...well, we're sisters. She loves and cares for me. She doesn't understand me, but she doesn't hurt me on purpose."

I choked out my last words. That was the thing with my family. They never hurt me on purpose. They weren't malicious. They were simply careless and selfish.

"I don't give a fuck if it was on purpose." Julien propped himself up on his elbow, locking eyes with me. "She is a grown-ass woman. If she can't see beyond her own nose to even fucking consider the repercussions of her actions, she shouldn't be getting married. You don't have to defend her. What she did to you is indefensible."

My nose twitched. My heart lurched. "I wasn't an easy sister to have, Jules. I'm not blameless."

"No." His jaw clenched as he stared down at me.

"No?"

"No. You don't get to take that on. Your family let you down. That has nothing to do with you. That's on them. You can keep telling me they love you until the end of time. They. Let. You. Down."

His anger made me flinch, and he immediately softened and lay down to gather me against him and kiss my forehead.

"I'm sorry," he soothed. "I'm pissed off for you, but I'll rein it in. I can see I'm not helping."

I threaded my fingers through his and held his hand to my breast. "Thank you for getting angry for me. Things are better with my mom now, but there was a long phase in high school where I didn't really talk to her or my dad. I got lost and turned inward, and they had no clue. Phe was this shiny, happy girl, and I was a black cloud. It was easier for them to focus on her."

A crevice appeared between his brows. "It's hard for me to imagine you ever being a black cloud."

I sniffed a little laugh. "High school me was so emo." I let my eyes close. "I can make fun of myself now, but it wasn't funny at the time. I spun out, you know? Every day was a trudge to get through, like walking through a swamp. Believe it or not, it wasn't easy being a geeky, short girl with frizzy red hair in the marching band. Kids were shit. Home was shit. I hated my reflection. And worse—I hated who I was on the inside. My cloud was black as night, and I saw what I was doing to my family. They pulled away because I was so incredibly unpleasant to be around. Who wants to be around a sad girl? I didn't want to be around myself, but I was stuck."

"Sera. *God*dammit," Julien gritted out.

I touched his clenched jaw, dragging my fingertips over it. "It hurt, Jules."

"What did?"

"Life," I whispered. Those years were burned into my memory. I couldn't bring back the anguish anymore, but I would never forget the way it had weighed down my bones. "Life hurt, and I hated myself, so I—"

"You what?" he asked sharply.

"I used to cut myself. I don't even know why I started. It doesn't matter. The first time, I felt like I was being split in two. It was the smallest little nick, but in my sick mind, I was bleeding the toxins out or something. I kept doing it and doing it. A nick here or there, when the pressure built back up in my body. I told myself it was a relief, but it wasn't. It was another way for me to hate myself."

When I thought of sixteen-year-old me, I wished I could go back and hold her. I would have told her there was nothing about her that deserved that kind of hate. That things would get better. God, if I could go back now, I'd tell her about Julien. Sixteen-year-old me would have been impressed by the hot, sweet guy I'd snagged. Obviously, I wouldn't tell her it was all pretend.

She didn't need to know that.

"One time, I cut myself too deep. It wasn't near an artery or anything, but the blood wouldn't stop. I tried on my own, but it kept bleeding, and I freaked out. So, I called my grandmother and told her what I'd done. A few minutes later, my parents broke down my door and got me to the hospital. While I was getting my cut stitched, they saw my scars. What I told myself were nicks had left my hips and upper thighs looking like I'd been rolling around in broken glass."

"Jesus," he muttered, gripping my hand tight.

"It was a wake-up call. For me, I realized I didn't want to die. For my parents, they had to come to grips with the fact that I had chosen to call my grandmother, who was thirty minutes away, rather than walk down the hall to their bedroom. They finally noticed the chasm between us and really *looked* at me."

"You got help?"

I nodded. "Yeah. Therapy and antidepressants turned my world right side up. But now do you see why I said I wasn't easy to have as a sister?"

"Abso-fucking-lutely not," he stated firmly. "I won't entertain that line of thinking. You were a kid who went through some heavy, heavy shit. Your sister has her head so far up her ass, she can't see the incredible woman she's lucky enough to be related to. I'm sorry but fuck her."

As much as him sticking up for me warmed my little wounded heart, I couldn't let him talk like that. "She's my sister, Jules."

He leveled me with an unwavering, stormy stare. I thought he would argue. Instead, he sighed. "I know. Shit, I know. It kills me she's not better at it. You deserve a rad sister."

"Yeah, well, she's getting the sister of her dreams through marriage. Maybe one day I'll marry a guy who has a rad sister I can stake a claim to."

Instead of laughing with me, Julien broke eye contact to look down at my hand in his. We lay together like that for a while, quietly holding one another. There was something about Julien that calmed me. Maybe it was his unwavering acceptance. I felt like I could tell him anything and he wouldn't bat an eye.

"Jules."

He raised his head, meeting my gaze. "Yeah?"

"I have scars, you know."

"Okay." His eyes flicked down, then back up. "I do too."

I huffed. "Mine are ugly."

"Mine aren't exactly beautiful." Letting go of my hand, he cupped my face. "You know there's nothing about you I don't like, right? You don't have to show them to me if you don't want to, but just know, if you do, I'll still think you're beautiful."

Experience had taught me not to believe what he was saying. Too many people who were supposed to care for me had hurt me. The people I'd loved had let me down. I shouldn't believe him, but I wanted to.

"I think you're beautiful too, and I don't want to hide from you."

Sitting up, I unzipped my dress and slipped the straps down my arms. Underneath, I wore a pale-pink slip, so I wasn't naked when I pulled the dress down my legs and tossed it on the floor. Julien was propped on his side again, watching me just as intently as he'd listened. My chest heaved as my heart pounded. Seth had seen me naked, but only in dim lighting or under the covers. He'd felt my scars, he had to have, but he'd never asked me about them, and I'd never come close to telling him my secrets.

When I raised my slip up to my waist, Julien didn't gasp or run screaming in disgust at the dozens of scars marring my hips. I pointed to one of them, the one I could find without even looking because it was so much bigger than the rest.

"This is the one that had to be stitched."

He leaned forward in slow motion. I didn't understand what he was doing until his lips made contact with my scar. His eyes flicked to mine. "Is that okay?"

I'd stopped breathing, but I nodded. "You don't have to touch them. I understand."

Frowning at me, he took my hand in his and brought it to his face. "Do you want to touch me?"

"Always," I said automatically. My thumb caressed the scar beside his mouth. I imagined he felt my touch less there, so I pressed a little harder, used firmer strokes. Julien's eyes fluttered as I touched him. It was only his cheek and beneath his mouth, but from the way tension seeped from his bones, it was like I was touching a lot more.

With a sigh, he opened his eyes. "I want to touch you too. Everywhere, Seraphina. Let me."

Lips parted, I nodded. "Okay." Later, I'd try to think of something profound to say or think or feel. For now, Julien had taken my thoughts and set them aside.

He pulled himself closer to me, tugging me lower on the bed. I shimmied out of my slip, leaving me in only lacy, nude underwear. Julien's mouth followed the band on my stomach to my side, kissing my hip over and over. Without looking, I knew he was finding each slice into my skin and soothing me now since he couldn't back then.

Rolling me to my side, he gave the opposite hip the same reverent treatment. I stroked his hair while he kissed me a hundred times. He wasn't erasing what I'd done, but he was acknowledging it with tenderness that struck me to my core. It was beautiful and careful. I wished he could give himself even an ounce of the same care he was giving me.

He pushed me onto my back, spreading my legs. I hadn't cut my thighs very often for fear of being discovered, but there'd been a few times. Julien found those scars too, only instead of kissing them, he traced them with his tongue.

Reaching up, he placed his palm below my belly button, slowly drawing it down my stomach. At the lacy band of my underwear, his eyes found mine. Breathless, I nodded, hoping I understood what he was asking.

He lowered his head, kissing and licking my inner thighs until his tongue ran into my underwear. He mouthed me through the material, making it even more wet. I arched into him, releasing a soft moan. Julien answered me with a hard grunt and nuzzled my clit with his nose.

The next thing I knew, he muttered a string of expletives and yanked my underwear off in one smooth, almost angry motion. It happened so fast, I wasn't prepared for the onslaught of his mouth.

My cry was high and shrill when his lips closed around my clit. Gone was the gentle, tender lover. Julien sucked me like he'd been wandering the desert for forty years and I was the only thing that could quench his endless thirst. My fingers tangled in the sides of his hair as he lapped at me, alternating between giving my clit all the attention and licking long strokes from my entrance all the way up.

The things he was doing to me were out of this world. I wouldn't discount that. But it was his blissed-out expression and the way he groaned as he had me in his mouth that brought my climax on quickly and with enough force to bend my spine like a rainbow.

I called his name over and over. How could I not? He was all I could think of. He was the only person who existed. The world had narrowed down to me and Julien, this bed, his mouth, our breath, his hands holding my thighs, his silky hair between my fingers.

I came again minutes later, my cry almost a scream. I had to remind myself it was the middle of the day and he had roommates. My daydream about us being on our own island was just that—a daydream.

I let my mind accept that this was real. Although Julien was only my pretend boyfriend, he was my real friend and lover. He cared for me. He *took* care of me. Even when I denied being able to have another orgasm, he knew what I was capable of better than I did.

When I was boneless, Julien climbed up my body, holding me against him. He'd gotten rid of his shirt at some point, so I sank into his heated skin, tracing the ridge of muscle along his spine. We were eye to eye, and he was watching me again. I grinned at him and stole a kiss from his swollen lips.

"They're so soft right now," I murmured.

"From your pretty, wet pussy."

Shuddering, I shifted closer, until our lips were fused. We'd talked ourselves to death. I wasn't really interested in doing more of it. All I wanted was to kiss Julien until I was so breathless, I was dizzy.

He gave me what I wanted. We kissed and kissed and kissed. I licked the scars around his mouth and nibbled at his lips. The guttural groan I elicited from him sent a wave of satisfaction through my limbs. I couldn't get enough of making him feel good.

Languid kissing morphed into touching. Remaining clothes were removed until we were fully skin on skin. Then, Julien lifted my leg, draped it over his arm, and slid into me. From this angle, he couldn't get quite as deep, but he was so long, I felt him in my belly anyway.

I made sure to pay attention to the scars on his face as we fucked. After this, I wanted him to think of slow, messy sex and sweet, wet kisses when he looked in the mirror. Like a Pavlovian response, the sight of his scars would bring him back to the moment, to my lips dragging along the raised scar on his jaw, my tongue sliding over the ones by his lip.

I knew for a fact I'd never, ever look at my own scars the same. Julien had utterly transformed them.

"Julien," I rasped. "You feel so good."

He gripped one of the metal slats of his headboard, using his upper body strength to fuck into me. This was nothing like the other times. Using slow, deep thrusts, he buried his cock inside me, stirring my belly with the shift of his hips, then retreating, only to do it all over again before I could catch my breath.

We went on and on like that, touching, kissing, fucking.

I was so swollen and wet between my legs, our bodies made squelching sounds each time he seated himself to the hilt. With anyone else, I might have been embarrassed, but with Julien, it turned me on. And out of nowhere, I was coming so hard, my body bowed and my forehead collided with his shoulder.

Julien groaned as my inner muscles flexed around him, and all his control evaporated. He gripped my ass cheek, digging his fingertips in, and rutted into me, his mouth latched to my throat. I continued coming with him, my orgasm renewed by his frantic thrusts.

When he spilled liquid heat inside me, we cried out together, clutching at skin, biting lips, winding limbs around limbs. We were a sweaty pile of pleasure, latched onto each other and woven together like threads in a tapestry.

• • • • • • • • • •

There was an "oh fuck" moment somewhere between Julien pulling out of me and the puddle forming beneath my ass on his sheets. No condom. But we'd discussed our recent test results, my IUD, and decided together it wasn't a big deal.

Which meant when we showered together a little while later, we were free to experiment with positions in there without pausing to find a condom. So, we did, and that experiment was a raving success.

Since I never wanted to wear my stupid dress again, I borrowed Julien's clothes. When he saw me in his T-shirt, he waited exactly ten seconds before ripping it off and starting our experiment all over again.

By the time we were sated, night had fallen, and I didn't want to go home.

"Can I sleep here?"

His brow furrowed. "Do you honestly think I'd let you leave?"

My feet found his under the covers. "I didn't know if you had a thing about sleeping with people. Like, do you hate hearing someone else breathe while you're trying to fall asleep? Does it drive you nuts if someone touches you in the middle of the night? Are—"

His hand covered my mouth. "Don't ask me hypothetical questions about some mythical 'someone.' You're sharing my bed, and I sure as hell won't mind getting to touch you in the middle of the night. Do you get that? After all that just happened between us, you get it, right?"

I nodded, and he dropped his hand. "I won't mind either."

He dragged his finger along my nose. "Good, because I'm fucking handsy in my sleep. Ask Amir about the one time we had a camp out in his backyard when we were kids. We woke up with me snuggling him like he was my teddy bear."

"Oh god." I snickered against his shoulder. "I'm dying. Does Zadie know about her big, scary boyfriend being snuggled like a teddy bear? In my mind, you guys were seventeen when this happened—and I don't want to be corrected."

Julien grinned at my laughter, which washed away the last of my sadness from earlier. I touched his smile with my fingertips.

"Thank you for being here, Jules."

He stared at me for the longest time, his breathing slow and steady. Then he nodded once and kissed my forehead. Sleep was creeping up on me, and Julien's warm, smooth chest was the most inviting pillow. I closed my eyes and sighed.

Right before sleep swept me away, Julien replied. "I've always been here for you, Sera. Nothing's gonna change that."

Chapter Twenty-two

Seraphina

After the bridal luncheon fiasco, my mother called to check on me. While that was nice of her, she also kind of inferred I was the drama in the situation. I had laughed and asked if she'd ever met her eldest daughter, since she was the very definition of drama.

Ophelia texted—not an apology, of course—but an explanation for her choice. Since I didn't loathe myself so much anymore, I chose to skim her paragraph and reply with a simple "thank you." There was no point in begging for a place in her wedding or a position in her life, so I didn't. It helped that Julien had been there when I received the text and had kissed my neck and shoulders while I dealt with it.

Honestly, I could have been walking the plank off a pirate ship, and as long as Julien had been kissing me, I would have done a swan dive and waved at the sharks on my way down.

A calm had settled over me throughout the last few days. I'd accepted the things I could not change while also accepting I had people in my life who would never, ever ask *me* to be any different than who I was.

Not gonna lie, it was pretty rad.

I pushed open the locker room door, and my stomach somersaulted at the sight of Julien leaning against the opposite wall, waiting to walk home with me after our pool session. I loved that he didn't have his hood over his head. When he peered at me, I got the full force of his crinkled forehead, perfect jawline, and crystal-clear gray eyes.

"Whoa," I whispered.

He cocked his head. "Something the matter?"

"No. Not at all. I just forgot how hot you are."

His eyes narrowed. "In the last ten minutes?"

"Mmmhmm." I eyed his position on the wall and heat flooded my belly. Dragging my finger through the air in front of him, I bit my lip, enjoying the sexy-as-hell view. "That is the sluttiest thing a man can do."

That made him laugh. "Wha-a-at?"

"That lean. So slutty. You know what you're doing." I crossed the hall and leaned into him, pressing my lips to his jaw. "You smell good. Underneath the chlorine, I mean." I sniffed his neck and sighed. "Yeah, delicious."

He wrapped his arm around me, chuckling lightly. "You're cute, Seraphina. You're also asking to get railed in that bathroom again if you don't get your tits and lips off me right now."

As much fun as our foray into semi-public sex had been, I backed away. I was not about that *getting caught going at it and being thrown out of the university* life.

"Fine then. Take me home."

He threaded his fingers with mine, and we started toward home. I liked being near him so much, I didn't mind that we were going slow, nor that he was especially quiet. I had no trouble filling in the silence. I was in the middle of talking about the latest chapter of the fic we were both reading when I noticed Julien grimace.

My heart lurched. Seth had made that face way too many times for me to be immune to it. When I turned my head toward Julien, I immediately saw his pained expression wasn't directed at me.

I stopped walking. "Julien, you're limping."

He chuffed and held up his cane. "It's a feature, not a bug."

"You know what I mean. You're in pain. Your gait is off. Did I hurt you in the pool?"

"No, absolutely not." He wiped his forehead with the back of his hand. "It's my knee. I have bad days, and today seems to be one of them. It'll pass. It always does. I just need to get home and put some ice on it. I'll be back to only semi-broken tomorrow."

"Shit." He was obviously trying to hide how badly he was hurting. Now that I knew, I couldn't miss how drawn and tight his mouth was or the beads of sweat along his hairline and upper lip. "Do you want me to call Lock or Elena for a ride? Actually, Alley should be finished with her class soon. She could swing by and pick us up. I wouldn't even tell her your knee is acting up. I'll just tell her I'm too lazy to walk home. She'll totally make me do a thousand squats to make up for it but—"

Julien dragged me against him and covered my mouth with his. He kissed me hard, but not fast, lingering on my lips until I started to melt into him. My fingers curled around his T-shirt, and I whimpered as his tongue slid against mine. He was tender and careful, sucking and nibbling at my lips. For a moment, I forgot what we'd been talking about, until I gave Julien more of my weight and he grunted.

Yanking my mouth from his, I stared at him in wide-eyed shock. He was gripping his cane so hard, it seemed like he was trying to fuse it to his bones.

"Jules," I whispered.

He raised his head, but he wouldn't meet my eyes. "You can call Alley."

Relieved, I did just that. And when she showed up shortly thereafter, I let her make fun of me the whole way back to Julien's house, though she sensed pretty quickly something was up with Julien. He sat in the back seat, silent, his jaw clenching. My chest cracked in two. There was nothing I could do for him, and I wanted to fix this more than anything.

He needed more than I could give.

• • • • ● • ● • • •

I followed Julien inside and basically shoved him onto his bed. Theo and Helen were on the back deck when I ventured into the kitchen to hunt for ice. I waved at them through the sliding glass door. Helen stuck her head inside.

"Hey, girlie," she greeted. "What's up?"

"I'm sorry for rummaging around the guys' kitchen, but I need some ice and a plastic baggie. I think I can find the ice, but the baggie, I'm not sure. I mean, I could look—"

Helen held a hand up and turned toward Theo. "Do you guys have sandwich baggies, Theodore?"

"Yep." The sound of a chair scooting across wood preceded Theo pushing Helen through the door and him following her inside. He shot me a wink on his way to a cabinet where he grabbed a box and handed it to me. "Take all you need."

"Thank you so much. This is for Julien, by the way. Not me."

Theo shrugged. "You're his girl. What's his is yours."

Helen ran a hand up her boyfriend's chest, grinning. "And there you go, saying all the right things." She shook her head at me. "We've been together almost a year and a half, and he's still bringing the charm. I thought it was supposed to wear off after the first year. I think there was a mess up in the factory."

I giggled. "Lucky you." I held the plastic bag under the ice dispenser in the fridge and filled it up. "Well, I better get back to Jules."

Theo nodded. "Take good care of my boy."

Helen brought her pinched fingers to her ruby lips. "Let me know if he needs a little smoky smoke, okay? Might help with the pain."

"Oh, he's not—" My eyes rounded. Julien was intensely private, and here I was, telling everyone his business. "I didn't mean—"

Helen laid her hand on my arm. "You didn't give away his secrets, babe. I figured the ice plus Julien's injuries might mean he's hurting so I offered. You know I'm going into healthcare when I graduate, so I'm all about natural remedies. Nothing's more natural than some herb."

"Thanks, Hells. I'll let him know you offered."

Julien was propped up in bed when I came back into the room. He'd taken an over-the-counter painkiller, but I had a feeling it wasn't going to touch this.

He allowed me to situate the ice on his knee and wrap a towel around his leg to keep it in place. Then I climbed on the bed beside him, unsure he even wanted me there since he'd retreated into his head. But he opened his arm, inviting me into his space. I lay down, my head on his chest, hand on his stomach, which was taut and straining.

"I don't want to talk about it," he gritted out. "Anything but this."

"Do you want me to be quiet or—?"

"No, never. Talk to me. Tell me anything. I like listening to you."

"Do you want some of Helen's weed?"

I lifted my head. His features were so pinched, it looked like someone had taken his skin and twisted, like the end of a balloon. I couldn't remember a time I'd felt this helpless—and that was saying something considering the dark places I'd gone to in the past. But this was Julien. Kind, grumpy, absolutely wonderful Julien. I wanted to lie down on top of him and absorb some of the pain straight from his skin. If only...

His nod was slight, but it was all I needed. I jumped out of bed, found Helen in the kitchen, and ran back to him with a lovely joint. While he smoked it, I told him a story my grandmother had told me. Her coworker had gone on a second date with this sweet man who had cooked dinner for her. He was vegan and had told her his food would taste a little different but promised it would be delicious. The coworker had a great time on the date, but the next morning, she became so violently ill, she had to go to the hospital.

"Never trust vegans," Julien said.

I snorted a laugh. "At least not this particular vegan. The doctors ran test after test and couldn't figure out what was making her so ill."

He exhaled a cloud of smoke. "I'm on the edge of my seat. What did this scary vegan do to her?"

"Well...my grandmother said there was this one doctor who'd studied rare diseases back in college and her symptoms made him suspicious, so he ran a test for this certain type of abnormal protein called prions."

Julien was listening with bated breath. The weed was working its magic, easing the tautness in his shoulders and face. I liked to think my story was helping a little too.

"The test came back positive, so the doctor asked my grandma's coworker if she had, by chance, recently consumed human flesh."

His hand came down hard on the mattress. "Fuck. No fucking way."

I nodded. "Yes fucking way. The vegan had served her human flesh. When the police went to find him, it turned out his house was a short-term rental and his social media was wiped. All traces of him had vanished. He made this woman a cannibal and went poof."

His head fell against my shoulder as he groaned. "I'm gonna throw up, baby. You can't do this to me. That's the most disgusting thing I've ever heard."

"I'm sorry, but I couldn't live with that inside my head another day."

"I think you could have."

I might have grossed him out, but he was laughing. His face was no longer contorted in pain. And he held me against him like he really, *really* liked me—stories about cannibalism and all.

• • • • • • • • • •

The next few days were rough, but Julien's pain eased as time went on. I forced him to accept rides from me and showered him with attention and affection. He grumbled about it but never once tried to make me stop, so I was fairly certain he actually liked it.

The thing was, I was worried about him. As much as I loved taking care of him, he needed to see a doctor.

We were getting dressed for class on Friday, and I found I couldn't bite my tongue any longer.

"Jules, I think you should call your dad about your insurance."

He looked up from his backpack, his brow pulling together in the middle. "What?"

"You haven't told me a lot about him. If he's, like, a murderer or if he'll hurt you in some way, then disregard me. If not, I think you should at least ask him if there's something he can do to extend your coverage. Is he even aware of the extent of your injuries?"

His jaw was hard. His nostrils flared as he inhaled a deep breath. "I don't know if he's aware. And no, he's not a murderer, as far as I know. He'd have to care about me in order to hurt me and he doesn't." He exhaled, his shoulders rolling forward. "It kills me to ask him for anything."

"Because he was a bad dad?"

He nodded once. "An absent dad. He let my mom struggle, barely took the time to see me *before* he had a legitimate family. After Beckett came around, forget it. I barely existed to him. Any time I've seen him, it was my mom or me initiating it. He didn't fight it when I went to live with Amir after my mom died."

"Do you hate him?"

"No. I don't know." He shoved his fingers through his hair. "Maybe I do."

"Do you think he hates you?"

He looked at me, his jaw working back and forth as he considered his answer. "No, he doesn't. He's...indifferent to me."

"I can't imagine anyone who knows you being indifferent to you."

His chuckle was desert dry. "That's the kicker. He doesn't know me. He never bothered with that. He made dad-like motions a few times. Set up a college fund. Paid Mom's rent and covered her funeral costs. Came to my kindergarten play." He shook his head. "Last time I saw him was at Beckett's birthday party. The kid had asked for me to be there. Dad pulled me aside to tell me Beck was going to ask me to come on their family vacation and I was to tell him I couldn't."

"Asshole," I muttered.

"Yeah. He explained it was because his wife was touchy about him having another son and wouldn't have been comfortable. Like I would've been comfortable in that situation? Come on. The kid never asked anyway. He probably saw the writing on the wall."

"I'm sorry you drew the short end of the dad stick. I hate that for you."

"Now you see why I'm reluctant to ask him for anything? I don't want to need him—and I sure as hell don't want him to *know* I need him."

I sensed Julien was about to dig his heels in, but I wasn't going to let that happen. His dad might be a giant dick, but he was the keeper of the insurance and money. Julien needed to call him, and I wasn't going to drop it until he did.

I put my hands on my hips, hoping the fact that I didn't have a shirt on yet would soften the blow.

"Yeah...well, what's that saying about pride? It goes before a fall? Don't be so proud you screw yourself. Suck it up, buttercup."

He sputtered a laugh. "Fuck. Is this tough love?"

"If it works, then yes. Your dad has the ability to help you in the way you need. I won't let you ignore that because he's a dick. It doesn't make you weak to ask for help. Putting aside ego and asking for help when you need it is so incredibly hot."

He put his backpack down on the ground. "Seraphina, it seems I need some help over here." He framed the bulge in his pants with both hands. "The kind of help only you can give me."

Scrunching my nose, I crossed the room to where he sat at his desk. "Maybe I should let you help yourself for being so stubborn."

He gripped my hips and tugged me down to his lap. His gray eyes grew calm, the clouds rolling away.

"I'll call him." His lips touched mine. "Thank you for saying what needed to be said."

"Always, Jules."

Chapter Twenty-three

Seraphina

A phone call didn't cut it with Julien's dad. Saturday morning, we were driving up to his estate. *Estate.* My family was wealthy by most people's standards, but we looked like paupers compared to the neighborhood Julien's father lived in.

I hadn't asked if Julien wanted me to come, nor had I waited to be invited. Once he told me he had to go to his dad's place, I asked him what time we were leaving. The relief that had flickered in his eyes assured me I'd made the right choice.

"This is it." Julien pointed to a set of intimidating wrought iron gates with a crest in the center. "The Savage Estate."

I slammed the brakes a little too hard, both of us jerking forward. "Savage? As in Savage River...that Savage?"

He nodded, his expression unreadable. "I told you he was rich."

"But...but our university is named after him. That's—"

"Not *him*. His great-great-great grandfather or something like that founded the town. It's all named for him."

I gave him a sharp glare. "Sure, sure. Definitely act like being a Savage isn't a massive deal."

I tried not to be miffed he'd never mentioned it. I got that he didn't feel like he was part of this family, and maybe he didn't want most people to know, I had just hoped I wasn't most people to him after all we'd revealed to each other.

"I'm not a Savage, Sera. I'm an Umbra."

He cupped the back of my head, turning me toward him. His gaze was steady on mine. There was nothing closed off there. He communicated so much in one look. He hadn't been hiding a secret identity from me. No malice was intended.

"I know." Reaching across the car, I took his hand in mine. "But maybe a tiny warning would have been okay?"

He brought my hand to his mouth and kissed my fingertips. "You're right. I should have told you. Forgive me?"

I rolled my eyes. "Obviously."

He could get away with a lot when he was sweet like that.

We were buzzed through the gate and parked at the end of a long, curving drive. As soon as we were out of the car, I threw my head back in an attempt to take in the sprawling house. It was Mediterranean style, with a red-tiled roof and beige stucco siding. And it went on and on and on. The entrance had double doors made of glass and curved iron. Before we could ring the bell, the door was thrown open by a gangly, raven-haired teenager in an untucked button-down and shorts. He watched us from beneath a furrowed brow.

"What are you doing here?" There wasn't anything friendly in his greeting.

Julien put his hand on my back, drawing me closer to him as we approached the house. "Hey, Beck. I'm here to see Dad."

He crossed his arms, guarding the doorway. "Does he know you're coming?"

"Yeah, he does." There were three steps to climb to get to the front door. Beckett observed Julien climbing them one at a time.

"What's the matter with you?" Beckett scratched the side of his head. His frown had morphed from suspicion to what I suspected was concern, but the way he expressed it was to get pissy with his brother. "You didn't have those scars the last time I saw you. Why didn't Dad tell me you have scars?"

Jules huffed. "I don't know how he is with you, but he's never been very forthcoming with information around me."

He took a moment to think about that then gave a slight nod. "That's him. Not very forthcoming."

Beckett finally moved aside to let us in the house. Great columns flanked the entryway, which led to an open foyer with an ostentatious chandelier hanging from the second-story ceiling. I got lost in the obscene display of wealth until Julien put pressure on my back.

"This is my girlfriend, Seraphina," he said.

Beckett kept looking at Julien then averting his gaze. He barely spared me a glance. At least, not my face. He did linger on my boobs in a way only a thirteen-year-old who thought he was being slick would. I had to bite the inside of my cheek so I wouldn't laugh. I truly didn't think Beckett Savage would appreciate being laughed at.

"You should greet people when you meet them, Beck," Julien admonished.

Heat reddened his little brother's cheeks and the tips of his ears. It was hard to tell if he was embarrassed or angry. From his scowl, I'd venture it was more the latter.

"Hello, my stranger brother's girlfriend." He glared at Julien. "Is that good enough? I don't know why I have to be polite to her. She'll disappear when you do—like you *always* do."

Jules held up his cane. "Sorry, kid. I had a lot going on the last ten months or so. But Sera isn't going anywhere, and if you're not an asshole, maybe we can make sure another ten months doesn't go by before we see each other again."

The kid rolled his eyes, but I was watching him close enough to see the tenseness in his shoulders ease some.

"I'll get Dad." He waved his hands around then shoved them in his pockets. "Just stay here, I guess."

I turned to Julien. "This place is crazy."

His smile was slight, but he gave it to me. "Yeah, it is."

"Your brother seems like he's a little shit."

That made his smile widen. "Yeah, he is."

I tucked his hair behind his ear. "I think he missed you."

He kissed my palm before I dropped it. "I got that sense. I never really thought he gave a damn whether I was around or not."

"I think he does."

"Do I really want a snotty little brother out of all this?"

"You definitely do. I'm a snotty little sister, and I know I enriched Ophelia's life by a thousand percent."

That made Julien laugh and kiss the top of my head. My stomach and chest filled with warmth, pleased I could make him happy in a place he was so deeply uncomfortable.

Within a minute or two, Beckett was back with his father in tow. He pointed to Julien, his frown deep and troubled.

"Did you know he had all those scars? If you did, I'm mad you never told me. I'm not a child. You don't have to hide things like this from me."

Under his father and brother's heavy scrutiny, I had a feeling Julien was wishing for his hoodie right about now. But here he stood, in this house that was nothing like him, completely exposed to the only people he had left in the world related to him by blood.

"Julien? I knew you were in an accident, but this—this is beyond a simple car accident."

Just like Julien and Beckett, his dad shoved his fingers through his hair, which was closer to Julien's color than Beckett's. In fact, Julien resembled his father so much, it was uncanny. Mr. Savage was tall and lean, with dark-blond hair sprinkled with a few white strands, and gray eyes. There was scruff on his jaw, but not enough to disguise the angular shape. From what Jules had told me, his dad was in his early forties, and though older men had never been my thing, Mr. Savage could get it.

He came forward and pulled Julien into an embrace, patting him firmly on the back. Jules stood stiffly in his dad's arms until he let go a moment later.

Julien stepped away from him, pulling me into his side again. "This is my girlfriend, Seraphina Ellis. Sera, this is my dad, Joshua Savage."

His dad held his hand out for me to shake. "It's just Josh. Nice to meet you, Seraphina."

"It's just Sera. Nice to meet you too."

His hand was warm and just a little too soft. His gaze was a little too assessing. His smile was a little too forced. I'd keep my mouth shut but I was pretty sure I didn't like Julien's dad.

After introductions, Josh placed his hand on Julien's shoulder. "It seems we need to have a conversation. Let's go to my office." Julien glanced down at me. His father followed his gaze. "I'd like to speak in private. Beckett can show your girlfriend the patio."

I squeezed Julien's arm before he could protest. "That's fine with me. I'm sure Beckett can keep me company."

He'd probably toss me outside and lock the door, but I didn't want Julien to worry about me.

"You sure?"

"Totally. Go talk to your dad."

He leaned down, pressing a kiss to my forehead, whispering he wouldn't be long, then followed his dad down a hallway off the entry. Without saying a word, Beckett swiveled in the other direction and walked away. I scrambled to catch up. There was a high chance I'd get lost, never to be found again, if I didn't stick by Beckett's side.

"This place is crazy," I said.

"It's whatever," he groused.

"I guess it's normal to you since you grew up here."

He peered at me over his shoulder. Well...glared was more like it. "Nothing's normal about living here."

He ushered me through a door leading to the patio. Patio was sort of an understatement. This was more like an outdoor oasis. I couldn't tell where the backyard ended, it was so lush with plants and flowers.

Beckett directed me to sit down on a low sectional—massive, like everything else in this mansion—then he went back inside, muttering he'd be back with a drink for me. Never mind he hadn't asked me if I wanted anything.

While I waited, I took out my phone to check my messages. I hadn't heard from my phantom in a while, but I didn't find myself tempted to text him. He had been my person to lean on when leaning on someone mostly anonymous had been easier than facing the people who really cared about me. Alley and Laura would have been my rocks if I'd let them, but my phantom had taken that place. I didn't regret that, but I was beginning to feel like that need had passed.

I hadn't really expected Beckett to reappear, but he did a few minutes later, carrying a bottle of water, which he shoved at me.

"Thanks." I laid it aside, craning my neck to look at him as he loomed over me. "Think you might want to sit down?"

"Whatever." He plopped on the sectional as far from me as possible—which was far, because, again, massive. Instead of taking out his phone and ignoring me, he stared at me unabashedly. It was actually unnerving.

"You're thirteen, right? Eighth grade?"

"Mmmhmm." He narrowed his eyes. "Are you really Julien's girlfriend?"

"Yes." I rubbed my hands on my thighs. Why was this child making me nervous? "Is that hard to believe?"

"He's never brought anyone here with him. I know he has friends, but I've never met them. He lived with them instead of living with us."

"I know. I've met his friends. His best friend, Amir, is sort of scary, but Julien told me a funny story about when they were kids and it made him a lot less intimidating."

I launched into the camping story. Beckett wasn't quite looking at me anymore, but as still as he was, I was almost certain he was listening.

When I finished, he stayed quiet. Slowly, his hands curled into fists on his thighs. Something was going on in his head. Though I didn't know him and he didn't seem to like me, he was Julien's little brother, so I wanted him to talk to me if he had something to say.

"You can ask me questions if you want. I'm pretty much an open book."

His eyes slid toward me before he turned his head. "Is he going to be okay?"

I nodded. "Yes, he will be. He might not be the same as before, but he'll be okay. He's made so much progress since last year. I know he'll keep getting better."

He touched his own cheek. "What about his face? Is it always going to be messed up?"

"It's not messed up. It's different than it was before, that's true, and I'm sure it's hard to get used to. I'll tell you the truth, though, Beckett, I think he's hot as hell."

He cringed, falling back against the cushions. "Oh, that's disgusting. Why would you tell me that?"

I shrugged, pleased with myself. "I'm just sayin', your brother has it going on."

"I'm going to throw up." He shook his head, his lips puckered. "That's not right. You don't even know me and you're saying all this stuff about my brother."

I giggled at his level of overreaction. "Yeah, well, now that we've met, I hope I can get to know you. I promise not to talk about how much I want to kiss Julien's face."

He held up his hand. "Please, make it stop."

"I can't help it, Beckett. He's just that swoony."

He cupped his forehead, groaning, which only made me laugh harder. This kid really was a little shit. One day, he was going to find a girl who got all swoony over him, and I hoped he remembered this conversation.

Finally, his groans subsided and he chanced a look at me again. "Can I ask you something else?"

"Of course you can."

"He never comes over. Do you know why?"

"I think...he hasn't felt welcome or comfortable here. It's definitely not something against you, I can tell you that. I think you're probably the only one he likes around here."

He sighed, raking back his hair. "I don't blame him for not wanting to be around. If I didn't have to live here, I'd never come back."

"I felt like that in my house too." I blew a curl off my forehead. "I actually still feel like that a lot of the time when I go home."

His attention sharpened. I wondered if this kid smiled. I hoped he did. Man, to be thirteen and so grumpy all the time had to be tough.

"What's your deal anyway? Were you with Julien before he got all cut up?" he asked.

I scrunched my nose. "My deal? That's kinda rude. And no, I didn't know him before. We met in class, I harassed him until he talked to me, and the rest is history. He doesn't mind if I talk his ear off and he reads fan fiction to make me happy."

"You *do* talk a lot."

"Oh, I know. It's something I'm working on, but not that hard honestly."

The corner of his mouth twitched, and I held my breath to see if he was going to smile, but at the last second, it fell back down into a flat line. Damn.

"It's not *that* terrible," he said.

I straightened, grinning at him. His frown deepened.

"Did we just become friends?" I squeaked.

"I don't know about that." He turned his head, and I swore I saw another twitch. It was now my mission to wear this kid down.

He cleared his throat. "But do you think you could ask Julien if maybe I could hang with him, you know, outside of the house? Dad would let me go with Julien." His eyes slid my way, then back to the distance again. "I mean, it's not a big deal or anything. It's just an idea."

"Of course. I think he'd be incredibly into that. He's got some baggage when it comes to your dad, but none with you."

"Okay." He scratched at the seam on the cushion beside him. "And maybe you could be there too. You could probably talk a little less, though."

My chest almost burst, but I tried to play it cool. "I might be into that. But I make no promises on the talking part."

"Yeah," he huffed. "I didn't think you would."

I had no idea what was going to come from Julien's talk with his dad, but at least he'd walk out of this house knowing he had a brother who wanted to be a family with him. And that wasn't nothing.

In fact, it was kind of everything.

Chapter Twenty-four

Julien

It was hard to concentrate on the upgrades my dad was pointing out on the way to his office when I was worried about Sera. Also, I didn't give a shit about the piles of money he'd thrown at architects to improve a house that was gaudy as hell and bore more resemblance to a Vegas hotel than a family home.

He gestured for me to step into his office. When I glanced back in the direction we'd come from, where I last saw Sera, he tsked.

"Your girlfriend seems like a nice girl," he remarked.

"She is. Think Beck's keeping her entertained?"

He chuckled. "In the way a newly minted teenager can. He's most likely snarling at her while drooling over her cleavage. That's pretty much par for the course these days when it comes to him."

For a split second, I had to battle the impulse to tear out of this room, find Sera, and protect her against my snarling little brother. But then I remembered the way she had completely disarmed me, even when I'd been a standoffish piece of shit to her. She could handle one middle school boy, even if he was more snarly than average.

Instead of circling around his desk, Dad settled in the club chair beside mine. He folded his hands in his lap and looked me over, from my cane to my scarred face.

"You told me you were in a car accident."

I nodded. "I was. Except...I wasn't inside the car, and it wasn't really an accident."

A gust of breath exploded from his lips. He pinched the bridge of his nose. "You were hit by a car. You didn't think I'd want to know that? From the looks of you, you were seriously injured." He held up his hands. "I'm at a loss here, Julien. Is there a reason you decided to hide the severity of your injuries from me?"

I shrugged. "I was in the hospital for over a month. I called you a couple days after I woke up from a coma. At the time, I wasn't really capable of going into detail and didn't know what my recovery would look like."

I could have beat around the bush or tried to spare his feelings, but I wasn't sure how deep my father's feelings went. Blunt seemed to work best with him anyway.

"That was almost a year ago. You didn't come to the hospital—"

"You told me not to," he interjected.

That was true. But I'd been drugged up, surrounded by people constantly. I hadn't needed another person hovering.

If he were any kind of dad, he would have ignored me and been at my bedside. Good thing I never expected him to play that role around me.

"You haven't checked in with me since, Dad. I know my medical bills have been going somewhere. I reached the cap on my insurance. You're telling me you had no idea about any of this?"

A deep line creased the center of his brow. "My personal assistant, Miles, takes care of that sort of thing. Obviously, there was a large oversight on both our parts. I'll be discussing this with him on Monday." He leaned forward, rubbing his jaw roughly. "As for not checking in, I could make excuses about being busy, but the truth is, I didn't know my concern would be welcome. You have never wanted anything from me besides financial support. You have a tight group of friends, and now, I see, a girlfriend too. I thought you were covered. Again, that was an oversight, and I apologize. I should have checked in."

I could have argued with him. Told him he was wrong, that I *wanted* more than financial support but had grown to only *expect* that. I could have said he should have been there anyway, whether he thought I wanted him there or not. But what was the point? He knew all this, and I wasn't a kid anymore. I didn't come here to ask for him to love me or coach my little league games. That ship had sailed a long, long time ago.

"Your concern would have been welcome, but what's done is done." I tossed my cane back and forth between my hands. "I'm going to need an extra semester at school. My recovery screwed up my semester last spring so I'm behind."

He lowered his chin. "Of course. That's not a problem. Your school will always be covered without question. You mentioned something going on with your insurance?"

"I reached my limit for the year."

He jolted, as if the idea was unfathomable. The Savages were a pretty healthy lot, after all. "All right. Miles didn't mention anything about that. I'll look into it. In the meantime, any of your bills come straight to me. Will you need surgery?"

"Yeah. My knee is jacked. I was supposed to go in a while ago, but I've been putting it off to get through the school year. PT was helping, but since I can't go anymore—"

"Goddammit, Julien." He pounded his leg, red climbing up his throat and cheeks. "There is absolutely no reason you can't get the medical attention you need. I should have been your first phone call."

"I thought I could make it through."

It sounded stupid now, sitting in this lavish house, across from a man whose pockets ran as deep as the history of this town. I guess I never thought I deserved it. Did he deserve this? Probably not. He spent the money all the same.

"My son doesn't just 'make it through.' You will have the best of the best. I would like you to see my doctor. I trust him implicitly, and he knows all the best specialists. There's surely something that can be done to…revise your facial scars."

There it was. The pride I'd inherited from him thrown back in my face. Literally. He cared about me, sure, I believed that. But he hadn't once asked what had happened to the driver who'd hit me.

He hadn't asked about the long-term effects of my coma. He hadn't even asked where I was living or how I was getting around. Nah, my image was his image. If I walked around looking like the Beast before Belle fell in love with him and broke the curse, Dad would feel the blowback.

He obviously hadn't yet, but that didn't mean he wouldn't.

"Dr. Abadir did my facial surgery." Everyone knew her. My dad's wife, Gretchen, knew her especially well since Dr. Abadir had basically rebuilt her from scratch. "If you think I'm ugly now, you should have seen me before."

My father's cheek twitched, but he wasn't amused. "Dr. Abadir does great work, but you'll see my GP, Dr. Simms. He might have another suggestion for you. You know what I always say: never take the first offer." He clapped his hands together as though he'd given me a pep talk and we were finished. The subject of my health was closed, onto the next. "So, that takes care of that. What else do you need? Are you working?"

"No, not now. I want to, though."

He nodded. "Good. A strong work ethic is invaluable." He got up, making his way around his desk, and clicked on the mouse a few times. With a furrowed brow, he bent over and typed on his keyboard for a protracted moment then flicked his eyes my way. "You'll work for me. I have a project I need an extra set of hands on. Nothing strenuous. You can work from home as long as you have a computer. I assume that won't be a problem?"

"What's the job?"

He chuckled. "Good on you for asking without blindly accepting. I just sent Miles your contact information. He'll be in touch with more information. It's mostly data entry, that type of thing."

"I can do that."

"Of course you can." He tapped his temple. "You're a smart man when you use your brain."

That sounded like a dig, but I let it slide. I had one more thing to ask him. It wasn't big, but it was important to me, and I didn't have the funds to do it on my own right now.

It felt like there was glass on my tongue as I formed the words. I hated asking for things more than I hated almost anything.

"There's something else," I said.

He sat down in his chair, folding his hands on his desk. "All right. Go ahead."

"My mother's piano is still in Amir's house. I'm not living there this year and—"

"You aren't? You didn't tell me." The good mood he'd gained from me semi-agreeing to work for him slipped into a frown. "Even if we aren't as close as we should be, I'm your father, Julien. I need to know where you're living."

"I couldn't do the stairs at Amir's house when I got out of the hospital. It doesn't matter. I'm living with friends now. I'm good. But I'd like to move the piano to my house."

He leaned back in his chair, his elbows on the arms, his fingertips pressed together in front of him.

"You're still playing then?"

"I did. I do. I mean, I will when I have the piano in my house again."

Something came over him. A wistfulness glazed his eyes as he stared at a spot in the corner of the room. Like he was remembering something that had happened there. Dear god, I really hoped he wasn't staring at the spot where I was conceived or something equally as fucked up.

Then he spoke, and I realized he wasn't thinking about that at all, he was simply thinking about *her*.

"Your mother was brilliant at the piano. When she worked here, I caught her running her fingers along the baby grand in the sitting room. I asked her to play for me. It took four or five times before she agreed. Did she play—" He cleared his throat. "Did she play until the end?"

"Yeah. She played until she couldn't."

"That's good." He cleared his throat again. "Give me the addresses and I'll have a piano mover arranged."

"Thank you."

Luckily, my father didn't seem to want to linger any longer than I did. We exited his office, and surprisingly, found Sera and Beckett out on the patio deep in a game of Ping-Pong, from the looks of them.

Dad chuckled as they whacked the ball back and forth. "That's the most enthusiasm I've seen Beck show since he turned thirteen."

Sera volleyed the ball back to him, hard, sending him diving for it. Beck barely missed it. She threw her arms up, howling in victory. He shook his paddle at her.

"You cheated. I demand a rematch."

"Sorry, kid. I can't think of how I could have possibly cheated at Ping-Pong. Just accept the *L* and move on."

My laugh drew both of their attention. She grinned back at me while Beck placed his paddle on the table and shoved his hands in his pockets. Back to being the cool guy. Too bad I'd seen him letting loose with my girl.

"You ready to go?" I asked.

Sera crossed the patio to me and tucked herself into my side. "Yes. I think I'll go out on a high note."

Now that she was beside me, all I wanted to do was carry her out of here and kiss her beautiful fucking face.

"Let's go." I raised my eyes to Beckett, who was watching us from the same spot on the other side of the patio. "Hey, Beck. Get my number from Dad if you don't have it."

Sera patted my chest. "Don't worry. We're already text buddies."

Beckett's cheeks flamed, and he scuffed his shoe against the stone patio. "She made me give her my number."

That made me laugh. "Sera has that way about her." I tossed him a wave and nodded at my father. "We're heading out now. It was good to see you both."

A minute later, we were in Sera's car, headed out of the Savage Estate. Fucking *estate*. I had a hard time accepting that was part of my lineage. Never really thought about it until I was here and it was impossible to ignore.

"How'd it go?" Sera asked.

"About as well as I thought. He acted like he was put out I hadn't told him how bad everything really was. He offered me money, told me I had to see his doctor, pounded his fists about 'no son of mine will go without' or some shit. There was nothing authentic about him. I don't know how we're even related."

"You look like him."

I chuffed. "Not anymore."

"No." She gripped my forearm. "You *look* like him."

"Maybe. That's not the worst fate. If anyone ever tells me I act like him, I'll jump off a bridge."

"I barely met him and can tell you with one-hundred-percent certainty you don't act like him."

My head fell back on the rest. When Sera had driven us out of the neighborhood and onto the main road, a knot in my chest loosened.

"I asked him for help moving my piano." I hadn't planned that, so Sera's surprise wasn't unexpected.

"You did? Really?"

"Yeah. He's going to arrange it."

She smiled, glancing from me to the road and back again. "I want to kiss your face right now but I'll crash if I try."

"Don't crash."

I unhooked my buckle so I could lean across the console and offer her my cheek. The bad one. A month ago, I would've never dreamed of willingly offering my scar-mottled skin to anyone, let alone *her*. My beautiful Seraphina. But I did now, and she giggled while she pecked kisses all over, pressing harder against the scarred areas so I could feel it.

When I settled back in my seat and buckled my seat belt, I told her the rest.

"The strangest thing happened when I asked about the piano. He got all misty eyed about my mother. He told me a story about her I'd never heard." I shuddered. "I don't know how much of what he said was real and what was a romanticized memory, you know? And I can't ask her because she's not here. It's like...I'm okay she's not here, I've had time to grieve, but then there are these moments, like right now, where I feel hollow in her absence. I'm still not ready to be without a mother, and she's been gone seven years."

"I'm sorry, Jules," she whispered, slipping her hand in mine.

"It kills me that *he* is the keeper of memories I don't have. And who knows if he'll give them to me." I balled my other hand into a fist. "Fuck. I hate going to that house. Never gonna go back."

"You don't have to. And you know you have the most important memories of your mom."

Exhaling, I held on to her hand tighter than I should have, but I needed her right now. This was real. That house, the people inside—that had been pretend.

"Even if you don't go back, you need to see Beckett."

"Yeah?" I kissed her hand. "You think?"

"He asked me to put in a good word for him. He's floundering in that house too, and he wants a big brother."

The rest of the knot in my chest unfurled. I liked that idea more than I would have thought.

"I could probably manage that...if you're there."

She snorted. "Your cool-guy baby brother said it would probably be okay if I was there too."

I barked a laugh, feeling lighter and lighter as the miles ticked by, putting more and more distance between me and that house.

"Was this before or after you trounced him in Ping-Pong?"

She sneered at me. "I can't help being a naturally gifted athlete. Hopefully Beckett will grow to respect my prowess on the Ping-Pong table."

"Give him time, baby. No doubt he will."

She grinned. I grinned too. It was easy to forget everything else with her. Easy to forget my loss, the strained relationship between me and Amir, the pain in my knee, and most importantly, that I hadn't told Sera the truth.

All those things were out there, waiting for me to tend to them. And I would. I had to. I just needed a little while longer to live in this daydream with my girl.

Chapter Twenty-five

Seraphina

For the entire drive back to Julien's house, and really since last weekend when he'd kissed my scars and held me when I so desperately needed it, I'd had a question on the tip of my tongue, but I hadn't let it escape.

As I parked at the curb in front of the house, I had to say it. Before Julien could get out, I clasped his hand.

"Jules."

He twisted from the door to look at me. "You're coming in, Sera."

"I have no choice?"

"Do you want a choice?"

I shook my head. "No. But I need to ask you something."

"Okay. Do it."

I rubbed my lips together, sucked in a breath, then went for it. "This is real, isn't it? We're not faking anymore. At least, I'm not. And I was thinking maybe you aren't either."

His breath hitched. "Sera." The tenderness behind my name made it almost unrecognizable. And it was an answer. The only one I needed. I wasn't alone here. This was real for him too.

He reached for me, tangling his fingers in the back of my hair, pulling me to his mouth. He kissed me with the same tenderness, sweeping his tongue between the seam of my lips so gently, it was a feather on a windy day. Touching my tongue and lips, so light, so careful, before floating away again. I fell over the console, seeking more of his feathery, tender kisses.

I cupped his jaw, his stubble tickling my palm. He spoke against my lips.

"We should go in."

I nodded against his forehead. "Okay."

The house was quiet, no one stopping us from locking ourselves in Julien's room. He kissed me there too, deeper, but still so careful. And I melted into him like I always did, glad for the door at my back holding me up.

He slipped the straps of my dress down my arms, and I shimmied so it fell the rest of the way to pool on the floor. Breaking away from our kiss, I helped him shed his layers until we were only skin and lips and tongues.

He held me tight in his arms. We were kissing and hugging, grazing fingertips and rolling nerve endings. There was more passion in those minutes standing just inside Julien's bedroom than I'd experienced in my entire lifetime.

He was hard against my belly, and I reached between us to take him in my hand. The groan that came from him heated my core to white-hot levels.

"Come here," I whispered. Taking his hand, I led him to the bed, where I sat on the edge. "Come here, Julien."

He was in front of me, his cock thick and throbbing. Wrapping my hand around the base, I brought it to my lips. Saliva pooled in my mouth. I wanted to taste him so badly. To prove to us both how real this was.

I took him between my lips, licking him from tip to root. He groaned, holding the sides of my head when he was all the way inside. We hadn't done this yet. I didn't know how he liked it. Then again, I didn't really know how I liked it.

At first, he let me set the pace. I felt him watching me, his head tipped down so he could have a clear view. I flicked my eyes up to his, and the ferocity in his stance nearly undid me.

"Touch yourself, Sera."

I hummed around him and pushed my hand into my panties. The wetness on my pussy lips and in between surprised me, but it shouldn't have. Pleasuring Julien was a treat. Seeing him above me, grunting as he slowly thrust into my mouth, turned me on so much more than I thought possible. My clit was like a little bead, so hard as I rolled it in circles.

"Yes, that's it. You look so beautiful right now. So sexy. You are so perfect."

He was being so careful with me, not putting pressure on my head or directing me. But he could. I would've liked that. I pressed the hand on the side of my head, showing him it was okay to hold me there.

"Yeah?" he rasped. "You want that?"

"Mmmhmm."

"Oh god," he groaned. "Your little vibrations are killing me, Sera."

He tangled his fingers in my hair and pushed his cock all the way in. He did it again and again, controlling my movement while I sucked. When he held me with my nose to his groin, his grunts were primal and from his belly. I looked up again. He was still watching me. He hadn't taken his eyes off me the whole time, and it was unaccountably hot.

My whimper broke him. The next moment, he dragged me onto the bed and tugged my underwear completely off. Then his mouth was on me, the flat of his tongue taking over where my fingers left off. I had been close before, but when he took over, it was a lightning strike to my nerves, bending me in half, making me scream.

"Julien, oh—" I clutched the sides of his head, watching him the same way he did me. When our eyes met, I felt like I was going to explode. Not from desire—although that was a close second—but from this mountain of euphoria Julien had built and carved inside me. I couldn't contain all these good, wonderful, out-of-this-world feelings.

"Julien," I cried. "Oh, that feels so good. I love it. I—" My mouth fell open, and whatever I was going to say was long forgotten. I burst into pieces, the tension in my bones scattering like confetti around my writhing body.

"Would you come here?"

He slid himself up my body, resting his hips in the cradle of my thighs. Thick and hard, I felt him throb on my belly.

He squeezed his eyes shut. "I don't think I can wait another second. Let me in?"

"Please. Please, Julien."

His arm tunneled between us, then his tip was at my entrance, pushing in enough to stretch me. A testing rock had me sighing and wrapping my legs around his waist.

Inch by inch, he sank into me. When his pelvis aligned with mine, we released twin exhales. He brushed my hair from my forehead then stretched his arms beyond me to grip the headboard.

"I can't go hard in this position, baby." His words were almost lost in my throat and hair, where his face was buried. I tugged on his hair, bringing him out so we were nose to nose, eye to eye.

"I don't want hard right now. I just want you deep inside me. Your skin on mine. I want to feel how real this is."

He kissed my mouth and started to move. He was so far inside me, I felt him in my belly. At my deepest point, he swiveled and stirred, touching every part of me he could. Even the shadows and hidden crevices others had overlooked.

I kissed his arms, which flexed as he used them and his uninjured leg to drag himself across the live nerves in my pussy and push himself back out. It was slow, torturous, and perfect.

"You are so good at this," I told him.

"Yeah? All I want to be is good to you."

"You are. So good to me, I don't know what to do with myself." I raised my knees along his sides so he could rock into me even deeper. "Oh, that's so right. The way you feel is so right."

"Never thought I'd be here." His brow furrowed as he swept his gaze over me and over me and over me. "Never thought I could have you, Sera. Not someone like me with someone like you."

"You can have me. You do have me."

He shuddered, his entire being vibrating against mine. I raised my head to kiss his chest and lifted my head to suck on the side of his neck. His groan was pained and so very sexy, shooting straight to my core. I thought I couldn't possibly come again, but all of a sudden, I was edging toward another release of this rapidly mounting euphoria I couldn't control.

"God, I feel that. I feel you getting wetter. You're soaking my cock, baby."

"I can't help it. It's you, Jules."

"Jesus," he gritted out. "How can you—"

He rolled us to our sides, pulling my leg up so he could open me to him. Then everything changed. Our slow, perfect lovemaking turned urgent, darker, harder. Julien's pelvis slapped into mine. My tits bounced as we collided. His mouth hungrily ate at mine.

I came, clutching at his shoulders and crying into his kiss. He answered me back with his tongue on mine, lighting a scorching path of white-hot ecstasy.

I was boneless and replete, but Julien was still on fire. Kissing me. Fucking me. Grasping my ass and digging his fingers into my flesh. He was relentless in his need for me. To find his way into the deepest part of me, that was his and only his. To suck on my skin and touch places that had once been forbidden but were now completely free for him to explore. Because I wanted him to know me, both inside and out. This was real, even if it felt like something I might have dreamed up for myself. Julien was real and he was mine.

"I'll feel you tomorrow," I whispered. "I won't forget I'm yours. You can come. I want you to come, Julien."

"Should I come inside you?" His control was on tenterhooks, but he still asked permission, which only made me sink into everything that was him even more.

I nodded. "Please. Fill me up and make a mess of me. I'll smell like you when I go to sleep. I want that so badly. Come for me. *Please.*"

"Sera," he barked, pumping into me like a man whose fuse had just been lit. He grunted and kissed me and fucked me so hard, my teeth rattled. And I held on to him, kissed him, let him take what he needed, give me what he wanted me to have. He disappeared into my body the rest of the day, the world melting away into this one moment. And holy Christ, it was a *moment*. Beautiful and filthy and sweaty and messy.

When he came, it was quiet and intense. So hot, almost boiling, my insides were coated and overflowing. I wrapped Julien's panting body in my arms and clamped my eyes shut. I'd never felt this way. So attached to another person. It hadn't been long enough. My loose threads shouldn't have been reaching for his to weave into something just for us.

But it didn't seem to matter how long it had been. My mind and heart were firmly in Julien Umbra's custody. My fake boyfriend turned real.

"I'm going to stay here tonight."

He burst out laughing, giving my butt a squeeze. "Are you asking?"

"Nope."

"You don't have to ask. You can sleep here every night if you want."

We eventually got out of bed and hung out with Theo and Helen in the living room, and then on the deck with everyone for a couple drinks. And all of that was nice. So real and perfect, it kept hitting me and hitting me how lucky I was to be here.

There were still things I wanted to ask Julien. Fears that had not yet been allayed. But if I said them out loud and his answer wasn't what I wanted it to be...well, I wasn't ready for that.

As we lay in bed together once everyone had gone their separate ways, I couldn't help the worries about what would happen after spring break. Carson would surely come to collect on our bet. There was no getting around that with him. I had to ask myself if I would give up drum captain for the chance to stay with Julien.

My instinct was to say yes, of course, but I'd given up so much of who I was in order to be liked by others, I wasn't sure I was willing or even if I *should've* been willing to give this up for him. On the other hand, no part of me wanted to walk away from this man. It was a punch to the stomach to even imagine.

We still had a couple weeks and had only just agreed we weren't faking it anymore. There was time for this conversation when I wasn't basking in the realness of us.

"Come here," Julien ordered softly.

I rolled into him, rubbing my face against his shoulder.

"Sleepy little Sera," he cooed at me. "Go to sleep now, beautiful."

"Only if you do."

"Oh, I will, and I'll rest easy having you here."

I knocked my forehead against his chin. "I'm glad you're my real boyfriend now."

"Mmm." He kissed my forehead and held me even tighter. "Can't get enough of you."

It was only after Julien drifted off to sleep and I was close to following that something occurred to me. In all my talk of us being real, he had never once agreed. It had been a kiss to the forehead, a hum which I took as agreement, my name said with so much emotion, I had heard it as a resounding *yes*.

The afterglow from my perfect day kept me cushioned and soft around the edges. Therefore, I chose to focus on the fact that Julien wasn't a huge talker. Actions were more his style, and he'd shown me in all the ways he could that I was important to him.

I let this particular worry slip through my fingers like wisps of smoke. I had enough running circles through my mind. The man who told me he'd have me sleeping in his bed every night if he could would not be one of them.

Chapter Twenty-six

Seraphina

As the semester wore on, I was doing my level best to keep my grades up, which meant studying. Although I didn't have to have complete silence, studying with Julien was a no-go. He managed not to become distracted by me, but I couldn't convince my mind to concentrate when he was in the room with me.

So, I was in my favorite nook in the student union with an iced coffee, a partially demolished muffin, and my laptop open. Music played in the earbuds nestled in my ears, drowning out the noise around me.

This was my favorite study spot because of the skylight overhead. The air conditioning was always blasting in the union, but the afternoon sunshine heated this little corner to the perfect temperature.

I was in the zone, absorbing the pages and pages of reading I had to get done, blocking out everything around me. That was my only excuse for not noticing his approach. If I had seen him before he sat down across from me, I would have slammed my laptop shut and made a run for it.

Seth's mouth was moving, but I couldn't hear him. Scowling, I threw my hands up in exasperation, then he pointed from his ears to mine. Understanding what he was saying, I yanked out an earbud.

"I'm studying," I stated. "Go sit somewhere else."

"I'm not here to attack you. I just want to have one fucking conversation with you without anyone else intruding. Give me ten minutes, then if you want me to go, I will."

The corners of his mouth were pulled down, and so were his shoulders. Overall, Seth seemed subdued, which wasn't like him at all. His hands were clasped in front of him on the table. There was something pleading about the way he was looking at me.

It was on the tip of my tongue to turn him away, but he was right. Once I'd seen the pictures of him with Katie, I hadn't allowed him to speak to me. As far as I was concerned, the pictures said enough. But if giving him ten minutes of my time granted him enough closure to disappear from my life, I had to try. It wasn't as if I trusted his word, but I happened to have ten minutes to spare, and I was in enough of a good mood to give them to him.

I closed my laptop and took out my other earbud, placing them both on top of it.

"Go ahead. You have ten minutes." I blinked at him, and he exhaled, his head dropping.

He wasted thirty seconds of his ten minutes just like that, head hanging low, audibly breathing in and out.

Clearing his throat, he raised his head, allowing his gaze to sweep over me before settling on my eyes. For the first time since I'd known him, he wasn't wearing cockiness like a mask. He looked like the Seth who only came out in the dark. Intensely insecure, sweet when he wanted to be, and vulnerable. He covered it all up with bravado and arrogance, but I'd seen glimpses of who he really was during the time we'd been together. Those glimpses had been enough for me to stay.

"I need you to know I'm sorry. I fucked up, and hand to god, it was only that one time."

I rolled my eyes. "Okay. Sure."

He held his hands out, palms up. "I have nothing to lose here, Sera. No one's around, I know you're not coming back to me, there's no reason for me to lie to you. I was incredibly wasted that night and made a really fuckin' bad decision."

"You sure did. I was at my grandmother's funeral while you were having sex with the girl you promised me was like a sister to you."

He grimaced, falling back in his chair. "That's not a lie. I was so grossed out with myself after it happened. Mostly because I cheated, but partly because of who it was with. I'm not into Katie, I don't see her that way, I never will." He rubbed the top of his head, back and forth, back and forth. "I'm sorry, Seraphina. I still love you. I get you're not gonna forgive me, but fuck, baby, I do love you, and I miss you like crazy. Your mouth—god, I miss you talking my ear off. I miss sitting in this nook with you studying. I miss all of you."

He almost got me. I almost let him crack me open and spill his lovely words into the cavity he'd carved out of my chest during the time we'd been together.

But then I remembered how many times he'd told me to stop talking.

I remembered he'd never held my hand in public.

I remembered him sitting in this nook but getting up and leaving for long periods of time before coming back without an explanation. Once, he hadn't even come back at all.

"You were a terrible boyfriend, Seth. What was up with you not allowing me to come to your party? Why'd I have to sit in my dorm and wait for your call?"

The crease between his brows deepened. "Uh...I don't even remember that. You sure that was me?" He tried to give me one of his charming smiles, but it hit about a mile off its mark.

"Yes, Seth. I'm absolutely sure it was you since you were my first boyfriend. Don't pretend you don't know what I'm talking about. It's insulting, and I really think you've insulted me enough."

He crossed his arm over his chest. "I don't know, Sera. I had a poker game to run that night. Shit to do I needed to dedicate my attention to." His jaw hardened, the Seth I had seen most often coming out to play. "Memories are coming back to me now. The minute I could step away from the game, I went to find you. You recall the position you were in? Baked out of your mind, all cuddled up with some random stoner. *That's* why I didn't want you there until I was ready to give you the attention you required. You were always so damn flighty, talking to whoever you met like you were besties. Even dudes who very clearly wanted to sink their dick in you."

"So? Just because someone wants me doesn't mean I'd allow anything to happen. *I* would never, ever cheat. Your presence had no bearing on whether I would be loyal, and I think you know that. No, you didn't want me there because then you had to act like a boyfriend instead of pretending to be single." I shook my head, suddenly exhausted with this conversation. "You gaslit me into believing the problem was me, when in reality, it was us. We didn't belong together. You couldn't get it up to treat me right, and I lapped up your crumbs because it was all I thought I deserved. Now, I'm with someone who has shown me I deserve to be their person—the one they want there before the party starts and in the morning to complain about the cleanup together."

Seth sputtered. "Oh, please. You're talking about the...the...disabled dude you're slumming with? I'm not too concerned about being compared to that guy. Of course he'd worship you. Kid doesn't have any other options."

A rush of heat licked at my cheeks, and my mouth fell open. "You have no idea what you're talking about," I rasped. "None at all. Don't you ever say another negative word about him. He's everything. Absolutely everything."

"Whatever." He waved me off. "What I really want to talk about is how you got those pictures. Who sent them to you? That's what I want to know. It's gotta be someone who has a grudge against me, and that needs to be nipped in the bud."

"I don't know."

I turned my head from him, taking shallow breaths, which did nothing to slow my racing heart. Anger surged through my veins. If I were a big, strapping guy like Seth, I'd knock his freaking lights out for speaking about Julien that way.

And me that way.

"You don't know who sent the pics? Or you're not going to tell me?"

"It doesn't matter. What's done is done."

I knew who sent the pictures. Clearly, I wasn't going to tell him. It was none of his business. My phantom hadn't told me how he'd happened to come across Seth and Katie going at it in Seth's car, but he'd managed to snap a few pictures without them noticing. He'd told me the flash had gone off and they hadn't even paused.

In between the lines, he was telling me they'd been so wrapped up in each other, a blinding light against the midnight sky hadn't been enough to tear them apart.

Seth cocked his head. "I don't know anyone who has vendettas against me. No one has said a single word to me since what I did came to light, and you'd think if this had been about me, someone would have gloated. So, I was thinking this might have more to do with you, Sera. Someone who wanted to get to you, possibly to get you to break up with me."

I wanted to throw my hands up. To scream. He wasn't accepting any culpability. Now he was trying to blame some faceless stranger for the demise of our relationship? That was incredibly rich.

I wasn't going to give Seth a reaction. He didn't deserve my anger or frustration or sadness. I was finished with him. He'd never get another thing from me. He'd already taken enough.

"I really don't feel like sitting here and throwing around theories with you." I tapped on my laptop. "I have studying to do, and your time is almost up."

He barreled on like he hadn't heard me. Nothing new there.

"I asked myself who had the most to win by breaking us up. Racked my brain, because it really didn't make sense. Then I saw you with *him* yesterday, and it hit me. That guy, your new *boyfriend*, is the one who came out on top in all this. We broke up, he got you a month later. I think it's way too much of a coincidence to be legit."

With a heavy sigh, I let my head fall into my hands. This was going nowhere. All I wanted was for Seth to realize that and walk away. "You have no idea what you're talking about."

"I think I do. I was going somewhere off campus yesterday. On my way, I drove through a neighborhood with a lot of rentals, and what the hell would you know? Out you came from one of them, followed by *him*. The next street down, I popped a U-ey and went back, because something was niggling in the back of my brain. The two of you were standing on this Craftsman porch, smiling at each other like a Hallmark movie or some shit, and foggy memories of the night the Katie thing happened—"

"The night you cheated on me with Katie," I corrected.

"Right." He exhaled. "So my foggy memories suddenly unfogged. That street is quiet at night, real quiet. Must be a bunch of nerds living around there."

Scoffing, I circled my hand in the air. "Is there a point to this? You have about one minute."

"I told Katie to park on that street. She was supposed to be my DD, but she'd been drinking too, so she wasn't thinking straight when she pulled up in front of this house." His eyes narrowed. "Your boy's house."

Something in the pit of my stomach squirmed, even though I should have been completely placid. I knew my phantom had sent me the pictures. He'd never explained how he'd gotten them or if he'd taken them himself, but I hadn't asked either. It had never been important.

The content had been important. Telling Seth he could go fuck himself had been important. But asking how my phantom had happened upon my boyfriend cheating on me? That question had never even occurred to me.

With a smug grin, Seth jerked his chin. "Yeah, you're thinking about it, aren't you? Were they sent to you anonymously? If they were, I bet you my championship ring your boy was the source. He must've spotted my sweet thing and wanted a piece for himself."

I didn't believe him. He was wrong. There was no way in hell Julien had taken those pictures. If he had, that would mean...

No. I'm not going there.

I bit down hard on the inside of my cheek to stave off the threatening tears. I would never cry in front of Seth again. He didn't care about my tears, anyway, nor did I believe he was actually remorseful. His whole act had been to make me let my guard down so when he dropped his bomb, it would hit as hard as possible.

Too bad his bomb had been completely off target.

"Your time's up." With shaky hands, I stuffed my laptop into my backpack. There was no way I was getting any more studying done. My only goal was to get away from Seth as quickly as I could, then I'd decide on my next move. "We're done."

With lightning-quick reflexes, he grabbed my wrist, keeping me at the table.

"I'm not done. I need to know you're hearing me, Sera. I messed up, I admit that, but I can't watch you move on with the guy who had a hand in breaking us up. Who knows? This guy could be some stalker who was waiting for me to make a misstep so he could tell you all about it and become your little limping hero."

I yanked my wrist out of his hold. "Even if that's exactly how it went down, you're the one who made the decision to cheat with Katie while I was most likely sobbing over my dead grandmother. If you insist on continuing to watch me, you'll absolutely be seeing me move on."

And then, because he still looked way too smug for his own good and I hadn't allowed myself the chance to really tell him off, I hit him even harder. "I am so done with you, I barely remember you anymore. When you sat down across from me today, I had to rack my brain for your name. You will be a minuscule blip on my time line. We are done, and I have nothing else to say to you. I also don't have to listen to you anymore since we're nothing to each other. I'm going to walk away, and you're not going to stop me. This is goodbye, *not* see you later. I hope you get yourself together and stop being such an asshole."

With my chin held high, I channeled Belinda Ellis and all her badassery and marched out of the student union without sparing my ex a second glance.

• • • ● • ● • • •

The only way to answer the questions Seth had raised in my mind was to go to the source. From the student union, I walked straight to

Julien's house. My knock went unanswered. He was most likely at the gym with Marco since I'd told him I'd be studying all afternoon.

There was no possible way I could wait until this evening to find out if my suspicions were right. I'd tear my hair out making up scenarios to either absolve him or find him guilty.

Jogging down the porch steps, I ran across the side yard to the house next door and rang the bell. Moments later, Elena answered.

"Hey, girlie. This is a surprise." She craned her neck, checking behind me. "Julien isn't with you?"

I scrambled to think of a reason I would be knocking on her door that would make sense without incriminating him. Because if I was wrong, I didn't want to look like a paranoid shrew. But if I was right...well, I guess I wanted to protect him until I heard the whole story from his lips.

"No, he isn't, which is the problem. I thought we were supposed to meet, but he's not home, so I'm thinking one of us got the time wrong. I would message him, but I'm such a dope, I've been messaging him through Savage Talk, which seems to be down right now. I never got his phone number."

Elena grabbed my hand, tugging me into her house. "Come on. Let me grab my phone in the kitchen and I'll send you his contact info."

I followed behind her, my stomach churning from the lie I'd just spun. My mother had always told me I was a terrible liar. I guessed I'd gotten better with age since Elena seemed to have bought it. I had to hope she wouldn't check Savage Talk anytime soon, because it definitely wasn't down right now.

Why hadn't I gotten his number? It had never even occurred to me to ask for it. Messaging through Savage Talk was just as easy as texting, and since we were together so often, actually speaking on the phone wasn't needed.

At least that was what I was telling myself to try to make sense of the situation.

She pointed to the island in the center of the kitchen. "Have a muffin. Zadie baked them this morning. You haven't lived until you've eaten your weight in Zadie's baked goods."

The riot going on in my stomach was too violent to even contemplate food, but I held back my grimace. "I just consumed a muffin meant for a family of five at the student union. I'll have to pass this time."

Elena chuffed as her thumbs darted over her screen. "And—sent. All of Phantom's contact info should now be in your phone."

"Okay, thank you." I didn't dare check the message while standing in front of her, so I stuffed my phone back in my pocket. It took me that long to register what she had called Julien. "I'm sorry, what did you say? Phantom?"

Elena propped her elbows on the island and twirled a piece of her white-blonde hair. "Mmmhmm. I started calling him that when he moved into the house last summer. He lurked in the shadows, only coming out after dark, hiding half his face, a la *Phantom of the Opera*. He told me he thought it was hilarious because he used to be obsessed with this terrible comic book movie from the nineties called *The Phantom*. No one's ever heard of that movie, but Julien watched it a hundred times when he was a kid." Straightening, she tossed her hair behind her shoulders. "Anyway, sometimes I still call him Phantom, but he's behaving much more like a real human being these days, so it's becoming a misnomer. I'll have to think of a better nickname soon."

I stared at her, aghast. My thoughts slipped by at warp speed. I couldn't catch a single one. My breath either. Heart racing, I pressed on the center of my chest, willing it to slow, for my lungs to fully inflate—anything so I could get out of this house before I passed out and made a fool of myself in front of Elena.

"I'm sorry, I'm all frazzled right now. I would love to stay and hang out and eat muffins, but I need to hunt Julien down."

"I get it." She picked up one of the blueberry muffins and wrapped a paper towel around it before offering it to me. "Take this one for the road. It will make Zadie happy. Actually, take one for Julien too. It will thrill her to no end that she's nurturing him from afar. And before you say no to the muffin, just know denying a nurturer an opportunity to take care of you is like spitting in their eye. You don't want to spit in Zadie's eye, do you? Of course you don't."

That was how I ended up with a paper bag filled with muffins, Julien's phone number in my pocket, my heart shredded in my chest, and a big hug from Elena before she sent me on my way. I had been upended before I knocked on her door, but I was dizzy and disoriented by the time I walked out.

I made it one block before I plopped down on the curb. I didn't know why I was waiting except that I didn't want to know the answer.

But I already knew.

With a deep breath, I dug my phone out of my pocket and turned on the screen, navigating to my texts. I clicked on Elena's, and with one eye barely cracked I pressed on the phone number. As soon as I hit "add contact," my phantom's info popped up. This contact already existed because it was the same phone number. Same person.

Heaving to breathe, I dropped my head between my legs. Each inhale I took was raspy and high pitched. Each exhale was shallow, barely clearing the air from my lungs before I sucked in more.

Julien was The Phantom. He was *my* phantom.

My phantom was Julien.

He was the guy from the party last spring.

The one who had sent me the pictures of Seth.

He was a liar.

Oh, Julien, what have you done?

Chapter Twenty-seven

Julien

Something wasn't right. I'd had this unshakable feeling clawing at me the last few hours, but there was nothing obviously wrong. My body felt good—strong—during my workout with Marco and Amir. Tension was at a low simmer between me and Amir, but I'd gotten somewhat used to that.

All my assignments were turned in. No papers coming up. No tests to study for. The doctor my dad had sent me to had come through, giving me a shot to provide temporary relief for my knee pain.

I'd hopefully be seeing Seraphina tonight.

At the spike of anxiety when my thoughts turned to her, I wondered if that was it. I'd let things get out of hand with her before having the conversation we needed to have. But she was just moving on from the wreckage her family and Seth had caused. The last thing I wanted to do was hurt her even more when I revealed myself as her phantom.

That wasn't the whole truth. I was holding back for my own selfish needs.

What were my needs? Seraphina.

Simple as that.

That wasn't what was scratching at my brain, though. Amir and Marco dropped me off at home, and the whole way through my shower, I filed through the events of the last couple days, trying to figure out what was bothering me.

Dried off and dressed, I shot a message to Sera. *Want to grab dinner with me?*

She replied pretty quickly. *Are you home?* When I told her I was, I waited for another response. Ten minutes went by before my phone alerted me to another message.

Except it wasn't inside Savage Talk. This was a text to The Phantom.

Sera: *I've been thinking about you a lot lately, and I think we should meet in person.*

Me: *Oh yeah, Dragon Girl? To what end? Don't you have a man?*

Fuck me. What was happening? I'd barely spoken to Sera as The Phantom lately. She'd never once mentioned wanting to meet up in the months previous. *Now* she was interested? What the fuck was going on?

Sera: *Things with him aren't going anywhere. My connection with you is so strong, I feel like we owe it to ourselves to explore it. I think about you when I'm with him. Do you think about me when you're with her?*

What the fuck? What. The. Fuck.

With a cry of pure fury, I flung my phone across the room. I staggered, almost falling over, but at the last second, I caught myself on my dresser. Heaving a jagged breath, I stared at my hands. White-knuckled, hungry for blood or pain or trouble. I wasn't a fighter, but I could have brawled right now. Rage mounted beneath my skin, close to bursting out, with nowhere to go.

I balled my hand into a fist and slammed it into the wall beside my dresser. The only blood I was letting was my own, and the throb in my knuckles didn't even begin to touch this agonizing, incendiary ball of anger filling me from head to toe. There was no one I could take it out on because I was the source.

Things with him aren't going anywhere.

I raised my head, and the mirror on top of the dresser reflected what Sera must have seen every time she looked at me.

Disgusting. Weak. Broken.

Not even close to good enough.

Of course they weren't going anywhere. How could I have thought they were? Our relationship was built on a wobbly foundation.

Fuck, Sera had only wanted our relationship to be real because she didn't have all the information. It was more like it was built on a daydream.

I think about you when I'm with him.

I knocked everything off the top of my dresser. The clunks as my books and clothes landed on the floor weren't nearly satisfying enough. Why the fuck didn't I have more breakables? I needed to shatter something. Destroy it. Grind it down until it was an unrecognizable heap on my floor.

The wall would work. I slammed my fist into it again, feeling every split knuckle, the dust and detritus invading my broken skin. I'd have to fix this. Couldn't leave Elena's house in disrepair. But first, I needed to break it a little more.

Someone banged hard on my door. "Julien!"

Whirling around at the sound of her voice, I stared at the door in confusion. Had I imagined that? There was no reason for Sera to be at my door. No fucking reason. She wanted someone else. The whole man she'd met at a party. She didn't want me. No, she wasn't here.

As soon as I convinced myself I was hallucinating, another bang came, this one sounding like a kick. "Julien, open the door right now or I'll get Lock to break it down. He's right here, and I'm pretty sure he could do it in three seconds flat. You don't want him to break your door down, do you?"

What the fuck?

Shoving myself off my dresser, I twisted the lock on my door and threw it open. Sera and Lock were crowded in my doorway. Lock's frown barely registered. It was Sera's red cheeks, wet with tears, that struck me to my core.

Fisting the hem of her shirt, I pulled her into my room and slammed the door shut behind her. From outside my room, Lock's voice rumbled.

"Be careful, Julien," he warned. "I'm not going far."

Yanking the door open again, I met his worried eyes. "I'm not going to hurt her."

He dipped his chin. "Never thought you would."

What he wasn't saying was he was more concerned I'd hurt myself. And fuck if he wasn't right to worry. I didn't think I'd ever hated myself more than this very moment.

"Jules," Sera rasped, beckoning my attention back to her. "What did you do to yourself?"

Closing the door again, I turned around, bracing my back against it. Sera was standing in the middle of my room, among the rubble, tears streaming down her cheeks, staring at my throbbing hand.

I cocked my head, unable to make sense of the fractured events that had just happened in rapid-fire succession. Searching inside myself, I found a switch to shut off the violence swimming in my blood. No matter the circumstances, no matter how far gone I was, I could never be that with her. That wasn't a choice I would ever make.

"What's going on?"

She swiped at her cheek. "I thought I could hurt you. I wanted to make you feel as badly as you made me feel." Her lips pinched, and she shook her head. "But I can't. I can't do that to you."

I took a step toward her but stopped. I still didn't know what the fuck was going on.

Pressing the heel of my hand into my forehead, I tried to get my brain to think straight. "I don't understand."

Her chest rose as she sucked in a deep breath. "I've been texting you for months, except I didn't know it was you. Not until today."

The ground beneath me trembled. Every lie I'd told collapsed beneath my feet. She knew. She knew, she knew, she knew. Shit, it wasn't supposed to go like this. I needed time to formulate my words. To help her understand what she meant to me—what she'd *always* meant to me. And here I was, bleeding and raw, and I had to try.

"Sera," I croaked, reaching for her. "I don't—"

"No." She snatched her hand up to her chest, taking a step away from me. "Don't touch me. You have to explain yourself. Explain why you pretended you didn't know me the first day of class. Explain why you let me talk about you and reveal my feelings for you in our texts. Explain all of it to me, from the beginning. Because right now, I'm not seeing how you can possibly justify any of this. Right now, I'm feeling like a great big joke to you—and it isn't a good feeling, Julien."

I shook my head hard. "You're not a joke, Sera. Never think that." I sank down into my desk chair, shoving my fingers through my hair. "You knew it was me when you sent me that text?"

She sat on the end of my bed, her fingers curled around her knees. "Of course I did. I would *never* go behind your back to meet up with another guy."

I exhaled, but only felt a small dose of relief. Relief I certainly didn't fucking deserve. I'd take it anyway. I still had a battle in front of me.

"Okay." I tried to organize my thoughts so I could make her understand my reasoning. I'd thought about what it would be like telling her, and it had never been anything like this—not with blood dripping down my fingers and accusation darkening her eyes.

Still, I had no choice but to make her understand. I could not let her leave this room until she saw what I did.

"I'm going to go if you don't talk," she warned softly.

I stared at her, but she wouldn't meet my eyes. They were over my shoulder, on her lap, on the floor—anywhere but on me.

"You stuck with me. I used to talk to everyone, go to all the parties, meet all the people. That shit filled me up. Then, one night, you sat down beside me, made fun of me for being all by myself, and talked my ear off. You stuck with me, Dragon Girl."

She flinched at my use of the nickname I always called her through texts.

"You didn't text me for months, so I find that hard to believe."

"The thing is..." I flipped my hands over, exposing my palms, "I was going to text you when I got home the next night—I'd been looking forward to bantering with you some more all day—but I was mowed down by an SUV and barely survived. My phone didn't make it. Fuck, a lot of my bones didn't either."

She gasped. Her hands flew to her mouth. "Oh no."

"Yeah. And when I woke up in the hospital a few days later, I was still thinking about you. I made Marco buy me a replacement phone, because I had it in my mind I could text you, make you feel sorry for me, get you to dump that asshole boyfriend and come visit me."

Her hands dropped to grab onto the comforter on either side of her thighs. "You never texted."

"I was on a lot of heavy painkillers. Thank Christ I didn't figure out how to text you. It would have been indecipherable. And once I started weaning off the meds, I was so messed up, Sera. You think I'm ugly now, I was a monster then."

Her nostrils flared. "I don't think you're ugly. How could you even say that to me?"

Bowing my head, I let my hair fall forward. "I'm not the way I used to be. You can say it. You didn't even recognize me from the party. I'm a different man now."

"You were in the shadows that night. I could barely make out what you looked like. This entire time, I remembered you having blue eyes, not gray." She squeezed her eyes shut. "Stop this. You're not the victim here. I'm the one who was lied to. You tricked me and manipulated me and I don't understand what you had to gain from any of this. Did Seth do you wrong? Is that what this is about? He seems to think the person who took the pictures of him and Katie has a vendetta against him."

"You spoke to Seth?"

She nodded. "Today. He was the one who made me see what was right in front of me."

"Are you getting back together?"

She stared at me without blinking. Her eyes were wide, expression incredulous. I'd taken a lot of missteps without recognizing them as such until I had hindsight and distance. But this was different. As soon as the question was out of my mouth, I wanted it back.

"Don't answer that. I know you're not with him." I scrubbed at my face with both hands. "You want me to keep going from the beginning or talk about the pictures?"

"The beginning," she hissed. I'd never seen Sera angry before. Not like this. It didn't suit her, and I hated with the heat of a thousand suns that it was directed at me—that I'd brought this out in her.

"Okay." This was it. The one chance I'd have to make her see. "I never forgot you, but I had nothing to give you. Never thought you could want me with how I looked. The way my body worked or didn't work. I had to put you out of my mind, and I did, pretty successfully, until you dropped Elena off at my house last fall. You were drunk, she was trashed, and I—"

"You made me cry."

"I did. Not my finest moment, but I was pissed she'd gotten that drunk, and then, when I realized it was *you*, I went into a blind panic, which turned me into an asshole—a bigger asshole than normal. The next day, I felt like shit about it, so I texted you. It was supposed to be a one-off. Check in with you and move on. But then..." I shook my head, pinning my gaze on her hands folded in her lap. "Then you were you. You drew me in in the way you do, and I couldn't stop. I never had any intention of seeing you again. Never thought we'd speak face-to-face, or I'd get to touch you, or have you in my room, or in my life. It was always supposed to be texting only."

She was picking at the skin around her thumb. Digging and digging. It was already raw and angry, a little bloody on one side. Sera didn't have a picking habit. That wasn't what this was. I'd hurt her, and she was trying to diffuse the pain through her skin.

"You keep saying 'supposed to,' as if your actions were outside of your control. The text could have been a one-off. I would have let it go. You didn't have to see me again." She smacked her forehead. "Holy shit, Julien. Did you enroll in our class because I told you I was taking it?"

I nodded once. There was no point in denying it now.

Her eyes rounded, and she hopped up from the bed, backing away from me. "Do you realize how insane that sounds? *Why* would you do that?"

"Why do you think?"

"Just say it, Julien!"

And because I would never lie to her again, I laid it all out there. The stark, honest, scary-as-hell truth.

"I wanted to be near you."

Her body caved in in the middle, as if my truth was a physical blow. She staggered back a step or two until she was leaning against the wall by the windows—as far from me as she could get without leaving the room.

"You should have told me who you were the moment I spoke to you." Her arms wrapped around her waist. "I'm so mad at you, Julien. So, so mad. I didn't think you would be this guy. Not you."

"I know."

Her disappointment and anger were so heavy, they felt like an elephant sitting on my chest.

"You're a liar. Why did you let me tell you everything?" She pressed her hand to her forehead. "I opened up to you. I told you so many personal things because—I don't know why! Because I didn't have to see you, maybe."

"Believe me when I tell you I *never* thought you'd see me. I'm so fucking sorry for not coming clean immediately, but I can't be sorry about texting you. I just can't, Sera. Those first couple conversations we had, I saw what you didn't see: you were accepting being given so much less than you deserve. You didn't expect more. You didn't even know how damn special you are. I couldn't walk away from that. I needed you to see it too."

She threw her arms out. "Why was that your job? Who made you my champion, huh?"

"No one. I did. I don't know what you want me to say."

"Say the truth." Her mouth flattened into a thin line. "Was I a project to you? Build the sad little girl back up and see what happens?"

"Fuck no." I got up from my chair and crossed the room, keeping my eyes on her until we were barely a foot apart. "I wanted you to be happy. I wanted you to demand everything you should have had without asking. That wasn't because you were a project. One conversation, and I cared about you. You had a piece-of-shit boyfriend who didn't prioritize you, and you took it. It drove me crazy not being able to do a single fucking thing about it. I tried to pull back, because I didn't know if what I was doing to myself was healthy, but I couldn't."

Her forehead crinkled. "What were you doing to yourself? I don't understand."

"I *cared* about you in a way that was impossible. One, because of the boyfriend. Two, because I never wanted you to see me. But each time I'd try to ghost our texts, I couldn't do it for long. I couldn't stay away. So, I decided to be there for you in the only capacity I could—to be your friend and listen to you. Hell yes, I wanted to build you back up when you were sad, but not because you were a project."

Blinking, she sucked in a deep breath. "Why?"

"Sera, I—" I raked my hands through my hair, most likely leaving the strands coated in blood, and tugged hard at the roots. I had committed to one-hundred-percent honesty, and I'd never felt so exposed and raw in my life. But if I didn't do this, I'd lose her. And losing Sera wasn't something I could recover from. "I love you, Seraphina. I don't know when it happened, but it was swift and complete when it did. I'm not telling you this as a way to excuse my dishonesty, but you asked why, and there it is. I love you, and there was no way I could stand by while you grieved your grandmother alone."

She winced, but it was true. Seth hadn't been there, and her parents had been more concerned with the party after the funeral than the loss of their matriarch. She'd been by herself, in this sea of grief, and had forgotten how to swim. I couldn't offer her a hand, not with my circumstances, but it had been impossible for me to watch her drown. So, I whispered to her every day, reminding her she knew how to swim. Reminding her how good she was at it. Making sure she listened to my quiet voice.

"You think I could have walked away when you were holding that razor?" I asked gently.

She bit down on the corner of her lip, rapidly blinking away the wetness in her eyes.

"I wasn't going to use it," she rasped.

But she'd thought about it, and instead of hurting herself, she'd texted me.

Sera: *I think I need help. Please.*

Me: *I'm here. Anything. Tell me. I'll help with anything.*

Sera: *There's a razor in my hand right now, and I want to use it. I haven't come so close to using it for a long time. But it hurts. It hurts so bad, and I want it to stop. I need to feel anything other than this hurt. Please tell me what to do.*

Me: *The first thing I need you to do is throw the razor away. You're not using it, Dragon Girl. Do you want to call me?*

Sera: *No, I can't. Not right now. I can't say these things out loud.*

Me: *I get it. Offer stands. Always. Did you throw it away?*

Sera: *I just did. I took it outside to the garbage can and stuffed it under some really gross casserole Susanne Jenkins brought us. I started spiraling by the garbage can and almost dug the razor from underneath all that cream of mushroom soup Susanne Jenkins used on a casserole that was supposed to comfort my family because my grandmother died. Do you know what my family is doing right now? They're at the movies. My grandma is barely in the ground. And I just...am I alone? I felt so alone in those seconds by the garbage can. But I closed the lid and came inside because I knew you were waiting for me. I'm here now, Phantom. No razor.*

Me: *That's my girl. My Dragon Girl, made of fire and light. You can't cut yourself or you'll burn the world down.*

We'd talked for hours that night, until the urge to hurt herself had passed and she'd sent me pictures of her hips as proof that she hadn't used it.

I nodded. "When we were talking, I needed air so I could stay awake for you, so I went outside. It was late, but there was a car parked in front of the house with the cabin light on. I would've gone back inside, left them to it, but there was something familiar about the guy. I went closer, and I knew it was Seth with a girl who very much wasn't you. I took the pictures that night—"

"You didn't send them."

"No. I couldn't do that to you, not after you'd just lost Belinda. Hell, I didn't even know if I was going to send them."

"So, why did you, Julien? Did you think if you sent them, I'd dump him and magically fall in love with you? Was that your plan?"

There was only a hint of venom behind her words. Mostly, she sounded exhausted, which I got like no one else could.

I needed to hold her like I needed to breathe. She was so close but completely untouchable. There was a tear on the top of her cheek. My hands twitched to wipe it away, but she wouldn't welcome that. Not now. I'd made no headway through her anger.

"No, Sera. I never once thought you'd want to be with me. I had no plans for the pictures, but I held on to them."

"And then what? Why did you send them a month later?"

"I don't...I don't think you need to know."

Her hands balled into fists. "You don't get to decide that, Julien! You said you'd be honest. Tell me why right now or I'm leaving."

The force of her voice sent her knocking back into the wall, and it pummeled the rest of the truth out of me.

"I saw Seth with another girl in the library. It wasn't Katie. Someone else. They were in the stacks, just kissing, but—" God, I didn't want to say this to her. Didn't want to add to the pain this kid had already left behind. "The way they were kissing, it was obviously leading to more. That's when I sent you the pictures. I put the choice in your hands, and I won't say I'm not glad you chose to dump his undeserving ass, but I'm so fucking sorry I had to be the one to tell you."

"Oh." Her hand flew to her mouth, and she staggered to the side. "Oh. Okay."

I caught her shoulders when she listed sideways and coaxed her to sit back down on my bed. If I could have dropped to my knees in front of her and begged her to understand, I would have in a heartbeat, but my fucking body didn't work that way, so I had to settle for sitting beside her.

"Sera, he was never good enough for you. He had to know it. I'm sure it ate him up on the inside."

She lifted her head, turning in my direction but not really looking at me. "Then why was I with him for so long?"

"I don't know." My knuckles dragged along her wet cheek. She didn't pull away, so I took it as a victory, but I didn't push my luck by trying for more. "I can't explain that guy or why you picked him. I only know for certain he isn't good enough for you."

She wiped her cheeks with the back of her hand and sniffled. Then she cocked her head, letting her gaze sweep over me. "You were in love with me?"

"Am. I am in love with you."

Nodding, she rolled her lips between her teeth, but she didn't respond. This was a lot. Way too much for one afternoon. I got that. But I was greedy for her words. As selfish as it was, I ached to know what she thought about my feelings for her.

I kept that desire inside, though. I'd burdened Seraphina enough. This ball was in her court.

"The second you spoke to me in class, I should have come clean. I know that. But every interaction, I kept thinking it would be the last one. Then you came back for more and more. I never once believed we'd be where we are. Never thought we'd—"

"Have sex?" she supplied in a flat, emotionless voice that sounded nothing like her.

I let out a dry laugh. "In my dreams, and only there."

"You had sex dreams about me?"

I scrubbed at my face with my hands. "Of course." Why not admit that too? I had no cards left to put on the table. Might as well share my fantasies. "You're always on my mind."

"That's flattering and crazy and—" She sucked in a breath and stared straight ahead. "I think...I think I need some time." One hand waved in front of her face. "My mind is jumbled right now, and I can't really process anything. You're telling me you love me, and that's big, and I don't even know what to say to it because I'm not sure I can trust you. But you're right, I needed you—*you*, Julien—and you were always there for me, without question. And if I consider the way you've been with me in person, you're the same as you were through text. I want to say I can get past this because you're so important to me, but I'm not sure I can. I think I need to go and get blind drunk with my roommates."

Sera rose from the bed, her head swiveling around like she was looking for something.

"I need to go now, Jules. I—" She clamped her mouth shut and shook her head. "I need to go."

Then she disappeared from my room, and a moment later, from my house. I'd see her again. That couldn't be avoided, even if she wanted to. But I really fucking doubted she'd ever set foot in this room again. She'd never let me touch her, hold her, kiss her, or tell me she loved me too. That last one had been a pipe dream anyway.

• • • • • • • • • •

Elena and Lock were in the living room when I finally emerged. I'd known they were out there. I also knew they weren't going to go away. Instinct had me wanting to bury myself so deep in misery, no light could get inside. That was what I'd done for months after the accident. Shadows were my most loyal friends.

Looking at the two people waiting for me on the couch, I accepted I'd been lying to myself. Shadows were nothing more than an illusion. *These* were my friends.

"I fucked up."

Lock cracked his knuckles. "Is this where I return the favor and punch you in the nose?"

Elena grabbed his hands, lowering them to his lap. "We don't punch our friends."

I raised a brow. "Really? I seem to remember you taking great joy in me punching Lock last semester."

Her eyes rolled. "That doesn't count. Lock was being an asshole. You look like a sad little puppy. Punches won't help your situation." She patted the couch. "Come sit down, tell us your woes. Fair warning, though, if you broke Sera's heart, I'll be very mad at you."

I sat down a couple cushions away from them. My bones felt old and brittle.

"I broke your wall. I don't know about her heart."

Elena blew out a puff of air. "Are you going to fix it?"

"The wall or her heart?"

Her brow arched. "Both."

"The wall, yeah, as soon as I can. Her heart? God, I would if I could. I'll try. The thing is, she doesn't want me near her. Probably not ever again."

"Did you cheat?" Lock ground out.

The laugh that came out of me was borderline maniacal. "Cheat? Fuck no, I didn't cheat. Even if girls were lining up—which they aren't—I don't want anyone but Sera. That won't ever change."

"Then what did you do that had Sera leaving this house looking like her heart had been stomped on and you with bloody knuckles and the saddest little face I've ever seen?" Elena braced her elbows on her knees, her chin on her fists. "Tell me and we'll figure out how to make it right."

I had to bat back my instinct again. Hiding wouldn't make this go away or prove to Sera I could be trusted. If there was a chance Elena or Lock could help me figure out how to navigate any of this, I'd take it.

"I lied to her for a long time. I guess I lied to you too."

There was a lot I wouldn't tell them, about the razors and catching Seth cheating the second time. But for the most part, I laid out my history with Sera, beginning at that party and ending with her asking for time.

"Shit," Lock muttered. "That's a lot."

"I don't see myself being able to come back from any of this." I rubbed at the ache in my chest. "It fucking wrecks me that I'm going to lose her, but I should have never had her in the first place, so maybe I should just thank my luck for the stolen time and accept what's never gonna be."

Seconds ticked by in loaded silence. Elena and Lock exchanged glances before they both stared at me. Finally, Lock threw his hand up.

"Bullshit," Lock rumbled. "That's pure bullshit."

Elena patted his thick thigh. "Babe, that's not very supportive. You could at least tell him his attitude is bullshit in a compliment sandwich. Here's how I would do it: Julien, you're a wonderful guy, but if you give up on Sera without a fight, then you're not as wonderful as I think you are. It's actually bullshit. But I know you well enough to know you're only frustrated and upset now. You won't give up on that gorgeous girl."

"Mine was more to the point," Lock said.

"Mmmhmm. Sure. But he'll listen to me because I built him up, knocked him down, and built him up again. Don't you see how dizzy he's looking?" Elena held her hand out to showcase me to Lock, like I wasn't sitting on the opposite end of the couch with them.

"He does look green," Lock agreed.

I swiped a hand in front of me. "All right. I get it."

Elena sat forward. "Do you? Because I'm not certain you do. The sad puppy look is adorable on you, sure, but it won't get you anywhere. You fought like hell to get where you are in your recovery. Are you out of steam? Is that what this is? I will push you down the tracks if you need a boost to go win your girl back. Tell me what you need."

"I don't know, El. I fought like hell to recover because it was good for me. I don't know if I should be fighting for Sera to take me back when she could do a hell of a lot better. She *should* do a hell of a lot better."

"With that attitude, sure she should." Elena rolled her eyes. "But you told me yourself you'll always want Sera and only Sera. That's a lot, Julien. Having loyalty and devotion from your boyfriend isn't trivial. Sera knows that all too well. Give her time, absolutely, but not too much. Then you have to actually put up a real fight to prove to her she can truly trust you. I've never seen you happier and more open than since the two of you started hanging out. That girl's as good for you as your PT was for your broken bits."

Lock reached out and hit my knee. "You want help, we're here. You knocked sense into me when I needed it. I'll be happy to return the favor for you."

"I might need that. I'm feeling all out of sense right now." Lock started to move, so I held up my hands. "Give me a minute to recalibrate before you bring down the fists of fury, man."

"A minute is all you're getting," Elena said.

I thought about the fact that I'd be sleeping alone tonight for the first time in weeks and turned into a wreck about it. But really, I'd been miserable since Seraphina had walked out the door.

"A minute is all I need." I flexed my hand in my lap, wincing at the sharp pain and stiffness. "Maybe a couple."

I may not have thought myself worthy of Sera, but she saw something in me that had made her reveal her deepest secrets not once, but twice. *She* thought I was worthy, and right or wrong, her opinion was worth a hell of a lot more than my own.

I had to fight for her, and I would when I got my feet under me again. Even if she didn't take me back, she had to see *she* was worthy of a fight. Letting her walk away for good without trying until I was bloody and my last claw had been torn out wasn't a choice I could even think about making.

Chapter Twenty-eight

Seraphina

I HATED THAT LAURA and Alley had to put me back together again for the second time in as many months. They dressed me, did my makeup, told me to hold my chin up, and shoved me out the door. Despite getting me drunk last night, they wouldn't let me wallow in bed today. It was to class with me.

The worst part was I was more torn up today than I had been at the beginning of the semester. Seth had humiliated and hurt me. Julien had blindsided me with bone-deep heartache. There was just no comparison to the pain between the two breakups.

Bile rose in my throat when the thought of being broken up with Julien flitted across my mind. That was the very last thing I had wanted. I wasn't sure if we were, but I also wasn't ready to find a way back to him.

I had promised myself I would no longer be the girl who gave chance after chance after chance. I had to learn from my mistakes at some point, right?

As much as I wished I could reason this out, tell myself half-truths—like Julien wasn't Seth and leave out the rest, that both of them had lied for their own gain—I couldn't. I was too mad at him for doing this to us to give him any kind of benefit of the doubt. Maybe I'd get past it, but I didn't know right now.

My stomach was cramping by the time I reached the class I shared with Julien. He wasn't in his normal spot in the front of the lecture hall, so some of the tension churning inside me calmed. I found a seat somewhere in the back of the hall. Not near my band friends, and far, far away from the front. That didn't mean I didn't notice Julien the second he entered the room. My body jerked involuntarily in his direction.

Even my cells wanted Julien. If only I could explain to them what it meant to have some pride. They were little sluts who liked the boy who gave us orgasms and snuggles, lying and manipulating be damned.

I only half listened to the lecture. Midterms were coming up, but my heart was nowhere in it. This was all about going through the motions so Alley didn't punish me with even more squats than usual.

When it ended, I forced my head to stay down. One gut-wrenching sighting of Julien Umbra was enough for one day. I waited in my seat until the room was half-cleared, then slowly made my way down the steps. I should have been paying closer attention.

Carson was waiting for me at the bottom, a smirk tilting his mouth. "Hey, Ser. What's up?"

"Oh, hey." I forced my hands to stay at my sides and not rub my sore eyes or brush my hair off my forehead. "Not much. Just class and studying."

He walked beside me toward the door, bumping his shoulder into mine. "We need an extra drummer this weekend at Savage Day. We're doing a little drumline performance on the green. Can you make it?"

"Yes, of course. Just let me know what we're playing. It won't be a problem."

Optimism lifted my ragged spirit. I'd expected Carson to be snarky, so this was a surprise. The fact that he was giving me something solid to look forward to made me lower my guard as he chattered away about which songs we'd be playing and what I should wear. I'd played at Savage Day—an all-campus open house for alumni, parents, and the local community—in the past, so I knew what to expect, but I let Carson talk because that was what he liked to do.

"By the way," he hooked his arm through mine, "I couldn't help noticing you and lover boy weren't sitting together today. Is there trouble in paradise already? Will you not even be making it to spring break?"

All my optimism vanished in a blink. Suddenly, I was pissed off, then doubly pissed off that I wasn't allowed to express myself. I couldn't tell Carson to shove his nosy questions up his tight ass because he still held a modicum of power over me.

I coughed into my hand. "No, that's not it at all. I went to the doctor this morning because I developed this cough overnight. He knew what it was right away and prescribed me meds that take twenty-four hours to kick in. I'll be fine by tomorrow. Until then, I'm super contagious. Obviously, I don't want to infect Julien, so I'm doing my best to stay away."

I coughed again for effect, but it wasn't really necessary since Carson had already scrambled away from me.

"Ugh, did you not think you should stay away from me too?" He swiped the arm that had been touching mine. "If I get sick, I *won't* be happy."

He didn't wait for me to giggle or tell him I was only kidding. I had a feeling once he had a chance to think about it, he'd realize I didn't have some rare coughing disease. He'd probably be pissy about it, but oh well. There wasn't anything else he could threaten me with at this point.

From the shadows, Julien appeared, startling me. My pulse rushed in my ears, and a hand flew to my chest to keep my heart from vaulting out.

"Holy crap," I wheezed.

"Sorry. The show ended, so I thought I should show my appreciation. Stellar acting."

"Yeah, well—" God, I wanted to run at him and forget everything bad. "—we're still working out the staging and props. With a one-woman show, you need a lot of props."

Shaking his head, he took another step in my direction. "I disagree. You don't need anything. Just you and a spotlight. That's all I want to see."

"You're biased."

"I don't deny it." The sweep of his gaze would have felt invasive from anyone else. From Julien, it made me feel intensely cared for. "Can we talk?"

I shook my head. "No. I'm not ready."

His head dropped. "This is killing me. Are you okay?"

"Not really. I wish I could rewind time and never listen to a thing Seth said. I wish I could unknow this."

He sighed, his chin sinking even lower. "I was always going to tell you. I let my greed for you get in the way of doing what was right."

When he said things like that—god, when he told me he loved me—every tiny little molecule of my being wanted to rub around in it and believe it to be true. But life, experience, Seth, my family, had all shown me I wasn't the girl who got to be loved that way, not without strings or deception or heartbreak. Maybe it was different with Julien—it certainly felt different—but my instincts were shit. I didn't trust my own judgment.

"It would have been awkward when I still didn't have your phone number ten years down the road." My quip came out sounding sadder than I'd intended, and Julien winced.

"Jesus, Seraphina, I'm a piece of shit. I'm sorry." He yanked at his hair, then raked his eyes over me. Tortured. He looked absolutely tortured. Three, maybe four feet separated us, but from the way he eyed the distance with hopelessness, it should have been miles.

"I believe that." I rolled my lips inward, sucking them between my teeth. This hurt so badly, I could have screamed. "But I really wish you didn't have something to be sorry for."

"You have no idea how much I wish that too. If I could cut open my brain and show you what I feel for you, how I think of you—well, you'd probably be scared. But you wouldn't question my motives. All of it has always been you. You deserve everything good and real—"

"Were we even real, Jules? Can something based on a lie be real? Or were we just something I daydreamed? I don't even know the answer to that, and I'd been so sure two days ago. It sucks that I'm doubting my own mind."

"We *are* real, Sera. I don't get why you chose me, but you did, and I chose you the second I spotted you at that party. I'm going to keep being here for you until you get that. Until you understand I love you in a way that's not going to go away. If you still want nothing to do with me, I'll let you go, but not before you see there's nothing pretend or fake about how completely devoted I am to everything about you."

I swallowed a flood of tears and curled my toes so I stayed rooted to my spot in the hallway instead of launching myself at him. I would have given almost anything to be able to get over this, to trust him and myself, allow myself to be back in his arms. *Almost* anything. Except my self-respect, which had been a battle to gain.

"I need some more time. Will you give me that?"

His eyes never strayed from me, even as his shadows tried to envelop him again. "Of course I will."

"Through the weekend. I don't know if I'll be able to make a decision or—I don't know. But we can talk again on Sunday, if you still want to."

He released a jagged breath. "Never gonna change, Sera. That means I'll always want to talk to you."

The barbs winding down my throat and into my chest were sharp and biting, but I managed a nod. "I have to go." If I didn't, I'd do something I might have regretted, and I didn't want to regret a single thing when it came to Julien.

At least not another one.

• • • • • • • • • •

I was in the middle of an intense session of staring at a wall when my doorbell rang. Laura answered it, and a moment later, she led Alley, Elena, Helen, and Zadie into the living room.

"We're here with the heartbreak cure," Elena announced.

"We're having a girls' night," Helen added.

"Long overdue," Zadie said, holding up a reusable shopping bag. "I have supplies."

I rubbed the grit from my eyes, offering them a weak smile. "Thank you for thinking of me. The thing is, I really don't want another hangover this week, so I'm going to have to pass."

A phantom ache passed through my skull from the memory of my last hangover.

Two days ago.

I did not want a repeat performance, even if the numbness of alcohol would have been a welcome reprieve.

Helen waved me off. "Pfft. I'm taking eighteen credits this semester. Getting drunk is a distant memory."

Alley leaned over the sofa and squeezed my cheeks. "We're going to get you on a sugar rush, my sweet little muffin head. Get your lazy ass into the kitchen and bake cookies with us."

"Cookies?" I mumbled around her hand.

Zadie waved her bag around. "You don't want to miss my cookies. They're almost better than sex."

Elena crossed her arms over her chest. "She doesn't lie—and that's saying a lot, given how...meticulous my boyfriend is with his hands. And his mouth. And his giant—"

Helen slammed her hands over her ears. "La, la, la. I do not want to hear another word about you and Lock rubbing your bodies together. That's like my brother and sister getting it on."

Elena rolled her eyes. "Need I remind you you were the one who brought our naked bodies into this? I was only going to mention Lachlan's giant, tender heart. Mind out of the gutter, floozy."

Alley let go of my face, only to take my hands. "Get up, lazy. Time to make the cookies."

• • • ● • ● • • •

An hour later, I stuffed my second chocolate chip cookie into my mouth. The chips were melty, and the outside edges were the right amount of crispness. Zadie was truly a goddess.

"Zadie, I love you," I cooed at her. "Marry me."

"Sure." She pointed at the piles of dishes in the sink. "But you're taking dish duty."

I picked up another cookie from the cooling rack Laura and I apparently owned. Who knew? "Worth the sacrifice."

We were gathered around the island in the kitchen. A batch had been made, and more were in various stages of prep. Elena was mostly supervising while nibbling on a cookie. Zadie was also supervising, but in a much more helpful way. Alley and Laura were rolling dough into perfect balls. And I, as I mentioned, was in the process of eating my weight in cookies.

Elena tore her attention from the action to look me over. "You know, if you want to rant about Julien, you can. Don't hold back because I'm friends with both of you."

"I don't want to rant," I told her.

Laura leaned into my side and kissed the top of my head. "Our beautiful Sera is sad."

Helen stopped mixing her dough. "Was he a dick to you? Theo was a major-league dick to me at the beginning of our relationship. I never thought I'd forgive him. But people change and surprise you. Rarely is it for the better. Lucky me, he was one of the rare ones."

My chest constricted, and I had trouble swallowing the cookie I was chewing. Finally, I got it down, but it tasted like sawdust.

"He's never been anything but wonderful to me. Well, there was one time he was a dick, but there were extenuating circumstances—" I pressed on the sides of my head. Even in those extenuating circumstances, he had texted me as my phantom to check in with me. He'd been struggling with his own turmoil, but he had put that aside to take care of me.

"He says he loves me."

"He does," Elena said nonchalantly. Like it was no big deal to be loved by Julien. It was a big deal. A massive one.

"You don't believe it." Zadie was soft all over, but the expression of understanding she gave me was like a bed of feathers. So comfortable and delicate, I could have sunk into her compassion and lived there happily. "If you don't believe it, is it even real?"

I winced at how hard she'd hit the nail right on its stupid head. I hadn't even told them why Julien and I were apart. Maybe a part of me wanted to protect him still. I didn't want any of them to look at him differently. Not when I still wasn't sure how I felt about him being my phantom. I was certain his deception would look even worse from the outside, and for reasons I couldn't quite articulate, I didn't want anyone looking at him like he was some kind of villain.

"I don't trust myself anymore. I never dated in high school, and when I got to college, I went out with this guy, Nate, who turned out to be a total monster. Luckily, Elena warned me away from him before I got too deep, but I hadn't seen him for who he was on my own. Then there was Seth. Beautiful, terrible Seth. I really thought I loved him and bent over backward to keep him, which was so, so stupid."

Laura palmed the top of my head. "Seth is sociopathically charming."

"Nate too." Elena snarled his name. "Julien is nothing like him."

"I know he isn't." I held her gaze, making sure she believed me. I would never compare Nate and Julien. Or Seth and Julien, for that matter. I was the common denominator here.

"It's just that...I want Julien so much, I can taste it, but I don't know if I can trust those feelings. What's real and what's wishful thinking?"

All my girls went quiet at that. What could they say? They could comfort me with cookies and support me with their experiences, but when it came down to it, it was me who had to take the risk. I had to be the one to decide if I could believe in us.

Right now, it seemed far-fetched that a man like Julien could truly love me in an honest, authentic, healthy way. Even as I thought it, I could practically hear my phantom telling me I wasn't allowed to think of myself as unworthy of everything good and right in the world.

I choked back a sob. I wanted to believe that.

Alley pounded on the counter. "Okay. Enough moping for all of us. We need music before this turns into the saddest party I've ever been to."

I had to laugh at that. "It isn't already?"

She waved her finger at me. "No, girl. I've been to some really tragic parties. I'm talking a singular bowl of chips and case of Bud for a hundred people. Yours might be sad, but at least there are cookies."

Zadie held up her mixing bowl. "Dozens of them."

Music kicked on, and Alley went into her automatic twerking position. Elena got behind her, grinding the air like a douchey dude at a club. The only difference was, El kept a respectful space between them. Laura watched with a raised brow, until Helen came over and smacked Elena hard on the ass.

"Stop hitting on a girl with a girlfriend. You have a man," Helen told her.

"Jealous?" Elena spun around. "You want some, Ortega?"

"Maybe I do, though I doubt you can keep up with me."

Helen shuffled closer to Elena, shimmying her shoulders. El took her by the waist and yanked her flush with her body. She slotted a knee between Helen's legs, and the two of them dropped low before working their way back up.

It was kind of hot. If Theo and Lock were here, their tongues would probably be rolling onto the ground.

Elena spotted me watching and waved me over to their side of the island.

"Get over here, Ellis. We have a little spot for you right in the middle," Elena called above the throbbing beat.

My first instinct was to say no, but I wanted to get a little lost from my instincts, so I danced my way over to them and got sucked into a Helen and Elena sandwich.

Elena was just as handsy as I'd expected, and Helen smelled like a field of wildflowers. They squished me between them, turning our dance into a moving hug. Both of them wrapped me in their arms, rocking me to the rhythm of the song.

"Smile, Sera!"

I turned my head, and Alley snapped a picture with my phone. Before putting it down, she tapped on the screen a few times, a devious smirk curling her lips. I almost asked what she was doing, but Elena spun me in a tight circle, replacing my questions with dizzying laughter.

They helped me let it all go. Spinning and dancing and screaming along with Taylor Swift songs. No decisions were made, but that was okay. I crawled into bed that night with a full belly and an even fuller heart. I was cracked but not broken.

Years ago, I would have taken a blade to my skin, telling myself it was to let out some of my pain, but really, it was a punishment. For not being pretty enough, smart enough, loveable enough, fitting in well enough.

For not being enough.

I couldn't keep punishing myself for just...being. This was who I was. That wasn't changing. It had taken me longer than most people, but I liked who I was. The problem was, I'd spent too long around people who'd tried to convince me to be someone else, and I'd gotten used to that.

Laura and Alley had taken to me as soon as we met, just as I'd taken to them. Helen, Zadie, and Elena had met me exactly where I was and folded me into their friend group without question.

But it was hard as hell to shake the ghosts of the past still very much present in my life. I was still bending over backward for Phe and my mother. I'd done it with Seth without thinking. I'd lost myself with him, and I was still recovering.

Which was why I couldn't rush back to Julien. I couldn't forgive him and sweep away his lies without really considering whether I was following the same pattern.

I picked up my phone to set my alarm before I went to sleep and noticed a few texts from Julien, who was no longer listed as

ThePhantom in my contacts. Against my better judgment, I opened it and saw he was replying to a text *I* had sent.

Freaking Alley.

She'd sent him the picture of me dancing with Elena and Helen, captioned "I'm not sitting around crying over you. You can suck it, baby boy." I would never have written something like that to him. I cringed at the thought of him reading it.

Julien: *Who has your phone?*

Despite myself, I had to bite back a grin. He knew me so well.

Julien: *Glad you're having fun, D.G. You deserve it. I'd never want you crying over me.*

Julien: *Remember when we danced? I'm not a dancer, but I'll always dance with you if you ask me to.*

Julien: *I miss you. I just need you to know that. I'll leave you alone now, like I promised. Have fun tonight, Sera.*

I touched his name on the screen and sighed.

"Good night, Phantom."

Chapter Twenty-nine

Julien

I hadn't expected the job my dad had offered me to be a cakewalk. For one, he was a dick. For another, he didn't get to where he was by paying his son to do busywork. The tasks his personal assistant, Miles, sent me—after profusely apologizing and begging my forgiveness—weren't anything strenuous but took hours of concentration to complete.

It couldn't have come at a better time.

Being chained to my computer was the only thing that got me through the week without breaking down Sera's door. Especially after that picture of her wedged between Helen and Elena. The words attached to it weren't hers. She might've thought I was a dick, but she wouldn't have put it that way. She'd remained radio silent after that, just as she'd said she would.

There was a tap on my open door. "Hey, you."

I looked up from my computer, finding Elena propped in the doorway. "Hey."

"You had the piano delivered. It looks good."

"Yeah. This morning."

Just like the job and the doctor, my dad had also come through with the piano. A weight had lifted off my chest the moment it was under the same roof as me again.

"Good. I'm glad you have it with you." She glanced behind her. "Lock and I are headed out. I just wanted to let you know about something going on tomorrow."

Groaning, I pushed my hair out of my face. "I'm not up for being social."

She rolled her eyes. "When are you ever?"

"Fair point."

"Tomorrow is Savage Day. Not your scene, I know, but I heard a little drummer girl will be performing at one on the green. I just thought you'd be interested." She shrugged and gave me a finger wave. "See you later, Phantom."

Fuck. Elena knew exactly what she was doing. I'd made a promise to give Sera time. Elena was going to make me break that promise, wasn't she? There was no way I could stay away.

• • • ● • ● • • •

I'd just gotten my concentration back when the front door rattled like a bomb had detonated. It wasn't just one boom, though, it was explosion after explosion.

Jerking to my feet, I grabbed my cane and left my room to check out what the fuck was going on. As I drew closer, I heard my name bellowed from the front porch, and I knew. I fucking knew. The confrontation I'd been hoping to avoid was about to come to fruition.

I yanked open the door as Amir prepared to pound on it again. I had to lean back so I didn't get knocked out by his right fist.

His face was mottled red. His eyes were black with fury. Marco stood behind him, pensive and silent.

"What the fuck, Julien?" Amir spit out. "What the actual fuck?"

I stood back, giving them room to come inside. Amir prowled in, his head swinging wildly before landing on the piano tucked in the corner of the living room. Marco followed him inside, kicking the door shut behind him.

"You're in trouble, kid," Marco muttered. "Big trouble."

Amir whirled around. "The fuck is this, Julien? You snuck your piano out of my house while everyone was in class, like...what? You think we wouldn't notice a big empty spot under the window?"

I lifted a shoulder. "Didn't want it to be a big thing. I didn't think you'd mind having some space freed up in your house."

The tendons in the sides of Amir's neck stood out like thick ropes, and his complexion went violently purple. I'd seen him angry. Homicidal even. I'd never once felt the full force of his rage directed at me.

"So, that's it?" He swept his arm in front of him in a savage arc. "Almost twenty years of friendship and we're done without a fucking conversation? You cut all ties with me?"

"No." I shook my head. "I wanted my piano. My dad paid for it—"

"Your dad?" He pressed his hands to the sides of his head. "You're talking to your goddamn dad?"

"Not by choice. I needed help with my insurance. While I was there, I asked for a job and the piano."

"Fuck, man. You're working for your dad?" Marco uttered.

"Need the money," I said.

Amir shook his head. "I would've given you the money. I would have moved the piano. Anything you needed, I would have given you."

"I know you would have. You've taken care of me for as long as I can remember. But this, the insurance, my tuition—that's my dad's job. He wasn't any kind of parent as you know, but his pockets are deep. He got me in with his doctor, got me scheduled for surgery on my knee—"

"Fuck that," Amir seethed. "I don't wanna hear about your deadbeat, piece-of-shit dad playing the hero."

My brow dropped. "In no way do I see him as the hero. He is still the same deadbeat he's always been. But shit, if I'm gonna have a rich dad, I might as well get all I can from him."

Amir's head lowered. He stayed silent as his chest heaved.

Marco squeezed my shoulder. "All of this is uncool, Jules. A conversation would have sufficed about the piano. You sneaking it out speaks louder than all the words."

"There was no hidden message. I wanted the piano. Obviously, I went about it wrong—"

"You're a liar." Amir finally looked at me again. "You're lying to us. You wanted to cut ties and did it the easiest way possible. A year ago, you would've talked to me about going to see your dad. Hell, you would have taken me with you."

"Sera went with me," I said.

He blinked hard. "You have a girl you care about enough to take to see your dad and I don't even know her. What the fuck happened to us, Julien? You're my brother. Closer than my brother. And all that's just...gone. It's gone, and I have no idea why because you won't talk to me. You talk to Marco. You talk to Lock and Theo and Helen—every-fucking-one except me. I'm not stupid enough not to take it personally. So, you gotta explain to me what the fuck I did to make you shut me out."

I didn't want to do this. I'd been avoiding this confrontation and had planned to keep on avoiding it for as long as possible—forever, hopefully.

Marco's grip tightened on my shoulder. "You gotta talk, man. It's time."

No matter how I felt about it, it was happening.

"You look at me like you wish you'd died that night."

Amir started, his limbs going stiff. "I don't."

"You do. You can barely look at me without wincing. Like my scars remind you of your failures or something. I can't stand it. I don't want to be around you because that look you give me reminds *me* of how fucking grotesque I am now. Like, to you, I'm so ugly, so messed up, you'd rather be dead than see me living in this body. You wanted to know, there it is. That's why I don't want to be around you, Amir."

"Grotesque?" Marco rounded on me, cutting me off from Amir, who'd staggered back into the piano bench. "That's what you think of yourself?"

I nodded sharply. "That's what I know."

Marco clicked his tongue against his teeth. "Maybe you were just too pretty before all this if you consider yourself grotesque now. You have scars now, sure, but chicks dig scars. Look at you, with a pretty little mama of your own. You think Sera's gonna stoop to be with a dude who's grotesque? She's nice, but not that nice, man."

"It's how I feel. Like I'm trapped in someone else's body. I don't know who I am on the outside anymore."

Intellectually, I knew Marco was right. I didn't look like a science experiment gone bad. Small children didn't scream at the sight of me. Sera wasn't superficial, but I really doubted she would have been kissing me and letting me touch her if she thought I was disgusting. But I was still trying to wrap my head around the way I looked.

It was impossible to explain to someone who hadn't been there. Waking up one day and not recognizing your own reflection was the biggest mindfuck there was. So, yeah, I felt grotesque. I wore a stranger's face, lived in a stranger's body, and I had to accept it.

Marco's dark gaze swept over me. We hadn't been friends for as long as Amir and I—he'd started coming around in middle school and never left—but our roots ran deep. When he pulled me in for a hug, my arms went around him automatically, and I shuddered in relief. His embrace was tight and said more than words could. We were cool. He heard me, understood why I was pulling away, but he wasn't going to let it happen.

When he broke away, Amir had crossed the room, closer, but still keeping his distance.

"There were times, while you were recovering, when I wanted to take your place." Amir's eyes held steady on me. There was none of his usual pity or guilt. "I would take everything you've gone through onto myself if I could, but I'm so fucking grateful you put yourself in front of me that night. It's easy for me to say I would have done the same for you a thousand times over, but you actually did it. You put my life before yours, took the hit intended for me, and I don't know what to do with that."

"You would have done it for me." My words came out gruff, but I didn't doubt them. "It's not about that."

"I know." His head bobbed. "I hear what you're saying, and I admit it. I've been carrying guilt on my shoulders since that night. It's my fault you were even in the position to take that hit. I thought I was keeping you separate from that life, but that was my ego. You wouldn't have been there that night if you had been separate."

With his head in his hands, he paced the length of the living room.

"And shit, I don't know how not to feel guilty about that. It burns me up from the inside out, Julien. When I look at you, maybe I do wince. Maybe I do. But the only fucking times I see you anymore are when you're struggling. After rehab, at the gym. When your physical limitations are getting to you. When you're sweating from pain and exertion. You expect that shit not to affect me when it's my fault it happened? I'm not a robot. It affects me down to my bones. I don't wish I was dead. My life is way too fucking good now to wish it away, and I have you to thank for that. But I wish I could take it all from you. If there was a way, I would."

He stopped and looked at me, absolutely ravaged. Amir didn't show vulnerability. He wasn't that guy, except maybe with Zadie. The fact that he was so nakedly torn apart made my already weak knees verge on collapsing.

"You can't take it. This is who I am now. That night is a part of me. If you want to be around me more, you're going to have to get over it."

Amir barked a laugh. "Get over it? That's what you want me to do?"

"Fuck yes." I pressed my palm to my chest. "This happened to *me*. You want to help me, be here for me, then get over it! That guilt on your shoulders is only pushing you further and further away from me. I can't help you hold it, I've got my own shit to bear. So find a way to get over it or accept that we're never gonna be like we were before."

His jaw went rigid. "I will never accept that."

I hit my chest. "Then get over it. This isn't about you anymore. This is about me."

Marco shook his head. "That's not fair, man. We're the ones who've always had your back. You think you being hurt doesn't hurt us?"

"I'm sure it does. But that needs to be processed privately. I'm telling you right now, I can't take on your pain along with mine. That's my line in the sand. You need support in any other area of your life? I'm there and always will be. But I will not be your shoulder to cry on about my own fucking circumstances. That's not how this works."

Marco let out a jagged breath. "You're an asshole. I see your point, and I hear it, but you're still an asshole."

"I know."

Amir had stopped moving. His hands were braced on the back of his neck, his head tipped to the ceiling. A distant clock ticked as seconds went by.

Finally, he looked at me again. "You think you could have said this to me, maybe six months ago?"

"No."

He raised an eyebrow. "No?"

"No. I wasn't in a place to say any of this. I barely left my room. It's taken me this long to feel like I'm a human being again, not just a combination of broken parts."

His face contorted with a kind of pain I recognized all too well. Chest rising and falling, he braced a hand on the wall. "I kept thinking I was gonna get a call that you were gone. I asked Elena to tell me if she thought you were close to leaving. She told me it was easier between the two of you because there was no baggage."

"That's true. I wasn't nice to her, and she was a bitch right back."

He brought his fist up to his mouth. "I guess I should have tried being a bitch to you too."

"Might've worked." I hit my cane against the ground. "Amir, look...I thought about leaving. You don't get that close to dying without thinking about it on the regular. But I never made a plan or anything. I didn't get that far. I haven't had any thoughts like that in a while now."

It turned out, helping Sera work through her darkness had gotten through to me too. I should have told her that. Maybe she would have understood.

"Shit," Marco muttered as he walked away from me. "Didn't know it had gotten that bad."

"Half of my body was broken. It was bad. But I'm not there anymore."

Amir raised his chin, searching me for answers. "Your girl?"

"Sera's the best thing that has ever happened to me. Knowing her has definitely helped me." I shook my head. "Don't know if she's my girl anymore, though."

"Zadie said the girls made cookies together." He straightened, moving toward me. "She said Sera doesn't know if she can trust her feelings for you. She said you love her."

I cocked my head. "Were you supposed to tell me any of that?"

He lifted a shoulder, his mouth curving slightly. "Probably not. If you tell Zadie, I'll smother you in your sleep."

"I won't tell her. I'd never screw that up for you."

"Appreciate it." He raised a brow. "You gonna tell us why the girl you love doesn't trust you?"

I shook my head. "Nah. I know what I did and what I need to do. Believe me when I tell you I'm working on it."

"She's treating you right?" Marco asked.

"Didn't you hear the part about her being the best thing that ever happened to me? I was the one who screwed up, not Sera."

Amir stopped right in front of me. "You said her name, you know. When you were all drugged up, you kept talking about Sera."

Marco chuckled, wagging a finger at Amir. "You just jogged my memory. This kid could barely keep his eyes open but he forced me to go get him a new phone."

"Same Sera?" Amir asked.

"Same one."

Marco covered his mouth, cackling. "Oh, shit. Now I know this is a good story. You're gonna have to spill this thing, Jules. I'm not leaving until you do."

I backhanded his shoulder. "Really? You want to braid each other's hair and talk about feelings now?"

He rubbed his cropped hair. "I'd like to see you try." Then he flicked the ends of my hair. "Now, this hair, I could braid. Can't believe you called yourself grotesque with this luscious mane."

I dodged out of his way, laughing. "Get your filthy hands off my mane. My girl is the only one allowed to braid it."

That had Amir laughing. "Now, I know it's serious. You let your girl braid your hair? Damn, I'm gonna need to have a sit-down with this girl if she's my future sister-in-law." He slung his arm around my shoulders, as natural as it had always been. "First, I'm gonna need to hear the story of how you met your kids' mother."

Marco flung himself over the back of the couch, landing with his arms behind his head, ankles crossed in front of him. "Yes, Julien. Do tell. And don't leave out any details."

Amir grinned at me.

I returned his grin without a second thought.

All wasn't right. We weren't back to where we once were. Only time would tell if we could be.

But I didn't give a shit about what was ahead of us. This, right here, was big. Monumental. For the moment, the two men in the room, my brothers, were all that mattered.

Chapter Thirty

Julien

Beckett Savage: *I knew you were a liar.*

I woke up to that very blunt and confusing message from my little brother. It'd been two weeks since I saw him last, and while I'd been meaning to text him, life had happened and the text hadn't.

I was getting the impression Beckett had gotten tired of waiting.

Me: *What's up, Beck?*

Beckett Savage: *Send me your address. I need to get out of the house. I'm coming over.*

Me: *Just like that?*

Beckett Savage: *Yes. Just like that. I obviously can't count on you, so I'm taking matters into my own hands. Send me your address and I'll be there in an hour.*

Me: *I've got plans today.*

Beckett Savage: *That's good, I won't be bored. Text the address.*

Little shit. So why was I doing what he said and sending him my address? Probably because he made me laugh, and somewhere deep, deep, *deep* down, I wanted a little brother. Maybe not this one in particular, but beggars couldn't be choosers. Beckett would've chosen a different big brother too, no doubt.

• • • • • • • •

"So, we're stalking Sera?"

As promised, Beckett had shown up in an Uber an hour after giving him my address. He walked around my house, declared it, "Okay for what it is," then pretty much ordered me to take him out for a late breakfast.

While eating, he then demanded to know where Sera was, when he could see her, and why she wasn't with us. I had to break the news that Sera and I were going through something rough and she'd asked for space.

Which I was giving her. But also not since I was going to watch her drum. With Beckett in tow. Which might have worked in my favor since I could put the blame on him if I had to.

"It's not stalking. We'll be low key about it, give her space like she asked," I told him.

"How's she going to forgive you if you give her space? I think that's a bad decision."

He gave me the side-eye as we walked across campus. We were bypassing all the other activities going on for Savage Day, heading straight for the green so we didn't miss any of the drumline performance.

"Do you think I want to give her space? I don't, but I have to respect her wishes."

He tsked. "If she was my girlfriend, I'd be doing anything to get her back. Space sounds like a bad idea. She'll forget why she likes you and maybe think how easy it is to live without you. You should disrespect her wishes before it's too late."

This kid was thirteen, and he was voicing every fear I'd been having. Sera's life *was* probably easier without me in it. It annoyed the hell out of me that Beckett recognized that.

"You don't know what you're talking about," I groused.

"Maybe not. But she seemed cool. Not many people are. So I want you to win her back. That's all I'm saying."

I glanced at him. "I want to win her back too."

"Then what are you going to do about it?"

That was the real question, wasn't it?

By the time we made it to the green, a wide lawn in the center of campus, a crowd had gathered around where the drummers were setting up. I easily zeroed in on Sera, who was laughing with the guy beside her. Stefan, I remembered.

Fuck Stefan.

Nice guy. Fuck him for getting a laugh from my girl. He didn't deserve it.

"Julien! Get over here!" Elena called out from the other side of the crowd. She knew exactly what she was doing too, because Sera stopped laughing and turned her head to find me.

I smiled and nodded.

Her smile wasn't as wide, but she gave me one and waved to Beckett.

I had a mountain to climb with her.

We joined Elena's group. They were all there. Amir and I fist-bumped. Beckett gave him a hard stare, and it didn't get any softer when Marco rubbed the top of his head.

"Little brother," Marco cried. "What are you, seven, eight?"

Beckett glared at him. "I'm thirteen."

Marco smirked. "Small for your age, right?"

"Dumb for your age, right?" Beckett shot back.

Amir cackled behind his hand. "Oh damn, this kid has fangs. I like it."

Beckett turned his glare on him. "I heard you let Julien snuggle you like a teddy bear. Cute story."

I thwacked the back of his head. "Time to shut up."

Amir grinned at me. "You've been telling tales about our childhood, huh?"

I glanced behind me at Sera, who was concentrating with all her might on her drum set. "It wasn't me."

"This one's thirteen too." Helen had her arm slung around a girl who was her mini-me. Somewhere in the back of my mind, I remembered she had a sister she took care of part time. I'd never met her, but there was no question this was the girl. She even had a skateboard in her hands. "This is Luciana. Make friends, children."

"Be nice," I murmured to Beckett, who had gone still as he stared at Luciana.

The first beat of a drum turned my attention away from my brother to the girl I loved. The drummers were in a semicircle, Sera's position near the middle. When I decided to come here, I'd been planning to get lost in the crowd so she didn't notice me. That plan flew out the window the moment Elena yelled my name, so I stood front and center, the best seat in the house.

Like at the party, Sera's drums were on stands. She danced while she played. Beautiful. So fucking beautiful. The rhythm resonated in my chest. I couldn't rip my eyes off her, even when Beckett said something about her being really cool. I nodded, but my tongue was tied. If this was how Amir felt about Zadie, no wonder he'd turned his life upside down to keep her. I'd turn the *world* upside down if it meant getting to have Sera.

They played for ten, maybe fifteen minutes. Not nearly long enough. If I'd been more cognizant, I would have taken my phone out to record it so I could watch it back over and over. And over. But I'd been stupefied through the whole thing. A slave to this girl.

When it was over, our friends clapped and yelled. Her grin was pure light, blinding and life giving all at once. She said something to Stefan, then jogged over to our group.

"Hey," she said softly to me.

"Hey. You were great," I replied.

Her cheeks flushed. "Thank you. Thanks for coming. I didn't know you'd be here."

Beckett pushed in front of me, and I'd never wanted to murder a child before that moment. "That was pretty cool," he said. "I know you didn't want Julien to come, but I appreciate that he chose not to listen or I would have missed it."

Her eyes flicked to mine, then she laughed. "Beckett! You're here."

"I am. I had to force Julien to hang out with me. I guess I'll have to force you to hang out with me too. This is doing wonders to my fragile self-esteem, by the way."

Still laughing, she hugged my brother. And yep, I was definitely going to commit fratricide.

"I'm overjoyed by your presence, Beckett Savage. I've never been happier a day in my life. I'm pretty sure rainbows are about to shoot out of my eyes like laser beams, but you know, the happy kind."

He pulled away from her, trying to bite back a smile. "I didn't consent to a hug." He scuffed his shoe on the ground. "But I guess it was okay."

Then Sera went around hugging every fucking one except me. Even Marco got a fucking hug. Beckett smirked at me as it happened.

Little shit.

"I have to go pack up." Sera tucked her hair behind her ear, but it popped right back out. "Thank you for coming, guys."

Helen grabbed her shoulders. "We're having a cookout on the deck. I've been promising Luc she could come to one of our deck parties for ages, so it's happening. I'll be personally offended if you don't show." Helen pointed to me and Beckett. "You guys too. Then Luc won't be stuck with all old people."

Luciana rolled her eyes. "Hells...you're not *that* old."

"Thanks, brat." Helen let go of Sera to sling her arm around her sister again. "You guys are coming, correct? The only answer is yes."

Sera glanced at Beckett then me. I nodded to her. Her mouth quirked. "Sure, I'll be there," she said.

"We're coming too," Beckett rushed out. I couldn't help noticing his focus had shifted to Luciana now, but she was more interested in her skateboard.

I locked eyes with Sera. Standing this close, feeling what I did, it took everything within me not to reach out for her.

"We'll see you there."

Her cheeks pinkened. "Good."

Good.

Maybe I did have a chance.

Chapter Thirty-one

Seraphina

I WAS RELAXED FOR the first time in a week. Truly relaxed, boneless, in the warm, early spring evening on my friends' deck. I'd eaten a lot of good food, had a couple drinks, played a game or two of badminton, and laughed a lot.

And as the day wore on, I'd found myself drifting closer and closer to Julien until I wound up in the chair beside him. He was holding a beer, casually kicked back, his long legs stretched out in front of him. I was curled up, sideways in my seat, sipping on a hard seltzer.

Beckett had just gone home in an Uber, and Helen's sister, Luciana, had gotten bored of us old people and went inside to hang out in Helen's room—a.k.a. use her phone in peace. So it was quieter now. Low music humming in the background. A steady din of conversation. I was half listening, half caught up in thinking about what I wanted to say to Julien.

I turned my head at the same time he did. Or maybe he'd already been looking at me.

"Hey," he said.

"Hey," I replied.

"It's not Sunday yet, but..." He raised a brow.

I unfolded myself from my chair and put my drink down on the table. "Let's go."

We snuck away without much fanfare and made our way next door to Julien's empty house. I noted the piano in the living room, and my stomach twisted with sadness that I hadn't been here when it was delivered. I'd missed that moment with him.

"The piano's here," I said.

"Yeah. It was delivered yesterday."

I looked at him over my shoulder. "Are you happy it's here?"

"Relieved." He raised his chin to the hallway leading to his bedroom. "Do you want to go in there or stay out here?"

"Your room is good."

The last time I was here, I wasn't sure I'd ever return. But when I stepped inside, it felt right. Julien had cleaned up, but the patches on the wall hadn't been painted over yet. That felt right too. We weren't quite the ragged mess we'd been when I left last time, but we were still nowhere near the same as before.

I sat down on the side of Julien's bed. He took his desk chair, pulling it close enough that our knees were almost touching.

"I'm sorry if my coming today crossed a boundary I shouldn't have crossed," he said.

I shook my head. "I don't care about that. I'm glad you were there. Even more glad you spent the time with Beckett."

His nose twitched. "He told me if I don't win you back, you're going to realize how easy your life is without me."

"It's not easier or harder without you, but it was better with you in it. I've missed you this week. Even though I saw you in class, that almost made it worse. Actually, it did make it worse. I could convince myself I was okay, then one look at you, and I had to force myself not to go to you. I really needed the time to think about what happened with a clear head."

"Did your girls help you sort it out?" he asked.

"No. They were there for me, but I kept most of it to myself. I don't think anyone outside of us will really understand."

He shifted in his chair, his brow pinching. "I told Elena and Lock. Not all of it. I'd never divulge the things you—"

I touched his knee. "I know you wouldn't, and I don't mind that you told them. I kind of figured you'd told Elena." I breathed out a sigh. "Can I tell you what I've been thinking?"

"Please."

I left my hand on his knee, because it was somewhat grounding, but also, it had been too long since we'd touched and I couldn't bring myself to pull away.

"There's a big part of me that's relieved you're my phantom. The things we shared, the feelings, the experiences—those were important. You saw my darkness and helped lead me out of it. And we formed this bond I don't think I could explain to someone else. For a while, when you and I were getting closer in person, and I was telling *you*, Julien, all the things I'd shared with my phantom, I felt guilty."

I waved my hand around, grimacing. "I'm not sure if this makes sense."

"I think it does," he said gruffly. "You had feelings for what you thought were two men."

"No." I was adamant about that. "No, the bond with my phantom wasn't romantic in any sense. It was like two soldiers who'd been through war together. And I was going to have to explain that to you eventually. In thinking about it, I probably should have told you I'd been texting another man during the time we were together."

The skin around his eyes tightened. "As the person on the receiving end of your texts, there wasn't anything inappropriate, Sera. Nothing to feel guilt over."

"Well, I do." I rubbed his knee a little. "I'm relieved I don't have to explain what my phantom meant to me, because it was *you*. You're the one I'm connected to. You're the only one who has seen inside my darkness. You stood on my battlefield with me."

"I always will. Always, Sera."

His hand came down over mine, lightly at first. When I didn't pull away, he curled his fingers to hold me. I breathed out something like a laugh.

"I should have known it was you, Julien. Now that I do, I feel so stupid. You have two little holes in your ear." I tapped my lobe, and he winced.

"I'm an asshole. I took the earrings out so you wouldn't recognize them from the pictures I'd sent."

"That was definitely a dick move," I agreed. "But I look at you now, and I'm perplexed I didn't know. Of course you're the guy from the party. You couldn't be anyone else. And it's not just how you look, though there is that. It's the way you've been so careful with me since the second we met. The way you make me laugh and feel safe. How you texted me to make sure I was okay after you were grumpy with me in person. Of course you're my phantom. How did I miss that?"

"I was actively hiding it from you, Sera." He squeezed my hand. "You don't know what it does to me to know I've made you feel safe."

"You do." I tilted my head. "You were the one to convince me to tell you about the fake dating."

Julien's expression grew sheepish. "I can't even be sorry for that. I know I should be, but I'm not."

"Because you wanted to be near me."

He nodded. "I wanted to be near you, even if it was fake for you."

I sucked in a breath. "But when I asked you if it was real, you avoided answering."

"Not because being with you isn't the most real thing I've ever had in my life. Never because of that."

"Then why?"

"I owed you the truth, Seraphina. I couldn't let myself believe we were real and going to last past the terms of your bet until I told you everything. You were right when you said we were built on a lie. I swear to all that is holy I was going to tell you everything so we could build on something true and solid. I kept finding excuses not to, but it had to happen, and I knew there was no avoiding it much longer."

I swept my eyes over him. I'd been hungry for this all week. I adored this man. I really did. And I couldn't get enough of looking at him. His beautiful stormy eyes and crooked lips made my stomach flutter. His long fingers wrapped around mine caused a knot to lodge in my throat.

"My trust is shaken."

As hungry for him as I was, I had to remind us both of that.

"I know it is and it kills me because I never wanted to be that person for you. I'm *not* that person. My book is wide fucking open with you. I have no secrets, no deceptions, no half-truths. It's easy for me to tell you that, but I get it'll be hard for you to believe now that I've rocked your trust in me. I get that, and I'm willing to do the work to prove I'm exactly who you think I am. I'm the soldier who went to battle with you, and I'm the guy who stares at your legs in class."

"Julien," I whispered.

"I don't deserve you, but I want you with every broken part of me."

I shook my head. "You're not broken."

"I am, baby. But I'll be as whole as I can for you."

"Am I broken?"

He reared back. "No. Why would you—no. You're not."

"Then neither are you. You're my Julien, and you're incredible. I refuse to hear you talk badly about yourself. How is it you spent so much time building me up and showing me I was worthy of everything good but you can't do the same for yourself?"

He opened his mouth like he had the audacity to argue with me, but I held my hand up.

"No, it doesn't matter. I'll stand on your battlefield with you until you see what's real and not what your mind is telling you."

His mouth closed, and he stared at me with something that looked a lot like awe and wonder.

"I love you, Seraphina. That is the truest thing I've ever told you."

"I believe you."

I wasn't quite ready to say it back, but I couldn't stop myself from climbing into his lap, my legs straddling his. He wrapped his arms around me with a fierceness that took my breath away, and I shoved my face in his neck, exactly where I wanted to be.

"Jesus, fuck," he murmured into my hair. "Tell me this means I get to keep you."

With a choked giggle, I nodded, my eyes squeezed shut. "You get to keep me as long as you keep your promises too."

"Always, baby. There's never going to be a promise I make to you that I won't be able to keep."

I lifted my head, finding his eyes shining back at me. Leaning forward, I touched my lips to each of his eyelids, my breath stuttering at the tears I found clinging to his eyelashes. I continued my tour of kisses along his cheekbones and jaw, finding a home on his lips.

We stayed there, holding each other, and kissed for so long, the room swirled and his breath became mine. Then we moved to the bed, clothes falling along the way. Our skin reunited first. Imperfection meeting imperfection flawlessly. And then I opened myself to him, and he fitted himself inside me.

We were chest to chest, face to face, riding lapping waves of pleasure and need. Lips were fused while hands were ever moving. He held my breasts, and I raked his back. I raised my leg higher on his hip. He cupped my ass to pull me closer.

"I'm not going to lose you again," he vowed.

"I wasn't lost." My fingertips touched his lips. "I was always yours."

"That's right, you were. Always."

I nipped his bottom lip. "And you're mine."

"Only yours, my dragon girl."

"My beautiful phantom."

That night went on and on. Napping, snuggling, and waking up reaching for each other. Like we'd been apart for a year, not a handful of days. But maybe this was the first time we were *really* together. There was nothing fake or pretend between us. We were finally our barest selves. Guilt and lies were dead and buried, leaving only us.

And for tonight, that was more than enough.

CHAPTER THIRTY-TWO

JULIEN

SERA STREAKED BY ME, squealing as I grabbed for her. "No, no, no!" she cried, darting in the opposite direction.

"You're not getting away," I called after her. My cane hit the marble floor. *Clip, clip, clip.* I followed her down the hall where she'd disappeared. If she thought I wasn't going to chase her to the ends of the earth, she hadn't been paying attention. I may not have been as fast, but I was fucking determined.

I pushed open the door, and there I found my Sera kneeling in the center of her bed, colorful toys laid out around her.

My mouth twitched, and blood surged into my cock. "My little dragon wants to experiment?"

She nodded. "I want you to pick."

A few days after we were good again, Sera asked me to stay with her at her parents' house during spring break. She tried to sell me on it by telling me they'd be away the whole time and we'd have the place to ourselves—and it was a couple blocks off the beach. I hadn't needed any of that. I said yes unequivocally. Sera was going to be there, and that was all I had to hear.

That was a week ago, and it turned out, there was something to be said for a huge, empty house by the beach. Sera spent the days in her bikini, and we fucked whenever and wherever the mood struck.

Crossing the room, I studied the toys she had for me to choose from. We'd started another scientific experiment: which sex toys makes Sera come the hardest. She'd already had a little collection, and we'd bought a few more together. Perks of finally having a job—buying my girlfriend all the vibrators she wanted.

I picked up the little glass plug with a rosebud on the end. "This one. I want to hear how loud you scream with this in your ass while I fuck your pretty pussy."

Her cheeks flamed, and she bit down on her swollen lips. We'd been leisurely making out on the patio for the last hour when she'd hopped up and ran from me.

"I want that too," she rasped. "Please."

Her bathing suit came off with a few pulls of strings, then she was spread out on white sheets, smelling like the ocean and sunshine and looking like my dream come true. I buried my face between her thighs, getting lost in her taste while I teased her with the plug.

Her fingers wove through my hair, holding the sides of my head like she always did. It was so gentle and sweet, even as she rocked her pussy against my mouth and begged for more.

While she was begging, I slowly, carefully pushed the lubed plug into her backside. She went still, panting hard, so I sucked on her clit to distract her from the new feeling.

"Oh, Jules, that's weird."

"Mmmhmm. Good, weird?"

She exhaled, then looked down at me between her legs. "You're so hot like that."

I laughed and gave her clit another swipe. "You didn't answer me. Good or bad?" Then I tugged gently on the plug while I flattened my tongue on her clit, and she moaned.

"Good, so good," she answered.

I licked her until she was shaking, writhing, yanking my hair to keep me in place. Her legs vibrated, clamping around my head, and her back arched. I loved the way Sera came. It wasn't small and delicate. She came loud, and full bodied, like she felt every single second of it in every part of her.

"That's my girl." Rising to my feet, I dragged her to the side of the bed and flipped her over. Then I gave her ass a smack. "Is my beautiful girl ready for more?"

"Yeah." She peered over her shoulder. "Always."

I wedged a pillow between her hips and the mattress, getting her at the right angle for me to take her like this. Then I spread her cheeks apart so I could see all of her. The gleaming gem in her tight hole, the swollen seam beneath it, her smooth, thick thighs, still quivering.

I was dizzy from the sight of her, and my cock was so swollen, I couldn't think straight. Sliding into slick heat didn't help me think. If anything, the moment I was fully inside her, she became my entire world where thoughts weren't required. The plug made her slightly tighter. She was wet beyond belief. And this position…fuck, she looked pretty, always, but seeing her like this really did me in.

I loved this girl beyond comprehension, desired her to the point of distraction.

"You're beautiful, Dragon," I told her.

She reached for my hand, pressing it against her hip. The skin that had once been a source of shame was where I held her and pulled her close.

She gave me a slow, sultry smile over her shoulder. "Do whatever you want with me. I'm yours."

I tried to go slow. This wasn't my first or even second time having her today. I should have been able to stretch it out. But Sera's head was turned to the side, so I could see the languid, euphoric smile curling her lips. And she was pushing back, fucking herself on my cock while holding on to the hand gripping her hip. It was too much. I was in over my head, lost to what she gave me—what she did to me.

"Oh shit, Sera. You feel too good, baby. Too damn good." I played with the plug, trying like hell to make this good for her, but Jesus Christ, I was losing my mind.

"I'm going to come again," she said. "Keep going. Just like that."

And I did, because she'd asked, and I'd always give her what she asked for. As soon as I felt her tightening around me and her cries turned into drawn-out whines of pleasure, I gave in and fucked her as hard and deep as both our bodies would allow.

My fingers dug into her hips, her hand tightened around mine, then I let go of the pressure, erupting inside her with molten ropes of my release.

Completely spent, we lay on the bed. Sera was sprawled on my chest, my fingers trailing down the length of her spine.

"I don't think I can go back to real life after this," she murmured.

I kissed the top of her head. "This is real." Then I let out a long exhale. "I get it, though. One day, I'm going to buy you a house so I can fuck you everywhere."

She slapped at my chest. "That's why you're going to buy me a house? Please do put that on your loan application. 'Reason for loan: Domicile for girlfriend fucking.' I think you'll be approved."

"Thank you. I think so too."

She giggled, then propped herself up on her hands. "Carson's going to expect me to break up with you when we get back. I'm not going to do it. I won't even pretend to do it."

I touched the pinch between her eyebrows. "You're worried, though."

Her nose wrinkled. "I feel like such a bitch for even caring about being drum captain at this point. I have you. I shouldn't ask for anything more. But I really, *really* don't want Katie to have it."

"And you really, *really* want it."

She nodded slowly. "Yeah, I do. It's been my goal ever since I joined marching band in high school."

"Then you'll have it. Fuck Carson. Fuck Katie. Stefan told me you were a shoo-in."

Her eyes rolled. "Stefan's great, but he also smokes a *lot* of weed. I don't know if I can really count on his read of the situation." She pecked my chin. "But it's okay. Whatever happens, I'll accept it. Just know, I might be extra needy and require lots of hugs."

"I think I can manage that." I pushed her hair back and cupped the back of her head. "You're going to have that position, baby."

"If only you could be in charge of voting."

"If only."

· · · · ●· ●· ● · · ·

We didn't spend every second of spring break fucking. I still had a job to do, so I worked on my laptop in the early morning and sometimes in the afternoon. Sera either slept in or went for runs on the beach while I was busy.

I knew this was somewhat of a daydream. Even when we graduated and had the money to get our own place, we weren't going to have leisurely days like this. Not a lot of them at least. But damn if this didn't feel like a sneak peek into our future together. It blew my mind that I could picture that happening.

Miles had sent me a stack of résumés to sort through. My dad's company liked to hire new graduates for entry-level positions, and they always received more applications than they could handle. It was my job to weed out the ones with absolutely no potential and set aside the most qualified. They weren't all from Savage U, but some were, and interestingly enough, I recognized a few names, which gave me an idea.

Sera burst through the front door, tearing my attention from my computer. She was red faced and wheezing, sweat pricking her forehead.

"Jules—she's coming."

I got up from the table I'd been working at and crossed the open living room. Sera met me in the middle, gripping my biceps.

"Run." Her eyes rounded with alarm.

"Hate to tell you, but running isn't my thing. What's going on?"

"Phe…Ophelia is coming. My mom texted while I was on the beach. Phe and her fiancé are coming to the house to spend the day at the beach. They were just going to show up and surprise us, but my mom thought it was better to give us fair warning."

Concerned at how frantic Sera seemed, my eyebrows lowered. "Okay. Your sister's coming. Do you want to leave? Or for me to leave?"

She shook her head, then nodded. "I don't know. I don't really want to see her, and I *really* don't want you to have to meet her and deal with her bitchtasticness. But she's, like, fifteen minutes away, so I don't think we can clear out before she gets here." Her forehead fell against my chest. "Jules...help."

New people weren't my favorite thing. I would have to go through the whole ordeal of them reacting to what I looked like, and from what I'd heard, I couldn't count on Ophelia to be subtle.

But this was inevitable. It helped that I was in a good, relaxed mental state, fairly confident I could handle whatever this woman had to bring.

"It's fine, baby. Let's go get cleaned up and presentable." I took her hand in mine and kissed her knuckles. "And make sure we put away the butt plug."

She groaned, falling against me. "Promise me you'll still want me even if this is a disaster."

"Promise."

Through narrowed eyes, she examined my expression. I could almost hear her remembering me telling her I'd never make a promise I couldn't keep. This one was easy as hell to make.

• • • • • • • • • •

Ophelia was the antithesis of her sister. While Sera was bright and out loud, Ophelia was muted and subdued. She shook my hand limply and gave Sera a half-hearted hug. If the two of them hadn't resembled each other in a skewed kind of way, I'd question if they were actually related.

The upside was, she barely looked at me. There was no shock and horror at my scars. In this instance, I was fine with being beneath her notice.

Michael, the fiancé, seemed okay. Preppy, and older—maybe thirtyish—he gave Sera and me both pats on the back then went to grab a beer from the fridge, asking what everyone else wanted to drink along his way.

Ophelia walked around the living room, straightening pictures and fluffing pillows.

"I'm surprised you guys aren't having a rager. I half expected the place to be trashed when I arrived," she said.

"The rager was yesterday," Sera shot back. "Did your invitation get lost?"

Michael snapped his fingers. "Damn. I think it did. It's been a while since I trashed a house. Oh well, maybe next time."

Ophelia whirled around on her fiancé. "Do you think trashing my parents' house is funny?"

He shrugged. "It is when the house isn't actually trashed. Relax, Phe. That's what everyone else is doing. Who wants to go to the beach?"

Sera folded her arms over her chest. "I think we'll pass. You two have fun. We'll try not to destroy my childhood home while you're gone."

Ophelia huffed. "Don't tell me you're still mad at me about the bridesmaid situation. I thought you understood. It's not like you'd enjoy being a bridesmaid anyway."

"I'm not mad, and I never was. Embarrassed, yes. Disappointed, of course. But not mad, and that's not why I'm skipping the beach. I got too much sun yesterday so I'm going to stay inside today."

"It sounds like you're mad," Ophelia muttered as she picked up her beach bag. "Fine. Be bums. Michael and I are going to soak up the sun. We'll be back in a couple hours and we can have dinner together."

They disappeared a few minutes later, and silence rang out in the house. There wasn't anything to say, not really, so I took Sera in my arms and held her tight.

"That's my sister," she whispered.

"Nothing about her surprised me." I kissed her forehead. "Should we make a beer run for Michael?"

She snuffed a laugh against my shoulder. "He's not a functioning alcoholic. He became an alcoholic to function." She peered up at me. "Sure you don't want to run?"

I shook my head. "Told you, D.G. Running isn't my thing."

There wasn't any way I'd be leaving Sera to deal with her family alone. Those days were done.

Chapter Thirty-three

Seraphina

Dinner was unpleasant to say the least. Ophelia barely acknowledged Julien and spent most of the time either gushing about her wedding plans or getting after Michael for every little thing he'd done wrong. He wasn't much better, antagonizing her while getting toasted on beer after beer.

Julien and I held hands under the table, silently communicating a vow to never be like them. I didn't think we were in danger of that, but my god, it was painful to watch.

When it was finally over and plates were cleared, I was hoping Phe would take her drunk man home and leave us in peace. No such luck, though.

She wrapped her fingers around my arm. "Let's let the boys clean up. I need your help with something. Can you come with me?"

"Uh—" I glanced at Julien. He nodded, mouthing, "Go ahead." I thought it was pretty safe to leave him with Michael. "Okay. Sure."

I assumed we'd be going to her bedroom, so when she steered toward mine, I had no idea what was going on. Possibly a real apology? No, I wouldn't expect that from her. I braced myself for whatever she had in store.

She sat on the corner of my bed—which I'd hastily made after my mother's warning text—and smoothed her dress over her crossed legs. If she knew what kind of debauchery had gone down on the cotton sheets right beneath the duvet her ass was on, she'd probably scream and faint. I, personally, was enjoying that secret knowledge.

"Did Mom tell you Beth hired a wedding planner for me?" She clapped her hands under her chin. "She's so perfect. I have a binder filled with all our plans. I feel so organized and official now."

I knew I loved my sister because I couldn't help the swell of excitement for her. Her dreams weren't mine, but I was happy she was getting what she wanted.

"That sounds amazing. I'm sure having a planner will take the load off your shoulders."

She crinkled her nose. "No, that's not how these things work. If anything, I have *more* work. All the little details I'd never think about. The most genius part is, even though the wedding's a year away, my tasks are front-loaded, so I can do a lot now and not have so much to do as it gets closer to the date. And that's where you come in."

I cocked my head. "Me? Do you need me to fold programs or something? I'm not the most crafty, but I can fold a straight line."

"Pfft, no. This week, I have to find my something old I'll wear on the day. *So*, I need Grandma's locket."

My heart stuttered. "What? Why?"

She kicked her feet out and stood, spinning to head to my jewelry box on my dresser. "Well, Victoria—that's my planner—wants to have the locket sewn onto a ribbon which will be wrapped around my bouquet. We'll have to send it to my jeweler first, to have the loop removed, since that wouldn't look very nice. That's why I need it now."

She opened my jewelry box, peering in. "Where is it?"

I was beside her in a breath, slamming the lid down, narrowly missing her hand. "You're kidding."

She blinked at her, her cheeks flaring pink. "No. I'm obviously not kidding. Give me the locket. It's not like you wear it, and she was *my* grandmother too."

I wanted to shout no, that I had worn the locket to *her* freaking bridal luncheon. I wanted to shove her out of my room and out of my life for even daring to ask. My grandmother had worn that locket every single day until I was hospitalized in high school. She gave it to me then, telling me I needed it more than her.

Because I had known the story behind the locket, I understood exactly what she meant. During those bleak days, weeks, months, I'd held it in my hand and rubbed my thumb over the grooved design, channeling Belinda Ellis's boldness. I didn't wear it often for fear of losing it, but it was the most important thing I owned, more so than my drums.

And even with all that, I was still tempted to give it to Ophelia. She'd be so pissed at me if I said no.

But then I heard both Julien and my grandmother telling me to be louder than the bullshit. She could be pissed, but that didn't mean I had to listen. She wasn't going to ruin my grandmother's locket—*my* locket—just because Victoria the wedding planner wanted her to.

"No. You can't have it."

Her mouth gaped as flames licked at her chest and cheeks. "Are you really that bent out of shape I chose Catrina over you that you'd want to hurt me this way?"

"No. One has nothing to do with the other. The locket is mine, and you can't have it."

With a huff, she opened my jewelry box again and started to riffle through it. I stood there, watching her with my arms crossed. It wasn't in there. She'd figure that out soon enough.

"Where is it?" she cried.

"Not in there. It's not in this house."

That had her spinning around, forgetting her search. "You'll ship it to me."

"I won't."

She actually stomped her foot. "You will. Grandma was important to me, and I want to have part of her with me at the wedding. I loved that locket, and it's really not fair that you have it."

"You love it so much you want to destroy it?"

Her perfect brows winged up in fury. "Don't be so immature. You can replace the loop after the wedding. It's not a massive deal at all. If you don't give me the locket, it *will* be a massive deal."

There was a tug in my chest to comply. To not rock the boat. To let my sister have her way so she'd be happy with me and like me.

But I'd worn the dress she'd told me to wear at her luncheon, and it hadn't been good enough. That was just the latest in a lifetime of bending to Ophelia's will to win her affection. I was finished doing that. I deserved more.

"Whose picture is in the locket, Phe?"

Her tirade came to a screeching stop. "What? Obviously Grandpa's."

"Nope."

She rolled her eyes. "Then our pictures are in there. What does it even matter?"

"It matters. That locket is invaluable to me, and I'm not giving it away since it means nothing to you."

Her hands flew to her head, pressing on the sides. "Cut the shit and tell me whose picture is in it."

"Phillip."

Her eyelids fluttered as her lip curled. "Are you messing with me now? There's no one named Phillip in this family."

"I know that."

She waved her hand in front of her. "Oh, stop being smug and come out with it. Just tell me who Phillip is."

Maybe I was smug, but it was a first when it came to me and Phe. She'd always, *always* had the upper hand in our relationship. Not right now.

"Phillip was Grandma's first fiancé. He gave her the locket. She kept it as a reminder to never settle and always be herself and follow her dreams, even if other people didn't understand."

For a split second, Ophelia let the hurt of not knowing this integral detail about our grandmother show on her face. Her eyes filled, and her mouth turned down in bitterness. Then Phe turned up her nose and stiffened her spine, the moment passing almost as if it hadn't happened at all. Her eyes dried as if she'd sucked the tears back into her body. My sister was made of steel, I'd give her that.

"God, fine. I'll just use one of Mom's pieces. Who even cares about that locket? It's ugly anyway." She started to storm for the door but stopped in her tracks and whirled around on me. There was something venomous in her gaze I did not like.

"What?" I asked cautiously.

"This boy, Julien, is it serious?"

"Yes."

"Isn't it too soon to jump into a new relationship after Seth? I didn't think things were really settled there."

"Seth is ancient history, Phe. He stuck his dick in other girls. That kind of settled everything."

She pursed her lips. "Sometimes that happens. If a man has other qualities that make up for a slip here and there, I don't think you should write him off."

"I disagree, but it doesn't matter. Seth didn't have other qualities besides his pretty face."

"Obviously a pretty face isn't important to you."

"Stop talking."

"No, I'm just saying, it's nice you can look past the outside. You've always been charitable like that. It's a quality I admire."

I knew she was saying this because she was hurt and angry about the locket. Ophelia could be a complete bitch, but the direction she was headed was so far beneath her, what she was doing was unrecognizable.

"I said stop talking, Phe. Don't say something you can't come back from."

"Hmph." She tapped her chin. "I'll have to ask Victoria to find a photographer who's an expert at retouching, in case your boyfriend is still around next year for the wedding. I wouldn't want any...*thing* to detract from my pictures."

Each of her words added a log to the fire burning bright in my belly. I was so heated, if I screamed, I imagined flames would come out instead.

"If you say another word, I'll slap you so hard, you'll need that retoucher to work on the bruises that will still be on your face next year."

I raised my hand, meaning every word even though I'd never hit another person in my life.

Ophelia laughed dryly. "You've lost your mind. Wait until I tell Mom about you threatening me over a joke about your boyfriend. If you can't handle it, maybe you should pick a boyfriend who isn't so—" The face she made was uglier than I'd ever seen her. Before I could follow through on my promise, a deep bark stopped us both.

"Ophelia, it's time to go." Michael stood in the doorway, his legs braced wide, arms crossed tightly over his heaving chest. The way he scowled at my sister sent shivers down my spine. I wondered how long he'd been there listening.

"Julien? Where's Julien?" I asked as my gut churned.

Michael jerked his chin. "He didn't hear anything. He's handling the dishes." Then he narrowed his eyes on my sister. "We're leaving your sister and her boyfriend alone now. Let's go."

"Michael," Phe cooed. "Wait, Sera and I weren't finished—"

He hit the frame of the door so hard, I jumped. "You're finished. Move it."

She tried to brush by me, rushing to Michael, but I caught her wrist. After all she'd said, I was still worried for her. I couldn't help it.

"Are you safe?" I asked.

Her head dropped, and she nodded. "He doesn't like when I"—she peered at me from beneath her lashes—"lose my temper and get mean. I promised him I'd stop. He's not happy with me, but he won't hurt me. He'd never hurt me."

"You're lucky Julien didn't hear," I murmured.

Her chin quivered. "I know."

"I don't think I would have been able to forgive you if you'd hurt him."

Her eyes darted to where Michael waited. "I need to go."

"Then go."

I let her tear away from me and watched her go. Michael gave me a curt wave before following her out. A moment later, Julien appeared in the doorway, drying his hands on a kitchen towel. When he saw my state, he wrapped me up with a fierceness only he'd ever shown me.

"I'm sorry I wasn't here."

"You shouldn't have to defend me from my own sister." My fingers curled into his shirt, clinging to him. "I stood up to her even though I didn't think I could. She didn't like it."

I would never, ever tell him what she had said about him. Not only to protect him—though that was the biggest reason—but because I hoped, one day, Ophelia would get over herself and we'd be able to have a normal relationship. I didn't want to ruin her completely in Julien's eyes. Maybe that made me stupid, but I'd rather be stupid while keeping hope that things could get better.

"I'm proud of you, baby," he said. "That couldn't have been easy, but you did it."

It was like peeling my skin off piece by piece, but I did it.

"I'm proud of me too." I tipped my head back to look at my phantom. "You know, I love you."

He sputtered a watery laugh. "I didn't know that." His hand went to the back of my head, holding me there. "Whoa. I didn't expect that."

I giggled at his discombobulated reaction. "I'm sorry to spring it on you. It's just that I do, I love you, and I'm so happy to call you mine."

His eyes squeezed shut as he drew in a deep breath, then my face was in his hands, his forehead on mine. "I love you too, Seraphina."

He didn't have to say anything else. That was everything.

Chapter Thirty-four

Seraphina

Today was D-Day. Spring break was over, and we were back to reality. My debt was being called in. I had to have an answer for Carson besides "Go fuck yourself with a rusty dildo,"—and I was coming up empty.

Julien kept assuring me he had it handled. He told me not to worry. *Promised* everything would be all right. And since he was in the business of keeping his promises to me, I had no choice but to believe him.

I only wish he'd tell me what was up his sleeve, but he was keeping me decidedly in the dark.

We were walking down the hall to our music lecture. I clung to Julien's hand, my nerves shot and knees shaky. He was far more steady on his feet than I was.

"It's all going to be okay," he soothed. "Trust me, baby."

"I do trust you. It's Carson I don't trust. And Katie. Don't forget her."

"I'd like to."

I tried to laugh, but my throat was too clogged with anxiety. "Me too."

Speaking of the devil, Katie was right outside the lecture hall, in what looked like a fight with Seth. They were hissing at one another, arms flailing, Seth's complexion a concerning shade of burgundy.

The thing was, I wasn't even curious about what trouble had come up in their paradise. I didn't care if they were together or not.

Neither of them mattered to me. I didn't pause as we passed them on our way into class.

When we were seated in the front row, Julien pressed his lips to my ear. "Seth applied to intern at Savage Industries."

"He did?"

"Mmmhmm. And you know how Miles loves me?"

"Yes. I heard something about that."

I felt Julien's smile, and it made me shiver. "Since he loves me, he'll do pretty much anything I ask. I told him what an asshole Seth was to you. This morning, Miles emailed to let me know he had Seth blackballed at Savage and had also contacted all the PAs he knows in the area to tell them to do the same. He's going to find it difficult to land an internship within a hundred miles."

I reared back so I could look at him. "Is this part of you handling things?"

"It is." He studied me, waiting for my reaction.

I ran my finger down his nose and tapped the end. "I never knew you could be so devious."

Okay, maybe I cared a little bit about what happened to Seth. This pleased the little black part of my heart that fed on vengeance. It didn't even matter that Seth wouldn't know why no one would hire him. I would know, and that pleased me very much indeed.

He held my chin between two fingers. "When it comes to you and someone who hurts you, there isn't much I won't do. I can reverse it if you think I went too far."

I shook my head. "I hope you don't think poorly of me, but no, I don't think you went too far."

He grinned. "I like that you can be a little devious too."

As he leaned in to kiss me, someone bumped into my shoulder, jerking us apart.

"Oh, excuse me." Carson stood over us, a smirk tilting his lips. "I didn't think you'd be there, you know, together. I heard the two of you broke up."

"Nope." Julien picked up my hand and kissed my knuckles. "You heard wrong, Carter."

"It's Carson, actually."

Julien winked at him. "That's right. I got it wrong because I don't care."

Carson gaped at me. "Are you going to let him talk to me that way?"

I shrugged. "I don't control him. I'm sorry he doesn't care enough about you to get your name right. That sucks."

He huffed, shooting murderous glares our way. My anxiety over the situation came flaring back to life. I'd choose Julien a thousand times over and give up drum captain every time, but I didn't know how far Carson would go when I crossed him.

I guessed I'd find out.

"You're done, Sera," he hissed. "Don't even think about drum captain anymore."

"We'll see." Julien kicked his legs out and leaned back in his seat like he didn't have a care in the world. "You can go now."

Carson tried to stare him down, but Julien was too busy kissing my fingertips to pay him any attention. Finally, after making angry sounds and flapping his arms, Carson whipped around and stomped up the steps to his usual seat.

The knot in my stomach tightened while Julien was more relaxed than I'd ever seen him. I wished I could have had whatever he'd taken to make him this way.

"Did you pop a Xanax this morning?" I whispered.

He chuckled. "No, baby. I'm just feeling good about how things are going to go after today. Wait and see, okay?"

I had no choice but to do just that.

Class began, and I did my best to pay attention. At least the topic of modern love songs was interesting, especially since I found myself humming them like a Disney princess whenever I thought of my Julien.

Our professor said we were going to listen to a medley of some of the most popular love songs from the last fifty years. This was my favorite part of the class. No matter what the lecture topic, we always listened to music at some point.

When Julien got to his feet, bewilderment struck until the professor told us our own classmate would be playing the medley. It was then I really registered the piano at the front of the class that normally wasn't there.

And Julien was heading to it, to play in front of hundreds of people. He wasn't wearing his hoodie, and when he sat down, his scarred side faced the audience.

I held my breath. His gaze found mine over the top of the piano. He grinned. I attempted to grin back, but my mouth was numb, so it might have been more like a grimace.

Then he lowered his head and started to play. But he didn't just play, he sang too. His voice was clear and smooth.

"Oh, my love, my darling..." He started with "Unchained Melody" by the Righteous Brothers, then transitioned to "Tiny Dancer."

Tears welled in my eyes as I watched him play. It wasn't just the songs, it was *him*. The confidence with which his fingers moved over the keys took my breath away. Not only that, but he wasn't hiding. This was the opposite of hiding. Julien was on stage, singing about love, and looking at me throughout. Anyone with eyes could see he was singing and playing for me. And he let them look.

He played Queen and Stevie Wonder, and I bit my lip through Cyndi Lauper's "Time After Time." I shouldn't have been amazed at him. I knew he was amazing. But I sat at my desk, gawking at this beautiful, talented man who was all mine, and I just...had to force myself to stay there and not burst like I was filled with confetti.

I never took my eyes off him while he took on Celine Dion, John Legend, and Coldplay. When he lifted his chin during "Yellow," making sure I knew those words were for me, I wondered if I was dreaming. I actually pinched myself to be sure this was real, and it was.

This was like my daydreams but real.

I had to swipe away tears when he sang "Chasing Cars" and nearly sobbed over "I Will Follow You Into the Dark." It was all so deeply beautiful and romantic. I almost wished away the rest of the audience, but the fact that he was doing this in front of all these people made it even more touching.

When he stood from the piano, he didn't pause to accept his applause—which was raucous with enthusiasm. He came straight to me, sat beside me, and cupped my cheeks.

"Was that okay?" he asked.

"I love you."

He gave me my favorite crooked grin. "I love you too."

We couldn't talk since class was still in session and the professor took over, leading a discussion about the songs Julien had played. It was all background noise. I clutched at his hand, trying to convey what I was feeling. But I couldn't really articulate it since this was so unfamiliar and unprecedented.

I knew I was happy and in love. And maybe that was the most important thing to know anyway.

When class finally ended, I thought we'd make a quick escape, but we were crushed by classmates who wanted to talk to Julien. He held me close, accepting their praise with humility.

Dina and Stefan stopped us. He waved his phone around. "I hope you don't mind, but I recorded that masterpiece and posted it...well, everywhere."

Julien shook his head. "I don't mind. Thanks, man."

Stefan raised a brow at me. "I hope *you* don't mind, but I might have swung the cam in your direction a time or two. You guys are the most adorable couple ever. I sent the video to the band discord. People are going nuts. If there was a marching band prom queen and king, you two would be a shoo-in."

"So cute," Dina agreed.

"I—thank you," I stuttered, then turned to gaze at Julien. "You're really okay with being splashed all over the place?"

He tipped his head down to mine, leveling his gaze on me. "I'm really okay with it."

Finally, we were able to break free and follow the flow of students out of the room. We made it all the way outside before Carson caught up with us.

"Hey," he called.

Julien held me firmly under his arm as we faced my nemesis. I was way too happy to deal with this guy, and from Julien's stance, he had it handled.

"Yes?" Julien asked.

Carson ignored him to glare at me. "We had a bet. Since you seem to be forfeiting, you can kiss drum captain goodbye."

Julien laughed, like that was the funniest thing he'd ever heard. "Do you really believe you have any pull anymore? A video of me singing love songs to my girl in front of hundreds of people is going around on social media. You can't touch us."

I was beginning to see just how devious my boyfriend really was. His performance may have been for me, but it wasn't *only* for me. He'd just cemented our love story in the hearts of everyone who watched that video. Even if it didn't go further than the band discord, that would be enough.

Carson sputtered. "Oh, I beg to differ. People listen to me. If I tell them your relationship is fake, they'll be pissed."

"There's nothing fake about us," Julien told him. "But if you insist on continuing to be an asshole, I'll go to plan *B*."

Carson sneered. "What the hell's plan *B*?"

"Ask me my father's last name." Julien took on the imperious stance of a true Savage. If I didn't know him, I would have been intimidated.

Carson rolled his eyes. "I don't care."

"You might." He stroked my side as he trounced all over Carson. "It's Savage. My father is Joshua Savage. Recently, I took a job with his company and came across an interesting résumé. What I do with it really depends on what happens in the next minute."

He swallowed, his face mottled red. "You're threatening me?"

"No," Julien answered with an eerie calmness. "I'm asking you to go away, forget this ridiculous vendetta, and back Sera during the vote for captain. That's all. It's so simple, I think even you can handle it."

"Then what? You'll give my résumé to your dad?"

He scoffed. "No. That would be something I'd do for a friend. You're a piece of shit. But I'll leave your résumé in the pile. I won't have you blackballed. You'll have the same chance as everyone else who applied. This is my one and only offer."

Carson worked his jaw back and forth, like he was considering it. The truth was, he was a weak bully whose tiny ounce of power had just been stripped away. He had no choice but to accept.

"Fine. Whatever," he spat out. "Katie would have sucked as captain anyway."

He stomped away, literally kicking rocks as he went.

Turning in Julien's arms, I cupped his cheeks. "You...are sneaky as hell. How did you do this? I don't—Julien! What did you do?"

He grinned at me, dipping his head to ghost his lips over mine. "While you were working on your tan over spring break, I was plotting. It worked out better than I could have planned." He kissed me again. "You're free, baby."

"I'm free," I whispered. "You sang love songs to me. Can you do that again when it's just the two of us?"

"Anytime you want."

"Julien..." I stroked his cheeks, still in disbelief. "You were up there in front of so many people. And the videos..."

He turned his head to kiss my palm. "I focused on you. That made it easy. It was all for you."

"And I love you for it, but I hate to think you did something that made you uncomfortable."

He exhaled a heavy breath. "A lot makes me uncomfortable. I didn't wake up liking my scars. I don't know if I'll ever get there. But I'm not gonna drag you into my shadows. You're fire and light—that's where you belong, so that's where I'll be with you. Fuck everyone else."

"Fuck everyone else." I circled my arm around his neck and released the breath I'd been holding for far too long. "I love you, Julien. I really do."

He bit my bottom lip then kissed it. "Love you too, Dragon Girl."

We started our walk toward home, holding hands and debating which love song Neville would have sung to Hermione. Me: none. That would *never* be a thing. Julien: adamant it would be something classic like "When a Man Loves a Woman"—the Michael Bolton version.

He was wrong, but, man, I really loved him.

As we walked, we left our broken pasts behind. He and I had started in the shadows, and we'd clung to them for far too long. That was over now. Ahead, as far as the eye could see, there was nothing but light.

Epilogue

Julien

Five Years Later

"Do we have everything we need?"

Sera patted her round belly. "Yep. Helen said to bring ourselves and nothing else, so I think we're good."

With my cane in one hand, Sera's hand in the other, we followed the path around the side of Helen and Theo's house. Beckett trailed behind us, his hands tucked in his pockets. He'd been a constant in our lives for so long now, it had become second nature to bring him with us everywhere we went. He'd just graduated from Savage Academy, so things would change when he went off to college, but the kid was attached, so he'd come back. Sera was just as attached, so she'd force him if he didn't.

And maybe I was too. He was still a little shit, but as far as younger brothers went, he was all right. More than all right, actually. He made being related to our dickhead dad worth it.

As soon as we reached the patio around back, Beck ditched us, as expected.

"I'm gonna go find a drink," he said.

Which was a lie. Luciana, Helen's little sister, was somewhere around here too. Beckett would find her.

Sera sighed when he left. "Ah, young obsession."

Laughing, I pulled her into my side and splayed my hand on her belly. "Speaking of obsessed, how are you and the little dragon?"

"The same as we were five minutes ago. Just fine. Ready for some cake, though. Do you think Zadie's here yet?"

We didn't have to wonder for very long. Helen and Theo found us first. Theo was carrying their daughter, Madelina—Lina for short—and Hells headed straight for Sera's bump.

"Oh my god, look at you, girlie. So, so cute!" she cooed. "Are you dying to find out what you're having?"

"I'm curious. I have no inkling." Sera rested a hand on top of her belly. Halfway into her pregnancy, she was like a flower, blooming more and more each day. I couldn't get enough of documenting every one of the changes in her body with my hands, mouth, eyes. My wife was so fucking beautiful, always, but pregnant, she was out of this world.

Theo nodded to me. "You have a guess?"

I threw out a hand. "Nah. No intuition, and no preference." I poked Lina's little tummy, and she gurgled. "What about you, little girl? Do you think it's a boy or girl?"

She blew spit bubbles at me and snuggled into her dad's shoulder. I wasn't up on baby lingo yet, so unfortunately, I couldn't interpret her message.

Helen pressed her hands together under her chin. "Well, I know, but I'm not telling. Not yet." She snagged Sera's arm to show her the decorations and food.

Theo shook his head as they left us. "Never thought my scrappy little skateboarder would one day be throwing gender-reveal parties for her friends."

I laughed, deciding to forgo mentioning Sera refused to call it a gender reveal since "gender is a social construct" and referred to it as a "penis or vulva reveal." I fucking adored that she was so thoughtful about things like that. Our kid was going to be lucky to have a mother who was so aware and open, but I didn't need to get into all that with Theo.

"Never thought I'd be attending one, much less for my own kid. But here we are. All grown up and shit."

He covered one of Lina's ears. "You have to cut out the cussing in front of babies, dude. It's frowned upon."

"Sorry, Lina. Uncle Jules will do better." She blew another spit bubble at me. "That means she forgives me, right?"

"Yeah. We'll go with that. Lina's pretty forgiving." Theo jiggled her and kissed the top of her thick, black hair. "Let's go grab something to drink. Everyone else should be here soon."

When he said everyone else, he meant *everyone*. Amir and Zadie had flown down from Oregon to be here. Lock and Elena were in from Wyoming, even though she was rocking a pretty huge baby belly—they were expecting a boy next month. Alley and Laura arrived with bells on, double fisting champagne and sparkling juice for the nondrinkers. Helen's high school friends who'd become part of the group over the years had shown up too. My dad couldn't make it, but that was no skin off my back. Sera's parents were in attendance, along with Ophelia, Michael, and their two-year-old hellbeast son, Dutton.

It wasn't Dutton's fault he was a hellbeast. Some of it was that he was two and it came with the toddler territory. But a lot of it was genetics. Had to be since Ophelia was just as beastly. Fortunately, Sera and I didn't spend a lot of time with her sister and brother-in-law, since Michael's firm had relocated them to San Francisco.

Sera had accepted her sister wasn't going to change. Things were as they'd always be. They loved each other, but they were too different to ever be close.

Thank Christ for that. I'd do anything for my girl, my wife, but I would never stop being relieved I only had to deal with Ophelia on holidays and the random FaceTime call.

Marco rolled in last, having taken a red-eye from god only knew where to get here. Since graduation, he'd been a rolling stone, with no real home base, jet-setting all over. He co-owned clubs in Vegas, Mexico, and LA. The kid was nowhere near settled, but that wasn't a surprise. If anything, the fact that Amir and I were married, me with a baby on the way, was the surprising thing. None of us had seen life going this way when we were younger. Then again, none of us had grown up with solid foundations. We'd had to build them ourselves.

Sera and I were so fucking solid, even an earthquake couldn't shake us. That came from complete honesty, pure devotion, and laughing at all the bullshit life threw at us.

And life had thrown us a few times. I'd had a complete knee replacement and a handful of other surgeries throughout the last five years. Physically and mentally, I was doing better than I'd ever dreamed, but it had taken *work* to get to this point, and patience from my wife.

Sera was so incredibly good at being patient with me. It came naturally to her, less so for me. When she was in grad school for physical therapy, I was a needy motherfucker, missing her like crazy while she was hard at work but sucking it up so she never once felt guilty about it. We got through that season and all the others.

Like the fact that I worked for Savage Industries and saw my dad semi-regularly. The dad part could go straight to hell, but the job was decent. I suspected I was grossly overpaid, but I wasn't going to look a nepotistic horse in the mouth—not when I had my own family to take care of.

And take care of them I did. Sera only had to work part-time as a therapist, freeing her up to assist with the band at Savage Academy. We had a nice house, with a place for my piano and a spare bedroom for when Beckett crashed with us—which was more often than not, much to Sera's delight.

I sat down beside my wife on an oversized lounge chair. She lifted her head so I could wrap my arm around her and sighed as she snuggled against me.

"I can't believe everyone came here just to find out which reproductive organs our baby has."

Snickering, I shoved my face in her curls. "I'm pretty sure they're here for you, maybe me a little, but mostly you. They wanted to see how incredibly adorable and sexy you look in person—"

"Only you think I look sexy like this." She poked her stomach out a little extra. "That's because you're responsible for this. It ignites your inner caveman."

"Damn right. That's my seed."

She snorted, shoving me away from her. "Don't ever say that again."

Laughing at her disgust, I fell back on the lounger, watching our friends, who were more like family, eat, drink, and be merry.

"Did you have any cake yet?" I asked.

"Not yet. Helen is making me wait until we do the reveal."

"She really hasn't slipped up about what you've got cooking in there?"

Sera shook her head. "Not even for a second. Her vault is sealed."

We'd had the twenty-week anatomy scan last week. The tech had written the baby's sex on a card and placed it in an envelope, which Sera had given to Helen, who had set up some grand way for us to reveal whether we were having a girl or boy.

When the time finally came, Helen made Sera and I stand in front of a blue-and-pink balloon arch, each of us holding smoke bombs. Our friends counted down, and on one, we pulled the wire, releasing the smoke.

Sera's eyes were on the smoke. Mine were on my wife's smile, which was so vivid, so wide and purely happy, I couldn't seem to look away. Even as she squealed and people around us applauded, she was all I saw.

And then she was in my arms, bouncing in my embrace.

"A boy," she whispered next to my ear. "A boy, Jules. Can you even believe it?"

All around us, there were clouds of blue smoke.

"A boy." There was wonder in that reality. My beautiful wife was growing my son inside her. "Holy fuck, baby. A boy."

She leaned back, her smile growing impossibly brighter. "Are you happy?"

"Is that even a question?" I felt it then. I was smiling back at her in the same way. Bright, wide, radiating a joy I thought only came in dreams. "We're having a son together, D.G. How could I not be happy?"

"You'd have to be crazy." She pressed a kiss to my lips. "Do you think he'll have red hair?"

"He might. Do you think he'll want to play drums or piano?"

"He'll probably pick up a basketball just to keep us on our toes."

I laughed, pulling her closer, feeling our son between us. "No second-generation drum captain?"

She tilted her head to the side, her smile turning peaceful. "He can be whatever he wants, can't he?"

All I could say was yes. He could be.

Sera and I had been broken in different ways, and in the darkest, most desolate moments, both of us had questioned if we wanted to be here any longer. That seemed like a lifetime ago now. A lot of work had happened between being broken and being made whole.

But we *were* whole. Not the same as before, but better. Stronger. And we would give our son what we'd never had—a life that was his, without expectations or chains, and with every ounce of support we had in our bones.

I kissed my wife softly on the lips. "I can't wait to do this with you."

She beamed. "It's going to be so great, Jules."

"It already is."

"Yeah," she breathed out with the same awe filling my chest. "I love you, my phantom."

"I love you too, Dragon Girl."

"This is like my very best daydream."

"Keep dreaming, Seraphina—I'll make them all come true. I promise."

She touched my jaw. "I believe you."

And she should have.

It had been 2,194 days since I first met Seraphina Ellis in the shadows, and 1,855 days since I made my first promise to her. Today was her twenty-first week in her second trimester. I was twenty-seven years old, and I'd been married for seven-hundred-fifty days. I'd made and kept countless promises since that first one, but it was still the most important.

I would never, *ever* make a promise I couldn't keep.

Savage Academy

Enter the hallowed grounds of Savage Academy in early 2023...

Find out what happens to Beckett Savage and Luciana Ortega-Whitlock when they meet again at Savage Academy!

Join my newsletter for updates on the release of the first book on my new Academy series:

https://www.subscribepage.com/savageacademy

Playlist

"My Love Took Me Down to the River to Silence Me" Little Green Cars
    "bad idea!" girl in red
    "fever dream" mxmtoon
    "Finally // beautiful stranger" Halsey
    "Comfort Crowd" Conan Gray
    "blame game" mxmtoon
    "Let Me Down Slowly" Alec Benjamin
    "Somebody to You" The Vamps, Demi Lovato
    "feelings are fatal" mxmtoon
    "Wildest Dreams" Taylor Swift
    "Hey Stupid, I Love You" JP Saxe
    "Dreamer" Dermot Kennedy
    "Two" Sleeping At Last
    "Cigarette Daydreams" Cage The Elephant
    "Tiny Dancer" Florence + The Machine
    "Till Forever Falls Apart" Ashe, FINNEAS
    "Fade Into You" Korey Dane
    "I'm With You" Vance Joy
    "The Safety Dance" Sleeping At Last
    "Cosmic Love" Florence + The Machine
    "Unchained Melody" Lykke Li
    "Time After Time" Iron & Wine
    "Slow Show" The National

"I Will Follow You Into the Dark" Daniela Andrade
https://open.spotify.com/playlist/72oNYjjeQ6DtKztzGlwcpn?si=02aa8237460f4e18

KEEP IN TOUCH

JOIN ME IN MY reader group for the latest book updates and to chat with other readers:
https://www.facebook.com/groups/JuliaWolfReaders
Follow me on TikTok:
https://www.tiktok.com/@authorjuliawolf

ACKNOWLEDGEMENTS

This book would not have been written without the brainstorming session I had with my son, P, before I started writing Bright Like Midnight. He told me to name one of the side characters Julien. I protested, telling him that it was too similar to my name. He held up his hands, looked me straight in the eye, and said, "Trust me."

I did, and look what happened.

Julien was never supposed to have his own book. In fact, I almost killed him in Bright Like Midnight. But I loved him too much to do that, and I knew you guys would hunt me down if I went through with it anyway, so I kept him around. I'm so glad I did. He deserved his happy ending.

I'd like to thank my high school classmate, Jess, who is a marching band guru. She answered my questions and set me straight on a few things.

Thank you to my girl, Alley Ciz, who beta read for me and pointed out minute details that only a fellow author would notice. And of course, thank you for allowing me to turn you and Laura Lee into the cutest little couple with the best boobs ever!

Thank you to Michelle Lancaster for the GORGEOUS photo. He is so, so Julien, I can't even stand it.

Thank you to Kate Farlow for the entire Savage U series covers (and most of my others!!). I love them so, so much.

And of course, thank you to my readers who have loved this series from the moment Helen fingered her bat under the counter in Soft Like Thunder, to Julien keeping all of his promises at the end of this one. I hope you'll stick around, because I'm not done with Savage River yet!